W9-CKI-764

THE
COMPANY

By K. J. Parker

THE FENCER TRILOGY

Colours in the Steel

The Belly of the Bow

The Proof House

THE SCAVENGER TRILOGY

Shadow

Pattern

Memory

THE ENGINEER TRILOGY

Devices and Desires

Evil for Evil

The Escapement

The Company

THE
COMPANY

K. J. PARKER

www.orbitbooks.net

New York   London

Orbit
Hachette Book Group
237 Park Avenue, New York, NY 10017
Visit our Web site at www.HachetteBookGroup.com

First Edition: October 2008

Orbit is an imprint of Hachette Book Group, Inc. The Orbit name and logo are trademarks of Little, Brown Book Group Limited.

The characters and events in this book are fictitious. Any similarity to real persons, living or dead, is coincidental and not intended by the author.

Library of Congress Cataloging-in-Publication Data
Parker, K. J.
    The company / K. J. Parker. — 1st ed.
        p. cm.
    ISBN 978-0-316-03853-9
    I. Title.
    PR6116.A745C66 2008
    823'.92 — dc22   2008035282

10 9 8 7 6 5 4 3 2 1

RRD-IN

Printed in the United States of America

To Pete Thompson, transport officer, A Company,
Brookwood irregulars, starer-down of lions, with thanks

THE
COMPANY

ONE

The boatman who rowed him from the ship to the quay kept looking at him: first a stare, then a frown. Pretending he hadn't noticed, he pulled the collar of his greatcoat up round his chin, a perfectly legitimate response to the spray and the cold wind.

"Don't I know you from somewhere?" the boatman asked.

"Wouldn't have thought so," he replied.

The boatman's frown deepened. He pulled a dozen strokes, then lifted his oars out of the water, letting the back-current take the boat the rest of the way. "I do know you," the boatman said. "Were you in the war?"

He smiled. "Everybody was in the war."

The boatman was studying his collar and the frayed remains of his cuffs, where the rank and unit insignia had been before he unpicked them. "Cavalry?" the boatman persisted. "I was in the cavalry."

"Sappers," he replied. It was the first lie he'd told for six weeks.

He felt the boat nuzzle up to the quay, grabbed his bags and stood up. "Thanks," he said.

"Two quarters."

He paid three — two for the fare, one for the lie — and climbed the steps, not looking back. The smell was exactly as he remembered it: seaweed, rotting rope, cod drying on racks, sewage, tar. It would've been nice if just one thing had changed, but apparently not.

As he walked up the steep cobbled hill, he saw a thick knot of people blocking his way. Never a good sign. It was just starting to rain.

It was as he'd feared. The short, fat man in the immaculate uniform was almost certainly the harbourmaster; next to him, two thin men who had to be his clerks; the old, bald man had the constipated look of a mayor or a portreeve. Add two guards and a tall, scared-looking youth who was presumably someone's nephew. At least they hadn't had time to call out the town band.

No chance of slipping past. He didn't look at them directly. At ten yards, they stood at sort-of-attention. At five yards, the presumed harbourmaster cleared his throat. He was actually shaking with fear.

"General Kunessin," he said, in a squeaky little voice. "This is a tremendous honour. If only we'd had a little more notice..."

"That's perfectly all right," he replied; his polite-to-nuisances voice. "Listen, is there somewhere I can hire a horse and two mules?"

Looking rather dazed, the harbourmaster gave him directions: through the Landgate, second on your left, then sharp right—

"Coopers Row," he interrupted. "Thanks, that's fine."

The harbourmaster's eyes opened very wide. "You've been here before then, General?"

"Yes."

One thing that had changed in seventeen years was the cost of hiring a horse in Faralia. It had doubled. All the more surprising because, as far as he could tell, it was the same horse.

"Is this the best you've got?" he asked. "I've got a long way to go."

"Take it or leave it."

The horse shivered. It wasn't a particularly cold day. "Thanks," Kunessin said. "Forget the horse and make it three mules."

The groom looked at him; cheapskates aren't welcome here.

Kunessin smiled back. "How's your uncle, by the way?" he asked pleasantly. "Keeping well?"

"He's dead."

Two things, then. "Not that one," he said, "it's lame." He counted out two dollars and nine turners. "Thank you so much," he said.

The groom handed him the leading reins. "Do I know you?"

"No," he replied, because at six and a half turners per half-dead mule per day, he was entitled to a free lie. "I'm a perfect stranger."

Climbing the hill eastwards out of town, his feet practically dragging on the ground as the mule panted mournfully under his weight, he thought: hell of a way for the local hero to travel. And that made him laugh out loud.

Because he took a long loop to avoid Big Moor, it took him two and a half hours to reach Ennepe, at which point he got off the mule and walked the rest of the way, to save time.

No change, he thought. Even the gap in the long wall was still there, a little bit bigger, a few more stones tumbled down and snug in the grass. Seventeen years and they still hadn't got around to fixing it. Instead, they'd bundled cut gorse into the breach and let the brambles grow up through the dead, dry branches. He smiled as he pictured them, at breakfast round the long kitchen table: one of these days we'd better fix that gap in the wall, and the others all nodding. Seventeen years; seventeen years slipping by, and they'd never found the time. For some reason, that made him feel sad and rather angry.

Walking down the drove, Stoneacre on his left, he could see Big Moor clearly in the distance. Seventy-five acres of bleak, thin hilltop pasture, a green lump. It cost him a good deal of effort to avoid looking at it, but he managed.

At the point where the drove crossed the old cart road (now it was just a green trace in the bracken; by the look of it, the lumber carts didn't come this way any more), he saw a boy sitting on a fallen tree, staring at him. He pushed his hat back a little, to show his face, and called out, "Hello."

The boy's head dipped about half an inch. Otherwise he didn't move. Kunessin understood the look on the boy's face all too well: the natural distrust of newcomers, at war with the furious curiosity about a stranger, in a place where strangers never came.

"There's a stray ewe caught in the briars up at the top, just past the deer track," he said. "One of yours?"

The boy studied him for three heartbeats, then nodded a full inch. His lips moved, but "thanks" didn't quite make it through. He stood up, but didn't walk.

"You'll be Nogei Gaeon's boy," Kunessin said.

"That's right."

"I'm on my way up to the house now. Is he likely to be in the yard, this time of day?"

Desperate hesitation; then the boy shook his head. "He'll be up at the linhay," he replied, "feeding the calves."

"Over Long Ridge?"

The boy's eyes widened; he couldn't understand how a stranger would know the names of the fields. "Thanks," Kunessin said. "How about your uncle Kudei? Where'd he be?"

The boy gave him a long, frightened look. "You from the government?"

Kunessin grinned. "I'll pretend I didn't hear that," he said.

He left the boy and carried on down the hill until he reached the top gate of Castle Field, which led into Greystones, which led into Long Ridge. The hedges were high, neglected, and they shielded him from the sight of Big Moor.

(Well, he thought, I'm home, as near as makes no odds; the last place on earth I want to be.)

Then, before he was ready, he was standing at the top of the yard, looking down the slope. Directly in front of him was the old cider house, which had finally collapsed. One wall had peeled away, and the unsupported roof had slumped sideways, the roof-tree and rafters gradually torn apart by the unsupportable weight of the slates; it put him in mind of the stripped carcass of a chicken, after the meal is over. A dense tangle of briars slopped out over the stub of the broken wall, and a young ash was growing aggressively between the stones. It must have happened so slowly, he thought: neglect, the danger dimly perceived but never quite scrambling high enough up the pyramid of priorities until it was too late, no longer worth the prodigious effort needed to put it right. There would have been a morning when they all came out to find it lying there, having gently pulled itself apart in the night. They'd have sworn a bit, shaken their heads, accepted the inconvenience and carried on as before.

A man came out of the back door of the house: tall, bald, slightly stooped shoulders. He was carrying a large basket full of apples. Halfway across the yard he stopped and looked up. For a moment he stayed quite still; then he put the basket down. Kunessin walked down to meet him.

"Oh," the man said. "It's you."

Kunessin smiled. "Hello, Euge," he said. He noticed that the apples in the basket were all wrinkled, some of them marked with brown patches. Forgotten about, left too long in store, spoiled, now only fit for the pigs.

"What're you doing here?"

"Visiting," Kunessin replied. "Where's Kudei?"

Euge Gaeon nodded in the direction of the foul, wet pasture beyond the house. "You still in the army?" he asked.

"No," Kunessin said. "I retired. How's the farm?"

Euge shrugged, as if the question didn't make sense: might as well ask, how are the mountains? Just behind him, a rat scuttled across the yard and vanished into a crack in the feed store wall.

"You staying long?" Euge asked.

Kunessin shook his head. "Flying visit," he said.

Well, at least he'd made somebody happy today. He left Euge to his melancholy task, rounded the back porch of the house (the midden was buried under the finest crop of nettles he'd ever seen in his life, but he could just see the remains of a dead sheep, and a large clot of sodden chicken feathers), climbed over the back rails and squelched across the small orchard to the beech-hedged bank that divided it from Little Moor. There was no gate in the gateway; instead, four or five broken willow hurdles had been wedged together and tied to each other with flax twine. He climbed over, grazing his ankle in the process, and saw a man in the distance.

Kudei Gaeon was standing a few yards from the single oak tree that grew in the top left corner of the field. He was watching a handsome heifer calf, which he'd clearly just tied to the tree with three feet of rope. The calf was tugging furiously, its feet dug into the soft ground, leaning back with all its weight, its head turned sideways. Ten yards or so beyond, a thin cow was watching, angry but too apprehensive to get involved. Kudei took a piece of rag from his coat pocket and bound it round his left hand; rope burns, Kunessin supposed.

"Hello, farmer," he said.

Kudei looked round and saw him. "Oh," he said. "It's you." For a moment he hesitated, then he grinned; it was as though his face was splitting, like a log to the wedge. "You're back, then."

Kunessin realised he'd taken a step back, just as he'd always done when talking to Kudei. Too close and he had to look up to him, because Kudei happened to be a head taller than him. He'd always resented that, for some absurd reason.

"How's the farm?" Kunessin asked.

"Could be worse," Kudei replied with a scowl. "Short on hay this year because of the rain, but the grass is good and fat, so we won't have to start feeding till late." He must have realised he was scowling; he deliberately relaxed his face, then smiled. "You didn't come all this way to ask about the farm."

"Actually," Kunessin said, then shrugged. "Hasn't changed much in seventeen years."

Kudei thought for a moment, then said, "It's changed slowly."

"The cider house."

"You noticed." Kudei laughed: a slight shudder in his massive chest. "Well, of course you did. Sorry about that. I guess we never got round to doing anything about it."

"There's always something," Kunessin said.

"Not when you had the place." Kudei frowned, then disposed of that expression too. "You really came back just to see what we've done with it?"

"No, of course not." The calf was twisting its neck against the rope. Quite soon, there'd be a sore patch. Dad would've padded the halter, Kunessin thought. "That's a nice little heifer," he said. "Going to show her in the spring?"

"We don't show any more," Kudei said. "No time."

Kunessin nodded. "Are you done here? I could do with a drink."

"Come up to the house. You'll have to excuse my brothers," he added sadly. "They haven't exactly mellowed with age."

"I met Euge just now," Kunessin said. "Wasn't he ever pleased to see me."

"I can imagine," Kudei said; he was pulling the rag tighter round his damaged hand.

"You should wear gloves when you're roping cattle."

"I would, if I had any."

For some reason, Kunessin was shocked by that. "You're kidding."

Kudei laughed. "Sort of," he said. "We've got seven pairs of gloves, actually, all of them with the palms worn through. And we've got three good cured sheepskins hanging up in the barn, going mouldy with the damp, but cutting a bit off and patching a glove..." He smiled. "It's a case of getting round to it, you see. Always tomorrow, always directly. Well, you know."

Shocked and, he realised, angry. "That's no way to live, Kudei," he said.

"We manage," Kudei replied quietly. "Come inside, we'll have that drink."

"Forget it," Kunessin said, more abruptly than he'd have liked. "I need to get back to town by nightfall," he lied. "It was good to see you again."

Kudei stopped dead in his tracks. "Is that it, then?" he said. "You came all this way to yell at me for not patching a pair of gloves?"

"You shouldn't have let the cider house fall down," Kunessin replied. "That was just idleness."

(He could always tell when Kudei was starting to get angry. It was a long, gradual process, and it always began the same way. He'd start to slow down, his movements gentler, his voice growing softer. Just before he got furious, you could barely hear him.)

"It hasn't been easy," Kudei said. "I was away for ten years."

"I know." Time for another lie. "It wasn't your fault."

"My brothers..." It was as though Kudei was searching the shelves and drawers of his mind for the right words. "They do their best," he said.

Which was true, and of course that was what made it unforgivable. But Kunessin hadn't come here to fight. "I'll be at the Glory of Heroes for three days," he said. "Drop in and I'll buy you that drink."

He started to walk away. Kudei didn't move. A pity, Kunessin thought; but when did we ever say a dozen honest words to each other without falling out? "If I don't see you, take care of yourself," he said, not looking round.

He took five steps; then he heard Kudei say, "If you can hang on an extra day, I've got to take a load of grain to the mill."

He had his back to Kudei, so it was safe to smile. "I'll see you then," he said, and walked away.

The sign didn't hang straight, and the paint was starting to flake in the salty sea air. It read:

Royal United School of Defence
Founder & Propr Thouridos Alces
Late Master Sgt at Arms 5th Infantry
All schools, styles & techniques expertly taught
Vacancies usually available

Under the sign was a small door that looked as though it had been made for a larger doorway and cut down to fit. The latch didn't quite line up with the keeper, so someone had bent it enthusiastically with a hammer. Beyond the door was a long, dark passageway leading to a flight of stairs; and at the head of the stairs, another door with another sign:

Fencing School
No Admittance While Class In Progress

Kunessin pushed it open and saw a large square room, brightly lit by a great bay window that occupied most of the outward-facing wall. The polished floorboards reflected the light, which meant that the man standing in the centre of the floor was a backlit silhouette. Nevertheless...

"Hello, Fly," Kunessin said.

There was a loud clatter as the man dropped the two-handed sword he'd been holding. "Teuche?" he said, in a bewildered voice, like someone woken up in the middle of a complicated dream.

"Yes," Kunessin said.

The man started forward, trod on the blade of the dropped sword, stumbled, jumped a foot in the air, landed perfectly and ran towards him—all, apparently, in one concerted movement. Instinctively Kunessin took a step back and sideways, but the man must have anticipated the move; he lunged, caught Kunessin round the waist and lifted him off the ground.

"For God's sake," Kunessin gasped. "You're breaking my bloody ribs."

Thouridos Alces laughed and let him go; he slid down the front of Alces' canvas fencing coat until his heels jarred on the floor.

"Teuche, you complete bastard," Alces said, gripping Kunessin's shoulders and shaking him. "What the hell do you mean by it, sneaking up on me like that? You might at least've let me know you were coming."

He'd forgotten, he realised, quite how short Fly Alces was: five feet four, five at the most. Hardly surprising: it was something you had to make a conscious effort to remember. For one thing, he never seemed to hold still for long enough to be quantifiable by any normal system of weights and measures; more like a wave than a solid object, someone had once said. For another, he had a knack of seeming to fill all the space available, regardless of whether he was standing in an empty barn or hiding in a flour barrel.

"You're a strange man, Fly," Kunessin said, pulling gently away. "First time I've ever come across someone who demotes himself when he leaves the army."

Alces' face became a total grin, from chin to eyebrows. "Professional licence," he said. "No bugger's going to pay money to be taught fencing by a captain. Got to call yourself a sergeant or they think you don't know anything." Kunessin didn't actually see Alces move, but suddenly he was a full pace closer and clinging to his elbow. "Come in the back and have a drink," he said. "My God, it's good to see you again."

(There was a scar, Kunessin noticed, running from the corner of his left eye to the lower edge of his cheekbone. He hadn't got that in the army.)

"Tea," he said, "or no deal."

"Sure." He was being towed along, like a cart, towards a green door in the far corner. "I'm a tea drinker myself these days. Haven't touched a real drink in five years. Mind your head on the beam."

Too late. He winced; for some reason, it was important to him not to yelp or swear. Alces opened the door, and Kunessin followed him into the back room.

It wasn't what he'd been expecting. Instead of chaotic poverty, he saw good furniture, silverware on a polished walnut table, a velvet-curtained alcove where he assumed the bed would be, a worn but good-quality imported rug on the floor, and (the last thing he'd been expecting) a wife.

"Enyo," Alces said, "this is an old friend of mine, Teuche Kunessin."

She wasn't impressed, he could see that. There were, in his experience, two sorts of wives. There was the easy-going kind, usually stout, plain-faced and harassed-looking, who smiled at the unexpected visitor and immediately set out an extra plate and spoon; and there was the other kind, who regarded their husbands' old army friends as marginally better than bailiffs but definitely worse than mice. They were the ones who kept tidy houses and cooked cheap, wholesome meals with plenty of fresh vegetables.

"My wife," Alces said, and although he sounded properly embarrassed, there was also a deep, unmistakable pride.

(Well, Kunessin thought. This makes things awkward.)

"You'll stay to dinner," Enyo said; not a question but a statement, a grim fact stoically accepted.

"Thanks, but no," Kunessin said. "I'm meeting some people in half an hour."

She made an unintelligible noise, turned her back on him and started peeling something; a dismissal, but also a withdrawal: just pretend I'm not here. Which, of course, he couldn't do.

"How's business?" he asked.

"Fine," Alces said, sitting down in a fine chair (he makes the room look untidy, but presumably she's learned to cope with that). "We've been running this place for—how long's it been, five years?" No confirmation from the other end of the room. "And it's turned out pretty well. Tradesmen's sons, a couple of the local gentlemen farmers; Faralia's changed quite a bit since our day, more money about since the war. No competition. We'll never be rich, but I do three classes a day, all fully booked. It's a living, and not particularly arduous."

The back of Enyo's head let him know exactly what she thought of her husband's summary, but he fancied that her definition of a living was rather different. He managed to keep his face straight.

"What about you, though?" Alces went on. "General Kunessin. Only goes to show, if you stay in the service long enough . . . "

"I retired," Kunessin said.

"I heard that," Alces replied. "What did you want to go and do that for? You'd done all the hard work; I'd have thought you'd have stayed on and taken it easy."

Kunessin forced a laugh. "Don't you believe it," he said. "I reached the point where I couldn't stick the aggravation any more. Best decision I ever made, actually."

Alces shrugged. "So, what's the plan?" he said. "Buy some land and play at farming?"

He knew Alces didn't mean anything by it, so he let it pass. "Sort of," he said. "I'll tell you about it some time. So," he went on, turning away a little, "do you see much of the others these days?"

A slight frown, but no change in Alces' tone of voice. "A bit," he said. "Not a great deal. I run into Kudei in the street from time to time, but he doesn't come into town much. Muri—you know about Muri?"

Kunessin nodded. "I don't get that," he said. "I thought he had plans."

"Apparently not," Alces replied. "Or else he changed them, or they fell through. He seems happy enough, which is what matters, I suppose."

"What about Aidi? I heard he's running a shop, for crying out loud."

Alces grinned. "Very successful," he said. "Got a real flair for it. Also, he got married about three years ago, but she died in the spring. Lost the kid, too, which must've been hard to bear."

Kunessin nodded. "I suppose it's something we never really considered," he said, "bad stuff still happening even when the war's over. It's so much easier when you can pile it all on to the enemy. Sometimes I wonder if that's what wars are really for."

Maybe a barely perceptible shake of the head; he wasn't sure. But he had the distinct impression that that wasn't a subject to be discussed, even in the presence of the back of Enyo's head. Fair enough, he thought. Any woman who married Thouridos Alces would have to be firm about what could and couldn't be talked about.

(And then he noticed; or rather, he became aware of the lack of it. Not on the wall, or leaning in a corner of the room; not in a glass case or over the fireplace or hung by two nails from a rafter. He couldn't have simply got rid of it, not even for her sake; but in a room so neat and orderly there were only so many places it could be, and it wasn't there—a glaringly empty space, like a place laid at the dinner table where nobody sits down. Could it have been in the rack of blunts and foils in the schoolroom? He'd have noticed it there, and besides, it was unthinkable.)

He planted his feet squarely on the floor and pushed himself up. "I really have got to make a move," he said. (Alces started to say something, then thought better of it.) "I'm in town for the next few days, I'm staying at the Glory..."

Alces grinned. "Haven't been in there for years," he said, and the back of his wife's head quite definitely twitched. "If you can afford to stay there, you can afford to buy me a cup of tea."

"Just about," Kunessin replied—it didn't even sound like him talking. "Pleased to have met you," he said to the room in general, and left quickly. Alces went with him as far as the green door.

(Outside in the street, he turned and looked up at the sign. Here lies Thouridos Alces, he thought, may he rest in peace. Not, he acknowledged with a faint grin, that there was much chance of that.)

After the visitor had left, she asked him, "Who was that?"

Inevitably. He marshalled his face and mustered his words. "Old army friend of mine," he said, picking up an empty cup and taking it over to the washstand. It was a valiant effort but tactically unsound; he never washed up dirty crockery.

"General Kunessin, you called him," she said, and he could feel her eyes on the back of his head.

"That's right," he said, up-ending the cup and swilling its rim in the washbasin. "He stayed on in the service after I quit. He's from around here, originally."

"He wanted something," she said.

"You think so? I thought he was just calling in to say hello, since he's in the neighbourhood. I haven't set eyes on him for seven years."

"He wanted something," she repeated. "But he wasn't going to tell you about it in front of me."

Retreat to prepared positions. He half-turned and smiled at her. "What could a retired general possibly want from someone like me?" he said. "Besides, he's retired. And so am I. You know that."

One of those looks: uncomfortable, like gravel in your shoe. Never for one moment had he regretted marrying her, but she could break his defences the way he used to break the schiltrons. "You want me to tell you about him?"

Shrug. "If you like."

He left the washstand and sat down in his favourite chair, where he could be besieged in comfort. "We were all at the Military College together, six of us, all from Faralia, which meant we had something in common; the city kids treated us like peasants, so we formed what you might call an offensive and defensive alliance, for mutual support. Then the war came, and amazingly enough the brass had the good sense not to split us up. They made us into a lance—"

"What does that mean?"

"Sorry? Oh, right. A lance is a military unit, an officer and ten men, only they were so short of manpower by then, most units were understrength. It was the six of us plus the officer, Lieutenant D'Eteleieto. Anyhow, we stayed together all through the war. One of us didn't make it, but compared to most we got off lightly. Specially since we were linebreakers. That means we were the ones who—"

"Don't tell me about that," she said sharply.

"Fine," he said, recognising the edge in her voice. "Anyhow, that's about it. The war ended, we went our separate ways. I always thought that afterwards we'd stay in touch, specially since we were all Faralians and all of us except Teuche—that's his name, Teuche Kunessin—came back here to settle down. But we didn't. There wasn't any grand falling-out or anything like that. I guess that once we split up—we'd been together twenty-four hours a day for ten years; just think about that—I guess we realised we didn't have anything in common worth holding on to." He paused, just long enough to breathe. "And that's all there is to it."

A lie so monumental you could have dug a moat round it and called it a citadel. He offered it to her with a sort of honesty; her choice whether to attack and invest or withdraw and leave him in peace. But she was a better strategist than that. "Those other people you were talking about," she said. "He seemed to know all about them."

Which hadn't escaped his attention, but he hadn't had time to reflect on the implications. "Presumably someone's been sending him news from home," he said. "Like I said, he's a local boy, grew up on a farm in the valley. Actually, there's a bit of a story there," he added, not sure whether it was a good idea to open another front but willing to take the risk. He paused, and she sort of nodded: yes, I'm waiting. "His family lost the farm just before we all went off to the College, and Kudei Gaeon's dad—Kudei was one of us—he bought it cheap and took it over, and Kudei and his brothers are still there, as far as I know. Now, Teuche and Kudei were best friends practically from the cradle, but I think that once the Gaeon boys got the farm, there was always this little bit of edge between them, buried really deep. Maybe that's why we've all lost touch, I don't know: Teuche was very much in charge, if you see what I mean; the rest of us were more or less pulled in, like filings to a magnet."

If he'd been hoping she'd lose interest, he was wrong. Her frown grew darker and deeper, and he wondered if something had snagged her attention that he hadn't seen for himself. He couldn't very well ask, though: might as well throw the key to the city gates down to the enemy. (Indeed, he thought; and what's all love except constant siege warfare with the occasional sortie and skirmish?)

She was looking at him. "If he wants you to go off somewhere with him, will you go?"

"Of course not," he replied, too quickly. "My life's here now, and besides, I'm through with all that."

"You'd better get ready for afternoon class," she said. "You were going to put new tips on the foils, remember."

The glue had set hard in the bottom of the little kettle he kept in the cupboard in the corner of the schoolroom. He lit the spirit lamp to warm it up, and eased the bristles of the brush against the palm of his hand to soften them and make them supple. Everyone lies to their wives, he thought. It's necessary, human beings couldn't function otherwise. Curiously, though (he broke off one of the old, worn tips; it came away quite cleanly, without splintering), he'd never really lied to Enyo, not that he could remember. She had a way of coming out to meet him halfway, so that either he told the truth or the subject was suppressed before a lie could take place.

If he wants me to go off somewhere with him — well, of course. Immediately, without hesitation, if needs be, without stopping to put on my shoes. That went without saying. But the situation would never arise, since what could General Teuche Kunessin possibly want him for? Where the case is so hypothetical as to be absurd, normal criteria of truth and falsehood can't be made to apply. He was sure she realised that. It was like asking him: if there was a fire and you could only save one of us, me or it, which would it be? To which the answer was: that's why I don't keep it here.

After he'd finished, he opened the window to get rid of the smell of the glue. From the window bay, he could see the corner of Latten-gate, where the Glory of Heroes was, and he thought: yes, but what could be tamer, safer, than drinking tea out of a blue-and-white cup in the parlour of the Glory? What possible harm...?

After class (at one point he allowed his attention to wander, and got rapped across the knuckles with a foil. The student actually apol-ogised), he went down into the street, turned right instead of left, walked up to the Merchant Adventurers' Hall, through the great double doors and down the circular marble stairs to the vault. The guard on duty recognised him but asked for the password anyway. He gave it, and was let through into the long corridor. Once, before the war, the hall had been part of the duke's palace, and the small, windowless rooms off the long corridor had been used for long-term storage of men. For some reason, he had difficulty turning his key in the lock.

It was, of course, much emptier than the rest of the cells in the row. The Adventurers kept their valuable stock in them: quality fabrics, mostly, some bullion, luxury goods (tableware, artworks, presentation-grade arms and armour), bonds, indentures, deeds, loan notes. In his cell, Alces kept the lease of the school, a thousand thal-ers in cash that Enyo didn't know about, five hundred she did know about, a chest of old clothes, a sallet and brigandine on a home-made wooden stand, and a cloth bundle, five feet long, slim, wrapped in two blankets, propped up in the corner. The blankets were soaked through with camellia oil, and the sweet smell stank the place out.

He unwrapped the bundle, just enough to see the white flare of the steel in the yellow glow of the lamp he'd brought with him, and to test the surface with his finger to make sure the oil hadn't dried out. Then he wrapped it up again, put it back and turned to go.

On the way out, he met the vault steward, and stopped him.

"I was wondering," he said. "What precautions do you take in case of fire?"

The steward looked puzzled. "It's all stone," he said. "There's nothing that could possibly burn."

Alces nodded. "Fair enough," he said. "Thanks."

"You're welcome. By the way, I think you'll find you're behind on the rent."

He smiled. "My wife handles all that sort of thing," he said, and left.

Even if he'd been a stranger in town, he'd have had no trouble at all finding the tanner's yard, even with his eyes shut, even with a scarf wrapped double round his face. Something you got used to, he presumed, if you really had to.

The foreman pointed him in the right direction, and he saw a wooden vat, seven feet tall and about the same in diameter, standing in the middle of a high-roofed wooden shed. Two men were next to it: one at the top of a ladder, the other down below, handing up a large wooden bucket. The man at the top dipped it in the vat and handed it back, and as he came closer, Kunessin saw that the bucket was full of greyish-white jelly. He shuddered. Everybody knew they used the stuff in the tanning process, but knowing and actually seeing are two very different things.

(Seen worse, he reminded himself, but it didn't really help.)

"Hello, Muri," he said.

The man on the ground looked round, saw him and (regrettably) dropped the bucket. His colleague on the ladder asked him what the hell he'd done that for. A fair question.

The last seven years, Kunessin couldn't help but notice, hadn't been kind to Muri Achaiois. His cheeks had turned into jowls, and there were pads of soft, folded skin under his eyes; his hair was thinning on top, and he'd made the mistake of growing a beard, or trying to, on a less than fertile chin, with the result that the sides of his jaw looked like briar patches, while his chin reminded Kunessin of downland pasture, sparse and closely cropped by rabbits. He'd put on weight, too.

"Teuche," he said, apparently unaware that his shoes were covered in spilled brains. "Where the hell did you jump out from?"

"Who's he?" the man up the ladder was saying. As far as Muri was concerned, he didn't exist.

"Can you get away for five minutes?" Kunessin asked.

"Sure." Immediately, Muri started to walk towards him; the

first step he took put him on notice that something was wrong. He looked down at his feet, and sighed. "Carry on without me," he said, to nobody in particular. The man up the ladder told him what he thought of that idea, but he didn't seem to hear.

"How'd you find me?" Muri said.

"Your cousin Erys," Kunessin replied, taking a step back as Muri came within arm's length. "She told me what happened. I'm sorry."

Muri shrugged. "Does everybody know? The others, I mean?"

"I don't think so. I just saw Fly; he knows you're working here, but that's all. I don't know about Kudei, we didn't have a chance to talk about old times, and I haven't seen Aidi yet." He frowned. "Your friend over there looks like he's a bit upset with you."

"Fuck him," Muri said succinctly.

"Fine," Kunessin said. "I don't want to be responsible for you losing your job, that's all."

Muri smiled broadly. "You know what," he said, "I'm not too fussed. Hang on, there's a trough out in the yard. I guess I'd better wash my boots off."

"No, it's all right." Kunessin shook his head. "You get back to work. I'm staying at the Glory. Drop by this evening and we can talk properly. All right?"

Muri scowled at him, like a child who thinks he's been cheated out of a promised treat. "At least tell me what's going on, Teuche," he said firmly. "You didn't come all this way just to see me drop a bucket."

"It'll keep," Kunessin replied. "See you tonight."

By the time he'd gone, the other man had climbed down the ladder, and was sweeping the white, dusty mess into the gutter with a yard broom. Curiosity had pushed out anger, and he asked, "Who was that?"

Muri Achaiois looked at him. "You were in the war, weren't you?"

"Yes, of course."

"That," Muri said, "was Teuche Kunessin."

The other man stopped what he was doing. "Oh," he said.

*   *   *

Aidi Proiapsen was easy enough to find. Left out of the tannery gates, down the hill until the narrow alley turned out into broad, well-paved Ropewalk, turn right and look for the biggest, bravest shopfront in town. Aidi was waiting for him in the doorway, leaning on a barrel of store apples; a tall, wide, curly-haired man behind a shield-like grin.

"Hello, Teuche," he said. "I heard you're back in town."

Kunessin nodded. "This is all very splendid, Aidi," he said. "You must be next best thing to respectable."

Aidi laughed. "You could say that," he said. "Vice-chairman of the Adventurers', deputy town clerk and justice of the fucking peace. Talking of which, I ought to have you run out of town for vagrancy. Unless you tell me what you're here for, that is."

Kunessin looked past him into the shop. He could see a boy unrolling a bolt of cloth on a long table, and a middle-aged woman weighing out rice from a big white jar. "Staff," he said, with a grin. "Do they know who they're working for?"

"God, no. They'd run home screaming."

"Justice of the peace is a good joke," Kunessin said.

"I looked them up in a dictionary," Aidi replied. "Justice and peace. Strange idea, both of them. You'd better come inside; you're scaring away the customers."

He nodded, and followed Aidi through the shop into a storeroom at the back. It was crammed with barrels, boxes, jars and cases, and there were rat droppings on the floor. Aidi pointed him at the only chair, and perched on the edge of a cider barrel. "It's good to see you again," he said.

Kunessin shook his head. "You won't think so in a moment or two, when I tell you what I'm here for."

"I gathered you've called a sort of army reunion," Aidi replied. "At the Glory. I can wait till then, if you'd rather."

Kunessin smiled. "You're going to say no," he said, "and I don't want you putting off the others. So I thought I'd get you over and done with first."

"Fair enough," Aidi said. "You've finally packed in the army, then."

"Yes."

Aidi nodded. "About time, too. No kind of life for a grown man."

"Quite," Kunessin said. "No, what I've got in mind is something rather more worthwhile, for a change. But I can see you're settled, doing well for yourself. You won't be interested."

Aidi yawned. "Probably not," he said. "But try me anyway."

There was no easy way to describe how Kunessin changed, but the difference was too extreme to overlook. He sat perfectly still, but he seemed almost impossibly tense, like a rope just about to snap. His voice was suddenly much softer; always a sign of trouble. "Did you ever hear of a place called Sphoe?" he asked.

Aidi thought for a moment. "It's an island, isn't it?" he said. "Somewhere off the northern peninsula. Didn't their third fleet have a base there, late in the war?"

Kunessin nodded slowly. "I've been there," he said. "Looting, basically. We went to see if they'd left any stores behind that we could use — masts, planking, that sort of thing."

"And?"

Kunessin wasn't looking at him any more. "Nothing we could use," he said. "They'd cleaned it all out before they abandoned it, but they left the buildings standing, and they'd done a lot of work there — wells, drains, storage pits, you name it. It's a wonderful place, Aidi. Nobody lives there, it's twenty square miles of good deep soil sheltered by a mountain range, with a big fat river running straight through the middle. We found a furnace they'd built, so we think they'd found iron there, and the entire south side is one big oak forest. You should see some of those trees, Aidi, there's nothing that size left on the mainland. There's deer, and wild pigs, bloody great birds living in the woods that'd feed a family for a week, and it's an island, so of course there's all the fish you could ever want, and there's a cove on the north shore where turtles come up twice a year..."

Aidi was looking at him, his head a little on one side, like a puzzled dog. "That's wonderful, Teuche, and I'm very happy for you, but what's this got to do with us?"

Kunessin could see in his face that he'd already guessed the answer. "I want us to go there," he said. "You, me, Kudei, all of us. Just take it for our own and live there, like we used to talk about."

The door opened, and a tall, thin boy, fifteen or sixteen, appeared in the doorway. "Sorry," he said immediately. "I didn't..."

Aidi beckoned him in with a flick of his hand, like someone swatting at a vexatious insect. The boy took a jar off a shelf and scurried away.

"For crying out loud, Teuche," Aidi said, and the edge to his voice was both annoyance and compassion. "You can't seriously think—"

Kunessin felt the anger spurting up inside him; the special anger, the sort that comes when you're explaining something to somebody who's too stupid to understand. "We used to talk about it," he repeated, "all the time. You all liked the idea. We had an agreement—"

Aidi laughed. In retrospect, he realised it was a serious error of judgement. "Oh, sure," he said. "And when I was seven years old, the girl next door and me agreed we'd get married as soon as we were old enough. I even made her an engagement ring out of copper wire. We were young, Teuche, young and stupid and cold and wet and convinced we were going to die. I think you'd have an uphill struggle trying to hold us to it in a court of law. And that's a justice of the peace talking," he added, with a false grin. "Look," he went on, lowering his voice a little, "that place we used to talk about finding. You know what it really was? It was being out of the army, where there wasn't a war. And you know what? The rest of us found it, all of us except you. We don't need any fucking island, Teuche. Really, all we needed was to get away. From the war."

Kunessin shook his head. "No."

"From the war," Aidi repeated. "From each other. Oh come on," he added, before Kunessin could interrupt. "You're supposed to be clever; surely you can see it for yourself. We all came back here, after the war, after the service. We all live right on top of each other in this rat-arse little town, and we never see each other or talk to one another from one year's end to the next. And you know why? It's not because we all had some grand falling-out or hate each other; it's just that there's nothing left to say any more. And—well—I suppose it's because we all remind each other of stuff we'd prefer not to remember. And you don't need a chequerboard and a box of counters to figure that one out."

Kunessin realised he was standing up, which meant he was about to leave, and his leaving would be a statement of disapproval, quite possibly a severance of relations. He was sorry about that. "Good to see you again, Aidi. You've done well for yourself, I'm really pleased about that."

Aidi was shaking his head. "They'll all tell you the same thing," he said, "and then you'll be pissed off with the lot of us and never speak to us again, and I don't really think you want that. Why not just drop it? Tactical withdrawal to defensible positions? You always used to say, nine times out of ten, the best battle's the one you don't have to fight."

"We'll see," was all he could find to say. "You never know, maybe the others are better friends than you give them credit for."

Aidi's face had frozen, as though he'd pulled down a visor. "So long, Teuche."

Kunessin walked out of the shop, and found that the sun had come out, slanting down over the roofs of the north-side buildings like a shower of pitched-up arrows. He found the warmth and light annoying, almost offensive.

For a long time after he'd gone, Aidi Proiapsen sat still and quiet in the back room, staring at a corner of the ceiling. Then he got up, opened a drawer in the desk in the corner, took out a ledger and went through it, quickly and with purpose, jotting figures down on a scrap of paper. His lips moved as he did the mental arithmetic. They'd laughed at him for doing it at the Military College, back when he was so young he actually cared what people thought about him. Now he did it as a deliberate affectation, because nobody would ever dare laugh at him again.

He found the total, added up again to make sure, and wrote the result down on the palm of his hand. Less than he'd thought; he sighed, and put the ledger away.

"Mind the shop," he told the middle-aged woman behind the counter. "I'm going out for ten minutes."

He crossed the road, turned left, headed up the Ropewalk as far as the corn exchange. On the corner there was a small, rather miserable tea-house, shutters down and almost bare of paint, a door that stuck in the damp weather. He went inside, waited a moment until his eyes adjusted to the gloom, found the man he was looking for and walked over to where he was sitting.

The man was drinking thin soup from a wooden bowl with an enormously wide spoon. At least a quarter of it was soaking into his shirt; his eyesight wasn't good, but he denied the fact, like a king refusing to acknowledge the existence of a rebel government.

"Proiapsen," he said.

Aidi scowled down at him. "You actually eat the muck they serve in here?"

"It's cheap," the man replied. "Food's just fuel. What do you want?"

"You know perfectly well."

The man grinned and laid his spoon down on the bare table. "It can't be anything to do with the offer I made you," he said, "because you told me you didn't want to know. In fact, you were quite offensive about it; a smaller man would've borne a grudge. So it must be something else, mustn't it?"

Aidi sighed and put the scrap of paper down in front of him. The man shook his head. "Can't read that," he said. "Your handwriting's terrible."

"You're going blind, you mean," Aidi replied. "Terrible thing that must be, blindness. It's the one thing I've always been really scared of. I feel sorry for you."

The man grunted. "The hell I am," he said, picking up the paper and holding it a hair's breadth from his nose. "The light's so bad in here. What's all these numbers?"

Aidi drew in the deep breath that's supposed to help you stay calm. "Stock at cost," he said, "fixtures, goodwill, accounts due less accounts owed. Take it or leave it."

The man made a performance of staring at the paper, spinning it out for as long as he could. "What's that?" he said. "Looks like a six."

"It's a nine."

"Can't do it," the man said abruptly. "It's not worth that to me. You know my offer. It's that or nothing."

If I kill him, Aidi thought, it'd count as a breach of the peace. "All right," he said. "Split the difference."

The man picked up his spoon. "I'll have to think about it."

"No." Aidi lifted the bowl out from under the man's nose and put it down on the floor. "This is your one and only chance, and I'll need the money in three days. Otherwise, no deal."

"Let me see those figures again."

Aidi screwed the paper into a ball and dropped it carefully into the soup bowl. "Yes or no."

"Ten thousand."

Aidi closed his eyes. "Fine," he said. "Three days' time, here, in silver money, and you can be absolutely fucking sure I'll count it. All right?"

The man sighed. "Soldiers," he said. "Why do you always have to be so aggressive about everything?"

Aidi turned to go, but as he reached the door, the man called him back. "Just out of interest," he said. "Why?"

"I'm leaving town."

"For good?"

"Yes."

"Ah." The man nodded. "Going somewhere nice?"

He had his back to the man, who didn't see him smile. "You bet," he said. "By all accounts, it's the earthly fucking paradise."

He slammed the door, presumably to make sure it shut properly. After he'd gone, the man picked his soup off the floor, fished out the scrap of paper, and finished his meal. Business and emotion, he fervently maintained, were all very well, but wasting food was a sin.

TWO

When the Confederation stormed the enemy stronghold of Ieres, the leaders of the allies expressed their thanks to Colonel Kunessin by giving him the wife of the garrison commander, who'd been killed during the assault. She was, they told him, the only thing worth having in the place, and it was the least they could do to show their appreciation.

Colonel Kunessin was, of course, notoriously shy around women, though the allies hadn't known him long enough to be aware of it. He knew they'd put the wretched girl in his tent, and he spent an awkward evening finding excuses not to go there, though he was painfully tired after a long, difficult day. Eventually, he couldn't hold out any longer. He rehearsed a little speech as he walked back through the camp, all about how he believed in treating civilians with proper respect and how magnanimity in victory was the mark of a civilised society. When he pulled back the tent flap and saw her sitting on the edge of the bed, however, all his well-chosen words evaporated like spit on a griddle, and he found himself stuck in the doorway, unable to go out again and desperately unwilling to go in. She turned her head to look at him; she'd been crying, understandably enough, and her make-up had run, leaving her with sooty black rings round her eyes, like a blacksmith.

"Look," he said, "I know you've had a rough day, but would you mind terribly sleeping on the floor? You can have all the cushions, and the rug. Only I really do need the bed."

She looked at him, and he was beginning to wonder if she could understand his dialect; then she said, "All right," and smiled at him. It wasn't forgiveness—he'd have been shocked if it was—but it acknowledged a gracious intention; and he realised she was the first person he'd met in a long time who actually came close to understanding how his mind worked.

"Thanks," he said, and sat down on the bed, just as his knees gave way. He heard the bed creak, and felt embarrassed. The best you could say for her was that she was attractively plain, but she did have rather fine grey eyes. "Is it all right if I put the lamp out now? I've got to get some sleep."

"I'll do it," she said, and the light went out. He yawned before he could stop himself, and closed his eyes.

Some time later, he wasn't sure how long, he woke up and found he was sitting bolt upright with his eyes wide open.

"Are you all right?" the woman's voice said.

He knew he was awake, because it was dark, and in his dream it had been broad daylight. "Sorry," he said. "Did I wake you?"

"You were having a nightmare," she said.

"Yes." He lay down again, but kept his eyes solidly open, just in case. He had no desire whatsoever to go back into the sunlight. "I get them a lot. You can probably guess why."

She didn't reply immediately; then she said, "If you like, I can tell you how to deal with that."

Naturally he was suspicious, but he said, "Can you?"

"It's quite simple," she replied. "My mother taught me. She was a doctor."

That didn't sound right, but then he remembered: they had women doctors in Coine Ariste, and women clerks and teachers and merchants. "I'd be very interested," he said politely.

"All you do," she said, "when you fall asleep and find you're in a dream, straight away you look round for a door. Doesn't matter where you are: in a field, on a beach, in the middle of a forest or a desert. You look round for a door, and you'll find one. Go straight through it, and as soon as you're through, you can decide what the dream's going to be; and if it starts getting nasty once you're there, just do the same thing over again. Look for a door and go through it. It works, really."

He thought for a moment. "I get these recurring nightmares," he said, "the same one every night for a week, sometimes, so I know them pretty well, and there's never a door in them anywhere."

"You need to look for it," she said. "Try it, it works. Only," she went on, "you do need to be careful, because sometimes there's two doors next to each other, and whatever you do, you must choose the left door—you're right-handed, aren't you?"

"Left-handed, actually."

"Oh. In that case, always take the right door. If you go through the other one, you'll find yourself in a memory, and you can't always choose where you'll end up. It's never actually happened to me," she added, "but my mother told me about it, and she was very firm."

He thanked her and lay back on the bed, trying to keep his eyes open, but he couldn't. Very soon, they closed and he was back in the dazzling sun; but this time, as he looked round at the terrible sight, he saw a doorway, set into one of the granite outcrops. Oh, he thought, and walked towards it. As he got closer, he saw that there were two doors, side by side, identical. He tried to remember what the woman had said, but the words were already drifting away, like the fragments of a dream when you wake up. Look for a door and go through it. It works, really. Yes, but there'd been more to it than that. Whatever you do, you must choose the—

Behind him, they were all looking at him. No, he thought, I really can't face all that again. Then he heard his own voice: left-handed, actually; and he felt his left-hand fingers flex. He reached out and opened the left door.

"General Kunessin," the woman said. "Are you all right?"

He opened his eyes. "What?" he said.

"You were shouting." She was tall and pale, with grey hair drawn tightly back in a bun. "I could hear you downstairs in the parlour."

Marvellous, he thought. "Sorry," he said, "just a bad dream." His left hand was numb; he'd been lying on it. He'd been doing that a lot lately, and it gave him cramp the whole of the rest of the day. "What time is it?"

She answered by pulling back the curtain and opening the shutters: broad daylight. "There's breakfast in the common room," she said, "or I could bring you something up."

She wasn't to know, of course. "Thanks," he said, "but I don't eat breakfast. Did you manage to get my boots mended?"

She looked at him. "He did the best he could," she replied, "but he said the leather's all perished, there's nothing left to sew into. I don't know why you don't get yourself a new pair. There's a very good cobbler in town, at the corner of Lattengate and the Ropewalk."

"I know," he said, "but I like that pair. I've got awkward feet," he lied. "It's hard to find boots that fit me."

He knew why he lay on his left hand, of course: so he couldn't use it. But it never worked. The pins and needles were starting now, particularly severe this morning. He'd been to see a doctor about it, the last time he was in Coine Ariste. Try lying differently, she'd said.

The woman was laying out his clothes for him, everything nicely pressed and folded, which made him feel ridiculous. He'd only started undressing to sleep six months ago.

"There was someone asking after you earlier," the woman said, draping his socks over the back of a chair. More holes than socks, she pointedly didn't say. "A farmer, by the look of him. He said he'd call back at noon."

"Thank you," he said, a little louder than he'd have chosen. "Tall man, broad shoulders, red hair, sunburnt, lots of lines round the eyes."

She seemed rather startled. "That's him," she said. "You know him, obviously."

He couldn't help smiling. "Since we were both three years old," he said. "We grew up next door to each other, and we both started at the Military College on the same day. But he came home after the war, I stayed in the service." I'll shut up now, he thought.

"Well, anyway," the woman said, "he called." The implication being: if he calls again, tell him to wipe his boots.

"Thanks."

She looked at him as she left, and he spared a tiny flake of compassion for her; farmers, in their work clothes, calling at the Glory of Heroes. The world was indeed hastening to its end, and here she was, caught up in its dying throes. But never mind, he thought.

Since we were both three years old. He frowned and swung his legs over the side of the bed. Scarcely a day out of each other's sight for twenty-seven years. The intriguing question was (and he'd never been able to answer it): which of them was substantial, and which the shadow.

Of course, he'd never be able to forgive him about the farm.

He pulled on his clothes, dragged a comb through his hair and beard, and put on his boots. He felt thick-headed, stupid; too much sleep, he decided. Kudei would be back again at noon. Something to look forward to.

He put on his coat, realised he'd forgotten something, took it off again, and picked up his sword-belt. Unlike most of his fellow generals, he'd never bothered with a special sword—blued and gilded blade, ivory grip, chiselled quillons, any of that. On the day he left the service, he'd sneaked into the armoury and helped himself to a standard Type Fourteen off the rack; hadn't even bothered drawing it from its sheath to examine the blade. Since then, he'd had it out to oil it once a week, scrub off the fine pitting of rust under the rain-guard with a handful of steel swarf, because he'd been taught to do that in college and old habits linger. But he'd worn it every day. When he was young, old soldiers had told him that after a while, a soldier can't walk properly without that three-pound weight on his left hip; you feel unbalanced, as though one leg's suddenly become an inch shorter than the other. Unlike most things the old-timers had told him, that one had proved to be true. He'd chosen a long coat, so only the chape showed under the hem. He'd gone for a Type Fourteen rather than a Fifteen because it was shorter. Even so, some people noticed, and he didn't like the way they stared at him, though he couldn't blame them for it. The chape bumped on the treads as he went downstairs. That's right, he thought, tell everybody in the building I'm coming.

Outside the air was cold and slightly damp, the remains of a sea fret blowing over from the west. There was just enough mist left to soften the lines of the houses, and he felt drops of moisture forming in his beard and moustache. I've forgotten how to be cold, he thought; careless of me. He walked slowly down the Ropewalk, stopping from time to time to stare in through the doorways of shops, until he reached an old stone building with a weatherbeaten frieze of a bee carved over the lintel. The door was closed, unlike those of the ordinary shops.

A young clerk scowled at him as he walked in. "Yes?"

"I need to see the resident," Kunessin said.

The clerk's face hardened, like red-hot steel quenched in water. "Is he expecting you?"

Kunessin took a packet from his sleeve: a sheet of paper folded small and sealed with a dark red blob. The clerk recognised it, and immediately turned into someone else. "I'll tell him you're here," he said brightly. "Please take a seat; he won't be long."

"Hurry it up a bit, can't you?" Kunessin said. "I haven't got all day."

The resident turned out to be a short, wide man who looked like he was trying to carry a cushion wedged under his chin. The letter clearly bothered him.

"I'm sorry," he said, "we don't usually hold sums like this on the premises. I'll have to send to Aeres for the balance."

Kunessin frowned. "How long will that take?"

"Two days there," the resident replied, "three, maybe four days back. The roads at this time of year..."

"How much can you let me have right now?"

The resident thought about it for a moment. "We can probably find you twelve thousand in ready cash," he said.

Kunessin nodded. "Write me bills of exchange for the balance," he said, "in units of one thousand. I take it they'll be good here in town."

"Of course," the resident said. Kunessin noticed that he was sweating slightly. "Will you be staying long?"

"Not six days," Kunessin said. "I'm disappointed," he added. "Your resident in Intera said you'd have the whole lot on deposit here."

"Under normal circumstances we would, General Kunessin," the resident said. "But with the milder weather, the farmers put off the cull, which means——"

Kunessin stood up. "I'll be back about mid-afternoon," he said. "If you can have it all ready for me by then, that'd be a big help."

One problem solved, at any rate. The two hired mules would be able to carry twelve thousand silver thalers reasonably easily. He'd have been reluctant to burden himself with a third mule; two would be bad enough. He tried not to think about the money as money, only as dead weight, heavy boxes needing to be transported from one place to another. Besides, he thought, it won't be long now, and I'll be rid of it for good. Is it possible for a human being, relatively sane and not in the grip of religious fervour, to hate money? Illogical, since money doesn't actually exist. A silver coin is simply a representative, like a delegate at a conference, participating in the general exchange on behalf of goods and labour. It's not to be held responsible for what it's exchanged for, any more than for how it was originally come by. Accordingly, hating money is like killing a herald: pointless, counterproductive and in poor taste. Even so, the thought of himself as a rich man had always bothered and disturbed him. Once it was all gone, he'd be relieved, like a man who's just carried a heavy sack up a mountain.

Down the Ropewalk to Spangate, Fish Street, North Quay, to the huge black shed at the end. The tide was in, and the slipway that led to the shed's enormous back doors was mostly under water, giving the impression that the shed was trying to drink the sea. Outside sat a stack of oak trunks, twenty or more, none less than five feet in diameter. A giant lives here, Kunessin thought.

He walked up to the front door, which was slightly open, and went inside. Nobody about; but in the middle of the floor, in a cradle of massive beams, lay the bones of a ship, a carcass picked clean by scavengers. The air was thick with floating dust.

"Hello?" Kunessin called. His voice echoed back off the high roof.

An old man appeared, apparently out of nowhere. He was small and thin, in clothes many sizes too big and lacquered like armour with tar. He looked at Kunessin with barely disguised horror.

"Good morning," Kunessin said. "I'd like to buy a ship."

The old man looked at him as if he was dangerous. "You don't look like a fisherman."

"I'm not."

"Or a trader."

Kunessin shook his head. "I'm not a trader," he said. "You don't remember me, do you?"

"Can't say I do."

He smiled. "I'm Teuche Kunessin," he said. "Heloria's son."

For a moment, the old man was perfectly still. Then he nodded, as though reluctantly agreeing to a deal that would end up costing him money. "You're back, then."

"Not stopping," Kunessin said. "More like a brief visit."

The old man frowned. "I heard you were still in the army."

"Retired."

At last, he'd said something the old man could bring himself to endorse. "That's right," he said. "That's no kind of a life. What did you say you wanted?"

Hard to believe, Kunessin told himself, that his mother and this creature had shared a grandfather. "A ship," he said. "For choice, I'm after a ketch, around a hundred and fifty tons' burden, square-rigged on the foremast, with the mainmast stepped well aft, and I need it as soon as possible."

The old man blinked twice. "You got any idea how much something like that'd cost you?"

Kunessin grinned. "About eight thousand," he said. "With all canvas, ropes and gear."

"Can't help you," the old man said. "I got nothing like that at all. Could build you one, take about three years."

"I need it now," Kunessin said firmly. "What've you got?"

The old man thought for a very long time. "I know for a grab," he said. "Three masts, two hundred ton. Head's all rotted out, mind, and shipworm pretty bad in the keel. Could have her seaworthy in nine months, but not before."

"No good," Kunessin said. "Anything else?"

"Got a brigantine," the old man said doubtfully. "At least, I know for one. Prize of war; it's with the agent now. He might take ten thousand for it, to be shot of it."

"Too much money," Kunessin said. "Nine's my limit, and that's pushing it."

The old man scrubbed his face with the palm of his hand. "There's a snow might suit you," he said doubtfully. "Belongs to a man out to Schetlia. Good ship, sound; had it from his brother who died, and he's no sailor, so he'd most likely sell for ready money." He shrugged. "I can ask."

Kunessin frowned. He'd done his best with the chapter on ships in Standing Orders, but that was the sum total of his maritime knowledge. "All right," he said. "What the hell's a snow?"

The old man looked at him as though he was simple. "Merchantman," he said. "It'd be around two hundred pushing two fifty, two masts, only the small mast back of the mainmast carries a mizzen. Well?"

Kunessin shrugged. "If that's all there is, fine," he said. "And you think I can have it for nine thousand?"

"Don't know about that," the old man said. "Reckon he'd want nine and a half, and that's without sheets and lines. I can ask."

"You do that," Kunessin said. "Tell him it'll be cash, no bills or letters, just silver money. That ought to make a difference, I'm sure."

The old man studied him for a while. "I thought you said you were in the army," he said. "Where'd you get hold of that kind of money?"

Kunessin smiled. "From dead people," he said. "A great many of them. I'm at the Glory; leave a message for me there as soon as you've talked to this man, all right?"

As he walked back into town, he thought: so I've just bought a snow. A snow, for crying out loud; what kind of name for a ship is that? Not, he reassured himself, that it matters, just so long as it gets us there and we can fit all the stuff inside. Still, if I'm spending that much money, I'd have preferred something I'd at least heard of.

(And supposing they refuse? Supposing they don't want to come with me, and the whole thing falls through? What the hell am I going to do with a two-hundred-ton mizzen-rigged snow? But if they refuse, none of it'll matter very much. So let's hope that won't happen.)

Nothing to do for the rest of the morning; no errands, no visits. He went back to the Glory of Heroes and sat on his bed, staring out of the window.

"Teuche Kunessin," he said, mouthing the words like a child playing with its food. "Now there's a name I haven't heard in a long time."

Alces nodded. "I never thought I'd see him again," he said. "I assumed he'd probably carry on in the service till he was a field marshal or something, then retire, buy a big country estate somewhere on the mainland, and spend his life riding to hounds and building ornamental fountains in the grounds of his mansion. That, or he'd buy a farm and settle down. I don't know," he added with a shrug. "I guess I just stopped thinking about him, once I came back."

"What do you think he wants?"

"I really can't begin to imagine." Alces hesitated, the glue pot in one hand, the brush in the other. "I don't suppose it'll be good news for anybody."

"What makes you say that?"

"I don't know," Alces said, putting the brush down. "There was always this rather scary streak in his nature. Don't know how you'd describe it. He kept getting big ideas."

Heure Alces grinned. "I can see where that'd strike you as dangerous," he said. "Never been a major fault of yours, thinking big."

"Thanks, Dad," Alces said grimly. "You were the one who said pack it in, settle down."

"True." Heure Alces nodded. "But maybe I had something other in mind. Damn it, son, when you came back from the war, you had money. You made damn sure you let us know about it. What happened?"

"Oh, well." Alces took the strip of rawhide and began stretching it over the glue-brushed handle, pressing out the air-bubbles as he went. "It didn't seem real, if you see what I mean. I guess I'd never really believed there'd be a rest of my life; after the service, I mean. So when I woke up one morning and found myself in it, I didn't really know how to handle it. I ended up treating being home as one long leave, the assumption being that sooner or later I'd be going back, so what I did couldn't possibly matter. And then, of course, I met Enyo and..." He shook his head. "Trouble was, by that point there wasn't quite as much money left as I'd have liked. But there's still some. A bit, just in case. And the school's doing all right. It's a living."

Heure held down the end of the rawhide with his fingertip while his son wrapped string round the handle to keep the hide pressed down firm while it dried. "You've never talked much about any of that stuff," he said. "I always assumed—"

"Nothing to talk about," Alces interrupted. "Mostly it was just boredom and hard slog: marching, sleeping rough, eating garbage. Waiting around. You'd spend a week sat in a tent in a muddy shithole in the rain, bored out of your head, and then suddenly it'd be forced marches, dragging yourself through a swamp to get somewhere in a hurry, then another week sat doing nothing and then back to where you started off from. Or else it'd be digging ditches, or building walls, and we never did find out what the hell it was in aid of. Some clown on a horse'd come along and say, 'You men, build a wall,' and that'd be that. Hardly ever came back to see if we'd done it how he wanted it; and then there'd be new orders, be twenty miles away by this time tomorrow." He shook his head. "Actual fighting time, maybe one month in every year. It was the least of our worries really."

Heure Alces waited till his son was looking the other way, then considered him carefully. Whatever else he might have been, he'd never been a liar before. But people changed at the war, he knew that, even though he'd never been a soldier himself. "Talking of which," he said, "I seem to remember you brought some other stuff home with you, besides the money. What became of it?"

Alces' head twitched, like a horse avoiding the bridle. "Got rid of it," he said. "Hardly likely I'd ever need it again. Why?"

"Just curious."

"Junk," Alces said, "cluttering the place up. And we're not exactly well off for space here."

"I guess not," Heure said. "Only, you could've made a display of it or something. Impress the customers, genuine war souvenirs. Something to show you'd actually been in the service."

"Maybe. Anyway, it's all gone, so it's too late now. All right, that ought to do it, you can let go now." Heure moved his finger, and Alces tied off the ends of the twine in a small, neat knot. "There," he said, "that's saved me a thaler fifty." He picked up the mended foil and put it back on the rack. "That's the Eridi boy," he said. "He loves to whack with the foil, like he's back on the farm threshing corn. God only knows why his father sends him up here, he'll never learn anything. Thinks he knows it all already."

Heure shrugged. "The public," he said, "bless them. It's the same in tailoring: they always think they know more about your job than you do, and then you get the blame when it ends up looking a mess." He grinned. "Do you remember Thoas Proiapsen? Great big fat man, but he insisted on trousers five inches too small in the waist."

"Oh God, him." Alces smiled. "Yes, and he used to come hammering on the door in the middle of the night, after he'd been thrown out of the Golden Bow, said you'd made him look like a fool and he wanted the alterations done then and there."

Heure nodded. "Your mother threw a bucket of water at him once."

"You're kidding."

"I'm not. She missed, mind, which was just as well, since the old bugger was a justice of the peace. Don't suppose he even noticed, though." Heure paused—in retrospect, just a bit too long. "You knew his son, didn't you? What was his name?"

"Aidi," Alces replied.

"That's right, of course. He's got the big mercantile in the Ropewalk now. Done very well."

"Indeed. A damn sight better than me, is what you're saying." Alces shrugged. "If he's done all right for himself, he'll have deserved it. Always very smart, top of the class at college. Of course, brains run in the family. His great-grandfather—"

"Yes, I'd forgotten that," Heure said. "The famous philosopher."

Alces grinned. "Aidi didn't inherit that," he said. "Always the practical sort. Saved all our necks a time or two, though. Now if he'd stayed on in the service, he'd be commander-in-chief by now. But he'd never have stuck it. Not exactly the fools-gladly type; and if there's one thing you get in the army, it's fools. You can tell them quite easily: they're the ones on white horses with gold braid down their fronts."

"Like your friend Teuche Kunessin."

"Ah well, he's the exception." Alces suddenly stood up, and Heure knew what that meant: end of subject. "You coming round later for your dinner?"

Heure shook his head. "Your aunt Theano asked me over," he said.

"Ah." Alces nodded gravely. "Run out of excuses, then."

"It's not that bad," Heure said. "At least she can't ruin bread."

After he'd gone, Alces swept the floor, checked the guards and buttons of the foils and trimmed the lamps, taking his time about it. It was getting dark outside. He went to the window; he could just see the glow of the porch lantern of the Glory of Heroes. Well, he thought. He sat down in the window seat, as the last of the light faded.

"Fifty thalers," the man said. "Take it or leave it."

Muri Achaiois turned his back on him for a moment, walked a step or two toward the door. "Sorry to have wasted your time," he said.

The man frowned, and maybe he moved just a little bit closer to the large wooden box in the middle of his shop floor. "You won't get a better offer," he said. "Not in Faralia."

"Then I won't sell them," Muri said. The man retreated as he approached the box, and reached down and slammed the lid. "You're quite right," he agreed. "You'd only have ended up losing money. It's not what you might call a big reading town."

The man was staring at the box. "I can run to fifty-five," he said.

Muri shook his head. "I wouldn't," he said. "You'll regret it if you do. I mean," he went on, flinging back the lid of the box and snatching a book at random, "look at this. *Types of Ethical Theory.* Who's going to want to buy that round here?"

"Quite," the man said nervously.

"Or this one. Neas' *Metaphysics.* You'd get so sick of looking at it up there on the shelf after a while, gathering dust, taking up space. No, I think you're wise to pass on this lot. Thanks for listening."

The man frowned. "Where'd you get them all, anyway?" he asked.

Muri shrugged. "My old college books, a lot of them," he said. "And others I picked up while I was abroad, in the service."

"That's right," the man said. "I remember someone telling me you were in the army. I was in the war too, you know."

Muri's eyes went blank, but the man didn't appear to have noticed. "Were you really?" Muri said. "What unit?"

"Commissariat," the man replied. "Master supply sergeant. How about you?"

Muri moved a little closer, just within arm's length. "I was a line-breaker," he said.

The man's lips moved, but no sound came out at first. "Is that right?" he said. "Well..."

"Anyway," Muri said. "That's where most of them came from, plus a few I bought since I got home. Not many, though. Not many booksellers come this way, after all."

The man was nodding. "So basically," he said, "they're imported books, right?"

Muri frowned. "You could say that, yes."

"Imported books are different," the man said quickly. "Imported anything's got to be better than the local stuff, hasn't it?"

"You think so?"

"Oh yes, no question about that. Cushions, lamps, crockery and tableware. Books too, stands to reason. I mean, I don't suppose there's another copy of—what was that one again?"

"*Types of Ethical Theory.*"

"Don't suppose there's another one of them anywhere in Faralia," the man said. "Scarcity value. Prestige item. Bound to find the right buyer sooner or later."

Muri considered that for a moment, then shook his head. "I doubt it," he said. "*Practical Carpentry*, yes, or *Secrets of the Bedchamber*. But not philosophy and ethics."

"You got either of them?"

Muri smiled. "Oddly enough, yes," he said. "They're down at the bottom of the box somewhere, I'm pretty sure."

"Good condition? All the pictures?"

"Unopened," Muri replied. "But some of the others are downright tatty. I mean, look at this one."

The man peered at the spine. "*Principles of Applied*... What's that word?"

"Geometry," Muri said. "It means the study of lines and angles."

"Sounds interesting," the man said, with less than total conviction. "Seems to me, if there's some kid going up to the Military College, he'll be able to buy all his books here before he starts. Give him an advantage over the other kids, I bet, if he's read the books before he gets there."

For some reason, Muri's face darkened. "Quite possibly," he said. "A bit of a long shot, though, don't you think? I mean, nobody sends their sons to the College these days."

"Tell you what," the man said desperately, "I'll give you seventy-five for the lot. Apart from *Types of*... that one," he added. "You can keep that. But throw in the box, I could use that myself. Well?"

Muri nodded gravely. "Deal," he said, and held out his hand. The man hesitated, very briefly, before shaking it, and he held his body out of the way, like someone stoking a very hot fire.

When Muri had left the shop, the man's wife came out from behind the curtain separating the front and back rooms. She marched up to the box, kicked it open with her tiny, delicate foot and said, "Are you out of your mind?"

The man scowled at her. "Bargain," he said. "We'll make a packet off this lot."

She swung round to face him, and not for the first time he wondered if he'd been sensible, marrying a woman half his age and height, who nevertheless had the knack of making him feel like he was six years old. "Books," she said. "College books," she added, making the word sound intolerably decadent.

"Like I told him," the man muttered. "Get a student in here, just off to the College —"

"Oh, right," his wife cut in, swift and sharp as an arrow. "Like we get a lot of them."

"We get all sorts," the man said firmly. "Anyway, they're not all college books. There's a *Secrets of the Bedchamber* in there, that's got to be worth —"

"That's going on the fire," his wife said. "And don't you let me catch you so much as opening it."

"Don't be stupid," the man pleaded. "To the right customer, it'll near enough pay for the whole lot, and then anything else we sell'll be straight profit. I'm not stupid, you know."

Her face told him she knew no such thing. "Who was he, anyhow?" she said. "You were practically licking his boots."

"Soldier," her husband replied, looking the other way.

She sniffed. "Soldier doesn't mean anything," she said. "Everybody's a soldier. *You* were a soldier. Doesn't mean anybody treats you like you're God almighty."

Self-evident, he thought; but it was far too late to do anything about that now. "He was a linebreaker," he said. "Got to show a bit of respect."

"What's a linebreaker?"

Muri Achaiois didn't go back to the tanner's yard. Instead, he crossed the road, walked up the alley between the livery stables and the tailor's shop, then up the steep, narrow street that led out of town, on to the hill. At the top, he paused and looked down at the town.

Faralia, he thought: a place to have come from, a place to get away from. People from Faralia tended to do well in the outside world, presumably because they had the extra incentive that if they failed, they'd have to go back home.

The seventy-five thalers filled both his jacket pockets; they bumped on his thighs as he walked, like saddlebags on a mule. The books had made Faralia bearable, and now they were gone; but that was all right (apparently), because Teuche Kunessin was back, back but not stopping, and wherever Kunessin was going, he was going too.

(He could almost hear her voice, in the back of his head: are you out of your mind? Going off with Kunessin, after the last time? Get real, Muri, you're too old for the wars, and if it's not that, it'll be something even worse. Mark my words, that man'll be the death of you.)

He thought about that. Probably not the wars, he decided. If Kunessin wanted to fight, he'd have stayed in the army; and besides, Kunessin had always been the one who didn't want to fight, only to stay alive and win if possible. The terrible thing about him was that, quite early, he'd reached the horrible truth that the best way to achieve those ends was to kill the enemy, as quickly and efficiently as possible.

Teuche wasn't to blame, he told himself, firmly and without conviction. He only did what was necessary. Without him, we'd none of us be here now. He was the only one who —

He realised he'd reached the edge of the cliff. Below (nothing between him and them but empty air) were the rocks of the North Shoal: Steeple Rock, Spit Rock, the Needles. Someone had said of Kunessin, years ago, that if he fell off a cliff, he'd learn to fly before he reached the bottom. The same, they said, was true of A Company as a whole. They were unkillable. Death simply didn't apply to them. He took one step forward, until the tip of his toe was just over the edge.

Not the wars, then; something else. Something even worse. Well, it could be anything, because nobody ever had more ideas than Teuche Kunessin. Anything from growing figs in the Stasin to gathering dried bat guano in the Iphthimous caves, and always the same tantalising promise to go with it: we could make a good living, we could put all this shit behind us, we could live like ordinary people, and nobody'd ever know. All my life, he used to say, I've wanted to be a stranger somewhere, I've wanted to go where nobody knows me. And they'd all grinned, and told him: fat chance of that.

Just think of it, though, Muri told himself. Just think of a place where we could be nothing more than five middle-aged men on a beach, walking up the road into town.

It's my own stupid fault, he thought. I could've said anything, but I had to go and tell that man I was a linebreaker. Couldn't resist, just once more, to see the shock in his eyes, the respect, the nervousness, the fear. They hate us really, Teuche used to say; they only tolerate us because they know we're not going to live much longer. And then he'd grin and say, wouldn't it be a laugh if we survived this war and went home? They'd have to either make us kings or poison our beer, or both.

He peered down, past his toes. Not the first time he'd thought about doing it. A cliff made it so easy, so convenient. You just had to take one step forward, until you reached the point where your centre of balance was over the edge. If you were scared or got cold feet, you could shut your eyes, so you wouldn't actually know when you'd passed that critical point. There'd be a short time, five or six seconds, when you'd still be alive, but falling, without any hope or possibility whatsoever of getting out of it. Then... It'd be over so quickly, you probably wouldn't even know. It was something you could do practically on a whim, in the split second when it seemed like a good idea, and once you'd committed yourself to it, there'd be no turning back, no resolution-sapping possibility of changing your mind. One step, and that'd be that. For two pins...

(His mother's favourite phrase: for two pins. As soon as he thought of her, he knew he couldn't do it; because just suppose there was a life after death, and when he got there she was waiting for him, bursting to tell him exactly what she thought of what he'd made of his life. It really was enough to make you determined to stay alive as long as possible.)

As soon as he'd reached that conclusion, of course, he felt sick and dizzy, and a gust of wind nudged him a little bit closer to the edge. He whimpered, twisted, felt his balance go and threw himself backwards, landing painfully, sitting down hard on a big chunk of stone. The jarring of his spine made him squeal like a pig (and you think that's painful, he pointed out to himself, think what it'd be like mashing your head on a big sharp rock. How stupid can you get?).

Fine, he thought, once he'd got over the pain and the panic. That's that settled, then. I'm going with Teuche Kunessin. But you'd decided that all along, hadn't you; and all this was just melodrama.

He turned his back on the sea and the cliff, as though it had insulted him, and limped back down the coast path into town. At the tanner's yard, the boss was standing beside the fleshing tanks.

"You've come back, then," he said.

"Yes," Muri said, "but I'm not stopping. I've decided to quit. You owe me four days' money."

"Oh, right." The boss scowled at him. "That's just fine. You take it into your head to piss off into the blue, and the hell with getting the order out on time, the hell with the penalty clause, I'm supposed to just hand over your money and wave you on your merry way. Well, maybe that's how you did things in the army, but in this trade—"

Muri nodded. "Point taken," he said. "You'd rather I worked out my notice, right?"

"You could bloody well say that, yes."

"Fine." Muri made a show of closing his right hand. The boss was a head taller than him, two handspans broader across the shoulders. Like that mattered. "Of course," he said, "if I smashed your face in, right now, you'd have no option but to sack me on the spot, and screw getting the order out. Otherwise you'd be a laughing stock."

The boss turned pale; not white, more a sort of dirty grey. Words seemed to have failed him.

"And I'd forfeit my four days' money, naturally," Muri went on, "so we'd both lose out. Me, my thaler twenty; you, all your front teeth. So tell you what, let's compromise. Well? What do you reckon?"

Slowly, the boss dug in his trouser pocket, withdrew his hand and dropped two thaler coins on the floor. "Keep the change," he said.

"Thank you," Muri said politely. He knew what was coming, of course. As he stooped to pick up the money, the boss aimed a kick at his head. It was a well-thought-out strategy; if he hadn't been expecting it, he'd have been in trouble, even with his reactions. As it was, he caught the boss's foot with his left hand and held it, firm as a rock, with just a little nudge to tilt him off balance until he'd finished picking up the coins. Then he let go, and the boss staggered back (just as Muri himself had done on the cliff: serendipity).

"Goodbye," he said, straightening up and smiling. It was a long time since he'd seen fear like that in anybody's face. He'd forgotten how little he liked the sight of it; quite disgusting, like something rotting. He turned his back on it and walked away, heading up the road towards the Ropewalk and the Glory of Heroes.

At the corner, he met Aidi Proiapsen. He was dressed in a beautiful new brocaded tailcoat, white breeches and black town shoes with silver buckles. It was enough to make a cat laugh.

"Hello, Aidi," he said. "How's the shop?"

"Sold it," Proiapsen replied. "How's the tanning business?"

Muri grinned at him. "Here's a riddle for you," he said. "What have a shopkeeper, a tanner, a farmer and a fencing instructor got in common? Three guesses, and you still won't get it."

Proiapsen nodded. "They're all stupid," he said. "You're going to the big meeting, I take it."

"You really sold your shop?"

"Gave it away's more like it. Still, won't be needing it where we're going, wherever the hell that turns out to be." He paused. "You seen Fly?"

Muri shook his head. "You think he'll be there?"

"To be honest with you," Proiapsen said, "I have my doubts. I'm not sure that wife of his'll let him."

Muri shrugged. "Assuming he's told her."

"Oh, he tells her everything, you can count on it. She's got him on a bit of string. You never know, he might even refuse to go. It's not likely, but it's possible."

"Fly Alces won't be left behind," Muri said confidently. "He never could bear being left out of anything. Remember that time when—"

"No," said Proiapsen.

Muri shuffled his feet. "Better be getting on," he said. "Did he give you any idea what this is all about?"

"Yes."

For a moment, Muri's face was blank. Then he grinned. "Come on," he said. "You can buy me a beer."

Proiapsen yawned. "No chance," he said. "And didn't I hear you were off the beer these days?"

Muri shook his head. "There's a difference between forswearing and not being able to afford," he said. "Of course, you've got a cellarful of the stuff back home..."

"Had," Proiapsen corrected him. "But that was this morning." He shook his head. "This morning, I even had a cellar. Not any more." He sighed. "It's wonderful, being friends with Teuche Kunessin. You get to lose everything, over and over again."

"I can see the appeal," Muri replied, "for someone like you. Gives you a chance to get it all back again, once he's finished with you. You enjoy doing that."

Without noticing, they'd started to walk, Muri lengthening his stride to keep pace with the taller man: second nature. "Just a little hint," Muri said. "I won't tell him you told me."

"No."

"But you're going, right? Or else, why would you have sold up?"

"Maybe because Teuche's back in town, and I'm getting out before he can talk me into doing some stupid, dangerous thing. Or maybe I got a good offer."

"At least reassure me it's not soldiering. I really have had enough of that."

Turning the corner, they walked into Kudei Gaeon. He was dressed in what were clearly his best clothes, and his boots were polished. He looked at them both for a moment or so, then said, "Kunessin?"

"Naturally," Proiapsen said. "What about you? On your way home from market?"

Kudei ignored him. "Haven't seen you for a while, Muri. I heard you're working at the tannery."

"I just quit," Muri said.

"How about Fly?" Proiapsen said. "I don't think he's going to show."

"Haven't seen him for a year," Kudei replied. "What makes you think he won't be there?"

"Aidi thinks his wife won't let him," Muri said. "I don't know her well enough to judge."

"She's all right," Kudei said slowly. "Mind, I'm not saying Fly didn't marry beneath him."

"That was inevitable," Proiapsen put in, "if he was ever going to get married at all. Any woman on his level would run a mile."

Kudei frowned. "They seemed happy enough, last time I saw them."

"I'm not saying they aren't," Proiapsen said. "Just like I was happy running a shop, and presumably you're happy farming. I always reckon getting well away from who you really are is one of the key elements of happiness in this world. I just think she'll stop him going, that's all."

Kudei shrugged. "We'll find out soon enough," he said. "Well, no use standing around here. If we're going, let's go."

For a moment or two, nobody moved. Then Muri lowered his head, like a calf driven into a stall, and stepped out in front of the rest, who followed in silence.

"What's a linebreaker?" she said.

Thouridos Alces frowned at her. "You said you didn't want to know."

"I changed my mind."

Alces sat down, his feet together, looking just past her. "A battle," he said, "is basically a shoving match. You've got two thick blocks of men, armed with pikes; that's a twenty-foot-long spear. When they're about to engage the enemy, the first six ranks level their pikes, so you've got six rows of needle-sharp points coming at you, with the combined body weight of a thousand men pushing them on. The idea is, nothing on earth should be able to stand up against something like that." He paused for a moment, as if thinking something through. Then he said, "You can imagine the mess you get if two armies of pikemen just crash into each other. Sure, they're all wearing breastplates and helmets, but that much weight pressing on a nine-inch spike, it's like driving a nail into a sheet of tin. Your only chance is if you can break up the enemy's line before it engages your pikemen. Punch a hole through the line, and the whole thing falls apart; and then your pikes come crashing in, and either the enemy breaks and runs away, or you slaughter them."

He paused again. For once, he had her full attention.

"Anyway," he went on, "that's what we did. Teuche, Muri, Aidi, Kudei, Nuctos and me. We ran out ahead of the pike wall, and we punched the hole. We were trained for it specially; they singled us out when we were at the Military College, told us we were going to be the flower of the infantry, and it was a great honour. They neglected to mention that most linebreakers don't survive more than two battles; a handful last for three, a very few make four. We fought thirty-seven times; thirty-seven major field engagements in ten years. It's a world record, actually."

There was a long silence. Then she said: "You must have been good at it, then."

"Oh, we were." He was staring at the wall, as if daring it, seeing who'd blink first. "There were different techniques. You could run up to the pike wall, then at the last moment you'd drop down, hit the deck, roll under the pikes and come up stabbing; we had short, wide swords, they used to call them cat-splitters, God knows why. Or you could try grabbing hold of an armful of spearheads and sort of jostle your way through — sounds impossible, but there was a knack to it, it could be done. That was how Aidi did it; he was so quick, he just dropped his shoulder and slid through, like a man in a crowd, and then he'd be at their faces, and there'd be nothing they could do. Muri and Kudei were droppers and rollers. I was the zweyhander-man; I had a great big two-handed sword, and I chopped the heads off the pikes. Teuche was the best of us, though. He'd push the pike heads down until he could jump up and walk on top of them, like someone crossing a stream on a fallen branch; he used a poleaxe, which is a pretty subtle tool, or you can simply use it like a hammer." He stopped; his nose had started to bleed. He wiped the blood off with his sleeve, and continued. "The worst of it was, you had to keep going, because if you stopped, you knew you had your own pikes coming straight up your arse, so if you slipped and fell over, or one of the enemy slowed you down, you'd be spitted on your own side's spearheads, and that was something you really didn't want to have happen to you. So you kept on cutting your way though, until they broke and ran or you came out the other side. It's quite extraordinary, actually, what human beings can do to each other, if they really have to. You get so tired, just from bashing metal and cutting meat; the last thing in your mind is that it's human beings you're driving a mineshaft through." He paused again, looking down at the blood on the palm of his hand. "Anyhow," he said, "that's what we used to do for a living. We did get paid a hell of a lot of money for it. Nothing was too good for the linebreakers. We used to buy the very best clothes to wear under our armour. Of course, after a battle it was all completely ruined, torn up, soaked in blood; all you could do was chuck it away and buy new, the next town you came to. Same with everything else, really. We could have the very best just for the asking, but either we spoiled it straight away or we didn't even bother with it. I mean, when that's what you do for a living, nothing else could possibly ever compare..."

She was looking at him. "You enjoyed it, then."

That made him laugh. "Of course we did," he said. "How else do you think we lasted? Oh, it was your worst possible nightmare while it was happening. We were so bloody scared, it hurt: real pain, right here in the chest. You got so cramped up with fear it was agony just breathing. And the exhaustion: it was sheer misery; such hard work you'd be nothing but a wreck of pulled muscles for a week afterwards. But of course we enjoyed it. We were heroes. We were practically gods." But then he shook his head. "That wasn't it, though. After a while, we didn't care a damn what anybody thought about us. Nobody else mattered, you see. The six of us, we were the whole world as far as we were concerned, as though we were the only six humans left in the universe, and everybody else was some other species that didn't matter; they were just there to feed and clothe us and be killed by us. We enjoyed it because it was us. It was love."

He closed his eyes. He knew she was looking straight at him, but he wasn't interested in her; she might as well have been a stranger, one of those useless, horrible creatures who'd sooner or later always ask: what was it really like? A question, of course, that he could never answer.

But instead she said, "You said six."

"What? Oh, right." He opened his eyes again. "There were six of us, to begin with. But one got killed. Right at the end of the war, would you believe? That was the really stupid thing."

For a long time, she didn't say anything. Then she stood up and left him alone. After she'd gone, he sat still and quiet, until the room was quite dark.

THREE

When Teuche Kunessin was thirteen years old, the war came to Faralia. General Oionoisin led the Seventh Regiment down the Blue River valley, trying to catch the enemy's last remaining field army before it could get to the coast, where the fleet was waiting to take it home. With hindsight, he admitted that he sent his cavalry too far ahead; the enemy dragoons cut them off and routed them at Sherden, whereupon their commander lost his nerve and withdrew them behind the defences of the coast fort at Greenmuir. The enemy immediately turned on General Oionoisin and, making full use of their cavalry superiority, forced him to fight a pitched battle six miles east of Faralia, on a high ridge of open moorland pasture. The Seventh fought well, holding off the dragoons for over an hour before their square finally broke. Once the pike wall was disrupted, however, the enemy infantry moved against them and their annihilation was inevitable. After the battle, in the absence of any effective opposition in the west, the enemy retraced their steps as far as Meshway, defeated General Houneka's Fifth Regiment and laid siege to the city. Most authorities now agree that Oionoisin's error of judgement at Faralia prolonged the war by ten years.

*   *   *

Teuche's father knew the soldiers were somewhere in the parish. He'd met Tolly Epersen as he was driving the herd back to the sheds for evening milking, and Tolly reckoned he'd seen them, a dark grey blur on the slopes of Farmoor. Teuche's father was worried, naturally enough. His sheep were on Big Moor, a hopelessly tempting prize for a large body of hungry men. He considered the risks and options: if Tolly had seen them on Farmoor an hour ago, even if they were coming straight down the combe, it'd still take them four hours to reach the pasture where the sheep were. There should be plenty of time, therefore, to get up to Big Moor and drive the flock into Redwater combe, where with any luck they wouldn't be noticed. Normally he'd have gone himself and left the milking to Teuche, but as luck would have it, he'd put his foot in a rabbit hole and turned over his ankle two days earlier, and was still limping badly. He didn't like the thought of sending the boy out where there might be stray soldiers, but he couldn't risk anything happening to the sheep. He called Teuche out of the barn, where he'd been mending hurdles, and told him what to do.

Teuche clearly wasn't wild about the idea, but he could see that it had to be done, and that his father was in no fit state to do it. He whistled up the dogs, put some rope in his pocket just in case he did meet any soldiers (if the dogs ran ahead, they'd give him away; once he got up on the top he'd put them on the lead, just in case) and set off up the course of the dried-up stream. It wasn't the shortest way, but he figured he could keep out of sight behind the high banks on that side, if there turned out to be soldiers on the moor.

The stream bed ran down the steepest side of the hill, but Teuche was young, fit and in a hurry. Because he was keeping well over to the lower side, in the shade of the ninety-year-old copper beeches his great-grandfather had planted along the top of the bank to act as a windbreak, he could neither see nor be seen, and the wind in the branches made enough noise to mask any sound he made, though of course going quietly had long since been second nature to him. It took him no more than an hour to reach the gate in the bank that led from Pit Mead into Big Moor. There he paused, pulled himself together, and peered over the gate to see what he could see.

To begin with, he had no idea what they could be. They were far too dark to be sheep, too big to be rooks or crows. If he'd been a stranger to the neighbourhood he might well have taken them for rocks and large stones; not an unusual sight on the top of the moor, where the soil was so thin and the wind scoured more of it away every year. But, thanks to his great-grandfather's windbreak, Big Moor was good pasture with relatively deep, firm soil; there were one or two outcrops down on the southern side, but none at all in the middle, and these things, whatever they were, were everywhere. His best guess was that they were some kind of very large birds; geese, perhaps.

At first, they only puzzled him; he was too preoccupied by what wasn't there, namely the sheep. He curbed the impulse to run out into the field and look for them. If they weren't there, it might well mean that the soldiers had got there first and were down out of sight in the dip on the eastern side. By the same token, the sheep might be down there too, though they only tended to crowd in down there when they needed to shelter from the rain. He couldn't decide what to do for the best, and as he tried to make up his mind, he considered the unidentified things scattered all over the field; not sheep or rooks, not stones, and there had to be hundreds of them. Thousands.

He stayed in the gateway for a long while, until he realised that time was getting on, and he still didn't know where the sheep were. Very cautiously, he climbed the gate and dropped down as close as he could to the bank, where he'd be harder to see. His idea was to work his way along the bank as far as the boggy patch, where he could use the cover of the reeds to get far enough out into the field to spy down into the hidden dip. It was a good plan of action. In spite of his anxiety, he felt moderately proud of himself for keeping his head in a difficult situation.

The first one he found was lying in the bottom of the narrow drainage rhine that went under the bank about a hundred yards down from the gate. Because of the clumps of couch grass that edged the rhine, he didn't see him until he was no more than five feet away. He stopped dead, as though he'd walked into a wall in the dark.

The man was lying on his face, his arms by his sides, and Teuche's first thought was that he was drunk; passed out and sleeping it off in a ditch, like old Hetori Laon from Blueside. He noticed that the man had what looked like a steel shell that covered his top half, from his neck down to his waist, and under that a shirt apparently made out of thousands of small, linked steel rings. Then he realised that the man's face was submerged in the black, filthy water that ran in the rhine. He ran forward to see if he could help, but stopped before he got much closer.

He'd never seen a dead man before. When Grandfather died, his mother had made him stay out in the barn; when he was allowed back inside there was no body to be seen, just a long plank box with the lid already nailed down. Maybe as a result of that, he'd always imagined that a dead body would be a horrifying, scary sight; in the event, it was no such thing. It looked just like a man lying down — a man lying down drunk, even, which was comedy, not tragedy — but he could tell just by looking at it that it wasn't human any more, it wasn't a person, just a thing. Teuche wasn't afraid of things. He went closer.

He knew the man must be a soldier, because of the steel shell and the ring shirt. From the available facts, he worked out a theory. The soldier had been drinking; he'd wandered away from the rest of the army, fallen asleep sitting against the bank, somehow slid over and ended up face down in the rhine, where he'd drowned without ever waking up. It struck him as a sad thing to have happened, sad and stupid but understandable. Something of the sort had happened to a tinker last year out over Spessi, and the general opinion had been that it had served him right.

But he didn't have time for any of that now, he reminded himself; he had to find the sheep and get them down into the combe. It occurred to him that the soldier's friends might be out looking for him, so he carried on down the bank towards the reeds, keeping his head below the skyline. He'd nearly reached the outskirts of the wet patch when he made the connection in his mind, between the dead man and the things he'd seen lying in the field.

Once the idea had occurred to him, he felt stunned, as though he'd just stood up under a low branch and cracked his head. If the grey things lying in the field were all dead men...but that couldn't be possible, because several thousand human beings don't just suddenly die like that, all together at the same time, out in the open fields.

But, he thought, they do, if they're soldiers, in a war. That's precisely what happens. He knew all about the war, and wars in general. He'd always liked hearing stories, both the old ones about the heroes of long ago, and the more up-to-date ones about how our lads were slaughtering thousands of the enemy every day, in victory after victory. It was almost impossible to believe, but maybe that was what had happened right here, on Big Moor; General Oionoisin had managed to catch up with the enemy and cut them to pieces, right here, on our top pasture...

He tried to think about the sheep, but he couldn't. He wanted to go further out into the field, to look at the bodies, but he couldn't bring himself to do it, in case some of them were still alive, wounded, dying. Shouldn't he try and do something for them, in that case? But the thought made him feel sick and terrified; the last thing he wanted to do was actually go near them, dying, as if fatal injury was something contagious you could pick up by touch. Nevertheless, he crept out from the fringe of the reed bed and walked quickly and nervously, as though he was trespassing, up the slope towards a clump of the things clustered round a gorse bush.

There were five of them. They all had the same steel shells and shirts; one of them had a steel hat, with ear flaps. It hadn't done him much good: there was a wide red gash in his neck, through the windpipe. The blood was beginning to cake and blacken, and the last of the summer's flies were crawling in it, weaving patterns with their bodies. The man's eyes were wide open—he had a rather gormless expression, as if someone had asked him a perfectly simple question and he didn't know the answer. There was another gash on his knee. His right hand was still clutching a long wooden pole, splintered in the middle. The other four men were face down, lying in patches of brown, sticky blood. Teuche noticed that the soles of their boots were worn almost through. A little further on, he saw a dead horse, with a man's body trapped under it. There was something very wrong about it, but it took him quite some time to realise that the body had no head. He looked round for it but he couldn't see it anywhere.

He tried to think what he should do. His first duty was to see if there was anybody he could help; but there were so many of them, and besides, what could he do? Suppose there were two or three, or five or six or ten or twenty or a hundred men lying here still alive, capable of being saved, if only someone came to help them. That made it too difficult. One man, one stranger, and he'd feel obliged to get him down the hill, somehow or other, back to the house, where Mother and the other women would know what to do. Just possibly he could manage one, but not two; and if there were two, or more than two, how the hell was he supposed to know how to choose between them? Besides, he told himself, these people are the enemy. They came here to kill and rob us and take our land. They deserved it. More to the point, he had to find the sheep.

He reverted to his original plan of action, though he knew it had been largely overtaken by events: down to the dip, where he found no live enemy soldiers and no sheep. That more or less exhausted his reserve of ideas, and he felt too dazed and stupid to think what to do next. After a minute or so wasted in dithering, he climbed up on the bank beside the southern gateway, where he knew he could get a good view of the whole of the river valley, from Stoneyard down to Quarry Pit. Of course, that wasn't Kunessin land; it belonged to the Gaeons, Kudei's family, but he knew they wouldn't mind if he went on to it to get his sheep back.

But there were no sheep; no white dots, only a scattering of the grey ones, stretching down the valley until they were too small to make out. That's it, then, he thought: the sheep have gone, the soldiers must've taken them after all. He knew without having to think about it that that was really bad, about as bad as it could possibly get. He tried to feel angry—bastard enemy coming here, stealing our sheep—but he couldn't. After all, the enemy had been punished enough, General Oionoisin had seen to that, and what good had it done? Thirty-five acres of dead meat wouldn't make up for losing the sheep. Then he told himself that the government would probably pay compensation, sooner or later; it stood to reason that they must, because otherwise it wouldn't be fair. You can't have armies come on to your land and kill thousands of people and steal a valuable flock of sheep and not expect to pay for it. The world wouldn't work if people could behave like that.

Anyway, he thought, there wasn't anything he could do, so he turned round and walked back. The light was beginning to fade and he had trouble getting the dogs to follow him; he'd let them off once he'd left the reed bed, since there didn't seem to be any immediate danger, and now they were sniffing at the dead bodies, completely fascinated. He wondered if the soldiers had got the Gaeons' flock as well. He knew, or he was dimly aware, that in the time since he'd left the house and climbed the hill, the whole world had changed completely and for ever, and naturally the idea troubled him. He knew that his father had borrowed money to buy the twelve pedigree ewes and the twelve acres at Lowertown, and that this seasons' lambs were supposed to pay off the loan, or the interest on the loan (all he knew about the business was what little he'd managed to gather by listening at doors and under windows), so they were in trouble to some degree. If the soldiers had robbed the Gaeons as well, maybe also the Pollons and the Alceses and everybody else in the district... The thought made him wince. If everybody was suddenly taken poor, what would happen? It was all very well assuming the government would pay for the sheep, but if all the sheep this side of Faralia had gone, money would be useless, because there'd be no sheep to buy to replace the flock with, no flock meant the loan wouldn't get paid back, and then where would they be? Then another terrifying thought struck him. What if it had been their own side, Oionoisin's men, who'd stolen the sheep? Would the government pay if it was their men, or would that count as contributions to the war effort, requisitioning and therefore perfectly legal? He had no idea how any of it worked, and that was incredibly frustrating. He found he was walking very fast, recklessly so; if he wasn't careful, he'd turn his own ankle over in the dark, and that really wouldn't help anyone.

He reached the top of the lane and realised he couldn't see any lights in the windows of the house. He had no idea what that meant, but it couldn't be anything good. He stopped by the yard gate, trying to decide what to do. He wanted to run straight to the back door and yell for his parents, but if something really bad had happened, and there were soldiers about…

(This, he thought, is what it must be like if you're a wild animal. People have it easy, now that there aren't really any predators left to hunt them. But rabbits and hares and deer must be like this all the time: danger everywhere, every movement and every moment of standing still a potential disaster. The strange thing was, the longer it went on, the calmer he felt: not a good calm, like midday break at haymaking, lying exhausted on top of the rick looking up at the clouds; more a sort of numbness, combined with vastly sharper senses. For some reason, he felt ashamed of himself for it.)

He took the long way round, skirting the vegetable garden, crossing the stream, edging right round the perimeter of the cider orchard so he'd have the poultry houses as cover as he approached the back door. He shoved the dogs in the woodshed and closed the door on them: one less thing to worry about.

At the back door he stopped again (but it wasn't indecision, panic, blankness of mind; he stopped to listen, gather intelligence, before planning his next move). He couldn't hear anything; if there were soldiers in the house, he'd expect to hear them, crashing about, stealing things, drinking the beer. Or else they were drunk already and sleeping it off. He decided it'd be safe to open the door a little.

"Who's that?" His father's voice, in the dark.

"Dad?"

"Teuche." He heard the scrape of a tinderbox, saw a little flare that became the glow of a single candle. "Where the hell have you been? Your mother's been worried sick."

"It's all right," he said, and realised that was a lie. "There aren't any soldiers, at least I didn't see any."

"Better safe than sorry," his father grunted, and the candle went out again. "The sheep. Did you find them?"

For a moment he had no voice. Then, quickly and concisely as he could manage, he gave his report. The sheep were gone, and Big Moor was full of dead bodies.

"What's that supposed to mean?" his father asked.

"Dead bodies," he repeated. "I think there must've been a battle. I didn't count them but there were a lot of them. I think they were all dead," he added, hoping that at least was true.

Dad didn't say anything for three or four heartbeats. "The sheep," he said, and his voice was disturbingly low and quiet. "Did you look in Gaeon's field? They may have..."

"They weren't there, Dad," he said, as gently as he could. "Nor Southside. I got up on the bank and looked down. If they'd been there I'd have seen them."

"Yes, but it was getting dark," Dad said (and Teuche thought: why's he being wilfully stupid?). "You could easily have missed them, specially if they've strayed up under the cover. That's where they'll be, you mark my words."

He didn't reply to that; he found it embarrassing. You couldn't make the bad stuff better by pretending it hadn't happened. "I don't think we need sit here in the dark," he said. "If there'd been any soldiers—"

"You shut your face," Dad snapped. "Only a bloody fool'd show a light, draw those buggers right here to us. You shut up and bide quiet, and then we'll go look for the sheep in the morning."

So he felt his way across the back parlour to the wall, where he knew the end of the settle was, sat down against it and rested his head against the side rail. The last thing he expected to be able to do was sleep, but he'd hardly closed his eyes when he felt something nudge his shoulder, and heard his father saying, "Come on." He looked up and saw the back door was open, a wedge of middle blue visible between the door and the frame, which told him it was just before dawn.

"We'll take the dogs," Dad said quietly. "We'll need them when we find the sheep."

The blue of the sky was thinning, and veils of early morning mist blanked off their view of the hill. They followed the dried-up stream; his father hardly said a word, which suited Teuche very well. He was ashamed of his own feelings, contempt and disgust; surely Dad had believed him when he'd said he'd looked for the sheep, so why was he pretending that finding them would be easy? He'd never known his father tell a lie, but now he seemed to be lying to himself, which was the worst kind of deceit. Pointless, he thought: he's just making it worse for himself, when the moment comes when he's got to accept what's happened. Only somebody stupid would do something like that, and weren't they in a bad enough mess already?

"Go steady," Dad said, as they came up on the gateway. "If we go rushing in, we'll only spook them."

He wanted to say: Dad, there aren't any sheep, just a lot of dead soldiers. He'd been brought up to tell the truth, hadn't he? In which case, why was he afraid to do so now? He felt as though everything was getting out of hand, coming apart, just when they most needed to stay sharp. Above all, he thought: it's not fair, it should be him being calm and sensible, not me.

Dad looked carefully up and down the line of the bank, then scrambled over the gate. In spite of everything, Teuche couldn't help admiring his father's grace and agility, exceptional for such a big, heavy man. He'd heard people saying he'd been a fine dancer when he was young, though of course he didn't have time for that sort of thing any more.

The ball of the hill was wrapped in soft grey mist, just beginning to burn off as the sun rose, so they couldn't see the bodies from the gateway. For a moment, he wondered if Dad would refuse to go out into the field to look for them: nothing here, he'd say, we'll cut back round the side and go down over Gaeons' after the sheep; and that'd be ridiculous, the sort of thing that happens in dreams, where you're shouting something important and obvious and nobody believes you.

But Dad walked out into the mist, whistling to the dogs, and for a moment Teuche wondered if he'd imagined the whole thing. Then Dad stopped, and stood still for a long time.

"Teuche." He sounded very calm now. "Come here."

Dad was standing over a dead body; a man splayed out as though he'd fallen out of a tree, his head on one side so Teuche could see the expression on his face, the eyes so wide they were almost comical, the mouth open, black jelly smeared over the chin and lower lip. "Is this the body you saw?" Dad asked.

"No," Teuche said. "I didn't come this way. But the whole field's—"

"We'll have to move him," Dad said. "Should've thought to bring a pick and shovel. Can't just leave him here for the crows, it wouldn't be decent."

Stupid mist, Teuche thought; if it wasn't for the mist, he'd see all the bodies and then we wouldn't have this stupid performance. "What about the sheep, Dad?" he said (and he was more ashamed of himself than ever). "Hadn't we better be looking for them?"

His father looked at him, and in his eyes Teuche saw a sort of panic, as though he'd been trapped. "Guess so," Dad said quietly. "This one'll keep, poor bugger. We'll split up: you go up the hill, I'll go round the headland."

But Teuche shook his head: he was in charge now. "Best if we stick together in this mist," he said. "It'd slow us up terrible if we got lost."

Quite soon they were in the thick of the bodies, and Dad was picking his way with exquisite care between them, like a man crossing a deep river on stepping stones. He'd started to mutter to himself, but Teuche made a decision not to be able to hear him. Then, without warning, Dad stopped still and turned to him.

"How many did you say you reckoned you saw?"

"Hundreds, Dad," he replied. "Thousands, maybe."

"Then that's it." Almost a whisper. "We've had it."

"Dad?"

"Don't you understand?" Dad snapped. "That's it, we've lost the farm. We're done for."

Teuche suddenly felt cold all over. "But the sheep..."

"Forget the sheep," Dad said. "That's the least of our worries." Teuche looked up at him, and saw that behind him the mist was thinning fast, and he could see the bodies, as many as the stars in the sky. He knew Dad had seen it too. "Don't you understand?" Dad said. "All this lot, hundreds of them, we can't bury them all, not in time. Can't burn them: there's not enough timber in the valley to fire this lot. We've lost Big Moor, Teuche, and without it, we can't pasture the stock. It's as simple as that. We're done."

Now he just wasn't making any sense at all. "But Dad—" Teuche started to say, but his father went on talking over him. "You know what'll happen," he said, "with the dew and a bit of rain, if we don't bury them? They'll start to rot, and they'll breed worms and flukes; the stock'll pick them up and they'll die. That's why, when an animal dies, you got to get it shifted quick. But we can't, not thousands of them; not even if we got the Gaeons and the Alceses and the Pollons up here helping, not in time. It'll be three years, soonest, before this land's fit to be grazed again, and by then, we won't be here. Do you understand me?"

Teuche almost laughed, because Dad was missing something obvious. "But it'll be all right," he said. "We'll go to General Oionoisin, he'll send his men up here and they'll—"

"No he won't," Dad said. "Don't you get it? These are our men, not the enemy. There's no army any more, there's no government. We got beat, boy, we lost the fucking battle, the enemy's in charge now. And they won't be coming up here to clean up their mess, you can bloody bank on that."

The shock hit him like a punch. It was losing the farm, going away, losing everything; but mostly it was the idea, the impossible idea, that they'd been beaten, that the enemy had won. Suddenly he was terrified, as if he expected savages to come rushing at them out of the mist, waving spears and swords. He wanted to run, but he had no idea which direction would be safe, or weren't there any safe places any more? "That can't be right, Dad," he heard himself say. "We can't have lost. General Oionoisin—"

"He might be here, for all I know," Dad said, and for some reason he was grinning. "Could be lying dead here right under our noses, like I could give a shit. If he's not dead, he's finished, just like us." Dad was twisting round on the spot, a frantic, aimless movement, like a pig in a sty when you're trying to catch it for slaughter. "The farm's gone, Teuche. If we're really lucky, we'll get enough for the land and the live and dead stock to pay off the debts, and then that'll be it. God only knows where we'll go or how we're going to live, and the war too. All because they had to go and have their stupid battle here, on our ground. Well, fuck them, they can stay here and rot and the crows can have them, because—"

That was enough. Teuche turned his back on him and walked away.

The outcome could have been worse. Dad sold the cattle at market, and prices were good because stock was short, on account of the war. The Gaeons bought the land, borrowing heavily from their cousins in Faralia. The Kunessins moved into the town, ending up in one dark room over a stable in Padgate. Teuche was lucky enough to get work in the tannery, washing down and cleaning out the troughs; it was filthy, poisonous work, but it kept him out of that terrible room, away from the silences and the bickering and the oppressive company of his beaten, humiliated family. Naturally, he lost touch with his friends, Kudei Gaeon and Thouridos Alces; but as he was leaving work one day, he met them both coming down the Ropewalk. He'd have preferred not to speak to them, but they saw him before he could melt away into the shadows. They asked him, sympathetically, what he was doing, and he told them. Neither of them had any comment to make; then Kudei said: "We're going to the Military College in the spring."

He'd heard of it, of course. "What d'you want to do that for?" he asked. "You've still got your farms."

Fly Alces scowled awkwardly, but Kudei replied, "I've had it up to here with my family. Dad and my brothers row all the time, and when they aren't doing that, they're picking on me. Besides," he added, looking away, "things aren't going so well. I'll be doing everyone a favour."

Teuche turned to his other friend. "Fly?" he said. "What about you?"

Alces shrugged. "It's boring at home," he said. "Dad's got Aclero to help him; they don't need me. And this war's not going to last for ever, and I want to be in it."

"It's not just us," Kudei put in, before Teuche could say anything. "Aidi Proiapsen and Nuctos Di'Ambrosies are going too, and the Achaiois boy, Muri, from the forge. So it's not like we won't know anyone there."

Teuche frowned. "I thought they only took gentlemen's sons."

Alces grinned. "Not any more," he said. "On account of they're running a bit short of fine gentlemen nowadays, the rate they're getting through them. You don't even have to pay: the government pays your fees and your board. So long as you can pass the tests, you get a place."

"You done the tests already, then?" Teuche asked.

Kudei shook his head. "We do 'em when we get there. But they're a piece of piss, everybody says so. We'll have no bother." He paused, and something seemed to be bothering him. "You could give it a go," he said. "Couldn't he, Fly?"

For a moment, Alces looked startled, then he said, "That's right, yes, why don't you, Teuche?"; and Teuche thought: they don't want me along for some reason; it must be because we lost the farm, so they're farmers' sons and I work in the tannery.

"I might just do that," he said. "When are you leaving?"

"Two weeks," Alces said reluctantly. "You'd need money for the journey, mind," he added, just a bit too quickly. "And there's your kit to buy, and books."

"How much?"

Alces looked scared. Kudei said, "A hundred thalers," quite quickly; he made that number up out of his head, Teuche thought.

"That's all right, then," he said. "I've been saving up, and I've got seventy. Dad'll give me the rest." He was lying, of course, on both counts, but that didn't matter; he already had an idea how to get the money. "Have you got to write and tell them you're coming, or do you just turn up?"

"I'm not sure," Alces said.

"Just turn up, I think," Kudei said simultaneously, then added, "I don't know that for a fact, mind. My dad arranged it all."

"I'll find out," Teuche said confidently. "I'll ask Aidi Proiapsen, I see him about quite often. That'll be good," he added spitefully, "all of us going to the College together. You got any idea what sort of thing they ask you in the test?"

They claimed to have no more information, and after thanking them for telling him about it, he let them go. As he walked home, he thought: the Military College, soldiering; what in God's name would I want to get mixed up in all that for? Just because Kudei and Fly didn't want him along wasn't really a good enough reason; on the other hand, why not? Working in the tannery was miserable, he certainly didn't want to stay there any longer than he could help, but what else was there in Faralia? Dad had muttered something about asking his boss at the sawmill if there was a place, but he hadn't done anything about it. Besides, the sawmill would be only a little better than the tannery. What Teuche wanted, more than anything, was to get the farm back, and any other sort of life simply didn't count. Day labouring, even training up to be a tradesman, wasn't going to get him the farm; but soldiering, being an officer... If you went to the College, a commission was practically guaranteed, and if you're in the army, what could you possibly find to spend your pay on? And there was other money to be had beside pay. He smiled grimly, remembering what Kudei had said, about things not going too well on the farm. He could believe that: the older Gaeon boys at daggers drawn with the old man all the time, and work not getting done. If things got really bad, and someone came to them with a good offer, they'd sell all right. It'd be only fitting really: since the war had taken the farm away from him, the war ought to give him the means of getting it back.

His father forbade him to go, which didn't really matter, except it meant he couldn't ask him for money. That was a nuisance. He knew there was still some left from the sale of the stock, two or three hundred, but he had no idea where Dad kept it. Not to worry: he still had the other source of funds to draw on, if it was necessary.

"He's going to make a speech," Aidi said.

Someone laughed nervously. Kunessin kept still for a moment, then grinned. "Officers make speeches, Proiapsen," he said. "I work for a living."

A grumble of laughter at the old joke; like believers intoning the responses at communion. "Anyway," Kunessin went on, "Aidi's already heard what I've got to say, so he can keep his face shut till I've finished."

"Yes, General Kunessin," Aidi replied, with a mock salute. "I'm only here in case someone feels like buying me a drink."

Muri wasn't laughing or grinning. "What's it about, Teuche?" he said. "For crying out loud, stop piddling around and tell us."

So he told them, in roughly the same terms he'd put to Aidi earlier, but with a little more restraint. Aidi was right, of course: it was a speech. The question was, had they noticed?

When he'd finished, there was a silence he could hardly bear. Then Muri said: "Count me in."

The silence resumed, and he thought: they aren't going to do it, and he was already asking himself why not: because they'd all got too old and too wise, or because Fly wasn't there? Then Kudei said, "We'll need money."

"All taken care of," Aidi called out. He was sitting in the window seat, at right angles to Kunessin, almost like the chairman of the meeting. "I sold my shop today."

Kudei looked as though he'd been slapped across the face. "I've got money," Kunessin said quickly. "Aidi, there was no call for—"

"Sod it," Aidi said firmly. "If I'm coming with you, I won't be running a shop in Faralia any more. It's not a gesture, if that's what you're thinking. Just common sense."

"I sold my books," Muri said.

"There's no way I can get anything out of the farm," Kudei said. "It's all tied up in some kind of legal trust, and besides, we're practically broke. Which is nothing new," he added.

"I don't need any money from any of you," Kunessin said. "I've already bought us a ship, and stores, everything we'll need. And there's money left over, plenty of it."

"You were a bit confident, weren't you?" Aidi said.

Kunessin shrugged. "I'm set on going," he said. "Obviously I want you all to come with me, but . . ."

Aidi waved a hand. "Let's not get bogged down about stupid money," he said. "Just to clarify, we're all going, right?"

Muri nodded briskly. Kudei kept still, but he'd have spoken if he didn't agree. Kunessin felt as though all the breath had been squeezed out of him, but he was fairly sure he hadn't let it show.

"What about Fly?" Muri said. "Maybe if we all talked to him . . ."

Aidi shook his head. "If he doesn't want to come, then fuck him."

"But he doesn't know what—"

"If he can't be bothered to come to the meeting, you can bet he's not interested," Aidi said firmly. "A pity, but there it is. I expect we'll manage without him somehow or other."

"Teuche?" Muri said.

Kunessin sighed. "Aidi's right," he said. "And I for one don't blame Fly. He's settled down—God knows how that ever happened, I never thought I'd live to see the day, but there it is. He's got a wife, and his business—"

"If you can call it that," Aidi growled. "I happen to know for a fact he made a loss last year, only just broke even the year before that. I think he's living off the farm money, plus whatever he's got left of what he brought back, though I don't suppose there's much of that. No, it's her. She had a saddle and bridle on him from the start."

"Maybe he likes it that way," Kudei said quietly.

Aidi shrugged. "Maybe he does, and why the hell not? Just don't expect him to come walking through that door any time soon."

For a long time nobody spoke, as though there was something that needed to be said, but none of them was prepared to say it. Then Kunessin shrugged. "Oh well," he said briskly. "Now, moving on. Like I just said, I've got a ship. All I know about ships and the sea is what I read in a book I liberated from Command before I left, but as far as I can make out, it's plenty big enough to get everything we need on board."

Kudei shifted in his chair. "Hang on a moment," he said. "Who's going to sail this ship of yours? We can't do it."

"We hire a crew, of course," Kunessin said. "In case it's escaped your notice all these years, Faralia's a seaport; we shouldn't have any trouble."

Kudei nodded slowly. "Fine," he said. "And once the sailors have taken us to where we're going, how are they supposed to get back?"

"On the ship," Kunessin said. "Once we've disembarked, they sail the ship back here, load up with supplies. Being realistic, we're going to depend on stuff brought in from the outside for quite some time, so a regular supply run—"

"Hold it a second," Aidi interrupted. "You're proposing we hand over the ship to a bunch of hired men and let them sail away, leaving us stranded with severely limited resources. That's maybe not the brightest idea you ever had in your life, General."

Kunessin raised his eyebrows. "I see what you mean," he said. "Well, I guess one of us'll have to go back with them. That shouldn't be a problem."

"That raises another issue, though," Kudei said slowly. "Not to put too fine a point on it, four of us — three, if someone's constantly on the ship shuttling backwards and forwards. I know it's quality that counts rather than quantity, but still, that's not a lot of manpower."

"Maybe I didn't make myself clear," Kunessin said. "I'm not proposing it should be just the four of us. Obviously we'll need more people. In fact, I was just coming to that."

Aidi was grinning. "Oh, I see," he said. "So basically we're talking about officers and enlisted men."

Kunessin frowned. "That's not really how I'd want to see it," he said. "Obviously we'll be leading the venture, putting up the money, claiming title to the land, so naturally that's got to be reflected in the way the colony's run once it's up and going. But it's got to be different from what we're leaving behind, or what's the point in going at all?"

Brief silence; then Muri said, "I haven't got a problem with that. Kudei?"

"I'm all for it," Kudei said, with a grin. "To be honest with you, I've never really seen myself as a peasant. Landed proprietor, now, that's perfectly fine, I could get used to that."

Kunessin raised his voice a little. "The buildings are already there," he said. "We'll have enough livestock to make us viable right from the start, and it's not like we're going to be clearing forest or scrubland. That's what's so special about Sphoe: with a relatively small amount of initial effort, we could have a functional settlement up and running within a year. All I'm proposing is that we take a few extra bodies — specialists: experienced stockmen, shepherds, foresters, tradesmen, either hired or indentured — to get us started. If some of them want to stay on, and they like us and we like them, then what's the big deal? There's plenty of space for everyone. I'm not suggesting we try and found the Great Society or Zeuxis' ideal republic. But like Aidi said, there's no reason why we should wear ourselves out trying to do it all ourselves. Once we've got enough land under cultivation, basic stuff in place like fences, it won't be much different from being farmers back here, except we'll be our own masters, not having to look over our shoulders all the time, no government, no taxes, nobody to tell us what to do. After seventeen years in the army, that's my idea of the earthly paradise."

He looked at them; he knew they'd all heard what he hadn't said. No war, no soldiers. He wondered if he'd lost them, at the last moment. "Kudei?" he said.

"Fine by me," Kudei replied. "You may've had seven extra years in the service. I've had seven years with my brothers. I've been on the point of just packing a bag and walking out for I don't know how long."

"Anyway," Muri said, "these are just details, we can sort them out later. The important thing is, we want to come with you, Teuche. We ought to be together again. It's been too long."

"Aidi?"

Aidi spread his hands in an exaggerated gesture. "Whatever you all decide is fine by me," he said. "Just so long as there's not too much digging, that's all I ask. And if we're going to take along a bunch of the common people to handle all that side of things, I really don't see a problem."

Kunessin frowned, but Kudei was grinning. Muri said, "It's just a shame about Fly. Do you think you could talk to him again, Teuche?"

"Just one thing," Kudei said. "You're sure this island's uninhabited? Only, if it's everything you say, it strikes me as odd that nobody wants it but you."

"There were people there once," Kunessin said, "but not any more. The military cleared them out when they built the station."

"No chance they'll come back?"

"No," Kunessin said. "I read the file. That's not an issue."

"And nobody else has got any sort of claim there?" Kudei insisted.

Kunessin shook his head.

"What about our lot?" Aidi put in. "The government..."

Kunessin smiled. "The military made a full report, compiled by a senior member of the general staff. Concluded the place wasn't viable. No realistic, cost-effective prospect of any further use."

Aidi raised an eyebrow. "Senior member of the general staff?"

"Me," Kunessin said.

"Ah. Very sensible." Aidi nodded gravely. "Well, in that case, I can't see there's any problems we can't deal with." He yawned. "I was getting bored with shopkeeping anyway," he said. "The money's good, but you've got to be polite to a lot of very stupid people you'd rather kick out into the street." He turned his head sharply and looked Kunessin in the eye. "Just so long as there's no fighting. I'm bored with that too."

Kunessin shook his head. "No fighting. Nobody to fight. And if it doesn't work out, we can always come home again."

"Yes, of course," Aidi said quickly. "Well, I don't know about you, but I feel this calls for a drink. On me, naturally. Muri, you're nearest to the bell."

"I need to get back home," Kudei said, standing up. "My turn to do the milking. When's the next staff meeting?"

"Tomorrow morning, early as you like," Kunessin said. "First item on the agenda: stores and supplies. I've already covered the basics, I think, but it's something we all need to talk about. Muri? Does that suit you?"

Muri smiled. "Sure. It's not like I've got anything else to do."

"Aidi?"

"Likewise." He frowned. "I gather we're not going to have that drink, then."

"Better not," Kunessin said. "Fact is, my drinking days are over."

"Well, you're no fun," Aidi said. "In that case, I'll see you all tomorrow." He stood up. "I have no idea what I've just got myself into, but what the hell. Good night, gentlemen."

Kudei left with him, but Muri hesitated. "I'm going to have a cup of tea," Kunessin said. "Join me?"

"Sure," Muri said, sitting down again.

Kunessin rang the bell. "Muri," he said, "I was so sorry to hear about what happened."

Muri shrugged. "It was just bad luck," he said. "You know what it's like. Just when you think you've got everything dealt with and settled."

Kunessin raised an eyebrow. "That's a rather odd way of putting it."

"You think so?" Muri laughed. "It's the way my mind works, when it works at all. Things to do today: settle down, achieve serenity, live happily ever after. Tick the box and move on. Of course, real life won't let you get away with an attitude like that, so the moment your back's turned, it slips in and trashes everything. It's probably just nature's cure for complacency, though why it needs curing I'm not entirely sure. Still, I don't make the rules." He'd been talking quickly; he stopped with equal abruptness. "What about you?" he said, after a moment. "I'll be honest with you, I never could figure out why you stayed in the service. I'd have thought you'd have come straight back here and bought a farm."

Kunessin pulled a face. "The farm I wanted wasn't available," he said. "Besides, it was different once the war was over. Less work and more money." He decided to change the subject. "It's a shame about Fly," he said. "But I can't say I'm surprised."

"I am," Muri said.

"I think Aidi was right," Kunessin said. "And the way I'm inclined to see it is, if he's got a real reason to stay, we should let him. We're only going because there's nothing for us here. I don't know," he added, looking away. "All those years in the job, daydreaming about coming home, planning what we were going to do. Then we get our wish, and somehow it has all changed. Not Kudei, of course. He had the farm to go back to, and his family. I really thought he'd have sorted all that out by now, but apparently not."

"His brothers gave him a hard time, I think," Muri said. "They didn't like that he'd gone away for so long, and then came back expecting to carry on where he left off. Also, he doesn't fit in with them. No disrespect, I know you've been close to them all your life, but Kudei's just not like the rest of them. Actually, I can see their point. It can't be easy having a brother who's so much smarter and better at everything than you are, specially if he's the youngest. You'd feel like you're always in competition, but you're never going to win. I can see why he's not been comfortable there since he got back."

Kunessin frowned. "It shouldn't matter, on a farm," he said. "That's what's so special about it. Every day should be the same, more or less; there shouldn't be anything to compete about. Dad and I—" He stopped. "I'm glad Aidi decided to join up," he said. "I thought we might have a problem with him."

Muri laughed. "You know Aidi," he said. "Because everything's always come so easily to him, he's not interested in success, like the rest of us. So he's built up a thriving business and he's making money; so what? Probably in his mind that counts as underachieving. No, I'm surprised he ever came back here at all. Except," he went on, "I guess being in Faralia's a wonderful ready-made excuse for not doing anything with his life."

Kunessin nodded. "You mean, if he thought this idea of mine stood a chance of succeeding, he wouldn't have agreed to come with us? Maybe you're right. Still, I'd rather have Aidi just playing at being involved than half a dozen other people doing their very best. You know that as long as he's around, you may not succeed but you won't fail, if you see what I'm getting at."

Muri smiled. "Remember what he was like about exams, back at the College? The rest of us'd be slaving away in the library, busting a gut. Aidi'd be swanning around, making sure everybody knew he hadn't done a stroke of work. Then, when the results came out, we'd find we'd passed with distinction, and so had he." He grinned. "He told me once that all he ever did was, the night before the exam he'd pick up the textbook, open it at random a few times and read a page or two, and next day he could absolutely guarantee that what came up in the paper was what he'd been looking at the night before. He said he had no idea how it worked, but it never failed."

"He told me that too," Kunessin said. "I'm not sure I believe it. But I can't remember ever seeing him in the library. I think he just sat down in the exam room, read the question and figured the answer out from first principles. I know for a fact that's what he did in our Tactics final, because the examiner made a point of praising him for a completely original answer. He told me once he didn't like reading books because it got in the way of thinking. Still," he went on, "maybe he was telling the truth, at that. He's always been outrageously lucky, as well as everything else."

Muri nodded eagerly. "Remember that time when we were pulling back after Bana, and they'd got us hemmed in on three sides and we thought we were completely screwed. Aidi couldn't have had any way of knowing the Nineteenth would turn up like that. But to listen to him talk afterwards, it was all part of a carefully worked-out plan, and he was slightly annoyed at them for being ten minutes late."

Kunessin frowned. "But he did know," he said. "Nuctos had slipped out just before dawn and spied ahead; he'd seen them coming—" He broke off, turning his head so he couldn't see Muri's face. "Anyway," he said, "there wasn't much luck involved there, just a bloody good piece of tactical thinking."

Neither of them said anything for a while. Then the door opened, and someone came to take their order for tea.

"I think I'll go home, actually," Muri said. "I've got a few things to clear up. See you tomorrow."

He left quickly, and Kunessin asked for a pot of black tea and a plate of barley cakes. The waiter appeared to disapprove, which amused him: the great General Kunessin ordering peasant food. Well, he thought, it'll be something he can tell his grandchildren.

Easier than he'd expected—but Fly Alces hadn't turned up, so on balance he had to put it down as a failure. Unless he had all of them, the complete set, it wouldn't work, and there'd be no point to any of it. He poured the tea—he'd forgotten to ask for butter, and of course they hadn't thought to offer it—and broke up a barley cake with his fingers. Would tea bushes grow on Sphoe? He very much doubted it. Still, there would be the ship.

There was a knock at the door, and for a moment he thought it might just possibly be the missing butter. But instead it was Thouridos Alces.

Kunessin looked at him. "You're late," he said.

Alces grinned. "I know. Sorry."

"You always were late for staff meetings, Fly."

"Fine. I'll go away again."

Kunessin shrugged. "You might as well," he said. "You've come to tell me you're staying here, and you didn't want to meet the others, in case they tried to make you change your mind. You reckoned you could handle me on your own, but you might not be able to stand up to Aidi."

Alces sat down, grabbed two cakes, slipped one up his sleeve. "Nice to see you too, Teuche. So, tell me about it."

Kunessin sighed and moved the plate, so that Alces would have to cross into his territory in order to conduct further raids. "We're going to found a colony," Kunessin said. "There's an island, ideal for comfortable subsistence agriculture. We'll have it all to ourselves."

"Sounds a bit bleak," Alces said with his mouth full. "Subsistence agriculture. That's living in a cave and wearing goatskins, isn't it?"

"Hardly," Kunessin replied, sipping his tea. Oily, and too strong without butter. "It's not like we'll have been washed ashore from a shipwreck. We'll take everything we want from civilisation with us."

Alces looked at him. "Brocade curtains?" he said. "Harpsichords?"

"Thanks for reminding me; I'll put them on the list. Anyway, what do you care? You're staying, aren't you?"

Alces stared down at his hands, folded in his lap. "I don't know," he said. "You're quite right, by the way. I've been standing in the doorway of the cooper's shop on Spangate, watching the front door of this place. When I saw Muri leave, I counted to two hundred, just in case any of them had any reason to come back."

"It's her, isn't it?"

"Yes," Alces said.

"That's funny." Kunessin broke up another cake; he hadn't eaten the first one yet. "Any of the others, not a problem. Even me," he admitted. "I can believe I could've met a girl and settled down, five years ago. But not you, somehow. Damn it, Fly, if you'd wanted to get old, why did you ever leave the farm in the first place?"

"Seemed like a good idea at the time."

"Yes, but a fencing school," Kunessin snapped. "Of all the bloody stupid things, Fly. Is that really what your whole life's been leading up to?"

Maybe Alces was offended, at what he'd said or how he'd said it. "Seems to me that what my whole life's leading up to is death," he said. "While I'm waiting, I might as well earn an honest thaler, preferably without killing anybody."

"So you teach swordsmanship. Not very well, if that's your mission statement."

Alces grinned. "Like the boxer's tombstone. You remember," he added, as Kunessin raised an eyebrow. "Here lies Mago the boxer, of whom it may honestly be said that he never harmed anybody."

"Oh God." Kunessin pulled the most dramatic of faces. "I remember, Menin's history lectures. Frankly, boy..." (His impersonation had become hopelessly stylised after twenty years, but Alces smiled nevertheless.) "And the knife as far as Ephianassa." His face fell. "We're both of us getting old, Fly, that's the awful thing. I'm not sure I can handle it."

Alces shrugged. "You should've stayed in the army."

Kunessin shook his head. "I can see why the fencing school," he said, and it was almost an apology. "You've got to stay light on your feet to teach fencing. You know what? I walked up to Little Moor yesterday and I had to stop three parts of the way up. That's terrible."

"That's just laziness," Alces said. "For crying out loud, Teuche, you're thirty-eight years old, that's hardly senile. My dad got married at thirty-eight, and his dad still referred to him as 'the boy.' Bide there, he used to say, I'll send the boy on after it. I remember him saying that, when I was a kid, and I thought he meant me. We're not old yet, Teuche."

"Maybe." Kunessin moved awkwardly in his chair. "But you know what they say: you're as old as you feel. On that basis, I'm about ninety."

Slowly and deliberately, Alces reached past him and secured the last barley cake. "I know exactly what you mean," he said. "It's because we'd all lived two lifetimes' worth of stuff by the time we were thirty. It's like the winter evenings," he went on. "It gets dark, you go home, take your boots off and get ready for bed, but really it's still the middle of the afternoon. All in the mind, of course."

Kunessin nodded. "So what you're saying is," he said, "I don't need to go to a remote island and found the ideal republic just to keep from shrivelling up and fading away. Yes?"

Outside, two women were screaming at each other, though Kunessin couldn't catch the actual words. It made him think of other screams, of orders frantically shouted that you couldn't make out because of the padding in your helmet.

"This colony," Alces said. "You're planning on staying there for good?"

"Yes."

Alces dipped his head to signify that the point was established beyond debate. "And what happens when you really get old?" he said. "I have this vision of you all hobbling round after the sheep on walking sticks. Not entirely practical, is it?"

Kunessin frowned. "What's your point?" he said.

"Simply this." Kunessin noticed that Alces' eyes were wide, his chin lifted, as they'd always been at the very last moment, just before he unsheathed the sword (and he thought: exactly when did I become the enemy?). "I'll come with you, Teuche, of course I will. I'd go with you anywhere, any time. But I've got to take Enyo with me."

He stopped talking, and Kunessin could feel the implacable force of his defence. The deployment wasn't one he'd been expecting, but still he said, "Of course you can, Fly, why the hell not? After all, we're going there to live, not just for two weeks' leave. And besides," he added, "she's your wife."

A sudden, unexpected attack in flank, throwing the enemy into confusion. "That's all right then," Alces muttered. "I thought you wouldn't like the idea."

"Really? You're a strange bugger, Fly. Assuming," he went on, "she's prepared to go."

Alces laughed. "No worries on that score," he said. "Enyo's a farm girl; she hates it in town. Her father was a farm labourer over to Actis."

"Family?"

Alces frowned. "Killed in the war," he said. "You remember, there was a lot of raiding there. It was while we were away."

"I heard about it," Kunessin said. "It's called Sphoe, by the way." Alces looked blank. "The island."

"Oh, right." Alces grinned. "You're not going to rename it, then. Kunessia."

Kunessin pulled a face. "I'm not sure I want you along after all," he said. "If you're going to be a disruptive influence."

"Surely that's the whole point of me going," Alces replied. "We can be five disruptive influences together."

FOUR

Cadet Muri Achaiois perplexed his tutors. One day he astonished them all with his brilliance; the next day, they could have sworn he was an imbecile. He worked harder than any of the cadets in his year, but made elementary mistakes through carelessness, and his greatest triumphs came not from diligence but pure untutored insight. All of the Faralia gang, as the tutors quickly came to call them, could be supremely exasperating on their day, but hardly a day passed without Cadet Achaiois' name being mentioned in the staff room or the faculty offices.

It wasn't just the tutors who were driven to distraction by Achaiois' bewilderingly paradoxical nature. One evening in barracks, towards the end of his first term, he was sitting at the table in the room where the cadets cleaned and polished their kit, writing frantically on a scrap of wrapping paper he'd salvaged from the stores. Cadets Kunessin and Proiapsen, who'd been waiting for him to join them in a raid on the buttery, found him there and asked what he was doing.

"Nothing," he said, and he made the fatal error of trying to cover the paper with his sleeve. Proiapsen immediately pinned his arm to the table, while Kunessin retrieved the paper and stared at it.

"Bloody hell, Muri," Proiapsen said. "It's maths."

Achaiois scowled at him. "So what if it is? Give it back, you'll smudge it."

Kunessin moved the trophy out of easy grabbing range. "But the maths isn't due in for a week," he said. "And we were going to do it together."

"That's not the assignment," Achaiois said, blushing red. "It's not anything."

"Ah." Kunessin nodded. "So if I chuck it on the fire, there's no harm done."

"Easy," Proiapsen said, taking the paper from him. "Here, let me see." He frowned, then turned the sheet the other way up. "He's right, it's not the assignment. Here, Muri, what's the big idea? You bucking for extra merit or something?"

Achaiois sagged a little and stopped trying to free his arm; Proiapsen let him go and handed back the paper. "It's just an idea I had, that's all," he said.

Kunessin looked at him. "What's that supposed to mean?"

"I don't suppose it's important," Achaiois said defensively. "It's just something that occurred to me, when I was reading up on right-angle triangles in geometry."

Proiapsen scowled at him. "He's doing it again," he said. "Reading ahead. Didn't we warn him about that?"

Kunessin ignored him. "So?" he said.

"Well." Achaiois smoothed out the paper on the table. "You've got a right-angle triangle, right? Now, two of the sides can be the same length or different, but there's always one side that's longer—"

"The hypotenuse," Proiapsen said.

"What?"

"That's what it's called. The hypotenuse."

Achaiois shrugged. "Whatever," he said. "Now, here's the weird thing. Suppose you were to turn each of the sides of the triangle into a square, like this, look." He scrawled a crude sketch on the back of his paper. "So you've basically got three squares sort of crowded round a triangle in the middle. If you calculate the area of the squares, it always turns out that the area of the two short sides put together is exactly the same as the area of the long side, the hypotenuse. Don't ask me why, it just is." He stopped, then shrugged. "I just thought it was interesting, that's all."

Kunessin burst out laughing, but Proiapsen gave him a look that would've soured milk. "Are you being funny, or what?" he said.

A worried look covered Achaiois' face. "Sorry," he said. "I don't know what you mean."

"It's all right, Aidi," Kunessin broke in, grinning as though his face had split. "He's not taking the piss, he doesn't know."

Achaiois now looked totally bewildered, while Proiapsen clearly wasn't convinced. "Your idea," Kunessin said. "It's absolutely right. Nail on head."

"Really?"

Kunessin nodded. "Absolutely. In fact, it's a famous mathematical law."

Achaiois' face fell. "You mean someone's already—"

"Yes," Proiapsen snapped.

"It's called," Kunessin went on, "Proiapsen's Law. After the bloke who discovered it—what, two hundred years ago?"

"About that," Proiapsen grunted. "Chalcis Proiapsen. My great-great-great-great-grandfather's brother."

Achaiois' eyes were very wide. "Oh," he said.

"Chalcis Proiapsen the world-famous mathematician," Proiapsen went on. "My illustrious ancestor, only member of our family who ever amounted to anything. Except," he added savagely, "you've never heard of him, apparently."

Kunessin started laughing again. Proiapsen made a disgusted noise and stormed out of the room. Achaiois watched him go, then turned to Kunessin, who noticed his face was as white as milk. "Well I didn't know, did I?" he said. "He never mentioned his stupid ancestor."

"Quite," Kunessin said. "And the way you figured it out like that, from first principles, all by yourself: fucking brilliant, if you ask me. Just unfortunate, that's all." He pulled Achaiois to his feet and clapped him on the shoulder. "It's all right," he said. "He'll be over it this time tomorrow, so long as you don't mind a few smart comments now and again."

But Achaiois had screwed the paper up into a ball. "He's mad at me," he said. "He thinks I was making fun of him. Damn it, Teuche, I didn't even want him to see. I tried to hide it."

Kunessin frowned. "Get a grip, Muri," he said. "It's funny, it's a laugh, right? For God's sake don't make a melodrama out of it."

"Yes, but now he thinks—"

"Shut it, Muri," Kunessin said. "That's an order." He stopped, took a breath, softened his voice. "You know Aidi," he said. "Not one of nature's grudge-bearers. For God's sake don't go getting in a state about it; you'll only make things worse."

Muri turned his head away, as if that somehow made him invisible. "It's not like I was trying to impress anybody," he said. "It was just my own curiosity."

Kunessin winced. It was like talking to a girl. "It's actually pretty bloody impressive," he said. "Just your rotten luck someone beat you to it. Otherwise, they'd be naming libraries after you."

Just the ghost of a smile; it'd have looked pretty on a girl. "Well, anyway," Muri said. "That's the end of my career as a mathematician. Look, explain to him, will you? Only, he'll believe you."

Not again, Kunessin thought. "Sure," he said, because it was easier than arguing. "Now forget about it, for crying out loud. Take your mind off it. Go and invent the waterwheel or something."

Muri laughed, and Kunessin thought: one of these days, this is all going to go wrong, and really, I'll only have myself to blame. For now, though, it keeps the peace.

In the event, Aidi had forgotten all about it by the time they came in for the evening meal, so there was no need to talk to him after all. Nevertheless, when Muri cornered him the next day and asked anxiously, "Did you manage to get things straightened out with Aidi?" he nodded and said, "You can put it right out of your mind." Which was, he told himself, not a direct lie.

"That's fantastic," Muri said. "How did you manage to talk him round?"

"He wants to come," Kunessin replied. "Ask him yourself."

Aidi looked up from the bill of sale he was examining. "No conditions?"

"Just one," Kunessin said. "But it's something we're going to have to talk about anyhow. He's just moved it up the list a bit."

"They're screwing you over these farm tools," Aidi said. "My supplier can get you exactly the same stuff, a third cheaper."

Kunessin frowned. "How long for delivery?"

Aidi shrugged. "Usually no more than a month. Depends when the ship comes in."

"Thanks," Kunessin said, "but I'd rather pay more and have the stuff right now. Besides, they're good quality. Guild-marked and everything."

"Sure," Aidi said. "Listen, there's a factory in a wooden hut outside De'Pasi where they do nothing except churn out amazingly good copies of Guild inspection stamps. Two dollars each, and you can turn any old junk into genuine Guild wares with one bash of a hammer." He smiled. "Where do you think I got all my hardware from?"

"Isn't that illegal?" Muri said.

"I've placed the order now," Kunessin said. "If I cancel, I'd probably have to go to law to get my deposit back, and that'd take years. Thanks, Aidi, but don't worry about it. So long as the hooks cut and the spades dig, that's fine."

"Money no object?"

"If you like."

Aidi sighed. "Where were you when I was in business?" he said. "Where's Kudei, by the way? He's late."

"Finishing up morning milking, I suppose," Kunessin said. He had a thick stack of papers on the table in front of him, but he hadn't even looked at them yet. "Don't you want to know what Fly's condition was?"

Aidi yawned. "At a guess, he wants to bring along that dreadful wife of his," he said.

Muri laughed, but Kunessin nodded. "I said yes," he said.

"Thought you might," Aidi replied. "You do realise it's just begging for trouble."

Kunessin picked up a sheet from the top of the stack. Calculations of how much flour they'd need for the first six months. "I don't see why," he said. "I mean, it stands to reason we're going to need women in this colony. Wives," he added, slightly awkwardly.

This time it was Aidi who laughed. "Fine," he said. "Where are you planning on getting them from? Not the same place you got the farm tools, I hope."

Kunessin made a show of studying the paper in front of him. "Arapese," he said.

He could feel Muri staring at him. Aidi said, "You're kidding."

"Not at all," Kunessin said. "It's a perfectly sensible, logical approach. We need women along, otherwise it's going to get pretty bloody awkward when we're all in our dotage and can't work any more. No free woman with enough brains to walk upright's going to sign on to a project like this. So, we do the obvious thing."

"Teuche," Muri said.

Kunessin ignored him. "Naturally, we set them free as soon as we get there," he continued.

"Sure," Aidi interrupted. "When they're trapped on an island with no way of getting off it, I'm sure freedom will mean a lot to them."

"It'll be a better life than anything they'd have otherwise," Kunessin snapped. "If you look at it calmly and objectively—"

"Teuche," Aidi said, "we used to kill slavers on sight, remember? No questions, no messing about: if we caught them on the road or hanging around near a battlefield, it was a rope over the nearest tree and bloody good riddance. You were always the one who said—"

"We were young and naïve," Kunessin said (and he thought: I'm practically shouting). "And yes, we lynched a lot of people, because we thought we were making the world a better place. And you know what? Nothing changed. Arapese's still there; in fact it's twice as busy as it was during the war." He made an effort and lowered his voice. "All right," he said. "I'm open to better suggestions."

"Don't look at me," Aidi replied quickly. "Sometimes there isn't a nice, clean alternative. That doesn't mean you've got to do the other thing."

"Fine," Kunessin said. "So what are you saying? You're not coming?"

"I'm with Teuche," Muri said. "Like he said, we'll treat them decently, like human beings. There's a world of difference between buying and selling."

Aidi leaned back in his chair. "Let's not start on that game, please," he said. "Every time I don't entirely agree with everything you say. Of course I'm still coming. I just think you haven't quite thought this one through. For one thing, what sort of people do you think you can buy for money? Someone you want to spend the rest of your life with?"

Kunessin turned away. "I'm not looking for true love, Aidi, I'm just being practical. We need children; therefore—"

"Fine," Aidi interrupted. "Buy some kids instead. Cheaper."

"Aidi." Kunessin could feel that horrible tightening in his chest. It hadn't bothered him for seven years. "Maybe I'm not explaining my position very well. Obviously, buying slaves isn't what I want to do—"

"Pleased to hear it."

"But it's got to be done," Kunessin went on, raising his voice a little. "Sure, in an ideal world we'd all bide our time till we met nice girls and fell in love and got married. But we're not living in Zeuxis' Republic, Aidi. The plain fact is, we're not the meeting-nice-girls type." (As the words left his mouth, he remembered he was talking to two widowers: too late, so he pressed on.) "We're going to Sphoe to build a colony," he said briskly. "We need..." (He scowled, searching for the word.) "Personnel, to cook food, mend and make clothes, all the stupid, trivial things that have got to be done, don't need strength or brains or courage to do them, but we can't do them ourselves." He took a breath. "We happen to lack those skills," he went on. "We could learn them, but why the hell should we? So—"

"You're talking about servants," Aidi said quietly.

"Up to a point, yes." Kunessin made an effort to slow his breathing. "But there's also the matter of reproduction. If it's really going to be a colony, it needs a future. Yes, you can go to Arapese and buy children, but you can't buy sons and daughters." He closed his eyes for a moment; he knew what he wanted to say, but the words evaded him, like the last two chickens in a big run. "You've never been a farmer, Aidi. If you had been, I wouldn't need to explain. Farmers understand this sort of stuff."

"Try me," Aidi said.

"All right." Kunessin sat down, took a moment. "When a farmer's son marries, he does it for the farm; like he does everything for the farm. So, when he's looking for a wife, he chooses someone who'll work hard, keep house responsibly, someone who understands what needs to be done without having to be told. Love..." He shrugged. "That comes later. It grows. It's built, out of respect, support, understanding. Where I come from, marrying for love would be like trying to build a treehouse in a sapling: you can't, because it hasn't grown yet. You can't really love someone unless you've known them at least ten years; it simply can't be done."

Aidi was looking at him as though he was watching a play. "I'm sure you're right," he said. "That'd explain why the world's such a miserable place. But that's not what we're talking about. You're making speeches about love. This is about buying slaves. Come on, Teuche, pull yourself together. You know we can't do it."

"I think he's making perfect sense," Muri said. "It's what they do in—"

"All right," Kunessin said wearily. "Fine, Aidi, you win. We can't do it. So what do you suggest?"

Aidi looked blank: victory's taken him by surprise, Kunessin thought. "I don't know," he said. "After all, I hadn't given the matter any thought before you sprang it on me just now. But at the very least, Teuche, they've got to be volunteers. You can't just go shopping."

"Volunteers," Kunessin repeated sceptically. It was his turn now. "Look, we're not storming a revetment or launching a night attack."

"Bad choice of words," Aidi admitted quickly. "But it seems to me there must be women in this town who'd be glad to go with us. I mean, you said it yourself, it's a good deal."

Kunessin smiled. "What you mean is, there's bound to be women whose lives are so wretched and horrible, anything's got to be better. Sorry, but I don't think they'd be quite the sort we're looking for."

"Maybe not." Aidi frowned. He'd picked up on the inconsistency, but apparently he didn't intend to point it out. "It's more like what you were saying, though, about farmers. Which is what we're going to be, after all. So what's wrong with presenting it in those terms? We've got plenty to offer: land, livestock, houses. Surely all we need to do is put the word out: four farmers in need of wives, good prospects but must be prepared to travel. At least try it," he added. "And if it doesn't work out, we'll stop off at Arapese on the way. How does that sound? Deal?"

Kunessin sighed. "You're quite right," he said. "Tell you the truth, I was having real problems persuading myself I wanted to do it."

Aidi nodded. "Lying to yourself's always a problem," he said. "You need to be really good at it, and I don't think you've had the practice. All right," he went on cheerfully, "how do you go about it, down on the farm? Are there still marriage-brokers, or did all that go out with wooden shoes and mutton-chop whiskers?"

Kunessin laughed. "Probably the best thing'd be to get Fly's aunt involved."

"Oh, God," Aidi said, "her. Yes, she'll have us all fixed up by this time tomorrow. You know what, when I was a kid and we came home for the holidays, I used to have nightmares about her. I'd be a hare, and she'd be chasing me through a wood with a pack of baying girls, with warts and missing teeth. Mind you, she must be about a hundred years old by now."

Kunessin nodded gravely. "I gather it's one of those skills that matures with age, like making musical instruments. Seriously," he added, "I think you're right. We'll do it your way."

Aidi nodded. "Only don't blame me if yours turns out to have only one eye."

Gorgo Alces expressed no surprise when her nephew gave her the commission. In fact, she said, it was quite a coincidence, because ever since General Kunessin (she let just a little stress lie on the word "general") came home, she'd been wondering if the Oxy girl might not suit him very well.

Alces frowned. "Hang on," he said. "The tall one, Sidery?"

Aunt Gorgo scowled at him. "Not her," she said. "She married Picron Oistun, the year before last, and they've got the farm over to Pickstiles now. Doing quite well, though he's an idle young devil. No, I was thinking of the younger Oxy girl, Dorun."

Alces raised both eyebrows, started to say something, thought better of it, shrugged and said, "Well, it's a thought. All right, so what about Aidi Proiapsen?"

"The other of the Doryclyta twins," Aunt Gorgo said, without hesitation. "Dolo married the Phrontis boy; they've got the lumber yard now that Eume Phrontis is retired, but Chaere's still at home, getting under her mother's feet. She'll give Councillor Proiapsen a run for his money, I'll be bound."

That was that settled, then. "What about Muri Achaiois?"

Pause: the longest he could ever remember his aunt going without saying anything. "I'll have to give it some thought," she said. "Maybe Clea Andron, in Lowertown. She's a widow now, so there'd be no problem with the parents."

"You're joking," Alces said; without thinking, because Aunt Gorgo never joked.

"I said I'll think about it," Aunt Gorgo replied testily. "Anyway, that just leaves the youngest Gaeon boy." She smiled. "And he won't be a problem. I've got just the girl in mind for him."

"Be reasonable," her father said wearily. "At least think about it."

She shook her head, and the ends of her hair slapped her cheeks. "No," she said. "Absolutely not."

Her mother pursed her lips. "You could do worse," she said.

"No I couldn't."

"You already did," her father muttered. "But you got lucky and he died."

She gave him the full force of her scowl. After twenty-seven years he was used to it, but it still shook him. Such an enormous force of malevolence trapped behind her eyes. "That's a disgusting thing to say," she said.

"It's true." Her mother couldn't be scowled down so easily. "He was a disaster. He got drunk, he hit you all the time, he chased other women, he never did a day's work in his life..."

"He was my husband," she said icily. "And I loved him."

"That's not what you said the time you came home with two bust ribs," her father said. "You wanted me and Ennepe to go round your house and kill him. You practically pleaded."

"I didn't mean it," she yelled at him. "I was upset."

Her father sighed. "Of course you were upset," he said patiently. "He'd been bashing you with a spade handle. He was a worthless, vicious bastard and he deserved what he got."

She turned her back on him, but all that achieved was to bring her nose to nose with her mother. "Be sensible, Clea," her mother said. "You're on your own, you're not young and you're not pretty. Take what you're offered and be grateful."

It could have gone either way, but in the event she dropped down on to the chair and started crying. If you could call it that, her father thought: there were tears, no shortage, but she roared like a lion. "Your mother and I love you very much," he said awkwardly. "But you've got to face facts. He left you with nothing, and who's going to look after you when we're gone?"

"It'd be different if you could even hold down a job," her mother added (her idea of reasonable, positive persuasion). "But you can't, can you? Even at the laundry you didn't last five minutes. You open your big mouth and that's it, finished. It's not like you've got a choice."

She stopped roaring like a lion and started bellowing like a bull. "Your mother's right," her father said sadly. "I'll be honest, it's not what I'd have wanted for you. But —"

"For crying out loud, Dad, he's weird." She broke off in mid-howl and glowered at him. "They all are, everybody knows that."

"Just because they went away for a while..."

"Dad." Instinctively, he moved out of the way. "You know what happened to his first wife. You want the same for me?"

"That was just wicked lies," her mother said.

"That's not what you said at the time," she pointed out, quite truthfully. "You said they should've thrown a rope over the nearest tree."

"Sometimes I say things I don't mean," her mother said briskly. "That's just silly gossip, it doesn't mean anything. You really think I'd let you marry him if I thought for one moment..."

Clea got up, deliberately knocking over the table with her hip. "I don't know why we're even talking about it," she said. "I'm not marrying him, and that's final. I'd rather starve in the gutter."

The house was only a wooden frame, boarded in with slats salvaged from big crates from the docks. It shook from floorboards to rafters when she slammed the door.

"She'll come round," her father said, after a moment's silence.

"Course she will," her mother said brightly, picking up her mending from the floor. "You know how she likes to have her bit of drama. But she's not stupid."

Her father pressed himself back into his chair, gripping the arms. "What do we know about this Achaiois man, anyway? He was a soldier, wasn't he?"

Her mother sighed. "He wasn't just a soldier," she said. "He was one of Teuche Kunessin's lot."

"Oh." Her father frowned. "What was all that about a first wife?"

Maybe she hadn't heard him. "It'll be all right," she said. "One thing's for sure, he can't be worse than Geraie Andron."

"True." Her father shrugged. "Ennepe'll have to be told," he said.

But her mother shook her head. "No time," she said. "It's all got to be done in a hurry, apparently, before they go away. Ennepe won't be back until after the wedding."

Her father stroked his chin. "I don't know about all that," he said. "Doesn't it sound a bit odd to you? Rushing it like that."

"They've got their reasons," her mother said firmly. "It's all to do with getting there in time for the planting season, otherwise they'll lose a whole year. Gorgo did explain it to me."

"That's another thing," her father said grimly. "All that way. We'll never see her."

"No different than if she married someone down in the valley," her mother replied. "Not being realistic it isn't. They get married, they go away, you don't see them from one year's end to the next, that's just life. Got to accept it."

He sat still and quiet while she unpicked a seam; then he said: "So they're all of them getting married, then. The whole lot of them."

"So Gorgo said."

"That's very strange," he said, his chin on his chest. "You can't say that's normal."

"Don't make difficulties," said her mother. "Look, you know as well as I do, nobody's going to want our Clea if they could get any-body else. Can't be helped, it's just the way she is."

"Kunessin and his gang. In the war. Weren't they some sort of special unit?"

Her mother shrugged. "Don't ask me, I don't know about that stuff. What I do know is, there's no shortage of money there. Take that Aidi Proiapsen, for instance. They're saying he's sold his busi-ness, got a very good price for it. And Kunessin himself, apparently he's been buying up everything in sight. Even bought a ship, would you believe."

"A ship." Her father stared blankly at the wall. "What's he want a ship for?"

"To get where they're going, I suppose. But what I'm saying is, he couldn't buy a ship if there wasn't plenty of money."

"But Achaiois works at the tannery."

"Used to," her mother corrected him. "Packed all that in when Kunessin came home. He's going to be footing all the bills, so they're saying in town."

"Well." Her father stretched his feet a little closer to the stove. He toyed with the phrase "rich son-in-law," but he was like a buzzard with a pigeon: too big to swallow. "All that way, though, some island nobody's heard of. What if she doesn't like it there? What if she's not happy and she wants to come home?"

Her mother didn't look up from her work. "She'd better bloody well like it, then," she said.

*   *   *

Gorgo Alces hadn't yet told Muri Achaiois about his good fortune; so far, she'd only reported back to Aidi Proiapsen and Kunessin himself. Aidi had taken the news rather better than anybody had expected.

"That's Teuche for you," he told the others. Kunessin was still at the shipyard. "He's out giving someone a hard time because some stupid little detail of the rigging isn't just so, but a really big decision, like who we're all going to marry, he delegates to a crazy old woman...No offence, Fly," he added quickly.

"None taken," Alces replied with a grin. "I hate her, always have."

"Quartermaster General Kunessin," Aidi went on, "issuing wives from the stores. Makes you wonder if there'll be kit inspection. Stand by your beds and look sharp for the officer." He smiled, but nobody followed suit, so he changed tack. "I'm not complaining, mind," he said. "Saves me a job, after all."

"Just a minute." Kudei Gaeon had been sitting still and quiet in the corner, reading through a stack of invoices. "You used to know her, didn't you?"

Aidi grinned. "Well remembered. In fact about three years ago I asked her to marry me."

Alces made a sort of neighing noise; Muri stared. "And?" he said.

"She turned me down," Aidi said, "needless to say. Her father wasn't best pleased, but she was adamant. She'd rather stick her head in the grist-mill, was how she put it, I believe."

There was a long silence, then Muri said, "And now she's changed her mind?"

"Presumably." Aidi was grinning again. "Bear in mind, three years ago she was eighteen, and there was still time. Now, I guess, she's coming round to the view that an old, ugly, creepy husband—her choice of words, not mine—is probably better than no husband at all. Or maybe I've mellowed, I don't know. Do you think I've mellowed, Fly?"

Alces smiled pleasantly. "Like store apples in April," he replied. "All wrinkled and soft, and rotten to the core."

Aidi shrugged. "I gather she had a string of disappointments, let's call them. No," he went on, "I'm quite satisfied with the way it's turned out. It's really just as well she turned me down when she did; we'd have made each other profoundly miserable. After all, what the hell would I have to talk to an eighteen-year-old about? Practically a different species at that age. Now, though... Well, we'll see. I have to admit, I had no plans to get married again until Teuche started giving orders."

"Who's this Dorun Oxy?" Alces said. "I can't say I've heard of her."

"They've got a farm over to South Reach," Kudei said. "I may have met her father once, I'm not sure. Hill farmers," he added, as if that explained everything.

"How does your aunt go about it, anyhow?" Aidi asked Alces. "Does she just draw names out of a hat, or does money change hands at some stage?"

Alces laughed. "Actually," he said, "I think she believes she goes to great pains to make a good, solid match. She knows everybody this side of the Mnester, and she reckons she's a fine judge of character. And from time to time she gets it right, in accordance with the laws of averages. This encourages her to carry on."

Aidi nodded. "Altruism," he said. "Next to earthquakes, the most destructive force known to man. That figures. Well, bloody good luck to her, and give her my sincere regards next time you see her."

"Which won't happen, if I see her first," Alces said. "Meanwhile, I've been looking at this map."

He had their attention. "Map?" Kudei said. "What map?"

Aidi was already on his feet and looking over Alces' shoulder. "A map of the island of Sphoe," he said quietly, "drawn by order of the surveyor-general." He frowned. "Why the hell can't they write their dates in numbers like everybody else?"

"Ten years ago," Alces said. "I found it under a load of other stuff in that pile over there."

"Let's see," Muri said.

"It begs the question," Aidi went on, "why we weren't shown this earlier. There's a distinct possibility we weren't meant to see it. Move your arm, Fly, I can't quite..."

"If that's the harbour he told us about," Kudei said, pointing, "then those must be the old ordnance department buildings there, look."

"Is that a river?" Muri said. "It's either a river or a road."

"You never could make head or tail of a map," Aidi said indulgently. "That's a river. It rises in these hills here, look, and flows down through these contours to the flat—I'll bet you that's all marshes there."

"That fits," Alces said. "You remember, he said there were bogs where you could pick up great chunks of iron ore, big as your fist."

"Forests all down the side of these hills," Kudei said.

"Birch, probably, or conifers." Aidi frowned. "If I didn't know better, I'd say that there is an extinct volcano."

Muri raised his eyebrows. "How do you make that out?"

"More or less round, with a lake right on the top," Aidi said. "In which case, all this lot here's probably rocky and barren, where the lava slopped down."

"These low-lying plains look promising," Kudei said. "Water-meadows here. A lot depends on which direction the wind's from. It could be everything he said."

"If they built the harbour here, on this side," Aidi said, "then the prevailing wind must be easterly. Otherwise they'd have used this big cove here, on the other side; it's a better position."

"If the wind's from the east, this whole valley ought to be nicely sheltered," Kudei said. "You could fetch the cattle down into these combes in autumn and not have to bring them in till February."

"Assuming the soil's any good."

"Bound to be," Kudei replied. "There should be plenty of good dirt washed down from the hills. There's nowhere else they can drain to."

"Why isn't there a scale on this thing?" Alces complained. "I've got no idea of the distances involved."

"Standard survey department practice is a mile to the inch," Aidi said. "Which fits more or less with what he told us."

Alces reached past Aidi's head and measured distances with his thumb. "Everything you could ask for in easy walking distance," he said. "That's good."

"Walking was never your favourite occupation," Kudei said with a grin.

"Life's too short," Alces replied. "Bear in mind, my legs aren't as long as yours. Well," he went on, "if this is anything to go on, it looks pretty good. Maybe Teuche wasn't exaggerating after all."

"Put it back where you got it from," Aidi said. "You know what he's like."

Alces put the map back, and arranged the other papers on top. "Yes, that's encouraging," he said.

"Makes me wonder why the government washed its hands of it," Aidi muttered. "I'm not sure about those marshes. I'd hate to have made it this far just to die of malaria."

"You're a cheerful bastard, Aidi," Kudei said.

Alces grinned. "He'll be on about wolves next."

"Unlikely, on an island that size," Aidi said gravely. "Snakes, now..."

"Don't encourage him," Kudei said.

Aidi sighed, as if to suggest that he'd been wilfully misunderstood all his life. "I'm still a bit puzzled, though," he said, "as to why Teuche hid the map from us. It'd be understandable if it contradicted every-thing he'd told us, or there was stuff on it he didn't want us to know about. But all it does is bear out what he said."

Kudei yawned. "It was under a pile of papers," he said. "That's not hidden, necessarily. By your criteria, I've got a whole load of secret unwashed clothes back home."

"Yes," Aidi conceded, "but you're a slob by nature. You couldn't ever accuse Teuche of that. Even Sergeant Major Mache had to work really hard to find something wrong with his stuff at kit inspection. So if Teuche puts a map under a pile of stuff, that's precisely where he wants that map to be."

Muri frowned. "If he wanted to keep us from seeing it, why not lock it in his trunk? Or keep it in his pocket? That's what I'd do."

"You're just trying to make trouble, Aidi," Alces said. "Admit it, you just love to brew up little mysteries wherever you go."

"True," Aidi conceded, with a broad, graceful sweep of his arms. "But if I'm devious and twisted, it's because I spent my formative years around you lot. As you know, I've always had a morbid fear of pranks and practical jokes, and you people—"

Alces threw a cushion at him; he parried it easily with his left forearm, caught it with his right hand and threw it back. Alces ducked; it cleared his head by an eighth of an inch.

"One thing that does bother me, though," Kudei said, ignoring the sudden outbreak of violence, "is why, if this place is uninhabited and the earthly paradise and nobody else wants it, Teuche feels the need to take quite so many weapons. Here, look at this," he went on, holding out a sheet of paper, which Alces intercepted just before Aidi could get to it. "That's a lot of stuff."

"What does it say, Fly?" Muri asked.

Alces cleared his throat. "Swords, Type Fourteen, issue, two dozen. Swords, Type Fifteen, issue, one dozen. Bows, long, self, yew, two dozen. Bows, short, composite, two dozen. Bows, cross... You're right, Kudei, this is quite a list."

Kudei nodded. "You haven't got to the field artillery yet. And this one here's armour," he added, showing them another document. "Two dozen black-and-white half-armours, a dozen almain rivets with bevored sallets, three dozen coats of double-riveted mail..."

"What's he paying for it, Kudei?" Aidi asked.

Kudei looked, then whistled. "Either he's being seriously screwed over by a very brave man, or this stuff must be premium grade."

"Dear God," Alces broke in. "He's only gone and bought a trebuchet."

"You're kidding," Aidi said. Alces handed him the paper, pointing out the entry. "He's right," Aidi said, his voice distinctly awestruck. "Nine hundred thalers. No, this is ridiculous. We've got to talk to him about it."

The room went quiet. Then Kudei said, "What did you have in mind?"

Aidi frowned. "I don't know," he said. "It's going to be awkward working it into the conversation." He noticed that Muri was looking agitated. Alces just looked stunned, Kudei was deep in thought. Part of Aidi wished he'd never seen the paper. "There may be some perfectly rational explanation," he said.

"Pirates," Muri said. "Well, you've got to cover every contingency, however remote. And if we were to get raided by pirates, bloody fools we'd look if we had nothing better than pitchforks and brush-hooks."

Alces nodded slowly. "You really think that accounts for the trebuchet?"

"Maybe he got carried away in the shop," Aidi said. "All it takes is a smart window display and a good salesman."

"Speroio's first law," Kudei said. "Force, to be effective, must be overwhelming." He shrugged. "You don't get much more overwhelming than heavy artillery."

"We need to ask him about it," Alces said. "It's no earthly use us guessing in the absence of hard data."

"For one thing," Aidi said, "who does he think's going to work the bloody thing? How many in a standard trebuchet crew, Fly? It's six, isn't it?"

"Depends on the size of the counterweight," Alces said. "But a minimum of six, yes."

"There's other stuff too, don't forget," Kudei said. "Two springals, two Type Six field catapults and an onager. That's enough for a brigade."

Aidi shook his head. "We'll have to ask him," he said.

Nobody spoke for a long time after that. Eventually Muri said, "I don't think there's anything sinister about it. Bear in mind that the colony's going to grow; the bigger it gets, the more prosperous we all become, the more inviting we'll start to look to pirates. Sooner or later we'll have to deal with that by getting some serious armaments. So why not start out with what we're bound to end up with?" When nobody reacted, he scowled. "Fine," he said. "If anybody's got a more plausible theory, let's hear it."

"Come on, Muri," Kudei said. "Even you've got to admit, it's a bit strange."

Muri shrugged. "If you think so, you'd better do as Aidi says. Ask him."

Alces shifted in his seat. "I think Muri may be right," he said. "After all, it sort of fits in with how Teuche's mind works. And if you look at the rest of his shopping list, he has covered every single possible contingency. Look at this one here: sixteen rolls of quarter-inch-thickness lead foil. Two hundredweight of copper nails. One hundred and forty-four pewter spoons. I'll bet you he's thinking: what if the ship gets wrecked and we're stuck there without a line of supply? So he's stocking up on everything we're ever likely to need that we couldn't readily make for ourselves. Into which category," he added, "field artillery definitely falls. Well? Any of you know how to go about building a Type Six catapult from things you find at home?"

"I think Fly's got a point there," Kudei said. "Remember how he used to pack for a three-day pass? Only man I ever knew who took a tent with him on leave."

Alces grinned. "God, I remember that. He just looked at me and said, 'But what if it rains, and all the inns are full?' That's got to be the funniest thing I ever saw."

"And that huge sack he carried his books round in," Aidi put in. "He always took every book he owned to every class, whether he was going to need it or not. And no one ever dreamed of taking the piss about it, because anybody who could lug that sack around all day without slipping a disc was obviously someone you didn't want to get mad at you."

When Kunessin got back from the shipyard, he showed them the map. He was pleased by their enthusiasm, but couldn't help noticing that it hadn't been where he'd left it.

FIVE

Cadet Nuctos Di'Ambrosies was invariably in the top three of every class, which probably accounted for the fact that he was never quite expelled, in spite of a record of misdemeanours and honour violations unparalleled in the history of the College. The authorities, who'd naturally seen it all before, were inclined to take a broadly tolerant view of Di'Ambrosies' activities, arguing that his sort of brilliant but unconventional cadet quickly knuckled down once they took their commissions and began active service. They were rather less sanguine about the effect and influence he was having on the other members of the Faralia gang: good students, all of them, but not good enough for their offences to be so lightly overlooked. There was the additional danger that Cadets Kunessin, Achaiois, Alces, Gaeon and Proiapsen might come to believe that, so long as they associated with Di'Ambrosies and followed his lead, they were untouchable as far as the authorities were concerned. College loyalties and allegiances were one thing; they had their well-attested uses in active service, reinforcing the usual bonds of loyalty between officers. A junior officer with his own private army, on the other hand, was quite another. The dilemma was, therefore, how to bring the lesser lights of the Faralia gang back into line without serving out equal justice to

Di'Ambrosies, which must inevitably lead to his expulsion. Efforts to split them up having failed dismally, the faculty finally arrived at a viable solution. Di'Ambrosies was appointed a college proctor—the youngest in a hundred and twenty years—with immediate day-to-day responsibility for the conduct of his classmates.

In time, of course, Di'Ambrosies and his cohorts found enough loopholes and grey areas in the regulations to allow them to continue their activities to a certain muted extent—the faculty would have been profoundly disappointed in them if they hadn't—but the Faralia gang's excesses were curbed sufficiently to allow the faculty to declare victory and look the other way. As for Di'Ambrosies himself, once he'd got over his resentment at being outmanoeuvred by an authority for which he'd come to have little respect, he professed himself grateful for a valuable lesson in both strategic thinking and military politics; it was certainly one he would never forget.

"Losing," Nuctos said, "is a matter of opinion." He pressed his ear to the door, turned the wire in the lock, and as he heard the soft click of the tumblers, his smile was as bright and as broad as the sunrise. "They think they've got us beat. I beg to differ." He got up off his knees, put two fingers on the latch lifter, and gently opened the door.

"Now what?" Teuche said.

Nuctos shook his head. "That's on a need-to-know basis," he said. "Muri, you're on watch. The rest of you, with me."

Once they were inside the room, Nuctos prised open the slats of the dark lantern just a little, revealing—

"Shit, Nuctos," Fly said, his voice hoarse. "How the hell did you ever—?"

"Foul language, Fly," Nuctos said. "Honour misdemeanour."

The reserve armoury. The most secret, the most secure room in the College. Rumour had it that only the principal and the dean even knew where it was. "What are we doing in here?" Kudei asked warily.

"Burgling it, of course," Nuctos replied, as though it was the most natural thing in the world.

"Are you sure this is such a good idea?" Aidi asked. "Only, I think they may take rather a dim view—"

"I should hope so," Nuctos said. "If they think they've beaten the Faralia boys, it's time they got a practical lesson in Rule Three."

Zeuxis' third law: never underestimate an enemy. "What do we want with any of this stuff?" Teuche said, though the distinct hint of passionate desire in his voice tended to undermine his implied objection. "You planning on starting a war, Nuctos?"

"Starting be damned," Nuctos replied. "They started it."

Weapons, beyond even the wildest dreams of Teuche Kunessin. The dim yellow light of the dark lantern made them glow like the gold of a dragon's hoard, perilous and precious. "The objective," Nuctos said, barely lowering his voice, "is to take something they'll be absolutely sure to miss. No earthly point in going to all this trouble if it's three years before they even notice."

He lifted the lantern, scattering light like a duke throwing coins into a crowd. Aidi was frowning. Teuche was balling his fists, locked in a desperate personal battle against temptation.

"The key thing," Nuctos said, "is to put yourself into the other guy's mind. So, if I was the principal, which of these delightful toys would I least want to fall into the hands of an unreliable and quite possibly disturbed student? To which question," he added, with a sudden smile, "there can only be one answer."

He reached out his hand, and from its place on the rack lifted down a small steel crossbow. It was no more than a foot long, ten inches between the nocks of the bow, which was easily half an inch thick in the middle. The string was steel wire, and it had its own built-in cranequin for winding it up. "Illegal to own in seven provinces," Nuctos said. "Come to Daddy."

"You really don't want to mess with that thing," Aidi said nervously. "Just looking at it's enough to get us all sent down."

"Trust me," Nuctos said. "I know what I'm doing."

He was looking for the arrows. He found them: a dozen barrelled steel bolts, like pins, bundled up with twine. "Attention to detail," he explained. "If you look closely, you'll see they're grooved along the top, so the retaining spring can stop them falling out. With ordinary arrows, it wouldn't be half such a threat to public safety. Right, I think we're all done here. Pass me the sack, Fly. Kudei, you take the lantern."

Nuctos left the door open. The others were in a hurry to get away, but Nuctos insisted that they wait while he poked about in the key-hole with a small, complex-looking gadget, something like a minia-ture outside calliper, with vernier scales and exquisitely fine set-screw threads. As he took each reading, he muttered the number three times to himself to secure it in his memory. "That ought to do it," he said at last, dropping the calliper back in his pocket. "Now then, let's take it nice and slow and easy. Nothing's more suspicious than a bunch of people walking fast."

So they strolled along the corridor and down the back stair, meeting nobody, observed from no vantage point, until they came to one of the garderobe ports: small doors in the wall that opened on to the chutes that conveyed the contents of chamber pots down into the covered drain and thence the soakaway. Smiling, Nuctos opened the port, then mostly closed it again, leaving it just slightly ajar. The impression, masterfully conveyed, was that someone had slammed it shut in a hurry, applied too much force and overridden the catch, so that it hadn't shut properly.

"They'll see that," Nuctos explained, "and they'll assume that the thief panicked and dumped the loot into the shit-pit. Which means," he went on, his voice practically a song, "that the prog's bogies are going to have to climb down in there on a long ladder and scrab-ble about in two hundred years' worth of vintage doodoo until they find it. Which they won't, of course, but most certainly not for want of trying. Economy of applications, my children, as expressed in Zeuxis' fifteenth precept."

Muri and Fly were grinning, but Aidi said, "Here's an idea, Nuctos. Why not dump the stupid thing down there for real? Look, we've got this far free and clear, let's for fuck's sake not push our luck."

"Your objection is noted, Lieutenant," Nuctos said, shouldering the sack. "Right, onwards. We've still got a lot to do today."

They walked in silence for a while, then Teuche said: "I realise the answer's obviously no, but I'm going to ask anyway. You're not thinking of actually using that thing, are you?"

Nuctos nodded. "It'd be a shame not to, don't you think?" he said.

"Nuctos…"

"Use your head," Nuctos said, firm and quiet. "Any one of you—on a good day, mind—any one of you could've found the reserve armoury, picked the lock and stolen the bow. So, if we dump it, you're all in the frame. But I want them to know it was me."

They knew better than to argue further. Nuctos had found the perfect hiding place: at the back of the gardener's shed in the dean's garden. Everybody passed its door at least twice a day, and behind the agglomeration of ancient and obsolete tools and junk, it was completely hidden from casual discovery. From there they made their way back to the dormitory, where Nuctos paused to write down a string of measurements on a scrap of paper, which he tucked into the toe of his shoe.

That night, at some point between the second and third watches, someone climbed the walls of the principal's garden and shot his wife's cat. Details of the crime spread quickly. The angle of incidence of the entry wound, for example, suggested that the shot was taken at extreme range, upwards of forty yards; a remarkable piece of marksmanship, given that the only light available was the glow from the parlour window of the lodge. Rather more sensational was the nature of the missile, an arrow unique to a special kind of miniature crossbow, very rare and highly illegal. This led in turn to the discovery that the College's legendary reserve armoury had been broken into, and the murder weapon stolen therefrom. All in all, it quickly became the most excitingly scandalous incident in living memory.

An exhaustive search of the entire College revealed nothing, even after the dean's officers dragged the cesspool and the drains, to the vast amusement of the student body. The student proctors were summoned to the principal's office and ordered to use all means necessary to find the missing weapon, and if possible to identify the thief. After a fortnight of frantic activity, however, no reliable leads had emerged and the weapon was still missing. It was at this point that

Proctor Di'Ambrosies made the suggestion that the principal write to the postmasters of all the students' home towns; since the weapon clearly wasn't on the premises, he argued, the thief must somehow have got it outside the wall. Since everybody knew that breaking out of the College after curfew was quite impossible — he'd learned this from personal experience, he admitted with disarming candour; he'd just spent three years trying — and nobody would be reckless enough to carry the thing out in broad daylight past the needle-sharp eyes of the porters, the only way to get rid of it was to break it up into its component parts and mail it home.

By this stage the principal was desperate enough to try anything, no matter how far-fetched, or how tainted the source. Letters went out by express government mail, which meant they stood a better than even chance of reaching the postmasters before the regular mail from the students. The search was made, and proved success-ful. The disassembled parts of the bow were found hidden in a large mechanical clock sent home by Cadet Haimatoenta, purportedly as a birthday present for his father; also inside were found a home-made key that fitted the armoury lock, and a specialised lockmaker's tool used for taking internal measurements. Further investigations revealed that Haimatoenta had bought the clock in the town the day before the robbery, and the cadet could give no alibi other than a fanciful-sounding story about receiving an anonymous note con-taining a mysterious summons to a rendezvous at the back of the archery butts, at which nobody in the event turned up. Haimatoen-ta's motive was easily supplied, since his resentment at Di'Ambrosies being made a proctor when he felt he was next in line for that honour was no secret. A disciplinary tribunal found him guilty on all counts, and he was immediately given a dishonourable discharge.

"Of course they know it was me," Di'Ambrosies said, after the assembly at which Haimatoenta's disgrace was formally announced. "Quite apart from anything else, they know Haima and his boys have had their knives into us ever since we got here. The old man had me in his office and told me he knew it was me; guess he thought he could make me break down if he yelled loud enough, but I just smiled sweetly and asked him for some proof. And since they'd got to nail somebody for it because of the scandal, they dumped on Haima; job done, and we won't have to see his ugly face around here any more. All in all," he concluded, as they collected their books from the common room, "I call that a satisfactory piece of work all round. One thing's for sure: they'll think twice before picking a fight with me again in a hurry."

"You reckon," Aidi said bitterly. "I don't think so. I think they'll have us for it, probably sooner than later, and it'll be your fault when we end up in the stockade."

But Nuctos only smiled. "You don't understand the way their minds work," he said. "Bear in mind, this is a military college. Stuff like this has always happened here; it's a sort of rough-and-ready way of choosing the brightest and the best. If you pull an outrageous stunt and get away with it, they know you've got the right stuff. Of course, if you try something and screw it up, they're down on you like a ton of bricks. Nobody loves a loser, see; but a winner can get away with anything. And that's all right, because one of these days, that winner'll go on to pull a stunt on the enemy general and win us the war, and that's the whole object of the exercise."

Whether what happened next proved or disproved Nuctos' theory was, essentially, a matter of opinion. On graduation (Cadet Di'Ambrosies was placed third in the year; Proiapsen was fourth, Kunessin sixth, Alces and Achaiois tied for ninth place, with Gaeon achieving a still entirely creditable twelfth), the Faralia gang were assigned to special operations, where they soon learned that they had been chosen, on the principal's recommendation, to be trained as linebreakers.

Clea Andron refused to marry Muri Achaiois, and nothing would make her change her mind. Even Gorgo Alces, who'd never had a failure in forty years, couldn't persuade her. She admitted as much to General Kunessin, who replied that it simply wasn't good enough. Each of them had to have a wife, or the whole project would fall apart.

Gorgo went home and thought about it; and in the middle of the night, on her way to the outhouse with a severe case of stomach cramps, she found the answer.

Clea wouldn't have to marry Achaiois; she could marry the youngest Gaeon boy instead. And Achaiois could have the Aeide girl, the one she'd lined up for Kudei Gaeon. Perfect.

Clea Andron shouted and cried and slammed doors and demanded to know if she was a human being or chopped liver, and then agreed quite cheerfully. Kudei Gaeon accepted the rearrangement with a shrug. Muri Achaiois asked, "What's she like?" and Gorgo replied that she was a nice girl, very quiet, brought up on a farm, very hardworking. Menin Aeide was told of the change of plan.

So that was all right.

"I'm sorry," Kunessin said, "but there's got to be a wedding. Otherwise the whole deal's off, apparently."

He was facing three blank, grim faces. It was like walking up to the hedge of enemy pikes (that strange interval between peace and war; like an actor going onstage, or a condemned man walking to the scaffold), but his only weapon was sweet reason, and he had no allies.

"All right," he said, lowering his voice, "so it's undignified. We're going to look stupid."

"Yes," Aidi said.

"But," he went on, "it'll take, what, half an hour, and then it'll be over, and we'll have the resources we need, and that'll be the end of it. And like I said, if we don't do this annoying but very minor thing, the whole deal grinds to a halt and we've got a serious problem. Come on, gentlemen, we've faced massed archers and heavy artillery in our time. We can do this."

Kudei looked up. "Did he just say 'resources'?" he asked.

"It's completely unnecessary," Aidi said. "There's a civil ceremony that's just as legal, and it doesn't mean standing in front of the whole town with garlands of flowers round our necks. Trust me on this, I'm a magistrate. In fact, I could do it myself."

Kunessin sighed. "I suggested that," he said. "They won't go for it. Traditional ceremony or nothing. It's your bloody aunt, Fly," he added savagely. "She's the one making all the trouble."

Alces, who'd been doggedly studying the map, looked up as if he'd only just realised there were other people in the room. "I believe you," he said. "Didn't I tell you she's pure poison?"

"Talk to her," Kunessin said. "That's an order."

"I will if you like," Alces said, with a broad shrug. "Won't make a blind bit of difference."

"It's all right for you," Kudei said bitterly. "You don't have to do it."

"Done it already," Alces replied, with just a trace of a grin. "And you're quite right, it's pretty bloody embarrassing and you do feel extremely stupid, with all those horrible old women staring at you and all the kids giggling. But if I had to go through it, I don't see why you shouldn't."

Instinctively, Kunessin looked towards Muri for support, and was depressed to see that his face was as hard and set as all the rest. "All right," he said, "I'm open to suggestions. Anybody got any ideas?"

As he'd anticipated, nobody spoke. He gave it a few moments, then targeted the ringleader. "Aidi," he said. "Think of something."

"I've already told you what I think," Aidi replied. "Tell Fly's aunt we're going to have a proper legal wedding, but it'll be the civil ceremony. Be firm. Don't take any shit."

Kunessin nodded. "Agreed," he said, "with one amendment. Aidi, I'm delegating this mission to you. I'm sure you'll make her see sense."

In their minds, they could all hear the clang of the trap as it closed round Aidi's ankle. "Fine," he said, after a long pause. "Leave it with me. It'll be the proverbial piece of cake."

When they met up again that evening, the first thing Kunessin did was home in on Aidi like a hawk on a pigeon and ask, in a perfectly clear voice, "Well? How'd it go?"

"All dealt with," Aidi replied, but he sounded tired and just a little fraught. "Civil ceremony, day after tomorrow. Oh, and I've checked up, I can do myself when I do the rest of you; it's perfectly legal. We just need two extra witnesses, but all that means is that for my entry in the register, all four of you sign. Otherwise, couldn't be more straightforward."

(Later, Kunessin found out how he'd done it. After shouting and pleading in vain for a very long time, he'd finally offered her a large sum of money; enough, in fact, to buy a small house for her retirement. Part of the agreement was that she wouldn't breathe a word of it to anybody, a contract term she breached within half an hour of being given the money.)

Since Aidi was still technically a justice of the peace—he'd resigned his post but stayed on the book until quarter sessions—he requisitioned the use of one of the public buildings over which he had jurisdiction, and the ceremony accordingly took place in the town jail. Fortunately, it was empty apart from one elderly drunk, who was fast asleep, and the deputy jailer, who locked all the doors before the proceedings began. It was Kudei's suggestion that a constable be put on guard at the foot of the tall ash tree in the courtyard, whose upper branches overlooked the exercise yard. Even that was a compromise: Aidi had wanted the tree cut down.

The brides arrived in a covered cart, hired from the livery stable and usually used to take cattle that had died out in the fields to the knackers. The front axle creaked twice each time the wheels turned, a noise uncannily like the braying of a donkey. The carter had brought a wooden crate to serve as a step; perhaps it was old and rotten, because Chaere Doryclyta's foot went right through it, causing her to stagger and graze her ankle on the splinters. Dorun Oxy refused to get down without a step, but there wasn't another box or crate to be had; eventually, Clea Andron jumped down, grabbed Dorun Oxy under the arms as though lifting a sack of onions, and hauled her out of the cart. Menin Aeide got down by clambering over the side, using the hub of the wheel as a foothold.

("I know her from somewhere," Kudei muttered, as he watched them arrive through the half-open yard door. "But I'm damned if I can remember..."

"Leave it, Kudei," Kunessin hissed. "It's supposed to be bad luck or something."

Kudei grinned. "You don't believe that."

"No, but they probably do.")

Thouridos Alces and his wife had been pressed into service as ushers. Alces hung back, but Enyo darted forward and gathered them up, remarkably like someone herding a parcel of skittish heifers to new pasture; she didn't wave her arms or prod them with a stick, but probably only because they chose to come quietly. Chaere Doryclyta was talking very loudly about her damaged ankle, which was bleeding rather spectacularly and leaving a trail of bloody footprints. She was wearing white satin shoes; the others all wore their yard boots, sensibly greased with goose fat. Alces held the door open for them and let them get well ahead before following them in.

The four bridegrooms were drawn up in a line with their backs to the front office wall. Aidi was holding a book, closed around his thumb to mark the place. He cleared his throat as the women advanced, also in line, but didn't actually say anything. Both lines held position about five yards apart. There seemed to be no way in which the silence could ever be broken.

Fortuitously, that was the moment when the drunk in the cell chose to wake up. He staggered to his feet, made it as far as the door and hung from the bars, staring. "Hellfire," he said. "What's all this, then, a dance?"

"No," Kunessin said. "It's a wedding."

"Ah," the drunk said, and stumbled back to his mattress.

That, apparently, was as much as Aidi Proiapsen could take. He sprang forward, making a large but vague shepherding movement with his arm, and saying, "Right, let's not stand about here all day. Teuche, you first." Kunessin took a step forward, like a very brave man volunteering for some desperate mission. Aidi turned, smiled at Dorun Oxy, and said, "You too."

She looked at him. "Where do I have to go?"

"Two steps forward and one left," Aidi replied promptly. "Right, hold still while I read the magic words. Oh, and when I ask either of you a question, just say yes."

She frowned, as though doing long division in her head, then moved forward; and it occurred to Aidi that she'd just made the knight's move, in which case, properly speaking, Kunessin was in check. Then he remembered that Chaere Doryclyta was reckoned to be a pretty fair chess player, and he smiled. He opened the book but didn't look down at it. "Fellow citizens," he began, in a clear and surprisingly steady voice, and got through his opening speech without a single stumble. After that, it went quite well, though Kunessin barked out his responses and Dorun chewed hers, like a dog with a crust. The whole thing only took three minutes, and then it was done.

"Thank you," Aidi said, "fall out." Kunessin knew what that meant, but Dorun clearly hadn't got a clue, so Kunessin reached out, caught her by the wrist and gently towed her out of the way. "Muri," Aidi said, and Muri stepped promptly forward and stood, feet a shoulder's width apart, weight evenly distributed, as though he was about to fight a duel. Aidi then realised he didn't know the woman's name. Fortunately, she didn't need to be called or told what to do; she took her place quickly and without fuss, then looked Aidi squarely in the eye and said, "Menin Aeide."

Aidi nodded gravely. "Thank you," he said. "Now, then. Fellow citizens..."

Three minutes later, Muri and his wife stepped away. She was watching the show; he was looking sideways at her, clearly interested in something. "Kudei," Aidi said. "And Clea Andron."

Clea took a step forward, then stopped dead. A man had appeared in the yard doorway. He hesitated for a moment while his eyes adjusted to the light, then darted into the room and stood facing Aidi and Kudei.

"Who the hell are you?" Aidi said.

"I'm Ennepe Andron," the man replied, his voice high and harsh with nerves. "Her brother."

"How did you get in—?" Aidi started, but Clea interrupted him.

"Ennepe," she said, "piss off."

Ennepe Andron ignored her. "I'm her brother," he repeated, "and I'm stopping the wedding. I'm her closest male relative, so I'm within my rights."

Aidi frowned, then grinned. "I know you," he said. "I gave you twenty-eight days for thieving, back end of last year."

"Ennepe, go away," Clea shouted, but he stood his ground.

"Well," he said, "you should know the law, then. And the law says you can't get married unless I say so. And there's no way you're marrying him."

Kudei looked frozen. Kunessin sighed. "Fly," he said. "Didn't your aunt sort all this stuff out?"

"Don't ask me," Alces replied. "But I'd have thought so, yes. She's usually very thorough."

"Ennepe!" Clea shrieked, and her brother winced, though he didn't look at her.

"All right," Kunessin said wearily. "You," he added, "with me."

Andron hesitated, but followed him into the far corner of the room. "I'm her brother, General Kunessin," he said. "It's up to me to make sure she doesn't do anything stupid. I promised our mum."

"When?"

Andron looked at him nervously. "Well, before she died."

"She's still alive," Kunessin said, "and so's your father. If you're going to shake people down for money, at least do them the courtesy of assuming they're not completely stupid."

"It's not about money," Andron said. "She's my sister. I'm not having her marrying that—"

Kunessin stood on his foot, pressing just hard enough on his instep to make him gasp. "Shut up," he said, "and listen. You don't have to worry, it's been sorted out. She's not marrying Muri Achaiois after all; she's marrying Kudei Gaeon, and she's quite happy with the idea, and so's he. All right?"

Andron shook his head. "I don't want my sister marrying any of you freaks," he said. "You're all wrong in the head, the whole lot of you. Killers, that's what you are. I've heard the stories. I'm not having my sister—"

He stopped short, suddenly speechless with pain. Kunessin had shifted his weight; just a little, but that was all it took. "If you make a scene," he said softly, "I'll cripple you for life. If you shut up and go away quietly, I'll pay you fifty thalers. All right?"

He was used to seeing that look in people's eyes. Andron didn't say anything, but he nodded. Kunessin smiled, and shifted his foot, releasing him. "Thank you so much," he said. "Your money'll be at the bank tomorrow morning. Now stay away from us till we leave town, or I'll have you killed."

Andron nodded again, backed away and fled, leaving the door

open. Kunessin closed it quietly and walked back to where he'd been standing. "Never a dull moment," he said. "Carry on."

Aidi cleared his throat and started the speech. Clea was crying, quietly, with the air of long practice, as though it was something she was good at. As Kunessin turned to watch, Dorun moved close to his shoulder and whispered, "Did you mean that?"

He frowned. "Mean what?"

"About having him killed."

"You heard that? You must have ears like a bat."

"Yes," Dorun said. "Well? Did you mean it?"

Kunessin shook his head. "No."

"Oh."

She didn't say anything else, but Kunessin got the distinct impression that something he'd done or said had met with her approval; quite what it was, though, he had no idea.

Aidi, meanwhile, was conducting his own wedding. It was, Kunessin reflected with an uneasy blend of annoyance, amusement and respect, a fine example of Aidi Proiapsen at his best. It was comedy, for sure, but not clowning. The question was, who was the audience? On balance, he decided, probably the girl. He watched her face with interest. She was stuck halfway between laughter and apoplectic fury. Well, he thought, she'd better get used to that. The men were enjoying the joke, forced to extreme effort to keep themselves from laughing.

"He's the shopkeeper, isn't he?" He'd forgotten about Dorun for the moment. He nodded.

"He's a very clever man," she whispered.

"He certainly thinks so."

"He likes her."

Kunessin nodded. "Proposed to her once. Got turned down."

"Ah," Dorun said. "That explains it."

He thought about that, and she was right, of course. To be sure, it wasn't a proper ceremony, just an official form of words to seal a contract. Even so, it was still a wedding; and Aidi was contriving matters so that this was one wedding where nobody was looking at the bride. She won't forget that in a hurry, he thought; so, maybe not so clever after all. "You're quite the judge of character," he said.

"Sh."

The ceremony was over, and Aidi was kissing the bride, who was holding still with the pained patience of a child having dirt wiped off its face with the corner of a handkerchief moistened with spit. A bit of her own back, Kunessin thought, but not nearly enough. "Right," Aidi said, breaking abruptly away and clapping his hands briskly together. "Now what?"

Kunessin hesitated. The women were all looking at him. Well, he thought. So everything has changed, after all. "Lunch, of course," he said. "We'll head back to the Glory. My treat."

Which was only a postponement, rather than a solution: sooner or later the situation would have to be faced, and new rules hammered out. For now, though, neither a victory nor a defeat, and Aidi had got them out of there in one piece.

When lunch was nearly over, he asked her, "Would you like to come and see the ship?"

The look on her face said: if you want me to. She nodded. "All right," she said; then, "Is it far?"

"About half a mile," he said.

She nodded. "You're precise by nature, aren't you?"

"Yes," he said.

The others watched them go. They left the Glory and walked up the Ropewalk, side by side. He matched his pace to hers. At the junction of the Ropewalk and Stilegate he said, "Do I owe you an apology?"

She thought for a moment, then said: "That remains to be seen, really. Is it going to be very unpleasant?"

He laughed. "It's what I've always wanted to do."

"I see."

"I haven't answered your question."

She shook her head. "I don't suppose you can," she said. "But it's all right. I'm fairly sure it can't be worse than home, anyhow."

He looked at her. "That bad?"

Shrug. "Well, not really. I don't know, it's hard to explain. Put it this way: when that dreadful old woman came round, my dad asked me if I wanted to do it, and if I'd said no, he'd probably have cancelled the deal. But I said yes. I guess mostly I'm just bored with Faralia." She looked sideways at him. "Was that how you felt, when you went away?"

He shook his head. "I didn't want to leave," he said. "But I had no choice. We'd lost the farm. I couldn't bear the thought of working for someone else. But I always had it in mind to come back."

She raised an eyebrow. "And now you're leaving again."

"That's right. As soon as I got here, I realised. It wasn't Faralia, it was the farm. And I'll never be able to have it, so..." He shrugged. "Next best thing."

"What you always wanted, you just said."

He smiled. "After the farm," he said.

"Ah."

A gust of chill wind, funnelled down Post Street, made him pull his collar tight round his neck. "Did I just say the wrong thing?"

She smiled. "Yes."

"I see. Do I get a hint?"

"No."

"Fair enough." He waited for a chaise to go by, then led her across the street. "So," he said, "who are you?"

She thought for a moment, then said: "I'm the elder daughter of Brotois and Oudemia Oxy. My father is a saddler and harness maker, my mother's family farm at Noen. I'm twenty-seven, which is far too old. This thing on my face is a hare lip, which I was born with; it's a damned nuisance, since without it I'd have been reasonably pretty, like my sister, and I'd have been married ten years ago. As it is, I've spent the last decade hanging round the house. My father has three apprentices, but none of them want to take over the business badly enough. I'm fully trained in all the usual domestic skills and duties, but I don't pull my weight around the house because I'm stroppy and miserable. Nobody's ever asked me what I want to do with my life, but if someone ever did, I'd probably say I'd like to learn to be a clerk. I can read, write and do figures, and apparently there are female clerks in some of the big Adventurers' companies on the mainland. I've been doing my father's books for six years, but apparently that doesn't count. That's it, really. How about you?"

Kunessin smiled. "I'm eleven years older than you," he said. "I was born on a farm a few miles north-west of town. All I ever wanted was to stay home, work hard, take over the farm eventually. But when I was a kid, they chose to fight a battle on our top pasture. We lost all our sheep, and because of all the dead bodies, the grazing was ruined and we had to sell the farm. My friend Kudei Gaeon's family bought it; there's a hell of a lot of brothers, all of them except Kudei with sons of their own now, so I'll never get the farm back. Anyway, when we sold out I went off to military college, joined the army, the same time as my friends there. We fought in the war; when it was over, they came home but I stayed on, somehow got made a general, stuck it out for as long as I could, then quit. Came back here, to see if I could get them to come with me to Sphoe. They agreed, and now we're on our way. And there you have it."

At the end of Post Street, they turned left along the sea wall. The tide was in, and the waves were brown with dredged silt. He could see she was cold but wasn't prepared to admit it.

"Tell me about Sphoe," she said.

The speech got more fluent each time he made it; part of the fluency was an improvement in natural delivery, so that it sounded almost as though he was making it up as he went along. She was listening, but without making an effort to show him she was paying attention, and she stopped him four times to ask questions. When he'd finished, he said, "Well? What do you think?"

"Could be worse."

He nodded. "What don't you like about it?"

"Oh, the obvious stuff," she replied. "Being so far from home, strange place, people I don't know very well, lack of creature comforts; and I don't mind hard work, but I'm not going to pretend I enjoy it." She frowned. "What exactly am I going to be expected to do once we're there? Apart from being a brood sow, I mean."

He raised an eyebrow but let it pass. "Really, that's up to you," he said. "There's basic housekeeping, of course, but as far as farm work goes, I don't imagine we'll need you out in the fields breaking up clods with a hoe. If you want to, you can be our chief clerk."

"I'll think about it," she replied. "So, how many of us will there be, exactly?"

He explained about the indentured servants. "They'll sign up for a minimum set term, for which they'll be paid a fixed sum of money, which is already on deposit at the bank here. If they want to stay on, they can either sign up for a second term, or they can ask to be accepted as permanent members of the colony; that means they get a say in how it's run and title to land. If they can afford it, they can bring in indentures of their own, but if they decide to quit and go home, they can't sell up; their land reverts to the founders: that's us. If everything goes well, in due course we'll start inviting free settlers to join us, but that's some way in the future. To begin with, until everything's settled down and running smoothly, we want to be in control."

"I see," she said. "So, not quite a model society, then."

"In time, maybe." He shook his head. "The truth is, I want to settle down, but I haven't seen anywhere I want to do it in. It's like houses: if you can't find one you like, you build one."

"Makes sense," she said. "So, if you've got all these servants to do the work, what'll you be doing all day?"

He laughed. "Not all the work," he said. "Just some of it, so we don't kill ourselves hauling out tree stumps and breaking up unploughed land. There's a certain minimum size the colony's got to be if we don't want to have to live like castaways after a shipwreck. The idea is to be sensible, make it as easy for ourselves as we possibly can and still live the way we want to. Which, I guess, is a reasonable definition of the model society."

"For you, yes." She grinned at him. "That's fine," she said. "If you were a bunch of idealists, I'd be worried. And like I said, it's got to be better than home."

They walked on a little further, until they could see the shipyard up ahead. "What was it like in the war?" she asked.

He didn't reply straight away. "It was great fun," he said. "It was worse than anybody who wasn't there could ever understand. It was boring as hell. It was so terrifying that sometimes you just lay on the ground and refused to move. It was about being quicker and smarter and stronger than anybody else in the whole world, and knowing no harm could possibly come to you, no matter what you did. It sounds unlikely, but fighting the enemy was almost beside the point. What I tend to remember is waking up in a ditch, in filthy clothes that'd been soaking wet for a week, starving hungry, constant diarrhoea, hardly any soles to your boots, and thinking: back home there's tramps better off than we are, and we're senior officers of the Grand Continental army. And then there was having to deal with the way that people disappeared: you'd spend a year with someone, practically every waking moment, till he was closer to you than family could ever be, and suddenly he's not there any more." He frowned, then said, "After all that, battles were a chance to let off steam, at least until the fear got to you. Once that started, you were done for, completely useless. Then it'd be up to the others to get you out of it in one piece."

"Did you kill a lot of people?"

"I suppose so, yes. I didn't keep score, or anything like that."

"Rough guess?"

He thought for a moment. "Hundreds," he said. "Probably not four figures. It's like everything, a knack. And we were better at it than anybody else, on either side. We were specialists, you see. I won't bore you with the details." He looked away. "Before I joined up, I worked in the tannery. We used to buy in all the barren, worn-out cows that were too old to be worth eating. I did three months on the slaughtering line. There were five of us, standing in stalls. They'd drive a cow into the stall, and I'd kill it, smack it between the eyes with a poleaxe, then tie a rope round its legs so the crane could hoist it up to the next floor, where they'd flay it. We did eight an hour, ten hours a day, seven days a week, and you had to hit them just right and very hard indeed. It was exhausting. My friend Muri Achaiois worked in the tannery too. His job was to crack open the skulls and scoop out the brains, which is what they use to cure the hides. Bone is a lot tougher than most people think; it's not like splitting logs. The closest thing to it I can think of is breaking very thick ice."

She frowned. "Can we talk about something else, please?"

"You asked."

"So I did."

They walked on fifty yards in silence, then Kunessin said: "If it was up to you, would you have married me? Do you want to come with us?"

She smiled. "That's a non-question," she said. "Like, if it was up to you, would you grow wings and fly like a bird? Well, yes, I would, but it'll never happen. How about you? If it was up to you, would you die?"

Kunessin sighed. "What I'm trying to say is, if you really can't stand me, or if the thought of going to Sphoe is utterly appalling, I'm sure we could sort something out—"

"It's all right," she interrupted him. "It really doesn't matter. The way I see it, it's always like the fairy tale—you know, the one where the hideous monster who lives in the castle in the forest forces the pretty peasant girl to come and live with him, or else he'll do something horrible to her family; and guess what, time goes by and the monster turns out not to be so bad after all. I think that's why arranged marriages are such a good idea. You're so sure you're going to get the monster, when he turns out to be just a human being, you're so grateful and pleased you really do your best. But a girl I used to know, she married for love—there were the most terrible rows about it, but she got her way and married this man she was crazy about; and he was handsome and charming and sensitive and considerate and kind, but as soon as they got married, he turned out to be just a husband, after all. The difference was, she thought she'd got the monster—the fairy tale in reverse, you see. Reckoned she was really hard done by. So," she said briskly, turning to look him in the eye. "What do you think is the moral of this story?"

"Well," he said, furrowing his brow as though doing mental long division. "I think you'd probably see the whole issue quite differently if you hadn't had the rotten bad luck to be born with that thing on your face. That said, I tend to agree with you. Also, I think you'll do well on Sphoe. Maybe you'll end up running the place."

She laughed. "Have we really got to go and look at the ship?"

"You don't want to?"

"No. I have an idea I'll be seeing quite enough of it in the next few weeks."

"Understood." Kunessin turned on his heel; she blinked, as though amazed he could move so fast, so precisely. "Well, we've got the next two hours free. What would you like to do?"

She thought for a while, then said: "What I'd really like is to get measured for two pairs of really comfortable yard boots. You know, ones that actually fit my feet. Ktesi Laon in Fishgate'll have them made by noon tomorrow, and I can't think of anything else that'd do more to improve my quality of life."

He laughed. "Good on you," he said. "There's an old saying in the service: an army marches on its feet. Never underestimate the crucial importance of good footwear."

For some reason that made her burst out laughing too; and Kunessin was reminded of how he'd felt in a battle when he'd looked round and seen the white helmet plumes of the cavalry in the distance, riding in to force open the crack in the line that he'd made, so he could pull back and rest.

SIX

When Menin Aeide was thirteen years old, the war came back to the Bluewater valley. General Anculometin and the Seventh Militia, squeezed between the two wings of the enemy's last and most desperate attempt to cut the loyalists in half and break through to the sea, fell back into the hill country where his predecessor had brought about his own total ruin six years earlier. Everyone, including General Anculometin, expected the militia to break and run when faced with massed pikes; but at Round Cop they held the line for six hours as the push of pike tried repeatedly to force the holm-oak woods on the steep western slope. Anculometin had already quit the field; ironically enough, he was caught and killed by an enemy scouting party as he withdrew his staff towards the imagined safety of the Aeide house. But the Seventh stayed put—as one veteran famously said afterwards, "We had no place to go"—and took their stand on the edge of Golden Hill Cover. At the end, when the archers had spent all their arrows, legend has it that the militiamen hacked at the oncoming pikes with felling axes and billhooks; rather more plausible are the accounts that lay stress on the marshy nature of the ground, where the surface water from the early autumn rain was soaking away down the valley, and the timely arrival of Auxin's light cavalry on the north wing. Even those factors, important though they might have been, do not wholly explain the crucial and entirely unexpected victory won by the leaderless Seventh on that day. Round Cop may not have been the turning point of the war, though most contemporary accounts saw it as such, but it left the enemy high command unable to avoid the harsh truth that they no longer possessed sufficient resources to hold the territory they had already acquired, let alone take the war forward; the only sensible course left to them was to withdraw to the mainland in the best order possible in the circumstances.

That was the day when Menin Aeide walked back from her aunt's house in Faralia with the month's supply of salt. Aunt had been in two minds about letting her go, because of the rumours of soldiers, but the Aeide family were due to kill the pig, and they needed the salt, and besides, the road back to Round Cop was straight across the ridge. If there were soldiers about, Menin would be bound to see them long before they saw her, in which case she was under strict orders to turn round and go straight back to town.

Menin saw the soldiers as she came up on to the top road from the Woodcombe side. She immediately ducked behind a clump of gorse, before realising that they were at least a mile away. Furthermore, they were quite far down in the valley; she guessed they were following the course of the brook, in which case going back down into Woodcombe was the last thing she should do. If she kept to the top road, on the other hand, she could see everything that moved for miles around, and she was only about a mile from the dense woods of Cylinder Hill Top, where she was confident she could creep past unnoticed even if the woods were full of soldiers. If the worst came to the worst, there was always the cave under the waterfall; as far as she was aware, only she and her brothers knew it was there. She could hide in the cave till it got dark, then follow one of the rhines down to the edge of Culin's duck ponds, and sprint the last half-mile home.

But the soldiers stayed down in the valley. She was almost disappointed; she'd thought up such a good, sensible plan, but it wasn't going to be needed after all. She saw more soldiers—loads and loads of them — in the distance, on Golden Hill, but nothing at all on her side of the Bluewater. She told herself that it was just as well and she was very lucky; also that her parents must be worried sick about her, and she really ought to get home as soon as possible.

At Cylinder Beacon, she paused to look out at the sea. If you could see the top of Stickholm, five miles out from Faralia harbour, it was a sure sign that rain was coming, but grey clouds and a smear of sea mist blotted the island out completely, so the weather was headed further up the coast, to Letho and Ennea, semi-mythical places she'd never been to. She could still see the soldiers on Golden Hill. They didn't seem to have moved in the last hour, so even if they left whatever it was they were doing and came charging straight at her, by the time they'd crossed the Bluewater she'd be safe in Cylinder Woods and as good as home. She sat down on an old, half-rotten tree stump, uncovered her basket and scrabbled around till she found the barley cakes that Aunt had put up for the family. Under normal circumstances, it'd be more than her life was worth to rob one. But, she decided, her parents would be so overjoyed to see her safe that one missing cake would hardly signify.

There was a little dip in the road between the Beacon and Cylinder Cop. She'd forgotten all about it, until she came over the top. On the brow she stopped dead, suddenly terrified. It was only a little dip, only big enough to conceal two or three soldiers, but two or three would be plenty. Her brothers had told her all about what soldiers liked to do to young girls, and although she didn't believe half of it, the other half was enough to give her nightmares. Ten more yards, and anybody down in the dip couldn't help but see her, silhouetted against the skyline. She could run quite fast, but outrun a grown man? Hardly.

Going back the way she'd come, on the other hand, was out of the question. The first lot of soldiers she'd seen would be in Woodcombe by now; for all she knew, they were coming up the lane making straight for the top road, and if she ran into them there she'd have nowhere to hide. Cylinder Woods, on the other hand, were only a couple of hundred yards away. If she could make it in there, she knew she'd be safe. She'd known them all her life; it was inconceivable that any harm could come to her in so familiar a place. All she had to do, she decided (it was hard to think with her heart beating so fast, and her stomach muscles knotted up like rope), was leave the road and sneak through the clumps of gorse and tussocks of couch grass. If there were soldiers in the dip, chances were they wouldn't even see her, if she went quiet and steady. If they did, she stood a much better chance of getting away from them on the rough ground than on the road. Grown-ups weren't very good at going fast through the couch bogs; they tripped over their feet or got stuck in the soggy patches, whereas she knew from long experience how to jump from tussock to tussock, and tread close to the clump roots where the going was soft. Taking a very deep breath — it was supposed to help, but it didn't — she left the road and picked her way with exquisite care in a wide semicircle until she was well clear. Then, crouching down low, she crept over the brow of the ridge and looked anxiously down into the dip.

She saw the horse first. It was off the road, no more than ten yards away, head down, nibbling delicately at the fine shoots of edible grass that grew under the crown of the couch tussock. She dropped down, nearly squashing her basket. A horse meant a rider, but she couldn't see one. What she could see was that the horse's front legs were tangled up in its own reins, effectively hobbling it. Deliberate? She didn't think so; it was too messy to have been done on purpose. That implied that the horse had bolted, got caught up and come to a stop, unable to go any further. Still dangerous; a bolted horse's rider might well come looking for it, if he was alive and capable of moving. Praying that she was as well hidden as she thought she was, she determined to stay perfectly still and quiet until something happened.

Later, she was quite proud of the way she managed to stick to her resolution, in spite of the damp and her own fear and merciless cramp in her left leg. She hadn't moved at all when the rider finally showed up.

He'd been there all the time, but she hadn't seen him because he was curled up in a soft patch under a clump of gorse. She saw him when he tried to move. First he lifted his head; then he reached out his arm (it was thin but very muscular, and filthy with bog mud), grabbed the stem of the gorse plant, and tried to drag himself along by it. He didn't get very far. It was obvious he was exhausted, badly hurt or both; no danger to anybody, in any case.

Even so, she managed to stay sensible. She crept forward, watching him intently for any sign that he'd noticed her, until she could see the glistening black mess of drying blood on the side of his head. She'd seen something like it before, when one of the woodcutters had been brought down to the house after a hanging branch dropped on his head. She'd had a good look at the damage, but Mother had sent her away after a while, so she wasn't there to see him die. This man's injury was just like the woodcutter's; as bad, possibly worse.

She stood up; he hadn't seen her. So she walked to the path — even if he got up, she was quite certain she could outrun him, in his condition — and, holding back a comfortable ten yards or so, cleared her throat and said, "Hello." It seemed a silly thing to say, but she couldn't think of anything else.

The man lifted his head — it seemed to cost him an absurd amount of effort — and looked at her.

"Hello," she repeated. "Are you all right?"

His eyes were wide. It was hard to tell, because of all the blood, but she reckoned he couldn't be much more than nineteen, six years older than her if that. She'd never seen anybody with brown eyes before.

He said something, but she couldn't understand a word. Not that she needed to; the tone of voice said, "Help me, please." She hesitated for a moment, then edged forward until she was close enough to reach out and touch him. It was then that she saw his left arm was broken, just below the elbow.

Her brothers always teased her about being strong; much too strong for a girl, they said. She knelt down, put her arms under his, her hands meeting at his solar plexus, and lifted him till he was sitting. It hurt him a lot, she could tell, but he didn't complain. He even tried to smile at her.

"Stay there," she said, though she knew he couldn't understand. "I'll get the horse."

It took her a minute or so to untangle the reins. It was a good horse, but thin. With an awful lot of heaving and shoving, she managed to get his foot in the stirrup iron; getting him into the saddle was more of a joint effort. He actually screamed at one point, just like a girl.

"I'm taking you somewhere safe," she said, slow and loud, as though that was going to make any difference. But he seemed to get the general idea; he smiled again, and said something that was presumably "thank you."

She led the horse down the road into Cylinder Woods. Each time she glanced back at him, he looked worse. His face was the colour of white clay, and he was clinging to the pommel of the saddle with his good hand; the other lay in his lap, and each time the horse stumbled on the uneven track, he shook all over. "Not far now," she said, several times, and hoped he understood that, too.

She stopped where the road met the forest brook and tied the horse to a tree with its reins. "We've got to walk now," she said, pointing towards the waterfall. "I'm sorry." She mimed getting off the horse; he looked at her very sadly, but she shook her head and repeated the mime. He understood. "Nice and slow," she said, trying to sound cheerful. "It's not so far really."

A bare-faced lie if ever there was one. She didn't make a very good job of helping him down off the horse; he fell, jarred his broken arm and howled quite shamefully, though she told herself to make allowances. How they got up the steep bank and under the waterfall she was never really quite sure. It was a terrible struggle, and of course they were both soaked. But at last they made it, and she helped him lean back against the cave wall and slide down until he was sitting, his legs out in front of him, his broken arm cradled in his lap. "You'll do," she told him briskly—it was what her mother said at times like this. He could barely keep his eyes open, but he nodded very gently and smiled.

"I'm going to get us some food," she said, "and some stuff to make you feel better." She mimed—looked more like a dog digging up a bone, she couldn't help thinking, but he seemed to get the message. She took the pudding basin and the tinderbox from her basket, looked back at him to make sure he was where she'd left him, and scrambled out through the curtain of water.

Just as well it was autumn; she found everything she needed quite easily, without having to go far. When she'd gathered enough, she scrabbled together a pile of dead twigs and brash, struck a fire and got it going, then put three large stones round the edge to rest the basin on. She filled it a third full with water from the stream, put in the herbs and mushrooms, and went back to the cave for the rest of the barley cakes. When the water was starting to simmer, she crumbled them in a bit at a time and stirred carefully with a clean twig.

"Here you are," she said, offering him the basin. "Eat it all up, it'll do you good."

As he ate — scooping the mush up with his fingers, then drinking the broth — she hoped it'd be enough. She was fairly sure it would be: four green death caps, two fly agarics and two of the tall, yellow ones that smelt of rotten meat, which people reckoned were the deadliest of all. As it turned out, she needn't have worried. About ten minutes after he'd finished the broth he started to shake all over. He kept trying to scream, but his mouth opened and shut and nothing came out. After twenty minutes he started rocking slowly backwards and forwards. Then he choked, made a dreadful rattling noise in his chest, and flopped sideways. She watched for another five minutes or so, just to be on the safe side, then leaned forward and touched him. He was already starting to get cold, and when she prodded his open eyeball with the tip of her finger, he never moved at all.

As she'd anticipated, her family were so pleased and relieved to see her, they took her story about having to hide from soldiers at face value and didn't ask any awkward questions, such as what had happened to the barley cakes and the basin. They were also extremely pleased about the horse, which was clearly worth a lot of money.

She didn't go back to the cave for a very long time. When she eventually did, he was still there, most of him; badgers and rats had been at the body, and ants and woodlice, so there wasn't a face left to recognise, but nothing bigger had found it, and certainly no other human. She looked at it for some time, feeling so very proud. The war was over now, so it wasn't quite the same. Still, she knew that when her country was in danger and so many brave men had given their lives, she'd done her bit too, killed one of them for her very own. She knew she'd never tell anybody, because they wouldn't understand; the nearest she'd come to mentioning it was when she asked if anybody on their side spoke a foreign language, or was it just the enemy? (She was glad to set her mind at rest on that point; she'd been quite sure at the time, but it had worried her nevertheless until her father confirmed it.) After that, she visited him once a year, on the anniversary of his death, right up until the time came for her to marry Muri Achaiois and emigrate to the island of Sphoe.

Loading the ship proved to be bewilderingly complicated.

Kunessin's original loading plan had been clear, simple and logical: bulk supplies in long-term storage — big barrels they wouldn't need to touch during the voyage — in first, at the back of the hold. Then the livestock; then the smaller barrels, bales and crates of long-term storage; then everything they'd need for the journey, at the front of the hold where they could get at it; everything else on deck, roped down under tarpaulins.

Aidi disagreed. He pointed out, as the hundred-gallon flour and malt barrels were being hoisted aboard, that Kunessin's plan would put most of the weight too far back, which would make the ship difficult to handle in bad weather and liable to capsize in extremely heavy seas. Instead, the main weight should be low and as central as possible; which in practice meant putting the bulk stores where Kunessin had planned to put the livestock. Kunessin pointed out that unless the stock was in the most stable part of the ship, they were bound to suffer dreadfully from being thrown about, even in relatively calm conditions; there'd be broken legs and other injuries, not to mention the risk of the animals getting spooked and breaking out, which would cause havoc. Alces suggested a compromise whereby the heavy stores should be distributed round the sides of the hold, to even up the weight, while leaving the livestock where Kunessin wanted them.

They tried that, but none of them (except Muri, who saw the problem but didn't say anything) realised how awkward that would be; with huge barrels all round the edges, there was hardly enough room to move around, let alone manhandle large, heavy crates down through the hatches. To make matters worse, it started to rain, which meant the perishable and imperfectly sealed and covered goods waiting on the dockside to be loaded were in danger of being completely ruined. But most of those stores couldn't be loaded until the livestock was in place, and the livestock couldn't go in until the pens had been set up, which couldn't be done until the heavy stores were on board. Meanwhile, the sailing master was muttering about the wind changing, which might mean that unless they got under way in the next eight hours, they'd be stuck right where they were for a month. Aidi took exception to that: he thought the sailing master was being far too pessimistic and started arguing with him, eventually convincing him that he'd been wrong. By then, unfortunately, rain was pooling in the tarpaulins and seeping through the cracks between the boards of the top layer of crates—mostly clothing, blankets, bedlinen and other fabrics, not to mention Kunessin's best-quality double-riveted chainmail shirts, which weren't likely to be improved by spending the journey soaking wet.

When this was brought to Kunessin's attention, he lost patience with the finer points and ordered the dockers to get everything on board and under cover as soon as possible: livestock first, then fit in all the rest of the stuff wherever it would go. Muri scrambled down into the hold and gave directions; he turned out to have a natural flair for sliding and stacking and double-banking, and he made scribbled notes as he went along so they'd have at least a rough idea of where everything was. Kudei dealt with the livestock (by this stage they'd been cramped up in temporary pens on the dockside for six hours and were in no mood to co-operate, but Kudei was a born stockman, and with the help of some fourteen-foot gates, stout willow hurdles and lots of rope, he managed to crowd and chivvy them out of the pen, up the ramp and into the crane-sling for lowering into the hold). In spite of Muri's efforts, there was a huge amount of stuff that couldn't be crammed into the hold. Alces took charge of stacking, roping and covering it on deck, and made a fine job of it in a surprisingly short time. A few minutes after the last barrel had been rolled into place, the rain stopped and the sun came out.

Aidi, meanwhile, had been taking an inventory of spoiled and damaged items. He negotiated an extra two hours from the sailing master, then rushed round Faralia buying replacements and persuading tradesmen and dockers to drop whatever they were doing and get the new stores aboard ship. There was no time to extricate the ruined stores and dump them, which meant the ship would be sailing somewhat over weight; Aidi talked it through with the sailing master and agreed a number of minor course and schedule changes, before reporting to Kunessin that everything was more or less in order, and there weren't likely to be any additional problems that they wouldn't be able to handle. The women and the indentured hands then boarded, and the ship finally left Faralia harbour, four hours late but helped by an unexpectedly fresh easterly breeze that promised to make up most of the lost time by nightfall.

"Well?" Chaere demanded.

Dorun was clinging to the rail with both hands. "Well what?"

"You know."

"Oh," Dorun replied, "that." A gentle wave nudged the ship against its direction of travel, and she jerked as though she'd been stabbed. "What about it?"

Chaere was looking revoltingly healthy and robust. "Well?" she repeated.

Dorun shrugged; the gesture cost her dearly. "If you must know," she said, "he fell asleep in his chair, in the middle of taking his boots off. Woke up this morning with a crick in his neck. Just tired out, I guess." The back of her throat was burning and her eyes hurt, but she knew Chaere would be mightily put out if she didn't ask. "You?"

Chaere smiled; probably been rehearsing that smile in a mirror since she was fourteen. "Let's say the jury's still out, but there are definite positive signs. Practice makes perfect, I guess." She frowned. "You look awful," she said.

Dorun didn't dare nod. "I think it's being on the sea," she said.

"You get used to it, apparently," Chaere said. "I think Aidi's got it too. He was massively sick over the side of the boat, and then he said he was going down into the hold to check the stores weren't shifting. Looked like death. Strange," she added, with a sweet smile. "A war hero and everything, you'd think he'd be able to cope with a bit of joggling about."

There were two reasons why Dorun didn't push Chaere into the sea just then. One was that she couldn't face the effort. The other was that she hoped she was a better person than that. "Teuche's fine," she said, "but he's used to sea travel." Slowly and bravely, she turned around, resting the small of her back against the rail. "What do you know about what they did in the war?" she asked. "Everybody seems to know some dark and deadly secret except me."

Chaere shrugged. "I've heard things, but it was all a bit technical for me. They were definitely heroes, though. Right there in the thick of it in every battle."

"I'd heard that too," Dorun said guardedly. "But you'd have thought, if they were so brave and did all sorts of glorious deeds and so forth, people would be, well, a bit more enthusiastic about them. The impression I get is, everyone's quite polite to their faces, but they aren't sorry to see the back of them."

Chaere nodded gravely. "You mean, if there's not something badly wrong with them, why did they end up having to marry us?" Dorun opened her mouth, but Chaere went straight on: "I don't know, is the honest answer. After all, think about it, we're the last people anybody'd tell. I know Muri Achaiois was married before, and his wife died. And when Aidi asked me the first time, you should've seen the way my parents reacted. Honestly, if I hadn't already turned him down, I'd probably have married him just to piss them off."

"But they agreed this time?"

"Yes." Chaere frowned. "But it was definitely anything's-better-than-nothing, and if I'd said no, they'd have backed me up. But I've been so desperate to get out of there..."

"Is that how you see it?" Dorun asked. "Anything's better than nothing?"

Chaere thought for a moment. "Not really," she said. "I mean, if it'd been one of the others, no disrespect intended to Teuche, I'm not sure which way I'd have gone. But I like Aidi," she said, sounding faintly surprised. "A bit," she added. "And it's not like he's a complete stranger or anything." She fingered a twist of damp hair out of her eyes. "Let's say I'm curious enough to be interested in seeing what happens. You?"

"Like you," she said. "Anything's got to be better than home. Except," she added, "being on a boat. If I'd known about this…" She coughed, spluttered, swallowed four times. "What do you know about the others?" she said hoarsely. "I've heard a few things about Clea—"

"Who hasn't?"

"But the other two are just names." Dorun half turned back towards the sea, got stuck and kept perfectly still, gripping the rail as though trying to strangle it. "Anything?"

"Enyo Aspida, as she was before she married, is a farm girl from the Ashmoor district. Menin Aeide's a complete mystery to everybody, except," Chaere added, suddenly looking thoughtful, "my cousin Thoas said he seemed to remember hearing she'd been on trial for manslaughter about five years ago."

"Manslaughter?"

Chaere shrugged. "Or arson, he wasn't sure. But she was acquitted," she went on, "and not long afterwards they caught whoever it was who really did it, and it was proved beyond all doubt that Menin had nothing to do with it. So Thoas said," she added, "and personally, I wouldn't take Thoas' word for it if he told me my name. But presumably that's why she landed up on the shelf," she went on, "because I can't see anything else wrong with her. Quiet, all-right-looking. Well, you can judge as well as I can. I overheard Kudei Gaeon just now asking where she was, and someone said she's down in the hold helping muck out the stock." Chaere shuddered just a little. "I suppose I'm going to have to learn how to do all that sort of thing."

Dorun grinned at her. "It's not so bad," she said.

"Easy for you to say, you were born to it." Chaere looked away. "I wasn't. And it's not my fault I'm not physically strong. I've got no strength in my arms at all. I tried doing exercises once, but it was a waste of time, loads of tiresome effort for nothing. So lugging buckets about and shovelling…" She made a complicated gesture with her arms. "I'm not even going to think about that," she said. "They can't make me do what I'm not physically capable of doing, and that's all there is to it. Besides, we've got servants for all that, so the question won't arise."

Dorun decided not to say anything. Instead: "I don't like the look of those clouds," she said. "Presumably if it rains we all go down into the hold."

"Presumably," Chaere replied, clearly preoccupied. "They can't expect us to stay up here and get soaked to the skin. Really, I wouldn't have thought it'd have been beyond the wit of man to put up a bit of shelter on the deck. Just a sort of shed thing with a roof and four walls would've done; it wouldn't have had to be anything fancy. And then we wouldn't be crammed in with all the animals." Her voice was high, loud, slightly brittle. "Actually, it might be worth having a word with somebody," she went on. "I mean, they've got loads of planks of wood and nails and tools and things down in the stores, and it wouldn't take them five minutes just to knock something up. What do you think? Should I suggest it?"

"See how things go," Dorun said sagely.

"Hmm." Chaere was looking at her hands. Town hands, Dorun thought; oh dear. "I really do think we need to start as we mean to go on," Chaere said. "I mean, they're dragging us out here to the ends of the earth; the very least they can do is have a little tiny bit of consideration. Really, I'm not the sort of person who complains all the time, but it's just common sense: how can anybody be expected to know what we're thinking unless we tell them?"

Dorun looked down at the deck. "It's worth trying, I suppose," she said.

"Well, I think it'd carry a lot more weight if we all asked," Chaere said quickly. "Start as we plan to go on. I mean, they can't ride roughshod over all of us. Maybe you could have a word with the others."

"I don't think so," Dorun said quietly, her hand over her mouth. "In fact, I don't think I'm going to be up to doing anything that means moving away from this rail. Sorry," she added wretchedly, "I don't want to seem difficult, but I haven't got a lot of choice."

Chaere sniffed. "Well," she said, standing up, "I'll talk to them later. But don't blame me if it all goes horribly wrong."

A perfectly reasonable request, Dorun thought once she'd gone, on the face of it. Any fool could see, of course, that a shed or canopy raised on deck wouldn't last two minutes once the wind started to blow. She smiled. Probably, Aidi Proiapsen would try explaining that to her, sweetly reasonable and wanting to tell her all the technical stuff—lap joints, stress points, shearing limits of materials—and that'd just make her irritable: you're supposed to be so clever, can't you do a simple thing like put up a shed? In the right conditions, a conversation like that could fester under both their skins for twenty years.

"How are you feeling?" She hadn't noticed him approach, but she turned her head and did her best to smile. "Not good," she said.

"No," Kunessin said, "I can see that. I got seasick once, when I was young. Lasted three days and I was sure I was going to die. In fact, I can't remember ever feeling worse, even when I was in the field hospital for seven weeks with blood poisoning, and they were convinced I wasn't going to make it."

"Thanks," she said. "I'm glad you told me that. Listen," she added on impulse. "Chaere—that's Aidi Proiapsen's wife..."

He nodded. "I'm gradually getting the hang of it."

"She's decided she wants a sort of covered gallery on the deck, to sit in when it rains. I take it that's out of the question."

He looked surprised, but nodded. "The wind'd rip it off in two seconds flat," he replied. "All it'd take would be a side-wind..."

"Maybe you should warn him," she said. "She's not the world's most tactful person."

He grinned. "I appreciate your concern," he said. "But Aidi's not that bad really. Let him handle it in his own way. They'll have to open negotiations sooner or later."

It was an odd way of putting it, but she could see what he meant. "You're very close, aren't you?" she said. "All five of you."

"In some ways, yes. But not in everything, by any means. We've been apart for quite a few years."

"Even so." The ship lurched, and she winced. "Oh God," she muttered. "Am I really going to have to put up with this all the way to Sphoe?"

He smiled. "Yes," he said. "But it stops as soon as you get off the ship. Or quite soon after, anyway."

"Fine. That's your idea of sympathy, is it?"

"Coming from me, that's sympathy on an unprecedented scale. Cherish it."

He left her and went below. As he'd feared, the cargo had shifted, so that three-hundredweight casks were jammed up against flimsy boxes and crates, ready to crush them as soon as the ship hit anything more boisterous than a gentle swell. The animals seemed quiet enough: the cows had backed into the far corner of their improvised pen, and the bull was standing in front of them, his tail swishing. Kunessin stuck a fork into the opened bale and threw him a mop of hay. He stared at it with contempt.

"He's not happy." He hadn't noticed Kudei, up on top of the hayrick, lying on his stomach looking down at him. "But I don't suppose he'll be any trouble, so long as we keep our distance for a bit."

Kunessin put the fork back. "How much of the hay got wet when we were loading?"

"Three score," Kudei replied. "I've put the wet stuff on top; it's drying quite well. It's the flour and the oats I'm worried about."

"Surely not. They're safely packed in barrels."

Kudei shook his head. "Someone down at the cooper's saw you coming," he said. "Green staves. With the damp and the warmth down here, some of them'll warp, you can bet on it. I'm not so bothered about the oats, if the pasture's as good as you say it is, but the flour was meant to be for us."

"It'll be all right," Kunessin said firmly. "We've got nearly double what we're likely to need."

Kudei jumped up. "Just as well," he said, hopping from the large to the small rick, and from there to the deck. "Also, Aidi's right. This ship is definitely too low in the water."

"For now." Kunessin manufactured a yawn. "But in a day or so we'll have eaten and drunk the excess weight, and then we'll be just right. The master reckons it's set fair for the next forty-eight hours."

"Well." Kudei picked up a small barrel that had rolled on to its side and set it straight again. "I hope he's right. I wish I knew about ships and all that stuff. It makes me nervous, having to rely on someone I don't know very well."

Kunessin grinned. "Aidi's a mine of nautical information," he said.

"Naturally. What does he reckon?"

"He thinks we'll be lucky to get to Sphoe without having to swim."

Kudei laughed. "Apart from that."

"Oh, he reckons I paid well over the odds for the ship, which isn't really suitable for what we want, and we should've had much more done to it before we set out; but that aside, it could be worse. Also, the master's reasonably competent, but his dead reckoning's out by at least two degrees, so we'll probably go right on past Sphoe till we hit the mainland, and then we'll have to double back against the wind, which at this time of year could take us a month."

"Apart from that?"

"No major problems," Kunessin said. "Oh, and he's wrong about the two degrees. I had Muri look at it, and he reckons the master's laid in a little bit extra to compensate for some current or other we'll run into while we're rounding the cape. I haven't told Aidi, needless to say." Using the flat of his right hand as a fulcrum, he levered himself up on top of the smaller hayrick, then pulled a face. "Damn it, Kudei," he said, "it's wet."

"Told you."

Kunessin shrugged. "Changing the subject," he said, "how are things going with...?" He froze, his face a study in acute embarrassment. "I really am most terribly sorry," he said, "but I've forgotten..."

"Clea," Kudei replied, grinning. "And not so bad, all things considered. We're both of us—well, cautious, so that's all right. I get the feeling she's making an effort to get off on the right foot."

"Good," Kunessin said; it was his commanding-officer-taking-an-interest voice, but it had come out like that before he could do anything about it. Kudei only grinned. "You know me," Kunessin went on awkwardly, "I haven't got a clue. But...well, it may just be possible that Dorun and I are going to be friends, if that's possible with women."

"Best way," Kudei said magisterially. "Just don't try too hard, that's all." He sat down on a heap of meal sacks, picking at some loose stitching. "I watched my brothers come to grief that way," he said. "Either trying too hard or not trying at all. Usually both," he added with a grin. "Euge always says we have women in our house the way other families have mice. Says it all, really."

Kunessin nodded.

"Dosei, on the other hand, says that a farm's got to have women, the same way it's got to have dogs." Kudei shrugged. "My father wasn't much better, come to that; when I think about it, I can't see my mother had much of a life, but she always seemed too busy to notice. Trouble is, you want it to be different, so you try too hard. Like my uncle Teleclidin, remember him? Wouldn't let his wife stir outside, or even make up the fire. Kept her stuck in that poky little upstairs sitting room all day doing needlework, like a gentlewoman. Thirty years, and she hardly ever set foot downstairs. And he was convinced he was doing her a favour."

"I remember him," Teuche said, after a while. "Little short man, always wore a scarf, even in summer. Looked a bit like a bundle of dry sticks in a sack. But I remember seeing him wrestle a bullock into a stall for debudding, all on his own. Always took three of us to do that."

"Oh, he was strong all right," Kudei said. "But how old do you reckon he was when he died?"

Kunessin frowned. "He was pretty ancient when I knew him," he said. "I don't know. Seventy? Seventy-five?"

Kudei shook his head. "Actually," he said, "he was fifty-seven." He looked away, then said, "When I was a kid, I really didn't want to be a farmer. What a total waste of a life, I thought. Everything you'll ever know you've learned by the time you're fifteen, and every year's the same as the year before and the year after. You know exactly what you'll be doing this day twelve months hence, because it's what you're doing today. I can't do that, I thought, I'll go mad. So I made them let me go to college and be a soldier." He grinned. "Thought it'd make a difference."

"That's a good joke," Kunessin said. "All I ever wanted was what you couldn't stand the thought of." He stood up suddenly. "You know something?" he said. "When we were at the war, I used to lie awake sometimes, making plans: how I could murder your entire family, one at a time or the whole lot of them together, so you'd be the only one left, and then I'd buy the farm off you. Oh, I thought of every possible way: poisoning the stream, boarding up the house at night and setting it on fire, killing them all in their beds and making it look like soldiers did it. It's a bloody good thing we were so far away, or I might have done it, too. I had it all worked out, times and distances down to the second, every eventuality covered with a back-up plan. When it was really bad, in the war, thinking about it was the only thing that kept me going sometimes. There was no ill will, believe it or not; I thought of them all as targets, like you do when you're fighting in a battle. It was one of the reasons I stayed on after the war: I didn't dare come home, in case I went ahead and did it."

Kudei thought for a while, then he said, "What if I'd refused to sell?"

"You wouldn't have," Kunessin said. "I've always known you didn't want the farm."

"Yes, but what if I'd refused?"

Kunessin looked down, at his hands steepled in his lap. "Then I'd have bullied you into letting me come and work for you," he said. "And then I'd have waited to see who died first. After all, we're a long-lived family, you're not. Anyhow, it wouldn't have come to that. I'd have talked you into selling."

He realised Kudei was looking at him. "What made you decide to tell me that?" Kudei said.

"I guess I thought you should know," Kunessin replied. "It's one of the few things I'm deeply ashamed of."

Kudei rubbed his eyes, as though he was suddenly tired. "You never did it, though," he said. "It was just daydreams. And we were all a bit off our heads back then."

"Not me," Kunessin said. "The only reason I didn't do it was because we were hundreds of miles away. If they'd ever given us two weeks' leave..."

"You shouldn't say any more," Kudei snapped. "And you shouldn't have told me. It's really not the sort of thing I want to know."

"It's why we're going to Sphoe," Kunessin said calmly. "You need to know the reason, or I'm leading you out here under false pretences. You ought to know the worst thing about me. There shouldn't be any secrets."

"Stuff that's just inside your head..." Kudei turned away, like someone avoiding a blow. "The way I'm going to choose to see it," he said, "you had some crazy ideas at one time, most probably because of the war and what it did to all of us; but you never did anything about them, and it's all over with now and out of the way. Just do me a favour and never mention it again."

"If that's what you want."

"Yes," Kudei said. "And if there's anything else you want to tell me..."

"There isn't."

"Good. Then let's forget it. All right?"

"All right," Kunessin said. "And I'm sorry, if that makes any difference."

Kudei got up and slipped past him; it reminded Kunessin of someone getting out of the bull's pen in a hurry, because he's starting to get agitated. "I'm going up on deck," Kudei said. "You might want to stay down here for a while and count something."

After he'd gone, Kunessin sat down again and thought long and hard about what had just been said. He took the conversation apart, broke it down into its functional components, searching for any ill-considered or insensitive things he may have said, or even implied. But there was nothing to find: he'd told the truth, advancing his pikes of honesty into the open ground. He'd told the truth and thereby flushed out and killed a secret; and secrets are just lies that haven't been spoken out loud, poisonous things that should be killed on sight. For some reason, however, Kudei had been upset by the simple truth.

Disingenuous, even when lying to himself. Of course Kudei was upset, because what he'd confessed had been a monstrous thing. But it too was dead now; and besides, all five of them had shared far worse, eaten from the same bowl. All in all, he felt hurt: he'd offered his friend something old and rare, and Kudei hadn't wanted it. He forgave him, of course, but he was still bothered about it; about why he'd rejected it, when it was offered with such good will.

Brooding on it wouldn't help, though, and he had other things to occupy his mind. He looked round at the stores, thousands of thalers' worth; the lives of killed men, represented by these barrels and sacks and boxes, like the people represented in parliament. Every copper penny he'd ever made out of the wars was invested here (and by the end, the money was just a way of keeping score, like entries in the game book: so many head killed on such a day, transferred to the larder and consumed); he'd made sure of it, so there'd be no going back, no chance of a return to Faralia, to the valley, the farm. Why hadn't Kudei understood that? It really was a most magnificent gesture, the abjuring of all his rights, claims and interests in what should rightfully have been his — if the war hadn't come, if thousands of dead men hadn't poisoned the grazing with the juices from their rotting bodies. Well, he'd spoiled any number of other men's fields, and some of it had been about staying alive and keeping death away from his friends, and some of it had been just work. But when it had been up to him, on those occasions when he'd had the choice, it had been for the money, because the money would somehow bring him the farm...

"A prize agent?" Aidi had said. "What the hell's a prize agent, and what do we need one for?"

He'd explained: the armour, weapons and military equipment of the enemy dead belonged to the state, just as their personal possessions belonged to the regimental treasury, but someone, a serving officer, had to be responsible for collecting and shipping it all and putting it in auction; for all which tedious, distasteful work he was entitled to five per cent of the gross. Apparently they had to have one, it was regulations. And so, if nobody else wanted the job...

"You go ahead, as far as I'm concerned," Nuctos had said, straight away. "We all get our cut from Regimental without having to lift a finger. You want all that aggravation, you're more than welcome."

Muri had agreed, of course; Kudei wasn't interested; Fly made a show of objecting, but changed his tune immediately when threatened with the job. "Really, it should be me," Aidi had said cautiously. "I'm the one with commercial experience. No offence, but what do you know about buying and selling?"

"I'll pick it up as I go along," he'd replied. "More to the point, Aidi, you don't need the money, I do. My family lives in one room behind the tannery, or had you forgotten that?"

Aidi: brave as a lion, but talk out loud about poverty and he'd run a mile. "Fine," he'd said, hands wide, "you carry on. If you need any help, just ask."

"Thanks," he'd said, and didn't add "but over my dead body"; Aidi could read a double page of accounts at sight, and the books he intended to keep weren't going to be honest: not to the government, or the army, or the other five members of A Company. He'd shed his blood for them, of course; he'd fight for them, endure anything for them, willingly die for them. But he had no intention whatsoever of being honest with the money. After all, he needed it; for the farm.

What he'd made during the war was, of course, small change compared with what he'd gouged the army for once he'd been made a general. Which was perfectly all right, after he'd first set eyes on Sphoe and known straight away what he was going to do with it. All along, ever since the beginning, when it was for the farm, he'd thought of himself as just a trustee. Once he'd seen Sphoe and given up on the farm, it was practically a duty. If any serving soldier had defrauded the government more remorselessly, ingeniously or comprehensively, he'd be vastly surprised, and it wouldn't have been for want of trying. Even when they charged the line, and he ducked under the needle-pointed pike-heads at the very last moment, coming up like a diver with the foreshafts on the tops of his shoulders, hacking into forearms and collar bones like a woodcutter, soaking wet with blood like a shepherd in the rain, and the jarring of his sword on their bones had made his tendons ache and his fingers go numb, the agency had always been in the back of his mind, the shine of the silver like dew on the grass, big five-thaler coins sprawled on a table like dead bodies littering a meadow…

And now it was all sacks of flour and barrels of malt, new ploughs still gleaming with the tempering oil, coils of wire, kegs of nails, cases of shoes and hats and long winter stockings, tin plates, spare blades for the bow saws, horseshoe blanks, buttons (five thousand buttons, various), seed drills, post mauls, hammer wedges, spikes you tied to your shoes when you crawled about thatching a roof; so much hard-ware, as though his father had taken one look at all the dead bodies on a battlefield, waved his hand and muttered an incantation, and turned all that foul, poisonous meat into good, useful household supplies. And why couldn't Kudei understand that, of all people?

(It had been in his mind to tell him about the fraud, too, but he decided to reserve judgement on that. Almost certainly it'd be different once they got to Sphoe, and Kudei could see for himself.)

He noticed that one of the crates was open; it had been thrown against a beam by the movement of the ship, and the lid had sprung its nails. He bent it up and peered inside, trying to remember what was in there. At first he couldn't make it out, a shape swathed in hay; too small for a shield, too big for a mirror. He pulled it out, teased off the hay, and grinned. It was a frying pan. Well, he thought, I've got twenty-four of them. Any man who can stand up and truthfully assert that he owns two dozen serviceable new frying pans has something to show for his time on earth.

He went back on deck. Aidi and his wife (he was going to have to make a very special effort and learn their names) had set up a chess board on top of the water barrel. Cautiously, so they wouldn't notice him, he craned his neck to see the board over Aidi's shoulder. He was startled to see that Aidi appeared to be losing; he was white, and there were only four white pieces left on the board. No, revise that: three.

"Check," she said.

He couldn't see Aidi's face, but the silence and the stillness were unmistakable. Aidi was thinking, very hard. She, on the other hand, looked bored. After two minutes, she yawned and said, "It's your move."

"I know," Aidi grunted. "I'm thinking."

He had a lot to think about. Teuche had never been a top-flight chess player like Nuctos Di'Ambrosies (or, come to that, Aidi Proiapsen), but he could read a board well enough. Mate in four, was his forecast.

"If you concede, we can start a new game," she coaxed.

"I never concede," Aidi growled.

"Then make a move."

He scratched his head. She sighed. He moved his knight, kept his finger on the piece, made a strange, baffled noise and put it back where it had been.

"Tell you what," she said briskly. "I concede. Now can we start a new game?"

"Don't be stupid," Aidi snapped. "You can't concede, you're winning."

"Matter of opinion," she replied. "You can still make checkmate with one knight and a king."

"Will you please be quiet and let me think?"

It was more than flesh and blood could stand, and Kunessin decided to stop it. He took a long, heavy stride forward and said loudly, "Aidi, there you are. I need you to—"

"Not now, Teuche, I'm busy," Aidi said, his eyes still fixed on the board. "Can it wait just for a minute or so?" he added, his voice less abrasive but just as resolute.

"General Kunessin," she said (which startled him). "Could you please take my husband away somewhere before I strangle him? I've offered him a draw, I've offered to concede, it's painfully obvious he's lost, but will he give in?"

Kunessin pursed his lips. "Looks like a draw to me," he said.

"I just need time to think," Aidi moaned.

"It's a draw, for God's sake," she shrieked at him. "You heard him. General, can you make that a direct order?"

Aidi made another strange noise and moved his king. "At last," she said, and her hand was on the piece; then she hesitated, and a bewildered frown spread across her face like the smoke from burning stubble.

"Now it's a draw," Aidi said, and he sounded very, very tired. "My knight takes your rook, my pawn makes queen, immediately gets killed by your bishop, which gets killed by my king, your knight takes mine, stalemate. Do you agree?"

She opened her mouth, closed it again and nodded; and he was right, there was no other way it could go. But where the hell had that last move come from? Kunessin traced it back in his mind. It was a perfectly legal move, there for anybody to see, but he hadn't seen it and clearly neither had she. "Right then," Aidi said briskly, scooping all the pieces together and shovelling them into a wooden box on the deck. "What was it you wanted me to do?"

Kunessin's mind went blank, but only for a moment. "You were saying something about our being off course two degrees," he said. "Can you do the sums and tell me what that's going to mean in terms of supplies? If we're going to run short of water—"

Aidi shook his head. "That's not a problem," he said. "Even if we overshoot by two degrees, we still reach the mainland long before the water runs dry. We can go ashore and refill." He frowned. "Was that it?"

"Thanks," Kunessin said. "Sorry if I disturbed your game."

Aidi gave him a poisonous look. Behind him, his wife was setting out the pieces on the board. Kunessin knew he shouldn't ask, but he couldn't resist. "What's the score?" he said.

Aidi looked at him. "Today?" he said. "Or since we left home?"

"Both."

"Today, six draws. Overall, she leads me two games to nothing, with fourteen draws. But there's still time," he added defiantly, "especially if we're two degrees off, and we get stuck on the mainland for a month waiting for the wind. I'm gradually learning her game," he said. "It's just that—"

"I thought you were good at chess," Kunessin said pleasantly.

"I am," Aidi replied, in torment. "In fact, I'm loads better than I ever thought I was. That's what's so terrible."

SEVEN

The second time that A Company, Sixth Battalion, the Ninth Regiment, engaged the enemy was shortly after the catastrophic defeat at Maxa, when General Euteuchida realised too late that he'd allowed himself to be caught in a simple crab's-claw trap by the enemy light dragoons. Maxa left the Ninth and Sixteenth cut off from what was left of Euteuchida's battered army, at the mercy of the enemy lancers and their crack Twenty-Sixth of pikes. Purely by chance, A Company hadn't fought at Maxa: Brigadier General Calodaemon had assigned them to cover an attack that proved to be a feint, and by the time they were recalled, the general retreat had already begun. Calodaemon, now in sole command of the two regiments, did the only sensible thing in the circumstances and fell back on the Mysartis river valley, allowing himself the option of escaping upstream to Shandra Bakt. Or so he thought: the escape route was, in fact, a fundamental part of the enemy strategy, although in all fairness there was no way that Calodaemon could have realised that from the information available to him. Once the ruse had become apparent, he resolved to make his stand on the eastern bank of the river, with his back to a small village called Pasen Far.

* * *

"You don't want to bother with anything the officer tells you," Nuctos said with a grin. "Just do as I say and we'll be fine."

The enemy were a grey rectangle, impossible, on the opposite side of the valley. As the wind fluctuated, they could hear snatches of the sounds they made: the thump of eight thousand pairs of boots on the dry chalk, the clatter of armour plates jostling against each other, from time to time the shrill, nervous voices of officers. Impossible, because they'd never seen anything like it before. Eight thousand, they'd been told, but they could only see one huge, solid grey object, sliding towards them down the gentle slope. It was inconceivable that anybody could expect them to fight that thing. They all knew stories about the heroes who'd fought giants and dragons; as far as Thouridos Alces was concerned, the whole point of the stories was the overwhelming size of the opponent — one lonely hero squaring up to a fifteen-foot man or a twenty-foot lizard. But this thing was a mile long. How could anybody fight that?

"You reckon," he heard Aidi say behind him.

"Trust me," Nuctos said; and his voice was different today, soft and slightly hoarse, almost as though he was looking forward to the appalling thing that was about to happen to them. "Come on, Aidi, we've been through all this. If we do it the orthodox way, we're packed lunches for the crows. Do it my way, they won't know what hit them."

Just for a moment, the sun came out from under the thick wad of cloud. It caught steel on the edges of the slowly approaching thing; like a silent roar, a predator showing its teeth. Alces tried to estimate the distance, just as an exercise in applied mental trigonometry (Muri and the right-angle-triangle law; couldn't help but smile at the thought of that), and decided they were still between six and eight hundred yards away. Now, if a marching man covers two yards a second, a hundred and twenty yards a minute, seven hundred divided by a hundred and twenty is five minutes forty-eight seconds —

"Where in hell," Aidi was muttering, "is our field artillery?"

"Basco," Nuctos replied promptly.

"Where's that?"

"No idea." Nuctos smiled. "Not near here, anyway. I heard the colonel swearing at a messenger. But the way I see it, who needs them? Sure, you throw a few rocks, you squash maybe three dozen of them, it really makes no odds in the long run. The only way we win is if we break them and they run for it. It's not about killing, it's about winning the battle. And that," he added, widening his smile to an enormous beam, "is why, right now, we're the most important men on this field. If we break them, we win. If not, it's goodbye Ninth Regiment, so long General Euteuchida, once this lot catch up and outflank him, and most likely pop goes the entire war. So," he added chirpily, "no pressure, gentlemen. Just go out there and do your best."

Behind them, they could hear their own pikes forming. According to the best authorities, if the enemy didn't get you, your own side would; when the line broke and the men surged forward to exploit the breach, there was virtually no time to get out of the way, nowhere to go, nothing at all you could do except keep cutting a path deep into the enemy formation, just to stay six inches ahead of the oncoming pike-heads. Keeping up with the enemy as they ran away was no good at all, since you'd be hampered by all the men in the middle and back rows. You had to chop and scramble. The best way was supposed to be to jump up and run on their shoulders, crushing heads as you went—the more you killed, the more dead bodies there'd be to get under the feet of your own oncoming line, slow them up, buy you time. That was, of course, too much to ask of any man, which was probably why most linebreakers didn't last more than one engagement.

"A bit closer," Nuctos was saying. He was nearly having to shout, because of the noise, the tramp and clatter and jingle. It really was true, the ground did shake. Alces could feel it through the soles of his boots. No more than two hundred yards now... "Not yet," Nuctos growled, "not yet, not quite yet." Well, Alces thought, I'm bound to have forgotten something, but it's probably too late now. "Draw and go," Nuctos yelled; and for a split second Alces thought: draw? And then he realised, draw the sword, and then he remembered he'd already done that; and next to him, Muri started to move, and it was as though they were tied together with rope, because he couldn't have stayed put if he'd tried.

Even so, he thought, this is stupid, we're running towards that thing, it should be the other way. Then the pike-heads were stupidly, dangerously close, you could do yourself an injury, and at the very last moment he remembered what to do...

(The trick, Nuctos had instructed them, was to jump, but just before your feet leave the ground, trip yourself up; so you go forward headlong, roll as you hit the deck, three rolls should do it to get well under the pikes; there's a knack to kicking away from the ground to get upright again all in the same movement, and use that surge to come up through the pikestaffs—like breaking ice from underneath [strange image, but they knew what he meant]—and bash straight into them, don't worry about trying to get your balance; there's nothing they can do about you, they're stuck in a bloody great hedge, both hands on the pike, helpless as kittens; and then, if you're quick...

Oh, and one other thing. Don't look at their faces, just at what you want to cut.)

He hit the soft grass with outstretched knees and elbows, but there wasn't time to hurt. The roll came out because they'd practised it so often, and the recovery came from the roll, and then he was crashing into a man's face and chest, remembering to turn his shoulder to crush the man's face out of his way while raising his arms for the first cut; not a big slash, not enough room for that, but instead a long, light-as-a-feather draw cut, pulling the cutting edge across nose and lips, to cause damage and pain, which disconcerts the enemy, putting him out of action for the fraction of a second it takes to get your balance, sway back and make the big cut. Mistimed: the face didn't go back far enough, so instead of the strong top third of the blade coming down sweet on the weak middle seam of the helmet, he jabbed the crossguard into an eye. Which worked just as well, even though it was a mistake and a mess, proving there's no justice.

The man obligingly dropped, showing the next target, and he redeemed himself with a perfect from-the-roof cut, on the neck just above the collar bone, missing the steel pauldron (try not to hit armour, it takes the edge off the blade); smart pull back to free the sword from the suction of the wound, and onwards (and remember, try and pace yourself. Don't waste your strength overhitting. If possible, get a rhythm going).

It occurred to him, quite suddenly, that he was seven feet deep inside the enemy formation and still alive; in which case, they'd probably done it, broken the line, in which case the countercharge should be coming up any second now. But there was no time to turn and look (he swung; too much weight behind it, because he split the helmet right down the braze line, through the bone, deep into the notoriously soft and clingy brain. He managed to get clear, but only just in time) and for a moment he had no idea where he was, lost, like a child strayed from its parents, because he couldn't see the others. Then he caught a glimpse of Muri—lunatic, he was taking the stuff about jumping up on their shoulders seriously, and it was working—and on the other side, the officer, Lieutenant D'Eteleieto, both hands on the hilt as he drew-cut a throat, then a perfect little shuffle to get into position for the next—

And then he didn't understand, because instead of a quarter-turn into the next target, D'Eteleieto lurched forward, bashing his nose and chin against the target's breastplate, and sort of slid down him to the ground; which could only mean he'd slipped, lost his footing on the blood-greasy turf, in which case...

There was no time to think, of course. If he'd thought about it, he'd have realised it was impossible, and that would mean leaving D'Eteleieto to die. So he turned his back on the man he had to get through and pushed with his legs, the way he'd learned how to get through a too-small gap in a thorn hedge. He felt something sharp brush across his face, a blade or the jagged edge of cut armour; it couldn't matter less. He was holding the sword high above his head, to keep it from getting caught in anything, and he turned round again, to see an enemy pikeman letting go of his splintered pike-shaft. He swung at him; no skill, just effort, and the sword-point skidded off the peak of his helmet and flew wide, though he'd hit hard enough to knock the man off his feet. But the enemy was now the least of his problems. The front rank of the Ninth was pressing a wedge into the breach; D'Eteleieto was on his hands and knees, about to stand up, just as the pike-hedge surged forward. Alces swung again, trying to bash the pikes down, but all he managed to do was smash one pike just below the socket.

It helped not to think. He knew what to do: dive, deliberate trip, roll, and come up under the pikes, burst upwards; just in time, he kept himself from swinging the sword and killing one of his own people. Instead, the man he'd just been at such pains not to kill barged into him. He felt his left knee give way, and a numbing, splitting pain in his head as the man stumbled over his bent back and landed on him with his full weight. He tried to move, but a boot slammed into his cheekbone, then another stood on his neck; they were trampling him as they jammed themselves into the hole in the line—they couldn't help it, almost certainly didn't know he was there until they felt him through their boot soles, but if he didn't contrive to get out of the way he'd be dead in a few seconds. So he reached up and grabbed, catching hold of a knee and hauling on it with all his strength; the man went down as he came up, he felt his shoulder ram the man's jaw, and something broke. His legs weren't working, but it didn't matter. He was being shunted forward by the men behind him, straight towards the levelled point of a pike. His outstretched hand caught and deflected it at the last moment—it went wide and in under the armpit of some soldier off to his left, and Alces was jammed up against the shaft, until the surge behind him snapped it and he lurched forward. Someone tried to jab him in the chest with a short sword, but he was either tired or not very strong. The sword-point skittered off Alces' breastplate and took a small nick out of the inside of his left forearm, and then the man went down, and Alces trod on his face as he was shoved forward.

Lieutenant D'Eteleieto, he remembered; where the hell was he? Pointless question; he couldn't go back. But he had to, so he twisted round, raised his arms, somehow got his elbows on the shoulders of two men, and hoisted himself off the ground. Then it was like climbing a horizontal, violent tree. He used his hands to grab handholds and hauled himself up; the support gave way and his feet touched down, so he did it all over again, swinging his head from side to side to butt obstacles out of the way. He could feel his strength starting to drain, like water out of a leaking bucket. Oh well, he thought, I'll get as far as I can and see if it'll be enough.

Then, remarkably, there was the lieutenant, at his feet; he had to stop sharply and take a knee in his stomach to keep from treading on him. It was bad enough already, so he stooped, put one arm under D'Eteleieto's knees and the other behind his head, and tried a straight lift. He felt the muscles of his back tear like rotten cloth, but he couldn't be bothered with that. Now all he had to do was keep his feet as the wedge squashed deeper into the enemy line, and hope he didn't get them both spitted on a pike. Quite a lot to ask for, and now there really wasn't anything he could do. He was exhausted, every last scrap of strength gone, his throat rasped raw with forced breathing. Mostly, he was furiously angry, because he'd got this far, and it wasn't going to be enough.

But it was, somehow. At some point the enemy formation finally splintered and ran, and the Ninth rushed forward into space that wasn't jammed with bodies, and there was enough room to fall over without being trampled. As he hit the ground, he rolled instinctively on to his side, curling round D'Eteleieto to cover as much of him as he could. His eyes closed, and everything went away.

"Fly," someone was saying. His name. No, his name was Thouridos Alces. "Fly, for crying out loud wake up."

Some fool, quite possibly the same fool that was yelling at him, was shaking him about. He lashed out with his arm, but it wouldn't lash; it was tied to his body. Odd, he thought. Odd enough to merit opening his eyes.

The light hurt, and Aidi Proiapsen was standing over him, his face unnaturally huge, yelling at him: "Fly, come on, wake up. We haven't got time."

His right arm was tied to his body with cloth; a sling. But he had the full use of his left.

"Ow," Aidi said, darting back. "Damn it, Fly, what do you think you're playing at?"

"Aidi?" He made his voice distant and dreamy. "Is that you?"

"Of course it's me, you clown. What did you go and hit me for?"

"Did I hit you? Sorry."

There was blood, he was guiltily pleased to note, smudged on

Aidi's lower lip. "Get up," Aidi said, and that didn't make sense at all, because a man lying on a bed in a tent after a battle with his arm in a sling is bound to be ill, and therefore excused getting up. "Come on. For God's sake, Fly."

"Where is this?" Alces demanded. "What happened?"

"No time." Aidi darted in; he was fast, had to give him that. Before Alces could deflect him, Aidi leaned forward, grabbed his left wrist, twisted it into a painful lock and dragged him to his feet. He staggered, throwing his weight on the wrist lock, which hurt. "Aidi," he protested, but a hand in the small of his back straightened him up, and he found he was being shuffled across the tent alarmingly quickly.

"It's all right," he gasped, "you can let go, I'm coming." But Aidi kept on twisting and pulling, and he stumbled badly, bashing his shin against the leg of a chair and howling. It didn't make any sense...

"Aidi." It was Muri's voice, but very high and weak. He looked round, but couldn't see him; the sound had come from the far corner of the tent, where a group of men were standing round a bed. Then he recognised the back of Kudei's head, and saw Muri turn and face them, and he was as pale as chalk.

Aidi let go of him and lunged forward, then stopped, as though he'd met an invisible wall. "He never woke up," Muri was saying. "Just stopped breathing."

Aidi; Aidi, Nuctos, Muri, Kudei, and on the far side of the bed, just straightening up out of a crouch, Teuche. And he'd saved Lieutenant D'Eteleieto, so who was dead? But Aidi had crumpled up, Kudei was standing perfectly still, Teuche was shaking, and there was someone lying on the bed, and his skin was grey.

"But that's not right," he heard himself say. "I got him out of there. He was alive."

"Well, he's not now," Aidi snapped at him. "Quite the bloody opposite."

"Aidi." Nuctos sounded tired, distant. "He did his best."

"Obviously," Aidi said, and moved violently away, colliding with a chair and smacking it out of his way with the flat of his hand. It was practically a formal challenge, but there was no feeling to it; like a ceremony performed too many times, or a religious service in a dead language.

"Well," Teuche said, "that's that, then. We're screwed."

Nobody said anything, but Alces thought: Aidi tries to pick a fight, Nuctos has run out of steam, Teuche's thinking about how there's nobody to lead us any more, Muri looks like his brain's stopped working, and Kudei's just slumped. And me? I'm watching the others.

They stayed there for a long time, restless, frustrated, for the first time unable to talk to each other. Then, at last, Kudei said, "I'm going to get some sleep," and Alces noticed his mouth was bruised and swollen, and blood was seeping through a fat bandage on his hand. Which reminded him.

"Teuche," he said, "did they say what's wrong with me?" And he flapped his tied-up arm, like a chicken's wing.

"Broken," Teuche replied. "If you look, you'll see it's all splinted up." He paused, looking thoughtful, and said, "You can go home with that, if you want."

"How long?"

Teuche shook his head. "They didn't say," he replied. "Anyway, as far as I can gather, we're all out of it for a bit. We won, by the way. We bolted them, and they ran smack into Euteuchida's men on the top road. Couldn't have been sweeter if they'd tried. So," he added, picking up the chair Aidi had knocked around and sitting in it, "nobody round here left for us to fight. They're pleased with us."

"Teuche, for crying out loud, shut up," Aidi said. "I couldn't give a shit about the war right now."

"But at least we won," Muri said, lifting his head. "It'd have been really bad if this had happened and we'd lost."

"If we'd lost we'd all be dead," Kudei said, and the way he stressed the word "all" made Alces frown. "But we're not, and I've had enough of today. Anybody got any idea where they dumped our stuff?"

"Hold on, I'll come with you," Teuche said. "Best thing would be to find the duty officer. Oh, while I think of it: Fly, they found your kit, I told them to stow it at the tent."

He couldn't think what Teuche was talking about; then he realised he must mean the zweyhander sword, and he felt a sudden lurch of panic, because he hadn't let it out of his sight since he'd been issued with it. And then Muri said, "What about him?"

Nuctos sighed. "We'll get up early in the morning and dig a grave," he said. "It's against regulations, would you believe, individual burials in an active theatre of operations, but I don't imagine we'll have any trouble. Pity. I could just feel like assaulting a superior officer right now. Which reminds me," he added sharply. "The captain didn't make it either." No reaction whatsoever to that. "So I spoke to the colonel, and we've been officially designated as a freelance; mostly, I think, because nobody's stupid enough to want to go with us." He shrugged. "Thought you ought to know."

Several days later, as they rode in a captured wagon in the rearguard of the reunified army, Teuche very tentatively raised the subject of Lieutenant D'Eteleieto's share of their account in regimental funds. "It's just that the bean-counters've been bugging me about it," he explained, "because we're a free company now. They want to know if we're tenants in common, a mutual or a tontine."

Kudei stared at him blankly, but Aidi said, "Tenants in common, I suppose. Really, if there's any money, we ought to send it back home to his family."

Teuche shrugged. "We can do," he said, "but apparently if we want to do that, we've all got to sign an indenture and get it registered at Battalion, and it'll all drag on for months. And, not to put too fine a point on it, since I'm the one who's got to do all the paperwork..."

"What's a tontine?" Muri asked.

"That's when everything goes to the last survivor," Aidi said. "A mutual's where we share it between ourselves as we go along, with dead members' shares falling in as they crop up. Tenants in common's where each man's share goes back to his family if he doesn't make it."

"Then let's make it a mutual," Kudei said. "I don't see why my useless brothers should benefit. They'll get my share of the farm, that's plenty."

"Aidi?" Teuche said.

"My lot don't need the money," Aidi said, "and presumably we're only talking about shillings anyway. A mutual sounds about right."

"Fly?" Teuche said.

"Whatever," Alces replied.

"Muri?"

"Haven't got any family I'm on speaking terms with," Muri replied. "How much are we talking about, anyway?"

"Shillings," Teuche said, "but who knows, we might get lucky. Nuctos?"

Nuctos looked at him without saying anything, then nodded.

Teuche licked his lips, like a cat. "So, we're all agreed, then. A mutual."

Aidi looked up at him. "Do we need any documentation for that?"

Teuche shook his head. "An oral agreement suffices," he said. "That's what the adjutant's office told me, anyway. Apparently it's the default position for free units; we only have to sign things if we want something different."

"A mutual sounds like it's the fairest way," Muri said. "Not that I'm in any hurry to contribute."

Nuctos suddenly grinned. "Right now, I'd settle for a new pair of boots," he said. "Without prejudice, in full and final settlement. These ones I've got on now are cut to ribbons."

"What is it with the army and boots, anyway?" Aidi demanded. "In the nature of things a soldier does a lot of walking, so obviously his boots wear out. You'd have thought your bloody generals would've realised that by now."

Muri nodded vigorously. "I asked the supply sergeant about that, just before we left Penna. He said we were second from top on his list, and we'd have them the day after tomorrow."

Kudei scowled horribly. "We ought to raise hell about that, now we're heroes," he said. "What we need is a company supply officer."

"We've got one," Aidi pointed out. "Teuche, didn't they saddle you with that?"

Teuche nodded. "Not a great deal I can do about it, though," he said. "I wrote Supply a snotty memo about it when we reached Silam Bet, but I don't suppose it even got there to be fair; it's not like we're still in barracks. The war gets in the way, you know."

"Even so," Aidi said. "I was talking to a couple of men from C Company, and they got new boots at Silam Bet. And I'd have thought we had priority over them."

Teuche shrugged. "You want the job, you can have it. Mine are size ten, with studs if they've got them."

"No chance." Aidi shook his head vigorously. "I don't work well with military bureaucracy, I tend to lose my temper and say things."

"Don't look at me," Kudei said. "I'm just a farm boy."

"I'm sure Teuche's doing everything he can," Muri said. "Maybe you can try again once we get back to the coast. I'm hoping we won't have much marching to do before then."

After that, the conversation veered away, somewhat to Teuche's relief. With luck, he told himself, they'd have forgotten all about it by the time they reached the fort, and he wouldn't be faced with the prospect of explaining to Supply why his company needed new boots when they'd been issued with two pairs each at Silam Bet. He'd sold them, of course, along with the clothing, bedding and eating utensils; they'd gone to auction along with the last consignment of enemy salvage from Regimental, and nobody seemed to have noticed that they were unissued regulation stores rather than bloodstained battlefield plunder. He made a resolution not to try it again for a while; no real need, now that there was likely to be a steady supply of salvage, and there were just the six of them.

Aidi was wrong. As the sailing master had promised, they made landfall on Sphoe just after dawn on the sixth day out from Faralia. A dense white fog kept them out of the harbour till mid-morning; it lifted quite suddenly, like a curtain.

"Are you sure this is the right place?" Aidi asked.

The harbour was a grey shale mouth wide open to swallow them. Beyond it, they could see the truncated cone of the dead volcano, scruffy with trees like an unshaven chin. A brown stone watchtower stuck up out of a huge fuzz of briars, next to the rotten remains of a jetty; from its top, a green and blue flag sagged on an ash-limb flag-pole. There was a revolting decaying-seaweed smell.

Kunessin was leaning over the prow rail, as if he wanted to pounce on Sphoe and catch it before it could get away. "This is it," he said.

Alces pointed at the flagpole. "There's someone here," he said.

Green and blue: navy colours. "There's nobody here," Kunessin said. "If there was anyone here, there'd be a ship."

They could hear the distant shrieking of a large colony of gulls. "Then someone's been here recently," Aidi said. "Or that flag'd have rotted away."

Kunessin straightened his back. "I personally am not afraid of a bit of old cloth," he said. "We might as well drop anchor here and take the boat in. I don't like the look of that jetty."

She came up behind him and looked round him. It reminded her a little of Chora Oudemia, ten miles down the coast from Faralia, where the old whaling station used to be. "Is it how you remember it?" she asked.

He hadn't realised she was there. "More or less," he said. "A bit fallen-down and overgrown, but that's only to be expected. We'll soon lick it into shape."

She doubted that. "Where are all the buildings?" she asked.

He pointed. "See that big sand dune? Behind there. You won't be able to see them till we're right up close."

"It's a decent enough harbour, anyway," Aidi was saying. "It's a bit like Chora Bay, back home. And we won't be short of building material, with all that shingle."

"They shipped in bricks," Kunessin said, "at vast expense. That's the military for you."

"I think there's someone already here," Alces said. "That flag..."

"Well, we'll know soon enough," Kunessin said, and she could tell he wasn't happy. He's told lies to someone about something, she decided, and he's worried about being found out. She found that puzzling. What was there to lie about? It was the flag, she assumed, because there couldn't be anything else.

They lowered the boat, and Kunessin scrambled awkwardly down a rope ladder into it, followed by the other four. (He's not extravagantly fond of water, either, she thought, but that just made her want to smile.) Kudei and Muri took the oars. Naturally, Kunessin steered. Now, she thought, if that boat were to sink and all five of them drowned, we could go home. She thought about that, but came to the conclusion that she'd rather they didn't. That caused her a degree of mild surprise, and also a very slight amount of pleasure.

"This is it, then." She hadn't noticed that Chaere was there. "Our new home."

She laughed. "Try and sound a bit more enthusiastic."

"It's a dump."

"Yes," she admitted. "Right now it is. We'll soon get it into shape."

Chaere sighed. "Optimism," she said. "Enthusiasm. Why do I always have to be surrounded with optimism and enthusiasm? Look at it, it's horrible."

So Dorun looked; and she saw a grey shingle beach sloping gently up to a tangle of furze and briars, with a few thin, wind-gnawed elms sticking up out of the mess, like an old man's remaining teeth. Behind rose a flat-topped mountain, grey and unfinished-looking in the mist. "It's not so bad," she said brightly. "You've seen the map."

"Actually no, I haven't," Chaere said. "I don't suppose anybody thought it was worth showing me."

"Well," Dorun said, "the buildings, where we'll be living, are just over there — you can't see them from here, the dunes are in the way. Then there's a wide, flat plain that goes all the way to the foot of that mountain over there. The foothills are covered in woods: oaks and beech on the lower slopes, pine and fir a bit further up; on the other side of the mountain, it's more hilly, quite like home, and there's more mountains over the other side. There's a river which—"

"Yes, all right, thank you." Chaere sighed again. "It's horrible barren wilderness, and we're going to be reduced to living like savages. And it's so cold. I feel the cold terribly. I bet you the wind comes howling in off the sea, and if we're going to be cooped up right on the edge here, it'll be bitter. Bitter," she repeated, and shivered. "It's all right for the rest of you, you were brought up on farms, you're used to cold and damp and squalor and brown muddy water to wash in. I want to live in a town, where it's warm and clean."

They hauled the boat up on to the beach, and looked around.

"Well," Aidi said, "here we are."

"We'd better take a look at the jetty," Kunessin said briskly. "If it's still in one piece, we can start unloading straight away. I want to get the livestock ashore before dark."

They trudged up the beach to the jetty, or what was left of it. Most of the planking had rotted through and fallen into the sea. Muri scrambled up and started poking about; Kunessin got the map out. "There's a cove about quarter of a mile down the coast where we should be able to beach the ship," he said. "It's pretty open, but if the weather stays like this it won't matter. It'll mean having to haul every-thing overland, but that can't be helped. It'll be better than trying to ferry all our stuff across a boatload at a time."

"We can patch it up," Muri called down. "There's enough sound boards here to make a walkway. It'll be a bit narrow, but we'll just have to look where we're going."

"Can we get out again?" Aidi said. "We're too far into the har-bour; we'll have to wait till the wind changes. Besides," he added, peering over Kunessin's shoulder, "this cove of yours is down the coast; we'll have a hell of a job tacking against the wind. Hold on, Muri," he called out. "I'm coming up."

Kunessin scowled at him. "There isn't time to fiddle about play-ing at carpentry," he said. "We want to get the stuff ashore today."

"We've got sawn lumber on the ship," Alces pointed out. "A cou-ple of boatloads of those long inch planks..."

"They're stuck in behind the flour barrels," Kudei said. "We'd have to shift them, and the pigs, before we could get to the planks."

Aidi was up on the jetty, sitting on his heels. "Muri's right," he said. "We can rip up this section here and lay the boards lengthways. If we get the flour and the pigs off the ship and on the jetty, we can get the planks, cover over this long gap here, and then we'll be fine.

It's a pity we didn't think to bring any withy hurdles. We could've laid them flat and used them as a temporary floor."

Kunessin was still studying the map. "There's another place here, where this offshoot of the river comes out, sort of a small estuary," he said. "That's up the coast, so we should be able to get there without waiting for the wind."

"It's all right," Aidi called back. "I told you, we can use the jetty. And then we won't have to lug all the stuff overland. Right, we'll need the long crowbars and a couple of sledgehammers, and a keg of the four-inch nails'd come in handy."

Kudei pulled his collar a little tighter around his neck. "Even if we can get the ship round to that estuary," he said, "there wouldn't be enough time to get unloaded before sunset. So, we might as well take our time and get everything straight, instead of rushing."

"Teuche?" Alces said.

Kunessin folded up the map. "You win," he said. "But we don't want to fool round getting out the planks. Get some axes and cut down that stand of birch poles there. We can lay them across the gaps and cover them in matting."

Alces and Kudei volunteered to take the boat back to the ship and get the tools. Muri was already busy pulling up planks with his bare hands. Aidi came down off the jetty and stood next to Kunessin, glancing round. "Let's take a look at these buildings," he said. "See if there's any with their roofs still on."

Kunessin hesitated, then shrugged. "Why not?" he said. "It'll be a while before they're back with the boat."

They walked together up the dune. At the top, they stopped and looked down. They saw a dozen long, rectangular houses, all but one roofless, their rafters bare like the picked-over bones of a chicken carcass. The exception was messily thatched with loose bundles of green rushes, tied with —

"Flag cord," Aidi said.

"Odd," Kunessin said; but Aidi was right. After so many years in the service, Kunessin could recognise it a hundred yards away. He also noticed that it was still white. Why would anybody use inch-thick soft woven cotton rope for tying up bundles of improvised thatch? Because—the only possible explanation—there wasn't anything else.

Aidi started off down the slope, and Kunessin hurried to keep up with him. It was only when they were quite close to the thatched building that he saw the thin stream of smoke drifting from a hole in the roof.

"Better go and see who it is," Aidi said quietly. Kunessin watched him stoop and pick up a two-foot length of broken paling. He didn't comment.

The door was grey planks, warped with the damp; to judge from the scrape it had made in the dirt, it hadn't shut properly for some time. Aidi opened it briskly, with his boot, and lunged inside.

There were two men, sitting on chairs on either side of a brazier. They jumped up as Aidi burst in. They were wearing the sad remains of regulation greatcoats, and home-made scarves of sacking.

"Hello?" one of them said. The other frowned, then said, "Are you the relief ship?"

Aidi had taken guard: sideways on, left shoulder forward, the length of paling in his right hand. Old habits. "Who are you?" Kunessin said.

The shorter of the two men stood a little straighter. "Lieutenant Aili Thraso," he said, "and this is Lieutenant Noi De'Pasi. You're from the ship."

Kunessin took a step forward, leaving Aidi where he was. "What are you two doing here?" he said.

Thraso frowned at him. "You're not from the supply ship," he said.

"No." Kunessin's scowl deepened. "Are you two some sort of..." He paused. "Garrison?"

"Look," Thraso said, and his voice was high, almost squeaky, "I don't know who you two are, but this is a military post, strictly off limits to civilians, so I'm going to have to ask you to leave. If you need water—"

"My name is General Teuche Kunessin." He tried to make it sound impressive, but he felt faintly ridiculous. They'd heard the word "general" clearly enough, though. "I'm here to take charge of this facility. I'm sorry," he added, softening his voice a little, "I wasn't aware we had anybody stationed here."

"We've been here eight months," the other one — De'Pasi, Teuche remembered — said quickly. "Waiting for the relief ship to take us off. We were starting to think they'd forgotten about us."

"You aren't supposed to be here," Kunessin said. "According to the file, this base has been abandoned for five years."

The two men looked at each other. "We've been here two years," Thraso said. "We had two companies to start with; then the rest got orders and left, and we were told to stay behind till the relief came. It was only supposed to be six weeks, and that was eight months ago. Fortunately there's plenty of supplies — food, anyhow," he added. "But we were starting to wonder."

"That's the army for you." Aidi came forward, dumped the broken paling in the brazier, and smiled. "Sorry to break it to you this way, Lieutenant, but it looks like they forgot about you. Just as well we showed up, or..." He shrugged. "Never mind," he said brightly. "Think of all that back pay you've got coming."

"Forgot about us?" Thraso looked as though his mother had just spat in his face. "No, that's not possible. We had our orders..."

"I've seen the file," Kunessin said gently. "There's nothing in it about any garrison. This island isn't even under military jurisdiction any more."

Thraso opened his mouth; then the realisation that he was addressing a senior officer hit him like a falling tree, and he shut it again. But De'Pasi said, "With respect, sir, can we see something in writing? Only..."

Kunessin smiled. "You've got to follow the chain of command. Well done." He reached into his inside pocket and took out a piece of lengthways-folded parchment. "Military conveyance," he said, passing it over. De'Pasi took it as though God had just pulled a star out of the sky and handed it to him. "I don't know if you're familiar with military property law," Kunessin went on. "The language is a bit abstruse."

"My father's a lawyer, sir," De'Pasi replied. "May I?"

Kunessin nodded, as De'Pasi unfolded the paper. "Basically, the government's transferred legal ownership of Sphoe to myself and my four fellow trustees, for the purpose of setting up a colony. It's part of an initiative to strengthen the outlying stations by establishing self-supporting settlements. That big red blob at the end is the seal of the adjutant general's office."

De'Pasi blinked and handed it back, as if afraid he might drop and break it. "So what are our orders?" he asked.

Kunessin smiled. "Our ship's going back to Faralia once we've unloaded our gear," he said. "If I were you, I'd hitch a ride, make your way overland to Seautou and report to brigade headquarters there. Do be sure to chase up your back pay, as Major Proiapsen said just now. While you're waiting, you might see if you can make yourselves useful with getting the cargo ashore."

De'Pasi nodded, and Thraso actually saluted; it took Kunessin a moment to remember how to salute back. "Before you go," he added, "you'd better show us where the rest of your stores are. You'll need me to sign them off."

When they'd gone, Aidi took a long stride, putting him a few inches from Kunessin's face. "What the hell was all that about?" he said quietly.

Kunessin shrugged but didn't move. "All perfectly true."

"That document." Aidi held out his hand for it. "You didn't just happen to have it in your pocket. You thought there might be someone here."

"It was a remote possibility, yes." Kunessin looked past him at the wall. "I ordered the recall of the garrison, but it's standard procedure to leave a couple of junior officers to hand over to the relief. I countermanded it, but there was always a chance the countermand wouldn't filter through the system."

"Teuche." Aidi lowered his voice even further. "You stole an island."

"No I did not." Kunessin took a step away from him. "It's a perfectly genuine document recording a perfectly legitimate transfer. There really is a civilian colonies initiative. I set it up myself. I had the transfer approved by the proper committee, who authorised the use of the seal. All honest and above board. All right?"

Aidi was silent for a moment or so; then he laughed. "This committee," he said. "Any real people on it?"

"All of them were real," Kunessin replied. "There was someone from Establishments, two men from the adjutant's department, a lawyer, a senile old fool from Supply, and me. Mind you," he added mildly, "the transfer they approved isn't quite the same as the one you're holding, not actually word for word. But it matches the file copy exactly, so who the hell's ever to know?"

Aidi made a curious roaring noise that had something in common with laughter. "I thought so," he said. "You stole an island."

"Nobody wanted it," Kunessin said mildly. "They were glad to sign it off the books and save the cost of maintaining a garrison. It's not as if it's worth anything to anybody but us."

"I'll say this for you, Teuche," Aidi said. "You're not cheap. Other people help themselves to penknives and inkwells; if they're feeling really daring, they might liberate a keg of nails or a few lengths of timber. You steal bits of geography."

"I earned it," he snapped, and Aidi took a step back. "We all did. So I got it, for us. It's no big deal," he added soothingly. "Command couldn't care less. You know the way things work."

Aidi didn't reply, and Kunessin couldn't help thinking of a boisterous puppy growled at and cowed by a senior dog. He decided not to think about the implications of the comparison. "We'd better be getting back," he said. "Kudei and Fly should have brought the tools by now."

Aidi nodded but didn't say anything; he always tended to go quiet when he was upset about something. Too bad, Kunessin told himself. But Aidi had always been scrupulous about money. If they bought a tray of cakes or a keg of beer, Aidi would be the one who worked out what everybody owed, exact to the last farthing. It was a curious, infuriating nuance of his character. He'd cheerfully burn down a farmhouse just so the smoke would cover his movements from the enemy, but if he took a chicken, he'd leave the money to pay for it. Kunessin had always wondered why Aidi hadn't volunteered to be the company's prize agent. Just as well, of course, that he hadn't.

Just to be on the safe side, as they walked back to the jetty he said:

"About all that stuff. Were you thinking of telling the others what I just told you?"

Aidi looked blankly at him. "I hadn't thought about it," he said. "Why, don't you want me to?"

"It's up to you," Kunessin said. "I'm really not bothered either way. I wouldn't ever lie to any of you, but..."

"Fly'd think it was funny," Aidi said. "Muri's hardly likely to give you a hard time about it. Kudei..." He frowned. "You know, I'm not sure I know what Kudei would think."

"He'd go by how likely it is we'd be found out. Which isn't going to happen; so I don't imagine he'd have any problems with it. I was more thinking about the women. I mean, they'd be bound to hear about it, and they don't understand about the military, the way we do. I wouldn't want them to be worried. And then there's the indentured men."

It was an excuse, and of course they both knew it: a compromise, a diplomatic solution, which Kunessin didn't like at all. He should have foreseen that Aidi might get stroppy about it; but then, he hadn't expected to find anybody here, and so the subject shouldn't have come up. He checked himself there; he could feel himself rationalising it into being Aidi's fault, whereas if anybody had done anything wrong (not that they had, of course) it was himself. "I'm sorry," he said. "I ought to have told you. And the others, too."

He saw Aidi relax, a little. "Forget about it," he said. "Is there really a — what did you call it? The initiative?"

"Of course," Kunessin said. "I set it up myself. It's a perfectly good idea. We've got garrisons of twenty, thirty men scattered about all over the place, in outposts of minimal strategic importance; we don't want to give them up completely, just in case they might come in handy some day, but they're costing us far more than they're worth, in money and manpower. Settling civilians on them keeps the presence but takes the strain off the military budget. The Treasury was very taken with the idea." He grinned. "Obviously I had an ulterior motive, but that doesn't make it any less beneficial to the commonwealth."

"Ah well," Aidi said. "That's all right, then."

When they reached the jetty, they found that the boat wasn't back yet; but Muri had pulled up nearly half of the sound but redundant planks and stacked them neatly against the rail. It made them both tired just to look at him.

There were problems, of course. One that none of them had anticipated was that the jetty's foundations must have sunk, because it was a good eighteen inches lower than it should have been. As a result, the angle of the gangplank was steeper than they'd have liked. It was hard to keep their feet as they manhandled the heavy barrels, and the livestock didn't like it at all. The bull slithered, panicked and tried to back up; some fool whacked it across the backside with a stick, which made it all the more determined to get back inside the ship; Kudei made them all stand back and let it calm down for ten minutes, then tried coaxing it down the ramp with fistfuls of hay, which would have worked just fine if a barrel hadn't shifted at the top of the ramp, rocking the whole thing and launching the bull into an even wilder panic. Aidi insisted on putting a rope through the ring in its nose — that's what it's there for, he said — and afterwards had to have his hands bound up in sheep's wool, because of the rope burns. Eventually, just as they were all starting to think it'd be better to get a heavy bow and shoot the stupid animal, it caught sight of one of the cows that they'd already landed, shuffled gracefully down the ramp and lumbered straight into the temporary pen.

The pigs were even worse. When all attempts at luring them down the ramp had failed, Kudei went behind them with a sheet of tin and got them halfway down; at which point, one of the big brood sows changed its mind, turned round, nosed Kudei out of the way and headed back up again. But by now the ramp was slippery with cowshit; it lost its footing, scrabbled helplessly and slid over the side of the ramp into the sea. There was nothing anybody could do, so they had to stand and watch it drown, a process that took a surprisingly long time. After that, it was something of an anticlimax when Chaere's trunk, with all her clothes and passionately cherished possessions from home, went over the side into the water. She wasn't in the least impressed when Aidi and Alces dived in after it, because by then it had come open, and those items that were recovered were soaked and covered in mud, while the set of painted plates and the silver milk jug were lost and gone for ever.

Nevertheless, they got all the livestock and most of the heavy stores ashore before nightfall, which was just as well. During the night, there was a torrential downpour, and they were too preoccupied with finding and stuffing sacks into the holes in the amateur rush-bundle thatch to spare a thought for the ninety bales of hay and twenty bales of straw that had been left on deck overnight. It was, of course, completely ruined, and went to join the sow and Chaere's milk jug at the bottom of the harbour; being waterlogged, the bales sank like stones. Twelve bales were salvageable, but only because someone had covered them over with Chaere's brocade bed-curtains — a far greater loss, according to her, than a load of old dry grass. It wasn't a view that found favour with the rest of the company, Chaere's husband included, which led her to say various things that might have caused serious offence if anybody had been listening.

Unloading the rest of the cargo took much of the next day, mostly because a large section of jetty floor planking that had been pronounced sound turned out not to be. That accounted for a butter churn, two three-hundredweight anvils and one of Kunessin's barrels of chainmail. When they cleared away the stub ends of the collapsed planks, they found that the main side-beam was cracked three-quarters of the way through. If it went completely, that would almost certainly mean the end of the jetty. Fixing it wouldn't have been too much of a problem, if only they'd had somewhere to stand while they were doing it. As it was, they had to bring the boat in under the jetty, and Muri cut and fitted the splice working over his head, standing on a precarious stack of boxes piled up in the bottom of the boat.

When it was too dark to work safely, they crowded into the thatched hut, lit a fire and sat round the walls, too tired to talk. After a while, Muri got up and fetched a sack of porridge oats from Thraso's supplies. It was their fifth meal of porridge in two days; and just after midnight, it started raining again. At that point, Kunessin remembered that there were fifteen sacks of bean seed on the deck of the ship. He was very tired, wearing his last change of dry clothes, and the repairs to the jetty floor weren't finished yet. He fumbled with his tinderbox, lit a lantern and got up.

"Where are you going?" Dorun muttered, her eyes firmly closed.

"Take a leak," Kunessin replied. He made his way to the door as quietly as possible, though he trod on someone's ankle and banged into the sharp corner of a box. He'd forgotten to find a hat, but he didn't go back for one, in case he woke anybody up.

Outside, the wind was up. In the pale glow of the lantern, he could see the rain; it was practically falling sideways. Something else he'd forgotten: boots. He squelched through the mud across the yard, up the dune and over to the jetty, half blinded by the rain. He figured that if he kept close enough to the left-hand rail that he could feel it brush against his leg, he'd be all right, so long as he went slowly and carefully. He climbed up on to the ship, put the lantern down and found the pile of bean sacks. They each held a hundredweight, he remembered that from the specification, but the wheelbarrows were ashore, in a lean-to next to the cattle pen. That reminded him: they'd forgotten to feed the pigs.

He swung a sack up on to his back, and staggered under the weight. Earlier, he'd seen Muri carry two of these sacks, one on each shoulder. Aidi could lift a three-hundredweight anvil on his own, and Fly was even stronger. He'd heard somewhere that it all depended on which body type you were: some people can build muscle easily, some can't. He shifted the weight as far up on to his neck as he could make it go, and tottered on to the gangplank.

Another thing they'd neglected to do was clear the cow muck off the ramp. True, the rain had washed some of it away, but the result was a deep, even coat of slurry. It hadn't been much of a problem going up the slope; going down was another matter entirely. He slipped and came down hard on his backside eight times in fifteen journeys, but at least he didn't end up in the water, like the brood sow. Small mercies.

Next, he had to find somewhere dry for the beans: easier said than done. The lean-to had a roof of sorts, but it was jammed full, as he discovered when he looked in there (that was when he dropped the lantern and broke the glass). Mostly by feel, he found the stack of planks they'd piled up to use on the jetty next morning. He used a dozen to cover over the sacks, and weighted them down against the wind with loose bricks from a collapsed wall. By this stage, he really didn't feel like feeding the pigs; the crushed barley meal was in the lean-to, and he didn't have a bucket, or a knife to open a sack with. His eyes were full of rain, and at some stage he'd trodden on a nail sticking up out of one of the jetty boards. He eventually found a bucket in the heap of jumbled gear in the yard, and used the edge of a sharp stone to worry through the stitching on the sack. The pigs were pleased to see him, at any rate.

When he got back inside, the fire had gone out. He crept back to his place on the wall, crawled down inside his wet clothes and tried not to shiver.

"You were a long time," Dorun whispered.

"Got lost."

"You're very wet."

"Yes."

"You smell of cow."

"Fell over in the yard. Go to sleep."

There was a hole in the thatch directly above where he was lying, and a continuous trickle of rainwater fell on him all through the night and pooled in his crotch.

EIGHT

Captain Kudei Gaeon was the first man in A Company to win the coveted Bronze Crown for exceptional courage in the face of the enemy. He tried to refuse the award, but was eventually persuaded to accept by his comrades in arms, all of whom went on to win the same honour before the end of the year. Ironically, the engagement which led to Captain Gaeon's award was a relatively minor affair...

On the second day after the battle, they crossed the bog. Aidi protested that there had to be a way round it, even though Teuche told him he'd seen the map and there wasn't. Muri insisted on going first, but his weight was a problem. He tried to do all the right things—treading on clumps of reed or the edges of the couch grass tussocks—but at every fifth step he went in up to his thigh, and the others had to fight their way over to him and haul him out. Teuche lost both his boots dragging him out of a black pool of slime he'd staggered into after sliding off a tree root. After that, he gave in and agreed to follow on behind, treading only where the others had gone.

Fly took the lead after that, being the lightest. It was Teuche's turn to carry Kudei, so he went in the middle, with Aidi to help him. At first they stopped every hundred yards; then every fifty; then every twenty; then every ten. After an hour, they ground to a halt and slumped where they were, hanging on to tussocks to keep their balance. None of them could talk for a long time. Finally Aidi, retching out a word at a time between gasps, said, "We've got to leave him. Otherwise, we're all screwed."

Teuche said, "No."

"Aidi's right," Fly said. "If we carry him, we'll just run out of strength, one by one. Besides, he's good as dead already."

"I'll carry him," Teuche said. "If I have to stop, you press on without me."

"Teuche, you're being stupid," Aidi snapped; and Muri looked away. "You can't carry him any more, and we're not going to try. No point all of us dying here."

"I said I'll carry him," Teuche replied. "You three keep going. Really, no hard feelings. You're quite right, all of you. Just let me keep going as long as I can."

There was a long, painful silence. Then Aidi said, "All right, then, if that's your decision. But we can't wait for you. Fly?"

Fly nodded. Muri didn't say anything. "Good luck," Teuche said. "I hope you make it."

They left him then, and stumbled for another hundred yards before collapsing. When he could speak, Fly said, "We ought to go back."

"No," Aidi said.

"Yes, we should." Fly's face was covered in black mud, from the last time he'd slipped and gone sprawling. He looked like the clown in a travelling pantomime. "Get real, Aidi, we're none of us going to make it out of here. I saw the map, this stuff goes on for miles. We're exhausted, we haven't got any food—"

"Yes, thank you," Aidi snapped. "I'm well aware of that, thank you ever so much. There's no need to ram it down my throat."

"If Nuctos was here, he wouldn't let us split up."

Aidi scowled horribly. "If Nuctos was here, none of us'd be here, because Nuctos can read a bloody map. But Nuctos is back with the column being cooed at by pretty young nurses, and we're here. All right?"

"All right." Fly held up his hand for a truce. "We've had it, agreed. So, I don't want to die thinking the last thing I ever did was leave two of my friends behind."

"Fine." Aidi sounded too weary to talk. "You go back and join them. Like you say, it hardly matters."

"We can't split up," Fly shouted back. "We ought to be together."

Aidi shook his head, like a cow trying to dislodge a buzzing insect. "You can sit down in this shit and die if you really want to. I have other plans. You can go back, or you can come with me and find a way out of here, on condition you stop talking. I'm getting just a bit sick of the sound of your voice."

Fly turned away from him. "Muri," he said, "you can see, can't you? We've got to go back for them."

Muri looked at him, and Fly was shocked at the expression on his face. His eyes were red and swollen, and tears had cut lines in the silt on his cheeks. "I don't know, Fly," he said. "I think Aidi's right. We can't just give up."

"You listen to him, Fly," Aidi said. "He's got some sense."

"Besides," Muri said, "Kudei's not going to make it. We should've just left him back in the wood. If we hadn't been trying to carry him, we wouldn't have worn ourselves out."

Fly looked at him for a few seconds. "If Kudei hadn't got cut up holding them off at the bridge, we'd all be dead," he said. "We owed it to him."

"Pointless," Aidi said furiously. "The whole thing's a fucking comedy. If Kudei had run when he had the chance and left us, he'd have got through, reached the cavalry before they took off, and be safe and dry back in camp right now. Instead, he's got to be a big hero and get himself carved up, we've got to be big heroes lugging him all this way, and now we're all going to die slow and miserable in this shithole. If I had the energy I'd piss myself laughing. And now you want to throw away the only slight chance we've got by going back for them. Give me strength."

"Muri," Fly said urgently. "That's Teuche and Kudei back there. We can't—"

"You go, then," Muri yelled. "I'm staying with Aidi. He's not stupid, like the rest of you."

Fly froze; then he shrugged, slowly and elegantly. "All right," he said. "I guess that constitutes a democratic decision. We leave them. I just hope you two can live with that."

"Chance'd be a fine thing," Aidi replied quietly; then, more conciliatory: "It doesn't matter, does it? You'd rather die knowing you tried to help your friends. I'd rather die knowing I'd done everything I could to stay alive. You don't want to feel bad, and I don't want to feel stupid. Go back if you want to. We'll understand. Or stay with Muri and me. It won't make any odds."

Fly seemed to have run out of things to say. He sat down on a tussock, his legs drawn up awkwardly under his chin. "Or we might as well just stay here," Aidi said. "It'll be dark in an hour or two anyway."

Fly laughed. "Listen to us," he said. "Doesn't matter what kind of a mess we get ourselves into, we just can't help bickering. Fifty thousand enemy soldiers out there, and we still manage to be our own worst enemies."

"Speak for yourself," Aidi said. "I don't bicker, I just try and make sensible suggestions. If you'd all listened to me in the first place…"

"Don't start," Fly warned him. "Teuche couldn't have known."

"Fuck me, you can't help defending him, can you?" Aidi tried to prop himself up on his elbow, slipped, and went down on one knee, splattering his face with mud. "In case you've forgotten, I warned him. I said, Teuche, there may be archers in that wood, we ought to take the long way round. No time, he said—"

"Quite right too," Fly interrupted. "The heavy cavalry were right on top of us, remember? If we'd stayed out in the open like you wanted, they'd have slaughtered us like chickens."

"For crying out loud," Muri wailed, and they both stopped and looked at him. "Like Aidi said, it doesn't matter any more," Muri went on. "But we're still alive—"

"For now," Aidi muttered.

"We're still alive," Muri repeated loudly. "We've still got a chance. We can get out of this. Like my dad used to say, there's no such word as can't."

Aidi rounded on him angrily. "Just goes to show how stupid he was, then," he said. "This isn't getting the ewes to load or pulling the cart out of the mud; this is it, the end, the one we don't get out of. If you can't face up to that, you're even more stupid than you look."

Muri tried to jump up, but instead he sank up to his knees, tottered and sat down, sending up a thick spray of black mud. Aidi burst out laughing; then, delicately as a crane fly landing on water, he straightened up, nudged with his feet to find firm standing, leaned forward, caught Muri's arm and pulled him upright. "You're a clown, Muri," he said. "Now, let's get moving while we still can."

He let go of Muri's arm, grabbed a handful of couch grass and hauled himself up to the tussock, then took a long stride forward, just managing to get his foot alongside the next one. The tangle of top-root took his weight; he paused to balance, then launched himself forward again. Fly tried to follow in his footsteps, but his legs were too short, and he went in above his knee, swearing and struggling until Muri dragged him out by his collar, like a dog carrying a puppy.

"We aren't making a very good job of this," Aidi said. "Come on, we can do better. What we need..." He paused, and looked round. "What we need is that."

That was a tree branch, blown off a dying elm, lying ten yards or so to their left. "Muri," Aidi said, and Muri plunged into the mud — there were no helpful tussocks — bent at the waist, grabbed a sparse handful of rushes and pulled himself across the surface ("One way of doing it," Aidi commented loudly); with a tremendous effort he managed to reach a large stone and hauled himself along by that; by his third stretch, he got a hand on the branch, towed it towards him and flopped on to it.

"That's the idea," Aidi said. "Now, can you get it over here?"

Muri hoisted himself round so that he was lying lengthways along the branch, then stretched for a handhold, edging along the branch until his fingers hooked round the stone he'd used on the way out.

With his other hand he gripped the branch so that, when he pulled on the stone, the branch came with him. Aidi, meanwhile, had waded out a long stride on to a small tuft of reed. As Muri dragged himself across the mud, he reached out, caught the end of the branch and pulled; but he couldn't get a firm enough grip to do any good, and his foot slipped off the reeds and deep into the mud. "Shit, I'm stuck," he moaned. "I can't move. Fly..."

Fly was already on his way, flat on his face in the mud, creeping forward an inch at a time; he was light enough to get away with that without sinking. When he was close enough, Aidi wriggled sideways and sat on his back as he dragged his leg out of the mud and back on to the tuft. Muri meanwhile had nudged the branch another few inches closer, so Aidi could reach it. He pulled, and the branch and Muri came across relatively easily.

"That's the idea," Aidi said. "Now we take it in turns. Muri, see that tussock over there?"

Still squatting on the reed tuft, Aidi pushed the branch towards the tussock, until Muri was able to scramble off the branch and on to the thin ledge of root; then he pushed the branch back, Aidi scrambled on to it, and Fly pushed him along to join Muri. Before Aidi pushed the branch back, he took off his belt and wrapped it round the end. "Now we're in business," he said proudly. "Come on, we can do this."

He was right about that. They took it slowly, one tussock at a time; it gave them each a chance to rest and catch their breath without the risk of being left behind. By nightfall, when they were lucky enough to find the roots of a beech tree, they'd covered three hundred yards. They hunched up with their backs to the trunk, closed their eyes and immediately fell asleep.

It was bright daylight when they woke up. "I can't move." Aidi said.

"No such word as can't," Fly replied. "Still, I know what you mean. I think I've pulled every muscle in my body."

Muri groaned, then shifted round and dragged the branch towards him. "Come on," he said. "We've got this far."

Fly was looking back, across the ground they'd covered the day before. "If you're looking for Teuche and Kudei, forget it," Aidi said. "If we only just made it, what sort of a chance do you think they had?"

"I think you've already made that point," Fly said. "Actually, I was just wondering if we've come the right way."

There was a long silence; then Aidi said, "I looked at the map..."

"So did I," Fly replied. "And that's the rising sun, which is east, and we should be heading straight into it. But we're not."

"Just a minute," Muri growled, but Aidi spoke over him. "The shortest way through the marshes isn't due east," he said. "There's a spur of dry ground—"

"Due east," Fly said firmly. "Starting from where we came in. You've been steering like we came in on the road, but we didn't."

"We were level with it," Aidi said defensively. "And besides, at that stage we were all just following Teuche."

"Yes," Fly replied. "But when we left him, we held too far south. Which means, if we carry on along this line, where we should be coming out of the bog, we'll only be just over half the way through. We need to change our line."

"You're forgetting something, both of you," Muri said. "There's the river."

"All right, so we've got to adjust a bit," Aidi snapped. "So we've come a bit out of our way. Big deal. If it wasn't for me—"

"Muri." Fly wasn't listening to Aidi any more. "What did you just say?"

"The river," Muri said. "If we head due south, we'll meet the river."

Fly laughed. "And the thing about fast, shallow rivers is, their beds are firm, stone and gravel. Muri, you're a genius." He swung his head round and looked straight at Aidi. "Well?"

Long silence; then Aidi said, "Good idea."

They went south. It was hard going. The couch tussocks were fewer and further between, and just before noon the branch broke, as Aidi was launching himself off it. He landed badly, going in up to his waist. Muri yelled at him to get on to the half-branch closest to

him, but instead he tried to crawl out, and got himself comprehensively stuck. By the time the other two managed to pull him free, the
half-branch (the half with the belt wrapped round it) had been trodden deep into the mud, and was lost to them.

"It's all right," Fly said. "It wasn't your fault."

Hardly said with ringing sincerity; and Aidi tried to make out a
case for it being Muri's fault, because Muri had been kneeling on the
branch, dragging Aidi out of the mud. Muri didn't reply, but Aidi
and Fly had a brief but furious argument about it, cut short by a violent squall of rain.

The loss of the branch slowed them right down. They used what
was left, but without the belt to drag it with it'd have been easier to
crawl, and in the process Muri hurt his back so badly he could barely
move.

"For crying out loud, Muri," Aidi yelled. "Now what? If you think
we're going to carry you..."

"Leave me," Muri replied.

"Don't be fucking stupid."

"You left Teuche."

That shut them all up for quite some time; then Aidi said briskly,
"It's not the same thing at all. Kudei was past saving, and Teuche
decided to be a hero. You've just done your back. Besides, two of us
aren't enough. We need three."

"Then we're all screwed," Muri replied. "I can't do it any more,
I'm sorry."

"No such word as can't," Fly said. "Listen," he went on, "we can't
be more than half a mile from the river. Half a fucking mile. How
big a deal is that?"

Aidi was thinking. "All right," he said, "we'll leave you. But we'll
get to the river, get out of this shithole, find a farm or something and
some sensible gear: ropes, boards. And then we'll come back and get
you. Agreed?"

Muri frowned, as though Aidi's suggestion was based on some
totally new kind of logic nobody had ever thought of before. "Sounds
good to me," he said. "Fly?"

"You're absolutely sure you can't move?" Fly asked.

"Oh, I can move," Muri replied. "It's dragging myself through this mud by my fingertips that's beyond me. Aidi's right, it's the only sensible thing."

"It's a deal, then," Aidi said.

"Just a second," Fly put in. "How're we going to find him again?"

Aidi thought for a moment. "Dead reckoning and luck," he replied. "And as soon as we think we're close, yelling at the top of our voices. Unless you can suggest anything."

Aidi and Fly ended up crawling most of the way, lying flat on their faces on the mud to spread their weight as evenly as possible. It was a cross between mountaineering and swimming. They didn't dare stop when it got dark, simply because there was nothing firm enough to stop on. Accordingly, they found the river by falling into it, down a surprisingly steep bank. As they stood up, waist deep in water, they were whooping and yelling like children.

They calmed down after a while, and Fly said: "Do you think we'll be able to find Muri again?"

Aidi nodded. "I got it figured out by the angle of the sun. It'll be all right, I promise."

Needless to say, the bed of the river was slippery, and they couldn't make particularly good time. Fly was anxious to force the pace, which meant he kept losing his footing and falling down. By the time the sun rose, they'd only gone a mile or so, and it was ten miles to the village. The current wasn't strong, but it wasn't negligible either. It was easier than the mud, but not by much. Even so, there was still enough light to see by when they finally stumbled up the bank and dropped on their knees on the gravel and cinder road that led up to the village.

"Just one thing," Fly said. "You got any money?"

Aidi stared at him, then replied, "I may have."

"I've got three thalers and some loose change. We'll need ropes and boards, and hiring a barge wouldn't be a bad idea. How much've you got?"

Aidi reached in his pocket, but the bottom was torn out. "Fine," Fly said. "Well, we can probably run to some rope."

It cost them the last of their strength to stand upright and walk up the gentle hill. The first building they came to was the post house. They clubbed the door with their balled fists until a scared-looking man with white hair and a beard opened it. When he saw them, he nodded and said, "You'd better come in."

There was a good peat fire in the open hearth, and four chairs. Two of them were occupied.

"Hello, Aidi," Teuche said. "What kept you?"

Teuche had remembered the map. Even so, he'd had to guess at his position and gamble; fortunately, he guessed well. Six hundred yards of murderous effort had brought him to the northern spur of the river. He'd arrived in the village the previous evening, and had spent the afternoon organising a rescue party, which had been due to set off at dawn the next day. Kudei was already out of bed. The mud had sealed his wounds, and the river water had washed them clean; so, against all the odds, he'd escaped infection. He was bandaged so tightly he could scarcely breathe, but he was still able to ask: "Where's Muri?"

Aidi didn't answer. Fly said: "We left him."

"Did you?" Teuche said.

"He hurt his back," Aidi said, quick and angry. "He could hardly move. I know exactly where he is, and we're going back for him."

Teuche didn't say anything.

They eventually found him — the innkeeper's twelve-year-old son practically trod on him; Aidi's dead reckoning brought them out two hundred yards short (not a bad effort in the circumstances, but in the marsh it might as well have been two miles) and they were on the point of giving up when they heard the boy yelling. It was just as well, they agreed, that the boy had brought along his dog, a lymer trained in following a blood scent. They shipped Muri out on one of the mud sleds the locals used for getting about on the marsh; an ingenious design, more like a raft than a sledge, propelled by hooks and long poles. The villagers made it look easy. Luckily, Muri had four five-thaler pieces in his inside coat pocket; together with Fly's three and seven and Teuche's twelve thalers, they were able to pay off the villagers for the rescue mission and Kudei's bandages, and still have enough for six loaves of bread and a small plaster-rind cheese. When they rejoined the regiment, Aidi tried to claim back their thirty-five thalers from Funds as legitimate military expenses; the claim was registered and sent back to Battalion, but they never heard anything more about it.

"Why do they call you Fly?" Enyo asked.

Slowly he straightened his back, like a scholar unrolling an old and irreplaceable parchment. "Nickname," he said.

His job was to put in the posts — seventy-two of them, six feet long and three inches wide — describing the perimeter of the permanent cattle pen. Kudei would be along later, with two of the indentured men, to nail on the rails, just as soon as they'd cut down the trees and split them lengthways with wedges. So far he'd managed twelve, and it was already mid-morning. The soil was thin, and every blow of the hammer on the bar seemed to find a new stone. Already, the top of the bar was mushroomed over, and he'd chipped the hammerhead.

"Of course it's a nickname," Enyo said. "What does it mean?"

He steadied the bar and twisted it round with his hands to start it off. "Fly as in small," he said. "Also nimble and fast. And," he added, "I think it means I talk too much. You know, like a fly buzzing."

"That's a bit unkind," Enyo replied, frowning. "You're not like that."

"I used to be." Alces grinned. "We were all pretty much full of it in those days. College did that for us, of course." He shook his head. "They didn't just teach us soldiering; they wanted us to be gentlemen as well. And now look at me, bashing in fence posts."

"You should leave that sort of thing to the servants," Enyo said. "That's why General Kunessin brought them, surely."

"They're not..." Alces shook his head. "I like putting in fence posts," he said. "Really. Well, it's better than some of the things I've done, anyhow."

She stood up. "I've got to go," she said. "It's time for my spinning lesson."

"Ah, right." Alces nodded. "I thought there wasn't anything to spin yet."

"Captain Achaiois says he's found a kind of nettle with suitable fibres. We're going to try using that."

Alces pulled a face. "Nettles," he said. "Trust Muri. Hold on, though. I thought you had to soak them till the fibres come free. Retting, it's called."

She shrugged. " I don't know, I've only just started learning."

"All right," Alces said. "But I can't remember Muri ever being a world expert on spinning. Probably he's just getting it out of some book."

She gave him a quick, dry kiss and walked quickly back to the main house, where Muri, Chaere and Dorun were waiting, behind a table piled high with wilted nettles. She said, "Haven't you got to ret them first before we can use them?"

Muri looked blank. "What's that?" he asked.

"You've got to soak them till the fibres come free. It can take several days."

Chaere sniggered. Muri frowned. "Are you sure about that?" he said. "I thought if we rubbed them between two stones..."

"You can try that if you like," Enyo said. "I'm not getting my hands stung."

"I'll get a basin of water," Dorun said, and left quickly. Muri took a nettle from the heap, picked at the stem, then dropped it quickly. "You just let them soak?" he asked.

"I think so," Enyo replied. "Of course, I'm not an expert."

Muri picked up another nettle, examined it, then snapped it off an inch above the base, pulled it into four strips, and teased the bark off. With his fingernails, he pinched out a bunch of short, fine fibres. "This'll do, surely," he said. "I've used stuff like this before."

"Captain," Chaere said. "Excuse me, but where did you learn to spin?"

Muri frowned. "In the service," he mumbled. "Making bowstrings. But the principle's exactly the same. In fact, bowstring's got to be spun to a higher specification than ordinary yarn."

Chaere pulled a slightly sour face. "My mother did a lot of spinning," she said. "I'm sure she never used nettles."

"No, probably not," Muri said patiently. "She probably spun wool, but we haven't got any, not yet. We will have, of course, later. Meanwhile, I thought we might as well practise the basics."

He looked hopefully at them all, and Enyo noticed he was rubbing his fingertips together. "Where's Menin?" she asked. "I thought she was joining us."

"She's still gathering nettles," Muri said. "Actually, she was the one who told me about them. She's very good on wild plants."

Chaere sighed. "Well," she said, "if Menin's stung her fingers to the bone picking the wretched things, we can't very well let them go to waste. We'll soak them for three days and see what happens." She stood up; the lesson was over. "After all," she said, "it doesn't actually matter, does it? We've got plenty of clothes, and cloth and yarn, more than enough to keep us going till the ship comes back. We don't need to learn spinning."

Muri looked at her as though she'd just kicked him. "We'll need to spin our own yarn eventually," he said, making an effort to keep his voice mild. "It's a good idea to learn now, while we're still—"

"Don't be silly," Chaere said. "Can't you see, this is all a game. It's your General Kunessin's hobby, that's all. It's what happens when men like that retire. Some of them take up hunting, or breeding horses; he's always wanted to be a gentleman farmer. Fine. He'll play at it for a bit, till all his money's gone, which won't be long, the rate he's going. Then we'll all pack up and go home and live normally again. We won't ever need to make our own clothes out of nettles." She smiled at him, pity and gentle contempt. "Aidi said I should show willing, so I have. Now I'm going to lie down and read a book."

She walked away, tall and magnificent. Muri watched her go, then started picking at another nettle. His fingers are too big, Enyo thought, but he's got the patience of a desperate man.

After a while, he said, "Is that what you all think?"

"Who do you mean?"

"The other wives," Muri said.

She shrugged. "I don't know, I haven't talked to them much. They're not the sort of women I'm comfortable with."

Muri nodded. "How about you?"

"Thouridos wants to be here," she said. "I don't particularly, but I don't really have a choice. I didn't much like living over the fencing school, either." She frowned. "What do you think? Are you happy here?"

"Yes," Muri replied. "We're all together again, where we belong. We need to stick together."

"Well, there you are, then," Enyo said. She stood up, then hesitated. "Can I ask you something?"

"I suppose so," Muri said.

"Why do you call my husband Fly?"

Muri looked at her as though he didn't understand the question, then laughed. "It's just a nickname," he said.

"The rest of you don't have nicknames, just him."

"Well, Thouridos is a bit of a mouthful," Muri said. "And he doesn't like being called Thouri."

She frowned. "That's what I call him."

"That's different, I guess."

Already he'd teased out a small pile of short fibres; about one per cent of what he'd need to weave one sock. She had a sudden vision of him dressed in a nettle-fibre coat; it'd be baggy and shapeless, probably frayed at the cuffs after a week. She had no doubt whatsoever he'd make one, if there was time. "It's a strange name, Fly," she said. "How did he come by it?"

"The human fly," Muri answered. "He was amazing at shinning up and down walls. We used to break out of the dormitories at night, when we were at the College. Fly would be the one who went ahead and opened the doors and windows."

"Ah," she said. "Thanks."

She left him and crossed the yard; as she did so, she saw Dorun coming back with the water, and in the distance, Menin with her arms full of nettles. She frowned, and went into the small hut that she and Thouridos had taken over for themselves. It was still pretty horrible. Thouri had nailed scrap boards on to the rafters, but that just concentrated the rain into miniature indoor waterfalls, and the floor was littered with pots and basins, full to the brim. The bare floor was damp. They had two stools, a chair and a packing case for a table. Thouri was out doing something for the general, something strategic and long-term. He only came home at night, usually either soaked or muddy; there was a special quality to the way he didn't complain about having to put wet clothes on in the morning. She took a handful of sticks from the basket by the door, and tried to get a fire going.

"We'll plough all this in the spring," Kunessin said. "I was thinking, barley this side of the river, wheat on the other, rye up there under the woods, flax in that big rap between the rocks and the lake. We might as well build the barns here." He pointed at something or other; Alces couldn't see anything that was any different from the rest of the flat, featureless plain. "We'll need to build a threshing floor, and a pen and stalls for the plough oxen. Some hard standing wouldn't be a bad idea; we can dredge stones and gravel out of the river."

Maybe, Alces thought, that's what it's like being an artist: you look at a blank canvas or a newly plastered wall, and you can see the picture in your mind. As far as he was concerned, it was just a lot of flat ground: ideal for cavalry, no cover for infantry, the river would be a death-trap if you got backed on to it. No general in his right mind would advance across it, unless he had to. "That sounds like a lot of work," he said.

"Yes," Kunessin replied. "It's frustrating we can't start now. I wish we could've waited till the spring. I guess it was me being impatient. Still, there's plenty to be getting on with."

Cue for a report; Alces felt more comfortable with that. "Kudei's got five men felling," he said, "and three more splitting the logs into rails. Getting the posts in isn't going too well, I'm afraid; the ground's so damned stony, even with all this rain."

Kunessin frowned. "That's a nuisance," he said. "I'd rather hoped we could have the pen and the sheds finished in the next couple of days, so we could move on to doing up the buildings." He shook his head, which Alces found mildly offensive. "How are the indentured men shaping up?" he asked. "You've seen rather more of them than I have."

"Not bad," Alces replied. "They do their work all right, not too much grumbling or skiving."

"But?"

Alces shrugged. "Depends on what you expect," he said. "After all, we've made it pretty clear who's the officers and who's the grunts around here. I don't think too many of them'll be staying on, though."

"We'll see," Kunessin replied. "It's early days yet."

"The farm boys are all right," Alces went on, "but the six or seven we recruited from the mines can be a bit of a handful." He frowned. "They work a good shift, but I get the impression they'd rather have something more interesting to do in the evenings, if you see what I mean."

Kunessin nodded. "We were short-handed," he said. "I never really expected them to stay on. We'll let them go when we get replacements."

"They aren't a problem," Alces reassured him. "Just not ideal."

Kunessin grinned. "You know me," he said. "I never could be doing with up-country people."

Kunessin still had surveying to do, so Alces left him and went back to the settlement. He found Aidi in the shed which Kunessin was already calling the forge. It was dark as he walked in, so he called out, "Aidi?"

"Over here." Aidi was on his hands and knees, doing something with a hammer and a wrench to what promised some day to be a machine. Alces couldn't figure out how he could see what he was doing.

"Why don't you open a window?" he said.

"Stuck," Aidi grunted. "Sills swollen in the damp. Soon as this is done, I'll have to take a look at them."

Alces knelt down beside him. "What is that?"

"This," Aidi said, "is a genuine Molosina double-action trip-hammer, or it will be if I can ever figure out how this thing's supposed to fit." He waved a bit of metal bar, something like a flat bone. "It's meant to go in between that lug and the flange, but there isn't room." He sighed, and lay flat on his back, staring into the jungle of works above his head. "Marvellous thing, but whoever designed it must've hated me; clever of him, since he died a hundred years before I was born."

"Impressive," Alces said. "What's it do?"

"Hits things," Aidi replied. "Very hard and very often. It runs off a paddle-wheel—we'll need to dig a race off the brook—and the power's transmitted through those gears there into this spindle." (Alces tried to see what he was pointing at.) "This arm thing turns the round-and-round motion into up-down-bang, but I can't—" There was a click as something slotted into place; immediately, Aidi pushed, straining against the steel bar, until the end came loose again and he shot forward, skinning his cheekbone on the side of the machine. He swore, straightened up, tested his face for blood with his fingertips and breathed out slowly. "They reckon this thing can do the work of two strong men with sledgehammers."

"Really," Alces said politely.

"Apparently. Of course," Aidi went on, "by the same token, two strong men with sledgehammers could do the work of this machine, and then I wouldn't have to drive myself nuts trying to put the fucker together." He dropped the bone-shaped bar; the clang it made on the floor sounded to Alces uncommonly like laughter. "Just think," he said. "Second year, I was top of the class in mechanical engineering."

"Second," Alces corrected him. "Nuctos was..."

He didn't finish the sentence. Aidi shrugged. "Anyway," he said, "it went together once, so it'll go together again. It's just a matter of being very patient and trying not to mutilate myself beyond repair in the process. How's you?"

"Worried," Alces replied, sitting down on the floor. "It's a mess, isn't it?"

"What, this, you mean?" Aidi picked up the metal bar, held it sideways and looked down it, checking it for straightness. "Minor setback. If I could just figure out—"

"The whole stupid thing," Alces interrupted. "I've just been listening to Teuche being lord of all he surveys. I think he's in a different world to the rest of us."

Aidi sighed. "The trouble with Teuche," he said, "he doesn't listen. You tell him things, he looks like he's listening carefully and taking it in, but really his mind's somewhere else, always four moves ahead.

Mark of a fine commanding officer, of course, but it's different in the service. You're always accountable to someone, you've always got the next man up from you in the chain keeping a watchful eye. Out here, he reckons he's God." He lay back, wriggled under the machine and offered up the bar the other way round. "Oh I see," he said, with a mixture of relief and exasperation. "That pin there goes in the little slot, and then it pivots." Two clicks, and Aidi emerged, wiping his hands on his chest. "Doesn't bother me particularly," he said. "It's not like I was doing anything interesting with my life, world's greatest underachiever. And you've got to say this for him, he hardly ever makes a mistake, overlooks a detail. No, I'm quite prepared to stick with him and see it through till he's got it out of his system. It's just important to bear his little frailties in mind, that's all. Pass me the jug, would you. Thanks." He took three enormous gulps, and water gushed past his mouth down his chin and neck. "We've all known each other long enough not to be too fussed at each other's faults," he said. "We make allowances, so that's fine. Not so sure about the girls, though. May be trouble there. Still, it's not like we're back at the war or anything. I mean, we've got food and clothes and nobody's trying to kill us; what serious harm could we come to?"

Alces thought for a moment, then said, "Malaria."

"Had it," Aidi replied briskly. "You've forgotten, haven't you? Fifth year of the war, I was sick as a dog. We were stuck for days in that fallen-down old barn, me babbling my head off, Muri with an arrowhead stuck in his hand, Nuctos with dysentery..."

"God, I remember that," Alces said.

"You weren't much better," Aidi reminded him. "You'd had a bash on the head, serious concussion; we had to take it in turns talking to you to keep you from falling asleep. Teuche was dead on his feet with exhaustion from getting us there. I think Kudei was the only one who wasn't at death's door, and he ran himself ragged looking after us all; by the time the foragers found us, he was in worse shape than the rest of us." He grinned. "We got through that in the end."

Alces frowned. "Death doesn't apply to us, you mean? You know, I always found that stuff mildly offensive."

"Never bothered me," Aidi replied. "Anyway, after that, this ought to be a piece of cake."

He stretched his arm for the wrench, but it was just too far for him to reach. Alces picked it up and put it in his hand. "We were younger then," Alces said. "Besides, surviving isn't quite the same sort of thing as actually succeeding at something. Failing to die's really just not being able to take a strong hint. Actually getting something to work takes different skills, and I'm not sure we've got them. Ah well," he said, with an exaggerated sigh. "Too late now."

"Quite." Aidi applied the wrench to a nut, gave it a ferocious tweak and swore viciously as the bolt snapped off. "Now look what you've made me do."

Alces grinned and stood up. "Always someone else's fault," he said. "Try and be a bit more careful, can't you?"

He headed for the door, but stopped as it swung open. A man he recognised but couldn't put a name to, one of the indentured men, burst in and looked round wildly, confused by the gloom. "Anybody in here?" he called out.

"What's the matter?" Alces said.

The man located him as soon as he heard the voice. "Big trouble," he said. "The grain store's on fire."

Without any conscious decision to move, Alces shouldered him out of the way and lunged through the door into the yard. The sunlight stabbed his eyes and he stopped, until Aidi crashed into the back of him.

They could smell the smoke. "Buckets," Aidi said.

"In the grain store," Alces replied.

"Shit."

Shoulder to shoulder, they sprinted across the yard. Fat red flames were licking the sills of the empty windows, like a tongue searching for the last smear of honey. Four indentured men, Enyo, Dorun and Menin were standing in a huddle ten yards from the door.

"Get away from there," Aidi screamed, his voice shrill with fear. If they heard him, they didn't move. Alces beat him to it by one stride; they grabbed shoulders and arms, hurling bodies across the

yard like woodsmen throwing logs up a hill. They only just had time
to get clear themselves before the first flour barrels blew.

It was sheer bad luck that Alces should have had his face turned
towards the shed. The blast of hot air hit him like a slap from a giant;
as he closed his eyes, he felt the sudden heat scorch his eyelids, and
the skin on his cheeks melt. A perceptible fraction of time passed
between the burn and the push that laid him flat on his back; when
he told him about it later, Muri thought it was most interesting, the
implication being that heat travels faster than air. He landed hard,
and for a few moments he wondered if he was dead, because there
was no air in his lungs and he couldn't seem to make them work.
When he did manage to fill them, the air was excruciatingly hot.
Then his whole face started to hurt, pain far worse than he'd ever felt
before. Hands fastened on his shoulders; he opened his eyes—they
still worked, a moment of overwhelming joy—and saw Aidi's face,
a most comical expression. He was being dragged by his feet, and
then Aidi lifted him and he was being carried. Once he was sure he
hadn't been blinded, he wasn't in the least scared.

As soon as he'd got Alces safe, Aidi took charge of the mess. The
shed was stuffed full of flour barrels, each of them capable of going
off like a potted volcano. (At the College they'd taught him flour had
to be soaked in oil to make it explosive; apparently not.) If it was
just him, or the five of them, and if every single bucket they possessed hadn't been in the shed, he might have considered trying to
put the fire out, or at least damp it down, before the rest of the flour
went up. But he had to consider the women and the servants, lesser
mortals. Frantically he tried to estimate a danger area, but he had
no data to go on. The first blast had nearly killed Fly at fifteen yards.
Thirty barrels going up simultaneously; not just the blast itself, but
a skyful of joists, beams and burning thatch. No guarantee they'd
be able to get clear in the unspecified time available. Not distance,
then; cover. "Get in the house," he yelled, and it was infuriating that
his voice should crack and come out as a loud squeal. "Inside, all of
you. Come on!"

Why couldn't people just do as they were told? At least the women
had some sense, or else they'd been trained from birth to obey when

men shouted at them. The servants just stood there looking at him, the dull, blank stares of cattle. He grabbed the nearest man by the collar, lifted him off his feet and sent him tottering and sprawling towards the house door. Later, he told Fly he was sure they only went inside because they were afraid of him, not because they had a clue about the danger. Simultaneously he was thinking: me, Fly, Kudei's up the woods, Teuche's surveying, where the fuck is Muri? And then he caught sight of him, bustling men in through the back door of the house like a sheepdog. No idea if all accounted for; didn't actually know offhand how many servants there were, let alone where. No time. He plunged through the door, slammed it after him and shot the top bolt.

Which wasn't quite enough, as it turned out. The blast, three seconds later, was far louder than he'd anticipated. It made the ground shake and the house shudder; he could feel the timbers bend, like trees in the wind. Then the door flew open; the ripped-off bolt shot past him like an arrow, as half a burning barrel sailed into the middle of the house. On the first bounce it smashed the long table the servants ate off. Next bounce it hit someone, he couldn't see who. Third bounce, it smashed a hole in the back wall and disintegrated in a shower of burning splinters.

He could hear women screaming; but the body on the floor was a man (small mercies), amazingly still alive, though both legs and the right side of his body had been crushed like a snail shell. The assessment was instinctive: won't make it, leave him. He took in the rest of the house in one looped glance. No other casualties, but there were shrouds and flowers of smoke drooping down through the thatch. Marvellous.

And no fucking buckets. But he wasn't prepared to lose the house as well. Cursing Teuche for not being there, he squeezed his mind till it hurt: no buckets, so what had they got?

"Muri," he shouted (still more a squeak than a shout), "we need ladders and rakes, hoes, billhooks, axes. Got to drag the thatch off before the rafters catch."

The slightest of nods and Muri was off running, drawing men with him like a magnet draws filings. He could trust Muri; who else?

"Dorun," he called out (surprised himself with the choice), "Chaere, get them out of here. Animal pen. It's far enough away, and open. Menin, Teuche's up the hill, run and find him, quick as you like." He didn't look to see if they were doing as they were told; he was kneeling to pick Fly up in his arms, like a baby, like Teuche had carried Kudei through the marsh. A wadge of burning thatch fell on the back of his neck as he scrambled out through the back door. He had a nasty feeling he should have coped better.

Outside, there was burning rubbish everywhere, but a breeze was clearing the smoke, thank God. He looked round, saw a cart blown over on its side, carefully laid Fly down beside it so its bed would shield him just in case any more flour barrels went off. He could smell burning hair; scared to death until he realised it was his own, still smouldering. He slapped wildly at it, like a blind man hunting a wasp, then hobbled (couldn't run; must've done something to his foot) round the side of the house, just as Muri and the servants brought up a ladder.

After all those years, of course Muri knew that Aidi was afraid of heights. Like all his fears, he suppressed it ruthlessly, but it was still there, a torment and a weakness, so it was only logical that Muri should be the one to go up the ladder, while Aidi took command at ground level. Unfortunately, Aidi didn't see it that way, and there was a ridiculous tussle, only lasting a second, at the foot of the ladder, before Muri gently but irresistibly shoved Aidi out of the way and started to climb. Only then did Aidi look down, mere curiosity, and notice a chunk of board stuck to the sole of his boot, attached to it by the long nail driven up into his foot. He stared at it, as though he'd just noticed an extra toe, then bent down and tugged it out. A spike of pain ran up through his leg to his heart, and he yowled like a cat; then he dropped the wood and hopped over to a couple of indentured men, who were bringing up the second ladder. Without a word he yanked it out of their hands, wobbled on one foot and fell over.

They were kind enough to help him up, and someone else gave him a shoulder to lean on as far as the doorway of the woodshed, where he collapsed in a heap, trying very hard not to whimper. He could see Muri up on the ladder, rake in hand, hauling sheaves of blazing thatch off the rafters; the fire fell all round him but he wasn't taking any notice. The rake handle caught fire; he dropped it and yelled for another one. Someone else had climbed the second ladder. He couldn't see who, or what he was doing. He felt useless, bitterly ashamed and angry; the fire was the least of his concerns.

Someone had gone to the feed store and fetched the pigs' buckets; only five of them, but soon a chain was in place, passing the buckets from hand to hand. He saw Chaere in the line, her hair tangled (she must hate that), and Menin, and Kudei's wife, Clea — a big, strong girl, he noted; she was passing the buckets up to the man on the lower rungs of the ladder, and a three-gallon bucket of water weighs thirty pounds. Someone else had had the bright idea of fetching fence-rails to push the thatch off with, much quicker and more efficient than nibbling away with a rake. For some reason he resented that.

He shifted, tried to get up, very quickly thought better of it. And then Teuche was looming over him, grabbing his shoulder, yelling, "What the hell's going on?"

"It could have been worse," Teuche said.

Thick twists of smoke were still rising from the ashes of the grain store; nothing left but a black ribcage of beams. "I guess," Aidi said.

"Much worse." Teuche pushed open the house door; it moved eighteen inches, then stuck. The impact of the flying barrel had twisted the hinges. He shoved through and stood looking up through the rafters at the blue sky. "We were going to have to do a proper job of thatching this anyway."

The floor was thickly covered in sodden wet thatch; Kudei and his team had done a savagely thorough job of damping down. The place stank of smoke and soaked straw. "The rafters are mostly all right," Teuche said, almost as though he believed it. "We'll need to replace a few, but we can use some of the beams we cut for fence rails."

It had rained briefly during the night; not enough to put out the dense heart of the embers, but more than sufficient to get everybody and everything thoroughly soaking wet. Aidi cleared his throat in an I'm-still-here kind of a way. "How's Fly?" he asked.

"Not so bad," Teuche replied. "Face is pretty raw, and the backs of his hands. Menin found some plant or other in the woods; she reckons it's good for burns. He was lucky he wasn't closer."

Always look on the fucking bright side. "We shouldn't have put all the flour in one shed like that," Aidi said.

"No." Teuche was still craning his neck, looking up at the rafters; probably trying to heal the cracks and burns by the power of positive thinking. "Won't make that mistake again. Of course, we never had that much flour all together at one time, back home."

He hasn't got it, Aidi realised; it hasn't sunk in yet, that the game's over. Someone really ought to tell him. "I've been doing some calculations," he said. "If we're careful about rationing, we'll be able to live off pork and beef till the ship gets back, assuming it's not held up, but it might be an idea to see if we can't spin it out a bit with other stuff. Kudei reckons there's deer in the birch woods, and he's seen duck on the lake. The main problem, as I see it, is going to be salt."

"Salt," Teuche repeated, as though he'd never heard of it before.

"Think about it," Aidi said. "It's not just our food that went up in smoke last night, it's the animal feed as well. Which means we'll have to slaughter most of the cattle and pigs quite soon, which means we need salt to preserve the meat."

Teuche turned and looked at him. "Who says we're going to slaughter the livestock?"

"We've got to," Aidi said, "otherwise there won't be anything to eat. Like I said, we should just about be all right till the ship gets here, but what we're going to do for provisions on the journey home —"

"We aren't going home," Teuche said. "Whatever gave you that idea?"

Well, at least he'd got it out into the open. Also, better to have a short, private blazing row about it now than let Teuche make a complete fool of himself in front of everybody. He took a deep breath, but Teuche turned his back on him and started to walk away. He opened his mouth, but somehow he couldn't launch the first word; just as sometimes, in a battle where two ranks of archers line up against each other at lethally close range, nobody can bring himself to loose the first shot.

NINE

The battle of Ceparouros, according to most authorities, marked the turning point in the war. General Euteuchida's advance forced an engagement in favourable terrain, and his pikemen, led by the legendary A Company, broke the enemy formation at the first attempt. Major-General Stethessi's heavy cavalry executed a flawless encircling movement, and a massacre was averted only because the lancers, instead of sweeping round to close off the only line of escape, stopped to plunder the baggage train. In spite of that, and a spirited counterattack by the loyalist militia, the victory was complete and overwhelming, leaving nothing between Euteuchida's triumphant army and the barely defended city except two regiments of regular cavalry and the sadly unreliable highland irregulars. No more propitious moment could be imagined for the arrival of General Arrabese with the long-awaited reinforcements: six regiments of pike, two of heavy cavalry and a field artillery train of sixty engines. Euteuchida immediately marched south to join up with Arrabese, pausing only briefly to crush the half-hearted resistance of the irregulars...

He opened his eyes, but he couldn't see anything. Panic; then he realised that the soft touch on his face was cloth, a blindfold.

Nor could he move. His arms were behind his back, joined at the wrists, there was a rope around his waist, and his feet were attached, at a guess, to the legs of the chair he was sitting in. Cramp everywhere. A thorough job.

No gag, though; so he said, "Hello?"

Stupid thing to say; somebody laughed. Perhaps the same man who hit him on the side of the head with something solid, quite possibly someone else.

"You're awake, then."

Strong accent, but fluent. Probably safe to assume that he was in the hands of the enemy. He tried to remember what had happened, but the smack to the head had confused him. He never could think straight when his head hurt.

Someone said something in a language he couldn't understand. It was a suggestion, and presumably someone else acted on it: another crack, this time on the other side, just above the ear. He yelped with the pain. More laughter.

"I'm disappointed," the linguist said. "They told us you soldier-boys were tough."

"Not me," he replied. Pause; then the linguist translated. This led to another suggestion, this time across his left collar bone. A stick, he guessed, maybe even a metal bar.

This time he didn't yelp. Instead, once he'd got past the immediate pain, he asked politely, "Excuse me, but you are who?"

Translation; muttering. Then the linguist said, "Us? We're Badadzes' militia. Thought you might've figured that out for yourself."

Loud muttering; he guessed that the rest of the gang weren't happy with the reply. The linguist didn't seem bothered. He said: "They reckon it should be us asking the questions. Can't see where it matters myself if you know who we are. Not like you'll live to tell anybody."

Well, he thought, but he found it impossible to feel anything except mild resignation. They were going to kill him, sooner or later, but somehow he didn't seem to be involved. A tactical error on their part, if they wanted to get information out of him. Without a faint, unrealistic chance of surviving, he had no incentive.

"Here's the deal," the linguist said. "We can do it quick and easy, or we can do it mean. Don't seem to me you like hurting all that much." Presumably to prove his point, the linguist hit him on the forehead, but he'd been expecting something and kept perfectly quiet. "Well?"

"What do you want?"

He could vaguely remember. A Company had split up, each of them on detached duty as scout for a battalion. His lot had been in the woods, quite near the front of the column. He'd heard shouting behind, then the whistle of an arrow, too close. He'd thrown himself to the ground, the way you do. Then he was in this chair, with a rag over his eyes.

"You're an officer, right? Got those fancy buttons on your coat. So, tell us all about it. Where you're headed, numbers, what you're figuring on doing when you get there. All that."

He had to make an effort not to smile. He hadn't bothered taking interrogation at the College; it was optional, and he didn't need the extra credit. But he knew that questions should be clear and precise, designed to impress the subject with the interrogator's depth of knowledge. You don't lie to someone who knows enough to be able to tell you're lying. All that didn't meet any of the approved criteria.

The linguist, not a subtle man, must've taken his silence for stubbornness. The blow was unexpectedly to his right kneecap, and although he didn't make a sound, he couldn't stop himself wincing. A small failure on his part; like losing a pawn in the first three moves.

"I'm sorry," he said mildly. "I don't understand the question."

Someone asked something; the linguist replied; another suggestion, but no attack this time. Instead, quite a debate, with tempers starting to fray. That didn't alter the fact of the ropes round his wrists and ankles, which meant that his life was very nearly over (trivial artefacts, bits of string, but they made all the difference in the world). Still, it was nice to know that his last stratagem looked like it might work. His teachers at the College would never hear about it, so they wouldn't be in a position to applaud him or give him a posthumous honorary degree in interrogation management; never mind. When captured and interrogated and all hope is gone, infuriate your captors so that they kill you in a rage before applying extreme torture; it will save you pain and deny them their information. He remembered writing that; copying out his lecture notes. Morbid, he'd thought, and he'd had grave doubts about whether he'd be able to be so clinical, or so coldly brave. He was mildly impressed with himself; not a bad state of mind to die in.

The debate seemed to have wound up, and he heard the linguist say, "Been a change of plan. Ain't going to kill you after all. There, isn't that a comfort?"

But—there was going to be a but. The voice sounded smug, and for the first time he felt a slight degree of concern. He waited.

"What we're going to do," the linguist went on, "is poke out your eyes, cut off your right hand and bust your left arm so it won't set right. Then we're going to turn you loose where your boys'll be sure to find you. Strong, healthy young man like yourself, could easily live another sixty years." He paused, then added, "Sixty years in the dark, and you won't even be able to wipe your own arse. We fancy that's quite mean enough, don't you?"

He couldn't help it; he shuddered, as the cold, twisting panic gripped him. "Course, you'll be a hero when you get back home," the voice went on. "The first three years, five maybe, they'll all be falling over theirselves to help you. After that, though—well, people do forget, don't they?" There was honey in the voice, and cream; pleasure, in a life that saw little enough of it. A unique chance to hurt a soldier without fear of repercussions. He could understand that. "And a blind cripple ain't no use, and he does so get in the way. You got any family back home?"

He tried to speak, but his tongue was swollen and clumsy, as though he'd been too long without water. He felt himself jerking forward against the ropes, which was ridiculous; and someone laughed. He felt a spurt of anger, the kind that comes when you're playing chess with a fool, and he suddenly takes your queen.

"Or," the linguist said, "you could tell us something useful. Course, we don't know enough about what you boys are up to, so we don't rightly know what to ask. Guess you'll have to think of something pretty good, so we'll be nice and grateful."

When captured and interrogated, and all hope is gone... if there was a course in being tortured, it followed that somewhere there must be a torturers' syllabus, with required reading, course notes, a series of lectures. He was inclined to doubt that these people had had that much formal education. An amateur, then; amateur, meaning one who does something for the love of it. Checkmate, he decided.

"Well?"

He had to concentrate hard to get the words out, as though he was the one speaking a foreign language. "The main army is heading for the city—"

"We know that, stupid," and a sigh.

"But six divisions of pikes under General Arrabese are looping round, following the river valleys, to come up on your blind side." Under the blindfold he screwed his eyes tight shut, desperate to get the message across crisp and clear. "When they reach the fork in the river, they'll set out in the middle of the night, leaving their watch-fires burning. They have local guides. If all goes well, they should reach the woods in the deep combe by daybreak, so you won't see them coming. General Euteuchida believes your regular cavalry will be waiting at the top of the valley to launch an attack on the main army as it comes through the pass. The pikemen will be there to take them by surprise. After that, he expects your militia will panic and melt away into the hills rather than risk getting cooped up in the city for a long siege."

Silence; then someone spoke, and several people laughed. "They're impressed," the linguist said. "They reckon you're probably telling the truth. They think we ought to show how grateful we are by letting you go." He paused, enjoying himself. "But I showed them the error of their ways," he went on. "I told them, that's the last thing on earth we want to do, considering as how we only picked you up and brought you on with us because your friends've got one of our friends, and we needed something to exchange."

It was like being in the marsh again: putting his foot down and feeling it sink, right up past the knee. Not to kill him; not to blind or maim him, because damaged goods are worth next to nothing; purely a commercial transaction, such as sensible, businesslike people engage in. They never intended to hurt him at all, they were trying it on, just in case he was stupid enough...

"Mighty gracious of you to tell us all that, about where the army's headed to," the linguist went on. "Reckon the regular boys'll thank us kindly for that, and it always does to keep in with them, in the way of supplies and all." A deep, happy chuckle. "Didn't think you were going to fall for it, all that acting ferocious and mean. Boys here've been having a hard time keeping a straight face — mind, they know me, wouldn't poke a pig with a stick, and you don't. Still," he added, after a tiny pause, "don't alter the fact, you must be dumber than horseshit to let a bunch of farmers make such a fool out of you." He let that sink in; no need. "But that's just fine, because if you don't tell nobody, neither will we."

A joke, then, like sending the apprentice for the left-handed screwdriver. Rustic humour (he knew all about that). But the army would march into an ambush because of him, his stupidity, his idiotic gullibility. Wouldn't poke a pig with a stick; he could imagine how they'd laugh about it later, probably for years to come, when the beer was slipping down nicely and they wanted something to feel proud of.

The linguist hadn't finished with him yet. He was still wallowing in his moment of triumph. "See, we're just plain country people hereabouts," he went on (his voice grated, like the heel of a boot on a blister). "We ain't soldiers, never will be. Thing about you soldiers is, you're all so damn cruel and mean, you get to thinking everybody's like you, all over the world. We were so scared of you when we heard you were coming; reckoned you'd drive off our sheep and burn our houses, do God knows what to the womenfolk and kids. But you're nothing special. In fact, you ain't even as smart as we are."

The linguist said something in his own language — probably his last devastating conclusion, translated for the benefit of his neighbours, who laughed and cheered. Country people, he thought, salt of the earth. Just like me.

"Anyhow." The linguist's voice told him the feast of good-humoured fun was over, and it was time to get back to work. "We'll drop you off somewhere, so's your people find you. You can spin them some yarn, they don't need to know we ever picked you up.

Course, you can tell 'em if you want to, that's your choice." Yawn; bored with this game. Also, a certain disdain, as of a man who's particular about the company he keeps. "You go to sleep now." He felt a brief but intense pain in the bone as something hard slammed into the side of his head, and then nothing at all.

"Well?" Kunessin said. "What are they saying?"

Dorun sat down beside him on the broken wall. The hem of her dress was filthy with mud and soot. "Is that what you think?" she said. "That I've been sent here to reason with you, like some kind of diplomat?"

He couldn't help smiling. "Diplomats negotiate," he said. "You look to me like you're here to try and make the stubborn fool see sense."

"True," she replied. "But nobody sent me." She nodded her head towards the long barn. "They're all in there," she said, "muttering."

He pulled a face. "Should I be worried?"

"Depends," she replied with a frown, "on the sort of thing you worry about. Your friends turning against you and leaving you here if you won't see reason: no, you needn't fret about that."

"Good," he said.

She rubbed her eyelids: cinders, or dust. "Aidi's telling them you're being stupid — which isn't disloyalty, just a plain statement of fact — but he's not suggesting a course of action; he's more sort of whining, in a very articulate way, of course, but he's not actually suggesting they dump you or anything. Kudei's on your side, except he thinks on balance we should go home. Muri's sticking up for you, of course, like he always does." She paused. "Doesn't he get fed up with nobody ever listening to a word he says?"

That took him by surprise. "What?"

She looked at him. "When he says something, nobody takes any notice. I mean, they don't reply or anything, they just talk across him." Her frown deepened. "Hadn't you noticed?"

He shook his head. "No," he replied. "Are you sure?"

"You mean you've never noticed?" She shrugged. "Well, anyhow, that's what they're saying, since you asked. I don't suppose you're interested in what the girls think."

"Actually..." he said.

She paused, then recited: "Chaere just wants to go home, or at any rate somewhere she can buy shoes. Enyo's far too worried about Thouridos to bother with anybody else right now. Clea doesn't want to go home, but she doesn't think we can stay here, either. Menin's out gathering things in the woods, which is all she ever seems to do. That's about it."

"You left out what you think," Kunessin said.

"Oh, me. I think we'd have to be mad to stay here, with no food unless we slaughter all the livestock, and if we do that we can't stay anyway. Oh, Muri offered to feed us all on venison, rabbit and squirrel. I can see why everybody ignored that."

Kunessin smiled. "Muri's one of the finest archers I've ever seen in my life," he said.

She looked at him. "Squirrel?"

"Don't knock it. You should try it pan-fried with almonds."

"Yes, but we haven't got any almonds. I don't know if we've even still got a pan. Seriously, we can't stay here. Or we can, but it'd be wretched. We'd be living like savages, and there's no need for that. Not when there's a perfectly good ship on its way to take us home." She looked into his eyes and said, "You do see that, don't you?"

He shifted away from her a little. "I know all about giving up, if that's what you mean," he said. "My dad gave up, when we found the dead bodies. He thought about it carefully, figured it all out, it was purely a matter of numbers, he said. So he gave up, we lost the farm, I had to join the army, and the best years of my life just sort of turned to smoke and drifted away. It took me all that time and more effort than you could possibly understand to get here—which isn't what I wanted, but I was sensible, I knew I'd never get that; this is instead of that, second best, the runner-up prize. I can't give up again, I'm too old and tired to go back in the army. I'd rather stay here and eat rats."

She was silent for a long time. Then she said: "Fine. And what about the rest of us?"

He shrugged. "They can do what they like. If they want to take the ship and go, that's all right by me. I never forced anybody to come here, and I won't make them stay."

Overhead, five rooks were mobbing a hawk, swooping under and over it, getting in its way, slowing it down, robbing it of the speed and space it needed in order to be effective. It had long since given up any thought of fighting, she could tell. It was worn out, and all it wanted to do was get away from those terrible nagging pests. She looked at him, but he was gazing at the burned-out store and the roofless house, and she had to admit she had no way of knowing what he could see there. She knew that he believed that what he'd just said was true. She wanted to walk away, but that would be cruel.

"It's ironic," he said at last. "That was always my worst nightmare, when I was a kid, growing up with the war so close. I'd come home one day and I'd find our place looking like that, burnt out, everything completely screwed. It never happened, of course: we lost the farm, but the farm never got touched. And now the war's over, I've left the army, there aren't any soldiers to be scared to death of any more, and this happens."

She didn't say anything; it was as though she didn't know the language. From where she sat, she could see the sea, a blue patch just visible between the bare rafters of the house.

"You're right," he said eventually. "We can't really stay here, not without food. Or at least, we can; but we'd be living like animals."

She felt as though someone had stopped crushing her neck. "I'm so sorry," she said. "What you'd always wanted…"

"We're not going back." His voice was as crisp as frost. "We can't. All the money's gone." He laughed, a sound like a dog snarling. "If only you knew what I had to go through to get that money, and now it's all gone."

He didn't seem to be making much sense. "I'm sorry," she repeated. "But it's like you just said. If we can't stay here, we've got to go back."

"No." She'd never heard that tone of voice before; she wouldn't have believed him capable of making such a sound. "We're staying here, and if we've got to rough it, it won't be the first time. Don't you understand? The money's gone." He was shouting now, and she wanted to put distance between herself and him, but she was afraid of what he might do if she moved. "I can't go back and get more; all that's over and done with now. This is my last chance, so we've got to make it work. I owe it to them."

She managed not to say anything; just keep quiet until he'd calmed down enough for her to get away. "You're going to have to help me," he said, quieter but no less intense. "I can handle Aidi and the others, but I need you to convince the women. If they agree to stay, it'll be easier on the men." (The men, she thought; he was thinking like a soldier now. How does a commanding officer get soldiers to launch a suicide attack, or hold an indefensible position? She couldn't begin to imagine, but he knew.) "Talk to them," he went on, "tell them it's not so bad. Tell them we've been in worse situations before, and it's not nearly as bad as it seems. Obviously it's not going to be comfortable, but we'll make it, I can guarantee that. You'll talk to them, won't you?"

"Of course," she heard herself say. Anything, to get clear, away and safe.

"Thank you." He smiled, but she could see he was still watching her, the way wolves watch potential prey in the distance; the thorough, methodical way a predator has of gathering the facts, weighing up the relevant factors and making an informed decision. He's got the patience of an animal, she thought; patient, clear mind and lightning reflexes. "I know I can rely on you."

She waited, for as long as she could bear to without screaming; then, as evenly as she could, she said, "Well, I'd better get on with it, then."

He nodded, but she couldn't go yet. If she broke eye contact now, he'd know exactly what she'd been thinking. Suddenly she understood what sort of soldier he must have been: a natural, unbeatably fast and unstoppably strong, a man-eater. She wanted to run away, like the little girl in the fairy tale, until she met a woodsman who'd come with his axe and kill the monster. She said: "I'll talk to them. I'm sure they'll understand."

He frowned, his face changing suddenly. "Don't say anything about the money," he said. "That's not something that needs talking about."

"No, of course." His eyes moved, just a little, and she realised she'd replied a bit too quickly; not enough to trigger an instinctive reaction, just enough to snag his attention. She could feel herself starting to panic. "I mean, that's none of their business, is it?"

"No."

She'd said the wrong thing. He was looking straight at her now, concentrating on her, and her mind had stopped working. She couldn't think what to say or do, but staying still and quiet wouldn't be possible for much longer. There was a calm about him that terrified her, like an animal saving its energy just before the quick, massive exertion of the kill.

Then, quite suddenly, he gave a little shrug and looked away. "Menin's got the right idea," he said. "There must be loads of things we can eat, quite apart from Muri's bloody squirrels. But I think the sensible thing would be for us to build a boat—nothing too fancy, just a sloop, something that'll get us to the mainland and back with a few barrels of flour; little and often, instead of trying to stock up all in one go. I've still got a couple of hundred in cash, and there's bound to be stuff we can trade. I mean, we don't really need three anvils, or all that mining gear. Come to think of it, I've got no idea why I brought it in the first place."

She laughed, although she was shivering. "That's a brilliant idea," she said. "There's plenty of cloth for a sail, too. How far are we from the mainland, anyway?"

He shrugged. "Two days, possibly three if the wind's being tiresome. I remember, when I was here after the war, four of us took a boat and went across, it was no big deal."

"Well, then." She gave him a big smile. "I'll be getting back to the house now." She didn't wait for a reply; she turned her back, catching her breath as she did so. She was quite proud of herself for not breaking into a run until she was inside the yard gate.

So they built a boat. Muri and Kudei felled the timber: tall, straight thirty-year ash from the top of the lower hills, which Aidi and Kunessin slabbed and planked in the yard, where they'd dug a sawpit. All but one of the long crosscut saws had been hanging up in the grain store when the fire started; the heat had drawn their temper and left them soft and useless, at least until someone could find the time to cook them up again. Aidi volunteered to do it, but Kunessin pointed out that he'd have to get the forge working first, and besides, they didn't have any charcoal. Aidi said he knew how to burn charcoal. Kunessin replied that he didn't doubt it, but they couldn't spare the time. Aidi started to explain that getting all six saws back in service would save them time in the long run; at which point Alces, who was listening to the debate from the chair he was confined to until his burns healed, suggested that if they were going to argue, they might as well saw wood at the same time. There didn't seem to be an answer to that, so Kunessin climbed down into the pit and they started sawing, still discussing the point at issue at the tops of their voices.

It was a good saw—Kunessin had bought nothing but the best; even so, it took them two hours to cut out one plank, a fact which Aidi took great pleasure in pointing out. Kunessin gave way more or less gracefully, and Aidi practically swaggered as he headed off to the forge. One of the indentured men took his place in the sawpit, and the next plank only took an hour and a half.

Kunessin was graceful enough not to make an issue out of the snags Aidi encountered once he'd got the forge going (charcoal wasn't a problem after all, once they discovered six full sacks of the stuff hidden among the heaps of rubbish at the back of the garrison's original storehouse). They had just enough whale oil to temper the saw blades in, once they'd emptied all the lamps in the main house; what they didn't have was a shallow container eight feet long to put it in. Eventually Aidi solved the problem by cutting one end off two drinking troughs and forge-welding them together, an extremely skilful piece of metalworking for which he got very little credit. The first saw he retempered snapped like a carrot as soon as they tried to use it.

In the end, they salvaged three of the five fire-softened saws, and dug three more sawpits. Even then, the most they could manage to produce was twelve planks a day (Kunessin soon had both hands wrapped in rags to cushion his blisters); the smallest number they could get away with was two hundred and sixty. At that rate—

Kunessin interrupted to say that he could do mental arithmetic as well as the next man, but what alternative had they got?

Kudei solved the problem. He cut a dozen oak wedges, and taught himself how to split the tree trunks lengthways to make rough but acceptable planks. A third of what he turned out were too bowed and warped to be any use except for cutting into short lengths, and even the good ones needed to be trimmed and fettled with adzes and drawknives. But with the sawpits working day and night as well, they brought their daily output up to twenty-one planks, which was generally reckoned to be enough to give them a fighting chance.

On the fifth planking day, Alces joined in. His hands and face were still heavily bandaged, but he declared that if he had to sit still and quiet for one more day he'd become a danger to himself and others. He was too weak to saw or swing a hammer, but he padded his hands with raw wool to the point where he could use a drawknife. They rigged up trestles to lay the planks on so he could work sitting down.

After thirteen days of frantic effort, they had their stack of planks (at which point, one of the indentured men pointed out that the floorboards from the main house were only a few inches shorter than the planks they'd just cut, and most of them were seasoned pine rather than green ash; the comment was received in stony silence and never referred to again), and it was time to face up to the fact that none of them actually knew how to build a ship. True, they'd all been in one, and all five of them had helped pass the time on the voyage out by studying how it was put together. That, Kunessin maintained, ought to be enough. Aidi then asked where they should start: should they lay the keel first and then fit the ribs to it, or should they begin with the ribs and shape the keel to fit? It was a very good question, good enough to push Kunessin to the verge of losing his temper. Aidi himself expressed no opinion, and the situation wasn't helped when Muri said that he'd heard of both methods being used, though he couldn't recall any details. At least that goaded Kunessin into making a decision: keel first, then ribs.

Kudei had found them a suitable tree: ridiculously tall and thin, with only a very slight taper. Aidi (Dorun reckoned he was still upset about breaking the first saw) then asked how Kunessin proposed bending it to shape, and was rather taken aback when Kunessin smiled and said he knew exactly how it was done. That proved to be something of an exaggeration. What he'd actually seen, once, was a bowyer bending a bow stave over a kettle, though he insisted the principle was the same.

They had a fifty-gallon iron cauldron. Nobody knew why Kunessin had bought it—Alces' theory was that he'd misheard the merchant who sold it to him, while Chaere took the view that he'd bought it for the sake of completeness, since he'd already stocked up with every other item of useless junk available for immediate delivery in Faralia. Now they lugged it out into the yard, lit an enormous fire under it, filled it with water and waited a very long time for it to come to the boil. Eventually it did; whereupon the five of them lifted the keel on to their shoulders and held the relevant place over the steaming cauldron for half an hour, which was the length of time the bowyer had given his slender wand of elm. Then they scurried it across the yard to the place where a massive forked-trunked beech grew, stuck the front end of the keel in the fork, and hauled sideways. They were all completely stunned, Kunessin included, when it worked first time. The wood bent smoothly and easily, and once it had cooled down, the carefully judged contour of the bend stayed there. They carried it back to the cauldron in thoughtful silence and repeated the procedure for the other end.

After that, there was no stopping them. They bent the ship's sixteen ribs in exactly the same way, using a curve scratched in the dirt as a template, and they were most put out, practically offended, when the fifteenth rib cracked as they hauled on it (on subsequent inspection it proved to have an unexpected twist in the grain, for which they refused to hold themselves responsible). Aidi wanted to go further and steam curves into the hull planks as well, but Kunessin said that wasn't necessary; they could be bent and nailed on, and the stress would keep them from warping as the green timber dried out. That sounded suspiciously as though he'd just made it up on the spot, but by that point they were sick to death of holding bits of wood over the cauldron, and nobody was minded to argue.

The rest, as Muri cheerfully told them, was just carpentry, which any fool could do. That analysis didn't hold up for very long. The three carpenters among the enlisted men quickly contrived to splinter two of the ribs as they tried to mortice them to the keel. When accused of carelessness, they objected that they were carpenters, not shipwrights, and only a fool would try and make highly stressed load-bearing components out of green timber. So Muri fitted the ribs himself; as he pointed out, he wasn't a time-served carpenter and didn't realise what he was doing wasn't possible, so he did it anyway. The carpenters watched him in grim silence; then, when he'd finished, they promised him faithfully that the whole thing would be firewood within forty-eight hours, and refused to implicate themselves any further. The ribs held, and so did the keel, but the carpenters maintained that it was a blasphemy and an abomination, and confined their involvement to planing the deck planks to a fine, entirely unnecessary finish while Muri and the others set about nailing up the hull.

While the ship was being built, nobody said anything about food, which was probably just as well. Nobody commented when bread was replaced with crushed-barley porridge made out of cattle feed, briefly supplemented with extravagant servings of pork. When the last of the pigs had been eaten, that was the end of the meat ration. Kunessin flatly refused to slaughter any of his pedigree Robur shorthorns, Muri was too busy cutting mortices to go deer-hunting, and all but three of the chickens had been killed by a fox on the night of the fire. When the porridge ran out, they ate the horses' oats; when the oats were finished, they broke into the two barrels of condemned beans that Kunessin had got cheap and intended to use for pig food; finally the seed-corn. The next night, after the assembled company had dined on walnuts, wild mushrooms and cranberries, someone went out while everybody else was asleep, took Muri's extra-heavy bow from the small barn, and shot a cow.

"It'd be a shame to waste it," Chaere said next morning. They'd been paraded at the scene of the crime, and nobody had said a word so far.

But Kunessin refused. He was clearly furious; quiet, nervous, as though bracing himself to do something he'd prefer to avoid. He told Muri and Aidi to drag the corpse to the latrine pit and throw it in.

Aidi looked at him. "Can I have a quiet word with you?" he asked.

Kunessin shook his head. "Are you going to do as I said?"

Aidi frowned. "We can post a guard on the cattle pen if you like," he said. "If we all take turns it won't be so bad. But—come on, Teuche, the bloody thing's dead and we're starving."

"Fine," Kunessin said. "Muri, get a rope."

Muri helped him rope up the carcass and drag it across the yard, while the rest of them watched in total silence. They had to use levers to get it into the pit; it fell with a loud splash and a sheet of nauseating spray, which hit Muri full in the face and drenched Kunessin's jacket.

Muri spent the rest of the day in the woods, and came home with a gutted roebuck on each shoulder. He was plainly exhausted, though he denied it, and spent the evening huddled by the fire, wrapped in a blanket. Precious little shipbuilding had been done that day, since the principal shipwright hadn't been there.

"I'll go tomorrow," Alces said. "I'm sick to death of sitting around all day."

"You're in no fit state," Kunessin snapped back at him. "We can't afford to waste time and manpower searching the woods for you if you flake out."

"Fine," Alces replied angrily. "Just leave me, I'll find my own way home." Melted-side grin. "I'll just follow the river."

(Later, Chaere asked Dorun if she had any idea why that particular remark had killed the conversation for the rest of the evening. Dorun replied that she hadn't a clue, but clearly Alces had deliberately hit a raw nerve.)

Alces left for the woods early next day, before Kunessin was awake. Muri volunteered to go and find him, but Aidi said no, let him get on with it; they'd all been in worse shape than that in their time and gone on to fight and win major battles. That was an exaggeration, but Muri nodded and carried on sawing a tenon into a brace. Earlier he'd said he reckoned they'd have the first planks on the hull by mid-afternoon, though nobody reacted to his claim one way or the other.

Alces came back just as the light was starting to fade, dragging an enormous wild pig on a sled of lashed-together branches. They didn't waste time weighing it, but Kudei reckoned it had to be at least four and a half hundredweight. Alces slumped in a corner without even taking off his mud-caked boots, and they had to wake him up for his dinner.

"We got three planks on," Muri told him cheerfully, handing him his plate. "If we really tear into it tomorrow, we'll have it done in a couple of days."

Dinner next evening was a thin, watery stew of store apples fried in pork fat, a chewy fungus Menin had found growing on the trunks of rotten trees, and three rabbits caught in wires set by one of the indentured men. Only Chaere commented on the taste; they'd got two thirds of the hull planked in, the mast was ready and Clea and Enyo had finished hemming the sail.

"It's ridiculous," Chaere told them, as they sat sewing in the door-way of the middle barn. "You're wasting your time, and that's all there is to it. That stupid boat's never going to sail anywhere. At the rate they're going, the real ship'll be here before they're finished."

Clea scowled at her; Enyo smiled and said, "Well, it helps pass the time. And I enjoy sewing."

Chaere could see blood and torn skin on the tips of her fingers. The sailcloth was too thick to be sewn with an ordinary needle (but ordinary needles were all they had), so it had to be forced through, using the already completed hem. Sometimes, the base of the needle punched through the hem and deep into Enyo's finger.

"Just as well," Chaere said. "Personally, I left Faralia so I wouldn't have to spend my life doing stupid, useless needlework."

The next morning, Kunessin got up very early, walking carefully across the floor so as not to wake anybody else. He went to the mid-dle barn and got a poleaxe, then crossed the yard to the cattle pen. The heifers were already crowding up to the rail, waiting for their ration of hay. He hesitated, choosing, then stepped up to the big-gest heifer and smashed her forehead with the hammer of the axe.

She dropped to her knees, then rolled over. The other heifers bucked and twisted away, as he climbed through the rails, opening his long-bladed pocketknife. He knelt down, lifted the heifer's head on to his knee, and stabbed the knife into the neck vein, dodging sideways to avoid the jet of blood. By the time the others came out to start work, he'd got the carcass hoisted up on the frame they'd used for the pigs. The steam rising from the opened belly looked like smoke.

They all worked well all day, lighting lamps and torches when the light began to fade so they could finish planking the deck. At one point, it looked as though they were going to run out of nails, until one of the indentured men found two full kegs in the lean-to store. Nobody seemed inclined to talk very much while they ate their evening meal (apart from Chaere, who complained that the beef was tough, though that was only to be expected if you left the animal too long before slaughtering it). There wasn't very much of it; the women had used up the last of the salt curing as much as they could.

After the meal was over and the trestle tables had been cleared away, Kunessin got up and walked over to the far end of the room, where the indentured men sat. They were huddled in a circle, studying what looked like a small handful of fine gravel heaped up on somebody's shirt. Kunessin stood over them till they had to look up.

"You two," he said (and there was no mistaking who he meant). "Outside."

The two men — he only knew their family names, Aechmaloten and Andrapoda — followed him into the yard. There was just enough moonlight to see by.

"Where the hell did you two get to all day?" Kunessin asked.

The shorter of the two, Aechmaloten, hesitated a long time before answering. "We went down the river," he said quietly. "Major Proiapsen wanted two sacks of fine gravel, for making cement, for the forge."

Kunessin could hear something in his voice, but he wasn't quite sure what it was. He said quietly, "That shouldn't have taken you all day."

"We found something," Andrapoda said.

Kunessin waited. Then he said, "Well?"

"Come inside," Aechmaloten said. "See for yourself."

Kunessin followed them, and soon found himself staring at the handful of brown silt on the shirt. "River sand," he said. "So what?"

The other indentured men were still and quiet, as though they were holding their breath, and Kunessin sensed danger; not the battlefield sort, but the uneasiness he used to feel when he had to climb into the bull's pen. Without saying anything, Aechmaloten prodded the sand with his finger. Something sparkled red in the dim firelight.

"We were going to tell you," Andrapoda said apologetically.

Kunessin wasn't listening. He didn't know much about the subject, but he remembered that Aechmaloten and Andrapoda used to be miners, working in the lead pits at the foot of the Blackwater hills. He knelt down (the others pulled away to give him room; the same sort of movement as bullocks shying away when you turn to face them, but immediately they start stalking you again), picked up a pinch of silt between his fingers and squeezed it, looking very closely. The same red sparkle.

"Where exactly did you find it?" he said.

"We can show you the place," Aechmaloten said. "But chances are the whole river's full of the stuff. We reckon it washes down from the knees of the mountain."

For a long time, Kunessin kept perfectly still. "You've seen this before," he said.

Someone else, another ex-miner, nodded. "There were always little bits of colour in the water back home," he said. "Where there's lead, there's quite a good chance there'll be gold as well. But usually just a few flecks, not enough to get fussed about." His voice was soft, like someone praying. "Nothing like this."

Kunessin looked round at their faces: strained, frightened, the expressions of men trying to decide something under enormous pressure. He could guess what was on their minds. After all, they had the advantage of superior numbers, though they'd lost surprise. The question occupying their minds was whether they felt up to taking on five linebreakers. Even with a river full of gold at stake, he was fairly sure they didn't. But he wasn't prepared to take any chances.

"We'll go and have a look first thing in the morning," he said. "If it's gold, we're going to have to talk about this, figure out what we're going to do."

He'd said the right thing, or he'd said it in the right way. He could feel the tension lifting, a little. One of the men nodded; a big, broad-shouldered bald man. "We understand," he said.

"This changes everything, naturally," Kunessin said. "I'll have to talk to my partners. After all," he added, listening to himself as he spoke, "we aren't miners, we came here to farm. And we still need to get the ship launched, or we're not going to have any food."

They hadn't been thinking about food, or shipbuilding. It was like the moment when two men on the verge of having to fight find a way out of the confrontation, and immediately change the subject. "Will she be ready tomorrow, General, do you think?" the big bald man asked. Kunessin got the feeling he was someone important; he wished he could remember the man's name.

"That depends on us," Kunessin replied. "But, obviously, the sooner we get her finished and launched, the sooner we can lay in supplies and get that problem off the slate. Till then, this" — he indicated the molehill of silt with a slight movement of his fingers — "is neither here nor there. I know it's hard, but best to put it to the back of our minds for now. What do you reckon?"

Of course, they didn't know him well enough; they hadn't been there when he'd used that tone of voice, ten, fifteen years ago. Aidi would've recognised it at once. "Fair enough," Aechmaloten said. "First things first, like you say."

Kunessin nodded. "Settled, then," he said. "And if I were you, I'd keep this a bit quiet. I mean, I'll tell my lads, in my own time, but there's no need to mention it to the women." He grinned, the universal-conspiracy grin of men talking about the opposite sex. "I reckon we want to keep clear heads for the time being. A load of yap from them's the last thing we need."

An appeal to the general, fundamental brotherhood of men; the carefully introduced misconception that common ground in one thing implies a broader sympathy. They'd been taught the principle in their second year at the College, in Logic and Rhetoric, learning to be young gentlemen as well as soldiers. He was glad he'd been paying attention that morning. Several of the men laughed, maybe just a bit louder than the comment warranted, and he felt a little more secure. You don't laugh at a man's jokes and then cut his throat in his sleep; not if you've missed out on the privilege of a first-rate education. But in his mind, he was thinking about the weapons: where they were, how quickly he could get to them, where he'd have to sit that night so he could keep an eye on both doors.

TEN

"Send them back," Aidi insisted; he was hissing like a snake. "As soon as the ship gets here. Otherwise we're going to get our throats cut in the night."

It was raining and the roof leaked, which really didn't help. Kunessin yawned; he hadn't slept. He looked round for the fifth time, just in case some enemy had crept into the lean-to store in the last ninety seconds. Rainwater dripped from the hole in the roof and puddled in the folds of his sleeve. "Two reasons," he said. "First, if we send them back, do you really think they're going to keep their mouths shut once they're home? I don't reckon so. I think they'll come back here with weapons and reinforcements."

Alces muttered something he didn't catch, but it sounded positive. Muri was nodding. But Aidi was still glowering at him.

"Second," he went on, "we may all think we're still twenty-one years old and a match for anyone and anything, but let's be realistic. I really don't fancy making them leave if they don't want to. It's not like herding cattle; you can't just crowd them with hurdles. I'm more interested in avoiding a fight than provoking one."

Aidi nodded. He had that look on his face that said he believed he was about to win the argument. "Points taken," he said, "both of them. We can't let them go, we can't make them go and we can't have them here, not if we want to stay alive." His mouth was thin and his eyes wide. "That only really leaves one course of action, doesn't it?"

Kunessin took a deep breath. He'd seen it coming. "I'd be reluctant to do that," he said, wiping rainwater out of his eyes. "Quite apart from the morality of slaughtering a bunch of unarmed men, I'd ask you to consider the likely consequences. We may be on an island, but we're not outside the jurisdiction. Sooner or later someone's going to miss them, and then we could be in more trouble than you can possibly begin to imagine."

Kudei, whose face hadn't moved, was now frowning. Alces said, "That's not a genuine option, surely." Aidi was already thinking about some other line of argument. Kunessin decided it was time to commit his reserve.

"There's another thing we could do," he said. "When the ship comes, we get on it."

That took a moment to sink in. Aidi got there first, of course. "Hold on," he said. "Are you suggesting we just sail away and leave a riverful of gold to a bunch of servants?"

Kunessin dipped his head, a polite gesture of acknowledgement. "It's an option," he said. "Not ideal, I'll give you that. After all, I'm the one who wanted to come here. It's my money." He paused there for a moment, not voluntarily. "But if it's that or a battle or mass murder, maybe we shouldn't dismiss it out of hand. If you think about it, I don't actually see we've got a choice." This time, the hesitation was deliberate. "We aren't miners," he said. "And since when have any of us—biggest collection of underachievers the world has ever seen—cared all that much about getting rich?"

He couldn't help holding his breath as he waited, but when someone eventually spoke, it was only Muri, who said, "I'm with Teuche," in a bewildered tone of voice that suggested he wasn't entirely clear about what he'd just agreed with.

"Have you told the girls yet?" Alces said.

Kunessin shook his head. "Let's get things sorted out in our own minds before we involve any more outsiders," he said. Then: "Come on, Aidi, spit it out. What do you reckon?"

But it was Kudei who answered him. "Suppose we do go home," he said. "What then? Personally, I'm damned if I'm going back to the farm. I can just see the look on my brothers' faces."

Kunessin ignored him. "Aidi?" he said.

"I don't know," Aidi replied. "I really don't want to turn my back on a fortune, but I can't say I like the thought of the servants breathing down my neck. I mean, think about it," he went on. "We've just seriously discussed the pros and cons of slaughtering them like sheep. If the same idea hasn't crossed their minds already..."

"They wouldn't dare," Alces said firmly.

"Under normal circumstances, yes," Aidi snapped back. "And suppose they try it and we win. It's the point Teuche raised. We'd end up trying to explain ourselves to the advocate general, since this is presumably still military jurisdiction." He glanced at Kunessin, who looked away. "Sorry, but I can't see an easy answer. Fly, what do you think?"

Alces frowned, and the thin, melted skin of his face stretched disturbingly. "It's one of those exam questions from college," he said, "where there's always the rider: would your answer be different if. Now, if we still had a barn full of flour, I'd say definitely, we stay. Fact is, though, we're screwed. We finish building the boat; fine. Who's going to sail it to the mainland now? If we send indentured men, what's to stop them recruiting a small army to get rid of us? If we go, I have an idea we might find it difficult getting ashore again. If, say, two of us go, that just leaves three here, which might well tempt them to have a go. If we don't send the boat, we just sit here waiting for the ship and getting thin; my guess is there'll be murder done over food, let alone gold. As to what's likely to happen when the ship gets here, I really don't want to think about that right now." He sighed, as if the whole business was bitterly unfair. "The safest option would probably be to slaughter the indentured men and make up some story about pirates, but we'd have to get the girls to go along with it; I don't think they're terribly good liars, any of them, and besides, I just don't feel like committing mass murder. Call me pernickety, but I can't help it."

Aidi lifted his head and looked straight at Kunessin. "There you have it then, General," he said. "You're the ranking bloody officer. Up to you."

Kunessin nodded slowly, though he felt anything but calm. "I think we should stay," he said.

It wasn't the answer they'd been expecting, but he could tell it was what they'd wanted to hear, though quite probably they hadn't realised that for themselves. "Mostly," he went on, "for the reasons Fly's just given us. Facts, gentlemen. There may or may not be gold in the river. But we can be certain bloody sure there's not enough food to keep us going till the ship gets here. Therefore, we need to finish the boat; either to get food from the mainland, or to take us there. We can't finish the boat and get it down to the water on our own, so we need the indentured men. If they're going to kill us, or try to, they'll do it very soon; otherwise they'll talk themselves out of it. So, the simple fact is, we're going to have to confront the problem whether we give up or not. If we're going to have to sort things out with the men, we might as well stay here. Like Kudei just said, what the hell is there for any of us back in Faralia?" He paused, a show of inviting reactions: none. "Personally," he went on, "I just want to farm, I'm not interested in gold-mining. But I spent every quarter I ever had getting us here, so it's here or nowhere. Therefore, I am not going back; therefore, I'm staying. If you boys want to dig for gold, you carry on. We'll still all be together, and that's the important thing."

He waited again, listening to the steady patter of rain on the roof, and a heartbeat later he knew he'd won. Then Aidi said, "It's all very well saying, sort things out with the indentured men. How, exactly?"

Kunessin shrugged. "Be straight with them," he replied. "Straight down the line, like we've always been with each other. Fair shares for all. Simple as that."

As he'd anticipated, Aidi jumped for the fly. "Now hold on," he said. "I'm all for equality and social justice, but I'm buggered if I'm going to stand for that. They're just servants, Teuche."

Kunessin smiled. Aidi had always beaten him in strategy and tactics at the College. "I said fair shares," he replied. "Not equal shares, necessarily. That wouldn't be fair, after all."

Alces laughed, Kudei smiled, Muri looked confused. Aidi was way ahead of them, but still waiting for the detail. "What I propose," Kunessin went on, "and what I'd like to put to the men, is that we organise it properly, like a trading company. That's your line, Aidi, you know what I mean. Equal shares for everybody, but only after deductions, the net profits. It's only right and proper we should get—what's the phrase, Aidi?"

"Interest on capital," Aidi said, nodding briskly. "We charge the company a percentage for rent, since it's our island, and another slice for using our facilities and tools. Or we could do it with shares, weighted to reflect capital contributions."

It had stopped raining. Kunessin grinned. "That's the stuff," he said. "It all sounds so reasonable when you say it like that. The main thing is to calm them down as quickly as possible. Put yourself in their shoes. Why risk taking on five linebreakers and committing murder just to save an extra five shares? They'll hear what they want to hear, just so long as it sounds reasonable."

Aidi frowned. "It is reasonable," he said. "Standard business practice. It's not like we're planning to rip them off."

"Quite," Kunessin said. "There you are, then, problem solved. Now, first things first, we need to talk to them, before we go and look at the river." He thought for a moment, then added, "We'd better get dressed first."

Alces looked at him. "Why? I thought the whole idea was—"

"It'll do no harm," Kunessin said firmly.

Getting dressed meant crossing the yard to the middle barn. "Just as well I brought all this stuff," Kunessin said, as they levered the lid off a barrel.

"Never leave home without it," Kudei murmured.

The mail shirts had been carefully oiled and packed in sand, but there was still a brown dew of rust on them, and that unmistakable smell. "Coifs but no helmets," Kunessin said. "We want to make a point, not scare them to death." From the weapon chests they chose catsplitters, the trademark short, wide swords of the linebreakers, with their distinctive double-ring hilts. "Where'd you get these, Teuche?" Muri asked.

"Government issue," Kunessin replied. "I had them booked out to a disbanded unit. When they came back, they were off the book, so the quartermaster just wanted rid of them. Shocking waste of tax-payers' money."

Everyone laughed, except Aidi. "Nice touch," Alces said. "Instantly recognisable, reminds them who they're messing with." He grinned. "Let's just hope we don't have to use them."

A Company despised the catsplitter. They'd traded the ones they were issued with to souvenir-hunters in return for Type Fifteens or civilian falchions. Aidi had moaned about that, too.

"Which raises the issue…" Kudei's head emerged through the neck hole of his mail shirt; his hair was messed up, and he had a smudge of brown oil on his forehead. "Rules of engagement."

Kunessin adjusted his belt. "Use your common sense," he replied. "We can't afford to take any nonsense, but the idea is, we've got to live with these people. If we start something, I'm afraid we'll have to finish it, and that's all our plans screwed up."

The yard smelt of fresh rain. It reminded Teuche of late spring back on the farm, and for a moment he couldn't think what the hell he was doing dressed up in armour like a soldier. He watched Alces skip lightly over a puddle, graceful as a dancer, only to have Muri splash him with muddy water as he stumbled in a pothole.

"Gentlemen," he said, and pushed open the door.

The indentured men were still in their huddle, at their end of the building. Kunessin could see Dorun and the other women staring at them, suddenly frozen by the sight of armour and weapons. The men turned to look at them; one started to jump up, but was quickly pulled down.

"General." Kunessin was relieved to hear Aechmaloten's voice. He looked for him and saw him sitting slightly to one side, with a tin dish on his lap. "You look like you're expecting trouble."

Bravely said; but spoiled by a very slight stammer on the "p" of "expecting." "Not me," Kunessin said, loud enough to be heard by everyone but still within his normal conversational range. "Join me outside; we want to talk to you."

He could read the looks on their faces easily enough, and silently congratulated himself. Aechmaloten didn't want to be a leader, let alone a ringleader, which was why he'd chosen him for precisely those roles. None of the others wanted to go outside with five armed and notoriously dangerous men, so Aechmaloten had just got himself elected spokesman. He tried very hard not to feel sorry for the man as he crossed the floor.

As soon as they were back in the yard: "Well?" he said. "Is it gold?"

Aechmaloten hesitated, avoiding the five stares. "We reckon so," he said. "There's proper tests, with chemicals. But we fancy we can tell gold when we see it."

Kunessin nodded. "No way of telling how big a strike, obviously."

Aechmaloten shrugged. "It was a lot of colour in a small place," he replied, "and all we did was scoop it up, not having a pan with us. We're pretty sure."

"Excellent." Big smile. "In that case, assuming you're right, we've got a deal we'd like you to talk over with the others."

He set out the terms: equal shares (after deductions, which he'd go into later), a formal partnership, with everything set down on paper so they'd all know where they stood; conditional, needless to say, on finishing the boat and stocking up on supplies first. Common sense. After that, though — well, by the sound of it there'd be more than enough for everybody.

"Well?" he said.

Aechmaloten was looking at him with big round eyes. "I'll need to talk to —"

"Of course," Kunessin said. "And I suggest you elect a foreman, before you go any further." (He knew exactly who that'd be.) "Best to start off properly organised, rather than let things run and get out of order. If we all know where we stand, there shouldn't be any misunderstandings."

He saw Aechmaloten look down, at the sword hilt Kunessin was lightly resting his hand on. He'd always prided himself on his ability to communicate.

"You go back and talk it through," he said pleasantly. "We'll wait for you out here. Oh, and you might ask our wives to join us." He grinned and lowered his voice. "Fact is, we haven't told them yet."

Not all that funny, by any standards, but it made Aechmaloten laugh (and to Kunessin that was the click of the lock). He gave them a comic mournful look and promised to send them out right away.

Later, they drew up a contract. Aidi wrote it down. A few years ago, he'd amused himself by learning law hand, the formal, abbreviation-filled, scarcely legible script traditionally used for legal documents. It wasn't a requirement; lawyers liked it because, unless you were used to it, you had terrible trouble reading it, and were therefore more likely to sign it unread. The indentured men (technically still, but only just; Clause 5 released them from their indentures, as part of the deal) were deeply impressed, which Kunessin thought was rather like fish admiring the craftsmanship of the net-maker.

After the recitals (Aidi put in a lot of those, mostly because each one started with a decorated capital letter, and he fancied he was rather good at the broad hooked loops), the document set out the basics of the agreement. All the named parties were to be partners in the gold strike, sharing the work and the net profits equally, with the usual penalties for not pulling their weight or trying to defraud the others, the obvious likely causes of disagreement. Net profits (and such a pretty net, Kunessin thought; but he managed not to smile at his private joke) were defined as the proceeds less expenses, which included rent paid to the island's five owners for the mineral rights — fifteen per cent of the gross — and fees for the use of tools and facilities: five per cent. A further two per cent went to General Kunessin, to cover the company's use of his ship, out of which the general undertook to maintain it and pay the crew. An additional clause, inserted at the general's insistence, conveyed the island, the buildings, fixtures and chattels to the five surviving members of A Company as a tontine. Although the ship was expressly excluded, the sloop currently under construction was to belong to the tontine, with all the partners obliged to complete and maintain it and act as its crew when required to do so. Apart from the sloop, any equipment and machinery built or acquired after the signing of the agreement was to be partnership property, to be paid for as an expense deducted from the gross.

All but three of the indentured men were able to sign their names; the illiterates each drew a cross, which was duly witnessed. One of them, a tall, nervous man with thin hair, objected to having his mark witnessed by a woman. He said he was sure he'd heard somewhere that it wasn't valid in law.

"I don't know about that," Aidi said irritably. "But nobody else can do it, because we're all parties to the agreement, and I know for a fact that doesn't count."

The man didn't reply, but he looked extremely sad, and some of the others looked sideways at each other. They think we're tricking them, Kunessin thought despairingly. As if we'd be that subtle.

"Forget about it," he said firmly, getting up from the table. "After all, this is our island, we make the laws here. In fact, let's make one right now. Law number one: a woman can act as a witness to a legal document. All in favour."

He waited; nobody moved, so he stuck his hand up in the air. Muri copied him immediately, then Aidi, Alces and Kudei. "Well?" Kunessin said.

Aechmaloten was looking at him. "What're you doing?" he asked.

"Voting," Kunessin said. "On the proposed new law. Stick your hand up; come on, it's not exactly difficult. Otherwise I'm going to have to assume you're against, in which case we can't have an agreement, with no witnesses, and we've all been wasting our time."

Someone else said: "We can do that?"

"I just said so, didn't I?"

Very slowly, like someone volunteering to be used for target practice, Aechmaloten raised his hand. When nothing bad happened to him, the rest of them did the same; cautiously, like newly weaned pigs leaving the sty for the first time. "Right," Kunessin said, loud and pointedly cheerful, "that didn't hurt, did it?"

Aidi was tugging anxiously at his sleeve. He allowed himself the gentle pleasure of pretending he hadn't noticed. Aechmaloten had, though; for some reason (not hard to find one), he seemed terrified of

Aidi. As well he might be. Occasionally, Kunessin tended to forget what sort of people his friends were, but never for long.

"Would you excuse me for a moment?" he said, frowning a little; then he turned to Aidi and whispered, "What?"

"I'd like a word with you," Aidi hissed back. "Now, please."

Kunessin smiled at Aechmaloten, and allowed Aidi to draw him away; five yards, no more. "Well?" he said.

"What the hell do you think you're doing?"

Kunessin nodded, as though Aidi had raised an obscure but valid point. "We'll talk about it later," he said.

"No we won't," Aidi replied. "What's the matter with you? This isn't what we talked about."

"Don't worry about it," Kunessin said, sharpening his voice a little. "It's no big deal. Everything's under control. Now let go of my arm, they're staring."

Reluctantly, Aidi did as he was told. Kunessin went back to the table and said, "I think that's everything for now, so I won't hold you up any further. Alexicacus, why isn't the mast up yet? You told me you'd fixed the problem with the retaining pin."

The indentured men left the hall quite soon after that, and Kunessin closed the door behind them. "Right," he said briskly. "I get the feeling you're annoyed with me."

"Not all of us," Muri said.

"Too bloody right," Aidi snapped. "What do you think you're playing at, Teuche? I mean, the company thing I can accept, but you've gone too far. Those men are servants."

Teuche sighed, and took his time sitting down. "Calm down, Aidi," he said, "before you get on my nerves. What about the rest of you? Kudei? Fly?"

"I'll admit I'm curious," Kudei said, sitting on the edge of the table. "Where did all this democracy stuff come from? I thought we were conning them, not building the ideal republic."

"Teuche wants to do both," Alces said.

Kudei laughed, but Kunessin's face didn't change. "This isn't like the army," he said. "We depend on their goodwill. For one thing, we've got to get the boat finished."

"How does voting on every damn thing help with that?" Aidi said.

"Use your head, Aidi," Kudei put in. "It's not every damn thing; just stuff that doesn't matter. That's right, isn't it, Teuche?"

"Better than that," Alces said. "Unsettle them. If they don't know where they stand..."

"Partly," Kunessin said, leaning back in his chair. His was the only one with arms; almost like a throne (a point that hadn't escaped Aidi's attention, though he'd made a joke of it). "Partly, I really do think we need to get them on our side, genuinely. Make them feel like they've got a stake in this. After all, what the hell do we know about panning for gold?"

Aidi scowled. "It can't be difficult," he said. "They can do it."

"And they'll teach us," Kunessin said. "And then we'll know. But we'll still need them after that."

"Really?" Aidi raised an eyebrow.

"Yes." Teuche nodded vigorously. "There's only five of us, remember."

"What's that got to do with it?"

Kudei stood up, but only to stretch his back. "We've discussed this before," he said. "Three options, remember? Kill them, or throw them out and risk them coming back with a small army, or learn to live with them in a spirit of trust and brotherly love. I'm not saying we made the right choice, but that's what we decided. What Teuche's just done is the next natural step."

"Lull them into a true sense of security," Alces muttered.

"Like I said." Kunessin leaned forward, arms on the table. "This isn't the army."

He was watching Aidi closely, and didn't mind everybody knowing it. "I don't buy that," Aidi said, with a feather of nervousness on the edge of his voice. "Even when we were in the army, we didn't do things the army way. We never bothered about all the service bullshit. We agreed everything among ourselves."

"Yes," Kudei put in quietly. "After Nuctos died."

"That's not strictly true," Alces said. "Teuche told us what to do, and since we never had any reason not to agree with him, the question never arose. You were forever arguing the toss," he added, smiling at Aidi, "but that's just you. I don't remember you ever pressing a point, or not going along with what Teuche said."

Aidi was starting to look harassed. "I don't know why you're all picking on me," he said. "I'm just saying, Teuche's line about this not being the service is completely beside the point. You want to know what I think? I think Teuche's scared of them, which is why—"

"No you don't," Kudei interrupted. "He's just being sly. Years of being on the general staff, having to get along with a bunch of people you wouldn't willingly piss on if they were burning. Maybe he's being a bit overcautious, but that's better than charging in bull-at-a-gate."

Kunessin acknowledged that with a polite nod. "Thanks," he said, "I think. And yes, Kudei's not far wrong. Over the years, I've had to learn how to handle stupid people if I wanted to get something done. And these men aren't particularly stupid, not compared with the average brigadier general. I think Aidi's forgetting he's not in Faralia any more."

Aidi opened his mouth, closed it again and indulged in a big, slow shrug. "The last thing I'd ever want to do is cause trouble," he said. "If you're all happy with this..."

"Yes," Alces said. "Now let's stop worrying about trivia and talk about something that really matters. Teuche, why the hell can't we tell the girls about the gold strike?"

Kudei laughed. Aidi had turned away—pretending to sulk, Kunessin decided, but Aidi never quite sulked. "You're quite right," he said. "We need to tell them. I've been putting it off, I'm not really sure why."

"Let's do it and get it over with," Muri said.

"They ought to be pleased," Kudei said. "Yours especially, Aidi."

Aidi groaned. "She's the last one we should tell," he replied. "Soon as she hears the G word, she'll be desperate to get back to Faralia and start shopping."

That's why, Kunessin realised. Not just Chaere; all of them. Their sentence of perpetual exile, punishment for not being married, suddenly commuted into the promise of wealth. Actually, he couldn't give a damn about the others. But Dorun—there was an old saying: it's not despair that hurts, it's hope. If Dorun started thinking there was an alternative to sleeping on damp straw on Sphoe, he'd probably lose her, and that would be a pity.

So he told her.

"Gold," she repeated, as though he was trying to persuade her to believe in some improbable mythical beast. "In the river."

"So they reckon," he replied.

She'd been combing her hair; now she was sitting with the comb in one hand and the mirror in the other, bewildered. It wasn't what he'd expected. "We've been out with them," he went on. "They showed us the place, and we dug out some of the silt from the river bed and they swirled it round in a dish, and there it was. Like little specks of yellow dust."

"Oh," she said.

"They think it's a substantial strike," he went on, supplying information she probably didn't want. "Apparently the signs are all there—they explained it all, but I wasn't really listening. Something to do with layers of rock and the action of the river eating into them. I think they really know what they're talking about." He stopped. She wasn't listening. "So," he said. "What do you think?"

"Me?" She looked at him. "What do I think about what?"

He sat down beside her; the stool creaked under their joint weight. "Well," he said, "it's not what we came for."

"True," she said, as though she suspected a verbal trap. "Does that matter?"

"That's what I'm asking you."

"I see." Her manner changed slightly; maybe it was just relief at understanding the question. "I think it's like everything. It could be good, or there could be all sorts of problems." She paused. Perhaps she thought she wasn't making a good impression. "Chaere'll be pleased," she said. "Clea too, I expect, she's never had anything. I'm not so sure about Enyo—"

"You're not answering my question."

"Aren't I? Oh." She frowned, a study in concentration. "All those long, earnest discussions you've been having with the servants. You're expecting trouble, aren't you?"

"Taken care of," he said firmly. "You're still not answering my question."

"Do I want to be married to a gold prospector rather than a farmer?" She shrugged. "Obviously it makes a difference. But it depends. Is it what you want?"

Kunessin smiled. "No," he said.

"But you haven't got any choice in the matter."

"No."

"Well," she said briskly, "if you don't have a choice, neither do I." She remembered that she was holding a mirror and a comb, and put them down. "You can't just leave them to it, because you've spent all your money setting this up. You're stuck with it." Like I'm stuck with you; but she didn't say that.

"We can leave," he said. "As soon as the ship gets here."

She looked at him. "What about the money?"

He nodded. "My friends will see to it that I get it all back," he replied. "It probably won't take them very long, if the strike's as good as they all seem to think. Then," he went on, looking over her shoulder, "we can go where we like and do what we like. It's not a problem."

"We could?"

Hope? He really wasn't sure. "Of course."

"You wouldn't mind?"

"I don't particularly want to be a gold-miner. I'm a farmer."

"It'd mean leaving your friends."

And still she hadn't answered his question; unless that was the point, unless asking her that was like asking the sea what it's like to be water. And, of course, he couldn't possibly leave them. Not like in the marshes.

"I'd rather not do that," he said.

"Well, then," she said.

Later, he called an informal staff meeting. Dorun had been right about Chaere's reaction, and Clea's, too. "Money," Kudei said ruefully.

"The moment I said the word 'gold,' it was like she became a totally different person."

"Less miserable?" Alces asked.

"There's worse things than miserable," Kudei replied. "She went all quiet. Now that's unsettling."

"There's a whole lot of things worse than quiet," Aidi said, with feeling. "Trust me on that."

"Muri?" Kunessin asked.

"I don't know." Muri was frowning. "It's as though she wasn't listening. No, that's not it. She was listening, but it's like she doesn't think it's any of her business."

"That's nice, dear?"

Muri grinned. "Almost. More like she's got something really important on her mind, and trivia like a massive gold strike just doesn't register."

"Enyo's not happy," Alces volunteered. "She's worried. Thinks it'll all end in blood and tears."

"That's what she says about everything, though," Aidi pointed out.

Alces frowned at him. "I explained that we'd taken steps to prevent any trouble with the indentured men—" He checked himself. "Mustn't call them that any more. Our new business partners. Anyhow, I told her about that."

"In detail?" Kunessin asked quickly.

Alces looked affronted. "Of course not. I just said we'd made a deal with them and they wouldn't be a problem. That just made her gloomy."

Kudei laughed. "Why a sensible woman like that ever married you, I can't begin to imagine," he said. "What about Dorun, Teuche? Is she all right about it all?"

"Yes." Kunessin said the word crisply, like the snapping of a twig. "Well, that doesn't sound too bad. Next item of business, the sloop. Why the hell isn't it ready yet?"

Muri and Kudei exchanged grins. "It's ready," Kudei said. "Only you've been so wrapped up in gold mines and establishing a democracy, we haven't had a chance to tell you."

Kunessin's eyebrows shot up. "The mast?"

"All done," Aidi said. "I had to rip out the brackets and cut in new ones, but it turned out to be much less trouble than I thought."

"Before you ask," Alces put in, "the sail's done, and the ropes. Fat lot of help I had from our new best friends, I might add. Too busy spending their limitless wealth in their heads, I dare say."

Kunessin felt oddly light-headed, as though he'd been hit by something. "Something's actually gone right," he said. "Well, that's a pleasant change."

"It could still sink," Kudei said soothingly. "Or the men might run off with the girls in it and not come back."

Aidi pulled a face. "We should be so lucky," he said.

The third day of the march, and the road was gradually climbing. White dust nestled in the folds of their clothes and the ridges of their boots like frost, and their pack straps were starting to fray against the steel rings of their mail shirts. Something had gone wrong with the supply train, though nobody knew exactly what; there should have been thirty wagons loaded with bacon, flour and apples waiting for them at the last crossroads. They'd waited for four hours (two hours either side of noon, no shade) before the general gave up and ordered them to resume the march. Now they were late, behind the clock, liable to miss the next rendezvous and be caught out in the open at nightfall. And if Supply hadn't made the last drop, was there any reason to believe they'd make the next one? What if something bad had happened?

"Muri, for crying out loud, put it away," Nuctos said, harsh and soft. "Unless you want to share with the whole army."

Muri froze, his mouth full, then shoved the rest of the cheese back in his coat pocket. A Company tended to make its own arrangements where essential supplies were concerned; nobody's business but their own, but it was sensible not to flaunt their superior foresight in front of the pikemen. Aidi, surreptitiously chewing a slice of dried apple, swallowed quickly.

"What do you reckon happened to the wagons?" Fly asked. He was trying to sound casual. "Just basic inefficiency, do you think?"

"Probably," Nuctos replied, shifting his pack a little.

"Probably," Kudei repeated.

"It's always the most likely explanation," Nuctos said. "You know Supply, couldn't drown in water."

"But..." Teuche prompted.

Nuctos shrugged, an uncharacteristically agitated gesture. "I don't know," he said. "It's probably just me, but I can't help wondering." He paused, frowning, a study for a monumental statue of Man In Thought. "Heading from the main depot to meet us here, the wagons'd have to come up the main east–west road, right?"

Muri looked blank. Aidi nodded. Teuche frowned, already half-way there. "Sure," said Fly. "I remember the map. So?"

Overhead, three crows were circling, doing complex geometry on blue paper. "Well." Nuctos turned his head. "If they're supposed to meet us at the foot of the mountain at dusk, we ought to have been seeing their dust for the last hour." He pointed at the horizon. "That's where the west road's got to be, all right? That green line in the distance must be the river, and we know the road follows the river bank the first third of the way. So, I'm thinking, thirty-odd wagons bumbling along the road should be kicking up a cloud of dust we could easily see from here."

Nobody said anything for a while. Then Teuche broke the silence. "That's not so good," he said.

Nuctos nodded. "It also begs the question of what happened to the wagons," he said. "Three possibilities. One, they're horrendously late leaving the depot; entirely possible. Two, they got lost — not so likely; even Supply'd be hard put to it to get lost in a desert with only one road. Three, someone cut them off." His frown deepened. "Not all that likely, because as far as we know there's no army, just a bunch of no-hope militia. But if there is an army..." He shook his head. "Not a happy thought, gentlemen."

Aidi said: "There can't be an army, we'd have seen their dust."

"Not necessarily," Nuctos replied gravely. "Not if they're drawn up on or just behind the mountain. Cavalry could take a long loop on the far side of the river, hit the wagons and go back the way they came, and we'd be too far away to see the dust. Of course," he went on, "that'd presuppose they knew our plans in some detail, if they know we're taking this route, and are going out of their way—literally—to make sure we don't see them." He scowled, then grinned. "Assuming there really is an army, for which we have no hard evidence. I think it's rather more likely that I've dreamed all this up to occupy my mind on this extremely boring march. You know me, morbidly active imagination."

Kudei shifted his pack straps on his shoulders and sighed. "Well," he said, "even if you're right, there's not a hell of a lot we can do about it, unless you fancy trying to make out a case to the general..."

"That famously open-minded individual," Nuctos said. "And even if we did, what's he supposed to do about it? We can't turn back, we're too far along."

"We could," Aidi said quietly.

"I don't think the general staff would be too impressed," Nuctos said.

"Screw the general staff," Fly said. "Starving to death in the desert's got to be the stupidest way to die."

"Bar being hung for desertion," Muri said.

"I don't think we'd make it back," Teuche said quietly. "Even with what we've got left."

Nuctos pulled a deep, comic frown. "Serves me right for raising the subject in the first place," he said. "Look, nobody's going to desert, all right? We've got no proof, just a load of idle speculation on my part. For all we know, the wagons got to the mountain early this morning, which is why we haven't seen any dust. Maybe they forgot about the drop at the crossroads and came straight on, or one of the wagons ran over a rock and busted an axle, and they've sent back to the depot for a smith. Could be a dozen other reasons, and they'd all be more plausible than an imaginary army suddenly rising up out of the dust like dragon's teeth."

That killed the subject, and left no real scope for a replacement, so they marched in silence for a while, only glancing at the horizon, with its blatant lack of dust clouds, when they thought the others weren't looking. Behind them, the main line was slowing down—lack of food starting to have an effect—but they were reluctant to slacken their own pace and so allowed the gap to widen, from the customary twenty-five yards to more like fifty. It didn't seem to matter; their place was, after all, at the front, on the march as in battle. Muri complained about his boots for the sixth time that day, but as usual nobody replied.

Nuctos noticed the dust cloud before anybody else; then Teuche, then Aidi, who pointed it out to the others. "Finally," Fly said cheerfully, but Aidi was frowning. Nuctos explained.

"Wrong direction," he said quietly. "Coming down the road."

Kudei squinted, then asked, "How can you tell?"

"Been watching it for some time," Nuctos replied. "It's headed away from the mountain. Hard to tell at this distance, but I could swear it's coming straight at us."

Muri looked worried. Aidi said, "Could be the wagons arrived early, realised they'd missed the first drop, and now they're coming looking for us."

Nuctos stopped for a moment, gazing at the white wisp, like a shred of wool caught on a briar. "Could be," he said.

"You don't think so."

"If that's wagons," Nuctos said, "they're moving at a hell of a lick."

They'd all stopped now. "We should tell someone," Muri said.

Nuctos laughed. "No point," he said. "If that's a squadron of enemy cavalry, the general'll see them for himself soon enough. Besides, what exactly do you think we can do about it? In the open, not so much as a pebble or a thorn bush. But," he went on, speaking a little louder, "there's a lot of us, and if they want to charge a square of pikes with cavalry, they've got my permission."

The dust cloud grew, from a wisp to a smear to an eyesore, and the general eventually noticed. He ordered a halt, and for two hours the army stood in the white eye of the sun watching the cloud grow. It sprouted men and horses, and the general wondered who they might be; he had no cavalry closer than Tenevris, and there was no enemy. The men and horses began to sparkle, and the general speculated as to who (apart from soldiers) rides with polished steel. Although there was no threat, he nevertheless ordered the pikemen to form a square, purely as a precaution.

The cloud became a wave. Nuctos counted them, or formed a reliable estimate: no more than five hundred, six at the very most. They weren't the cavalry from Tenevris.

"Which means," he said, "they're the enemy, or an enemy. Like it matters. There's too few of them to be any threat to us."

Even so (purely as a precaution), he led A Company inside the pike square. Once inside, they couldn't see what was going on. The first arrow, therefore, came as a complete surprise.

It floated, on a high, decaying trajectory, just over the heads of the back row of pikemen; then, like a wounded bird, it lost its momentum and pitched in the dust, a yard or so from a colour sergeant, who had his back to it and didn't see. Someone must've told him; he turned round and stared at it, then took a long stride and picked it up. As he straightened his back, another (it flew tired, as though it had just crossed an ocean) dropped in two feet to his right; he looked round at it, frowning, as though someone was playing a joke on him, and so didn't notice the third arrow until it pecked him in the chest. His mail shirt stopped it, of course, but he jumped a foot in the air; someone laughed, but not for very long. Then it started to rain.

They came in on a steep angle, like those short, frantic showers that arrive out of a blue sky. Instinctively, the men in the middle of the square looked round for cover, but there wasn't any. Someone gave the order to kneel; it was standard procedure for pikemen under fire in the open, designed to reduce the size of the target, but against arrows dropping in practically from overhead it had no real effect. They were weary arrows, with no real spite left in them; they pattered off helmets and armoured backs and shoulders, stinging as they pecked but making no more than an irritating dent in sixteen-gauge plate. The pikemen crouched forward as they knelt, tucking their chins down on their chests, hiding their hands under their armpits, just like men caught out in the rain. From time to time an arrow might skip or skid as it bounced, and fly off unpredictably, grazing a knee or slapping a face with its shaft, but there was no genuine chill of danger; just the misery of getting drenched and having to huddle.

Nobody spoke, so the only sound was the tapping, pinging, pecking, like a workshop full of silversmiths. It couldn't last long, at any rate.

It didn't. The shower stopped as suddenly as it began, and men stood up, wincing at cramps, pins and needles from crouching awkwardly, and all started talking at once. The officers were yelling to make themselves heard; men were scooping up arrows, to look at them, maybe secure one as a souvenir.

"Archers," Fly said. "But they haven't got an army."

"Horse archers," Nuctos replied. "Which is impossible. Nobody's used them in civilised warfare for two hundred years."

Aidi stood up; his legs were white with dust, and he looked like a clown. "If that's the worst they can do," he said, "I don't see there's anything to worry about. They'll have to come a lot closer than that to do us any harm."

And they did. An hour later they were back, and the arrows came in on a steeper line, and with a livelier bite. They still weren't hitting hard enough to penetrate helmets or mail, but this time they punched and slapped instead of pecking and kissing; enough to force the air out of a man's lungs or slap his brain against the inside of his skull. They huddled and made themselves small, like someone being beaten up by a mob; men were screaming, or in tears. The noise was far louder this time—blacksmiths, not tinkers—and it drowned out the orders the officers were still insisting on calling out, though nobody showed any inclination to move. Aidi was hit seven times, Muri five, Fly and Kudei four each, Teuche and Nuctos twice. About a dozen yards away, a pikeman in the back row suddenly jumped to his feet and started to run, in no particular direction. An arrow hit his kneecap and he stumbled and fell, rolled on the ground, hugging his knee and bawling like a calf penned away from its mother.

The second shower lasted two minutes, more or less, and when it stopped and it was safe to unclench and look up, the ground was stuck full of arrows, like a stubble field. Later, once the order had been given to move out and they'd left the site of the square (a strange plantation of red-and-yellow-flowered canes in an otherwise empty wilderness of dry dust; it reminded Teuche of something, but he didn't share with the others), Aidi did the multiplication: six hundred archers, shooting for two minutes, nearly five thousand arrows.

"Which means," Nuctos pointed out, "they can't keep it up indefinitely. Say they each started out with fifty rounds. They've each used twelve, so—"

He broke off. Not as comforting as he'd intended it to be.

They marched quickly, as if there was some safe place to go; but they hadn't gone more than five hundred yards when the dust cloud appeared again, and the general ordered halt and form square. This time it was no more than a minute and a half, and instead of lobbing their arrows high, the horsemen closed the range and concentrated on the front ranks. It was an experiment, suggesting an enemy with a methodical approach. He learned from it that too many arrows weren't making it through the forest of levelled pikes, and when he attacked again, half an hour later, the archers went back to shooting high. By now, they'd found the optimum range for pitching down into the inside of the square, where the canopy of pikes offered no shelter. This time the arrows got through, hitting hard enough to puncture a helmet or split the links of mail and just about draw blood. The punch was harder, enough to knock a man down; the point of the arrow sticking through a helmet, or the sharp edges of the cut metal, gouged a furrow with every movement, and the hooked barbs of the arrowheads made it impossible to get them out. Even so, nobody who'd been hit took his helmet off, though some snapped off the shafts; most didn't, and quite comical they looked, as though they had twigs growing out of their heads (but each time an arrow shaft snagged on something—a neighbour's back, the victim's own shoulder—it moved the head, which cut another furrow). It wasn't long before somebody noticed how rusty the heads of the arrows lying on the ground were; just one more thing to be depressed about.

The attack seemed to go on for a very long time. When eventually it stopped, the general, who'd noticed that the enemy was concentrating his efforts on one section of the square, tried to move his men about, so the same ones wouldn't come under fire the next time. This manoeuvre didn't go as smoothly as it might have done, and the men were still bustling and shuffling around when the arrows started falling again. There was a general rush for places, which meant a dozen or so men were still standing, their arms and legs exposed. Three of them were hit, right in the middle of the square where everyone could see. Meanwhile, news had filtered through from the front ranks that four more dust clouds were on their way.

That must have prompted the general to do something. He ordered the square to advance, a complicated business at the best of times, requiring a quarter of the men to turn their backs on the enemy. The invitation was gratefully accepted. With no hedge of pikes to obstruct them, the horsemen crowded in, shooting from as close as ten yards. The back rank melted like ice, leaving a mess of bodies behind. Immediately the general ordered a halt. The archers kept on shooting as the pikemen struggled to turn; as soon as the pike-hedge came down, they drew back and resumed their patient, practised lobbing. The square crouched, aware that it had been outsmarted.

This time, the arrows didn't stop; the five cavalry units were taking turns to advance, loose six shots and retire, and they didn't seem to be running short of arrows. Aidi did his sums once again: at most, they'd lost twenty to thirty-five men, no big deal, nearly all of them the victims of the general's error of judgement in trying to march the square. While they were crouched under the shelter of the pikes, they were mostly safe...

"Which is the beauty of it," Nuctos muttered, in the tiny reprieve as two units changed shift. "We daren't move, we stay here, sooner or later we'll parch, starve or cook to death." He had an arrowhead lodged in his mail shirt just below his left collar bone. The barbs on one side had got under the links, and he was gingerly trying to work it free. "Or we rush them, and they shoot us dead. Either way..." He shrugged, then winced as the arrowhead cut him. "I'm not usually in favour of running away in the middle of an engagement, but in this case I'm prepared to keep an open mind."

"Fine," Aidi said. "And how exactly do you propose—?" But then the arrows started pitching again, and the noise drowned him out.

This time, they must have managed the shift change rather more smoothly, since there was no break to speak of between the two-minute barrages. The next change wasn't so smooth. The arrows stopped coming, and that was enough for one wall of the square. They jumped up, knocking over and trampling the men who weren't quick enough getting off the ground, and streamed out in a ragged wave, while the officers yelled at them.

"Now," Nuctos said. "Come on."

As they stood up, the horsemen wheeled in, and for the first time A Company saw the enemy. They were nothing much, by any standard: small men on ponies, many of them old men or boys, very few of them armoured, most just wearing their one tired, everyday coat over a homespun shirt and trousers. They looked like farmers riding to market, except that they were drawing their short curved bows and loosing, horribly fluent, letting the weight of the bow snatch the string off their fingers as soon as the nock touched the lobes of their ears; if they were aiming, it was just a glance, casual and expert, the way country people do any familiar task. The front rank of fugitives collapsed like an undermined wall, the second rank swept over them and fell on top of them; and Nuctos, judging the moment, shouted, "Go!"

He'd chosen well: a gap between two enemy surges. Six men running off to one side weren't worth bothering with, when there was a gaping hole in the square to be mined and exploited. They put their heads down and sprinted, glimpsing the legs of the horses sweeping past them, going the other way; and then nothing, just the flat plain and the white dust. They ran until the hammering and the yells had faded into an indistinct jumble of noise; then they stopped and fell over, and after some time, turned back to see what was happening.

They'd come eight hundred yards or so, and there were no horsemen to be seen, just the collapsing square, an unidentifiable shape made up of small movements too distant to mean anything, shrouded in a white veil of dust. They couldn't have stirred if they'd wanted to; their lungs were raw with effort and their legs didn't seem to be working. So instead they took the roll, and counted five.

For a long time, nobody said anything. Then Teuche said, "It looks as if Nuctos—"

"Shut up, Teuche," Aidi said.

They looked back, trying to see a body between the square and where they lay, but the dust was too thick. So they watched, though it was virtually impossible to make out what was happening, until the horsemen pulled out and rode away, taking the dust cloud with them.

"Do you think...?" Muri said.

Teuche stood up, straightening his back with an effort, like a man who's been hauling timber all day. "We can't stay here," he said. "And we can't go back and join the others. If we do..." He didn't need to finish the sentence. The enemy had won; they could all see that. Whether the horsemen came back and finished them off, or whether they left them to huddle in their wrecked square until the sun killed them, they were dead already.

"We head for the mountain," Teuche said. "There's water there, if I remember the map right."

None of the others spoke. He reached down, grabbed Aidi's arm and pulled him to his feet.

"What about food?" Fly asked.

"Don't ask me," Teuche replied. "We'll pool what we've got left, and try and make it last. When that's gone..." Big shrug. "If you ask me, we're probably just as dead as those poor buggers over there. Still, I suppose we ought to make an effort."

Fly stood up, then Kudei. Muri said, "Teuche, what about Nuctos? Shouldn't we...?"

"No," Teuche said (a harsh voice, like salt in a cut). "Try and keep up, Muri, or we'll leave you behind."

The good luck came later.

Instead of stopping when the sun set, they kept going, trusting their sense of direction in the pitch dark; and after four hours of blind trudging, they saw a light. It was the orange glow of a single small fire. Without discussion or debate, they headed for it.

Several hundred yards before they reached it, they heard voices. That made them slow down, and they took pains to walk quietly, so they could listen. At two hundred yards, more or less, they could make out some of the words but they couldn't understand them. Foreigners. The enemy.

They knew what to do. Really, it was no different than going after rabbits with the long net. They walked in, nice and slow and easy, until they were close enough to count seven men sitting round a fire. Two of them were playing chequers, three were passing a big tin cup round, one was mending a bridle on his knee and the last one was asleep. Behind them, A Company could just make out the silhouettes of horses. They looked hard for a sentry, but couldn't see one. They closed to fifty yards before making the final dash.

Wasted effort. Apart from their bows, unstrung and cased against the dew, the horsemen had no weapons to speak of, didn't look as though they'd have known how to use them if they'd had them. Aidi killed the chequers players with two quick, easy slices. One of the drinkers managed to run about ten yards before Fly jumped on his back and cut his throat. The others died where they sat, giving no indication that they realised what was happening to them.

"Get the horses," Teuche said.

Nine horses; two over, to carry the supplies. They recognised the flour sacks and the water skins, which solved the mystery of what had become of the supply wagons. They left the fire to burn itself out.

"Change of plan," Teuche said quietly, as they tacked up the horses. "Back the way we came."

Daylight showed them where they were. Somehow they'd managed to turn right round; a mile or so away to the east, they could see the shape of the square, though whether the men forming it were alive or dead they had no way of telling. There was no sign of the enemy, no dust clouds. Presumably their seven unwilling benefactors had been scouts.

Later, when they'd been back at Tenevris for a week, they heard the news. The grand army had been completely wiped out, somewhere in the open plain. If there were any other survivors, they hadn't been heard from. Apparently there was an enemy of some kind out there; scouting parties had found the wreckage of the supply train, abandoned wagons and the bodies of men who'd died by violence. That, however, was all anybody knew. It was just as well, they were told, that they'd got separated from the main army so early in the march, and had had the wit to turn round and come back to base instead of ploughing on, or otherwise they'd all be dead too. Teuche agreed that it was a sobering thought.

"Of course," they told him, "it means the war's more or less over. We can't recover from this. We'd hoped to press on to Coile, do to them what the bastards did to us. But now…"

(Teuche thought: they were farmers, protecting their land. Only, they had the good sense to leave the dead bodies out in the desert, rather than ruin good pasture.)

"It's you we feel sorry for," they said. "Everything you fought for, all the men who died, and what's there to show for it? Basically, we're right back where we started."

He thought about that. "I'm not," he said.

"You're going home," they told him. "That's good news, isn't it?"

He assumed it was a question that didn't need to be answered. "How soon?"

"Soon," they replied.

"I'm in no hurry." He stood up to go, then hesitated. "Do we know what happened?"

"Not really," they admitted. "Hell, we didn't even know they had an army. At the moment we're working on the assumption that somebody betrayed us, but we've got nothing to go on."

Teuche nodded. "It's academic, though, isn't it? I mean, presumably the traitor died along with everybody else."

Pause. "It'd be convenient to assume so," they said. "We can't see what good it'd do, looking into it too closely. Bad for morale back home, and that's rocky enough as it is."

Soon, they'd told him; a vague expression, meaning anything from now to a few years. When Teuche reported back to the rest of A Company, they seemed unusually subdued, and didn't press him for a more precise definition. "It's a pity we're not going to Coile, though," Aidi said. "I was looking forward to it. Apparently they've got the most amazing library."

"Just as well, then," Teuche said. "We'd probably have burned it down."

Muri said: "Do they know what happened yet?"

"No," Teuche said. "They think it may have been treason, but—"

"Highly unlikely," said one of them. "Who'd do a thing like that?"

ELEVEN

Menin Aeide had wanted to help the men, but they sent her to gather food instead. You'll be far more use, they told her. You know about all that stuff.

So she went to the woods with a basket and picked wild garlic. It was just coming into flower, and the smell of the crushed stems on her fingers was overwhelming. When her basket was full, she sat down beside one of the little brooks that ran down from the outcrops in the clearing, washed her hands and waited for a while.

She saw him coming, long before he noticed her. "Hello," he said; he had a deer on his shoulder, freshly dressed out, and his sleeve was dark and damp with its blood. "You're Captain Achaiois' wife, aren't you?"

"That's right," she said. "I don't know your name."

"Terpsi," he replied. "Terpsi Cerauno."

"Why aren't you helping with the ship?"

He smiled. He had a nice smile. It'd been the first thing about him she'd noticed. "I'm a lousy carpenter," he replied. "Neither use nor ornament, as my gran used to say. But I'm a fair shot, and I like it in the woods." He grinned. "That's why I like it here," he said. "Never allowed to go hunting back home; didn't even have my own bow."

He hesitated, then sat down on a log, six feet away from her. "Do you like it here?"

She nodded. "Better than home," she said.

"How's married life?"

"Fine," she said, looking away.

"I mean to stay on," Terpsi said. "Especially now there's the gold. I plan to make my pile, go home, marry the girl next door and come back and live here for good."

She smiled awkwardly at him. "What's her name?"

"Theano," he replied straight away. "She said she'd wait for me, and I believe her."

"That's nice," she said, watching a drop of blood swelling out of the cloth at his elbow. "Are you going on the boat, when it's ready?"

He laughed. "Catch me going on a boat if I don't have to," he said. "I was sick as a dog all the way here. Which is crazy, really. My dad and two of my brothers are fishermen."

"I hate sailing," Menin said. "I'd rather stay here for ever than get on a ship again."

He nodded, and they were both quiet for a while. Then he said, "Mushrooms?"

"What? Oh, I see. No, wild garlic."

"That's the smelly stuff with the white flowers, right?" He frowned. "Can you eat that?"

"Oh yes. Raw in a salad, or cooked like spinach."

He didn't look keen. "I was hoping it was mushrooms," he said. "Venison stew with mushrooms; can't beat it."

She smiled. "I like that, too," she said. "All right, I'll see what I can find. There's not a lot about at the moment, but..."

"Thanks." He stood up. "I'd better get back," he said. "I'm going to dump this one, then I thought I might try my luck out the far end. There's a track they've been using lately; my guess is they're going back that way in the middle of the day, to lie up in the holly grove."

She nodded. "Good luck, then," she said.

After he'd gone, she sat still for a while, looking down at her hands. Then she stood up and followed the path he'd taken.

*   *   *

"Someone ought to make a speech," Aidi said.

"Go ahead," Kunessin replied.

Aidi scowled. "I didn't mean me," he said. "I just thought…"

He sidestepped to let Muri get past him. "Is that the last of it?" he asked.

"One more load," Muri called back over his shoulder, "and then we're ready."

Muri scrambled up the steeply angled gangplank, dumped the sack of oats on the deck and scampered back down again. "Sure you don't want to come along?" he asked.

Aidi shuddered. "Absolutely sure," he said. "You wouldn't get me in that thing for cash money."

"You helped build it."

"That's why."

Kunessin laughed. "Is that the last sack of oats?" he asked.

Muri shook his head. "There's two more left in the store."

"Let's hope we won't need them," Kunessin said.

Aidi yawned. "We'll be all right," he said. "We've got the last of the salt beef, and I found out one of the servants is pretty handy with a bow and arrow. I sent him off to the woods this morning, and he's had one deer already."

"Tell him to leave a few for me when I get back," Muri called out, as he darted off to the sheds.

Kunessin got up and went on board the sloop for a last look round. Aidi left him and walked across the yard. On his way, he met Menin, Muri's wife.

"Can I carry that for you?" he said.

She shook her head. "It's not heavy," she said. "Just leaves."

He frowned. "What is that stuff?"

"Wild garlic."

"Ah." Pointedly, he didn't say anything about the smell. "Salad," he said.

"Or you can cook it."

All sorts of things you can cook, but it doesn't mean to say they're edible; not by any civilised criteria. "Splendid," Aidi said. "Well, mustn't keep you."

He went back to the house; nobody about, as he'd expected. He made sure, then, using the point of his sword and the back of a big iron spoon, he levered up one of the floorboards. As he'd hoped, there was quite a lot of room underneath; he'd studied the house carefully from the outside, and figured there ought to be at least eighteen inches. In the event, more like two feet.

He left the board up while he darted out to the lean-to, where he'd previously hidden a couple of sacks behind a row of barrels. He picked them up, one in each hand; the weight made him stagger, but he really didn't want to make two trips. He trotted back to the house, half carrying, half dragging the sacks. They clanked every time they touched the ground.

He had to stop for a minute and rest after that; his elbows hurt, and he'd felt a warning twinge in his back. Then he opened the first sack and began unloading its contents into the gap under the floorboards. He ended up having to lift the neighbouring board, to make a hole big enough to get some of the stuff through. The job took him a while, and he was slightly concerned that someone might come in and see him, but he'd chosen his time well; everybody would be down at the jetty, fussing over the launching of the sloop. On that assumption, he risked the noise, took off his boot and used the heel to hammer the boards back into place. No sign of what he'd done; just to be on the safe side, he pulled the table across so one foot was resting on the newly replaced boards. He stared hard at the place, to make sure he'd remember where to find it again, then went outside, just in time to see the sloop pull away from the jetty.

"You missed it," Kunessin said.

Aidi shrugged. "Well," he said, "since there wasn't going to be a speech, I couldn't be bothered."

Kunessin pulled a face and left him, heading back to the house. He'd asked Aechmaloten to meet him there, while the rest of the indentured men were busy with other things. Sure enough, Aechmaloten was waiting for him, a desperately worried look on his face.

"Thanks for finding the time to see me," Kunessin said (because nothing confuses a scared man more than politeness and old-world courtesy). "Please, do sit down. Make yourself at home."

Aechmaloten balanced awkwardly on the edge of the long table. "What—?" he began, but Kunessin cut him off.

"Now we've got that out of the way," he said, "we can get on with the job in hand. When can you start?"

Polite but brisk, a gentleman terrier. Aechmaloten's mind must have gone blank; he stammered a bit, then mumbled, "Any time you like, really. We don't need—"

"Fine," Kunessin said. "Right now?"

Aechmaloten's big goat eyes widened. "Sure," he said. "I mean, yes, right away. All we need's a tin plate."

Kunessin smiled. He'd put one on the bench earlier. Now, as he produced it and held it up, it must've seemed like he'd magicked it out of thin air. "This do?"

"That's fine," Aechmaloten said. "Oh, and a shovel. We'll need a shovel."

"I've got one outside ready," Kunessin said. "That's everything? You're sure?"

Aechmaloten squinted at him as though it was a trick question, which of course it was. "I think so," he said cautiously. "Oh, and a bag or something. A sock, even. For the dust. If we get any."

Kunessin nodded, and took a sock from his pocket. "Right," he said. "Off we go, then."

It had clouded over, and a chilly wind was blowing. Kunessin pulled his collar tight round his neck. "Aren't you going to wear a coat?" he asked.

Aechmaloten shook his head. "We'll soon warm up," he said.

Nobody about in the yard. They picked up two shovels on their way through, left the yard and followed the river as it wriggled away over the flat. On the way, Kunessin tried to make conversation, but it was a bit like a god trying to chat to a sacrifice chained to an altar; which was, after all, the effect he'd been working for. He gave up, and followed in silence as Aechmaloten led the way, walking faster than he'd expected. By now, of course, he knew every bit of the plain almost as well as he'd known the pastures back home: the dips and rises, the wet spots and the rocky patches, the lone trees and the withy thickets, the place where an old willow had split apart under its own weight, and dense stands of saplings had grown vertically from the fallen branches. Aechmaloten was looking for something, but Kunessin couldn't figure out what it was; and when they stopped, and Aechmaloten nodded and said, "We'll try it here," he couldn't see anything different. So he asked: why here?

"Well," Aechmaloten said, and launched into a rapid, barely comprehensible lecture about seams, layers, different kinds of rock and clay and how to recognise them. "That's a good place to try," he said, pointing to a long bar of silt and gravel just breaking the surface in the middle of the stream. "Or over there, see that large rock lodged in the side of the bank, where it's formed that deep pool? Anywhere the silt's likely to get trapped. Even an old tree root sticking out into the water can be worth a try. Here's good, because we're just downstream from where the rill comes down off the slope; means that when it rains there's a good head of water coming down there. You need the pressure to grind the gold out of the seam. Nearer you can get to the outlet the better, of course."

"I see," Kunessin said, though he was exaggerating. "So, what now?"

"Take this." He gave Kunessin the plate to hold, then plunged into the stream. "Come on," he called back (not so nervous now, Kunessin thought), and Kunessin followed him, wincing as the cold water filled his boots; apparently, real gold-panners didn't care about getting their footwear saturated. He understood why as his soles crunched on the gravel bed; not nice to stand on in bare feet for hours at a time.

"Now, then." Aechmaloten stooped, dug a spit of silt and gravel out of the side of the bar. "Of course, you can simply use the rim of the plate. Easier that way if there's just one of you, but if there's two, this way means less stooping." He spooned silt into the plate, then propped the shovel up against his leg, took the plate from Kunessin's hands and peered into it, the tip of his nose practically touching the silt. "Can't see anything," he said, "but that doesn't mean much. Got to wash it first."

He stooped and pressed the plate down through the surface of the stream, just enough to flood it; then he began wobbling it from side to side, nudging water and silt over the rim. "Gold's so heavy," he said breathlessly, his lungs cramped by crouching. "It sinks right down to the bottom and stays there. Means you can wash off the shit, all the light stuff, and the gold's still there, so long as you're careful. Really, there's nothing to it," he added, his hands moving the plate in a series of twists, thrusts, nudges and jerks, flicking off waste from the edge of the silt deposit while stirring the middle. "It's all in the wrists and the elbows. Once you've got that, it's a piece of piss."

You could, of course, say the same thing about playing the harp, or surgery. "You've done this before," Kunessin said.

Aechmaloten nodded, his eyes still fixed on the plate. "There was a strike at Forches when I was a kid," he said. "What, thirty years ago. Me and my dad went, but we came in just on the tail end, when it was nearly all gone. Ended up spending out more than we brought back; we'd sold the farm to pay for the stake, see, and of course, everything costs so much where there's a strike; food and lodgings — the locals are the ones who make all the money. We came back poor, but I did learn how to pan. It's a mug's game, though, unless you're in right at the start."

He'd got rid of nearly all the silt; just a few spoonfuls left, swilling round in the bottom of the plate as he twisted and turned it. "There," he said, and his voice was high and a little shaky. "Come here, you can see it. There."

It was like a little sky, trapped in the bottom of the plate: black silt, and a few bright twinkles, like yellow stars. "Is that ...?"

"That's it," Aechmaloten said, "that's the good stuff all right."

Kunessin thought: there's not a lot in there, for all that work. Enough to plate the head of a small pin, if that. "Is that good?" he said. "I mean, is it promising?"

Aechmaloten laughed. "Tell you what," he said. "If Dad and me'd ever seen this much colour back in the old days, I wouldn't be here, I'd be home on my country estate, drinking wine and eating grapes." Another precise flick, and a fingernail-sized dollop of mud flew off the rim. "Best I've ever seen, and that's the truth."

It all seemed to take a very long time, and it made Kunessin feel tired just watching. In the end, though, all the silt was gone, and in the bottom of the plate lay a sprinkle of yellow grit, like shiny dust. "The sock," Aechmaloten said, and Kunessin only just managed to keep himself from laughing.

"Won't it get trapped in the weave?" he asked.

"Burn it out, when we're done." Aechmaloten was completely pre-occupied, hardly acknowledging his presence. He tapped the rim of the plate with his fingernail until the dust hopped across and over the rim into the sock. "There you are, then," he said, straightening up and beaming like an idiot. "You got the idea now?"

"More or less," Kunessin lied. "You'd better show me again."

Aechmaloten was delighted to oblige; he was almost frantic with energy now, impatient, obsessed. As soon as the plate was filled with silt, he started twisting, tilting and shaking it, dribbling off tears of dark brown water. "Really," he said, "you need a pan with grooves in it, so you can catch the dust easier." He didn't seem to be having much trouble without a grooved pan, and his hands never stopped moving until all the silt was gone, and a few more specks of dust shone against the grey tin.

"Just once more," Kunessin said, two or three times. His feet were frozen numb in the cold water, and his back hurt from standing still.

"Your turn," Aechmaloten said mournfully, handing him the plate as though they were in the desert and he was giving up the last mouthful of water. "I'll shovel, you just do the sifting."

Five minutes later, Kunessin's wrists and forearms ached from the unrelenting effort, and he was holding a perfectly clean, newly washed plate. Aechmaloten was frowning at him, as though he'd just discovered an entirely new species. "You're too rough with it," he explained, though Kunessin couldn't see how that could possibly be. "You're not digging a fucking ditch. Here, let me show you again."

And again, and again. Kunessin was in no hurry. But eventually he got the plate back; and this time, just as he thought his hands must be about to shake loose and fall off his wrists, he ended up with a half-spoonful of sparkly black sludge. "Right," Aechmaloten said. "Now you want to take it a bit steady."

Kunessin nodded. He'd been moving the dish with just his

fingertips for as long as he could remember. "A bit steady," he repeated, and Aechmaloten confirmed that that was the way to do it.

Kunessin took on a little water, which he swirled round the coast of the sludge island, teasing and smearing the silt across towards the rim, then tricking, betraying it over the edge. The island grew a golden heart—the grains seemed to be getting bigger the more he stared at them—while its black beaches were gradually eroded away by the action of his tiny artificial tides. He smiled. An island of gold, he thought; who could possibly ask for more? Present company excepted.

"There," Aechmaloten said, "I knew you'd get the hang of it." He was nervous, restless; he wanted to snatch the pan back and carry on working for himself. Strange, Kunessin thought. Here's a man, apparently quite rational and sensible, who wants to throw away the soil to get the gold; and here I am, by definition supremely sensible and rational, having done the exact opposite. He considered that proposition; it was elegant, if a bit forced, but too shallow for anything except a rhetoric tutorial, and he hadn't had to endure one of those for twenty years.

He noticed he'd got rid of the last of the dirt. "There," he said, "how's that?"

"Not bad," Aechmaloten said, and as he spoke he reached for the plate. Kunessin moved it just out of his reach. "I think you may have lost a bit at the end there. Be a bit gentler."

Any gentler and I'd be dead, Kunessin thought. "Understood," he said, and he let Aechmaloten take the plate. "I'm not sure I'm cut out for this," he said. "Doubt I'd have the patience."

Aechmaloten was bending over the shovel, stabbing it into the silt like a soldier killing a prisoner. "It's hard slog," he said, "long, hard slog." He straightened up. "If the stuff's there, it's worth it. If it isn't, forget it. Simple as that."

Kunessin nodded. "And how do you know beforehand?"

Aechmaloten was loading the pan. "You don't," he said.

He watched for two more platefuls, and then he'd had enough. "I'll be getting back now," he said, and he doubted Aechmaloten was listening, or even remembered he was there. "Thanks for the lesson."

He left him shuffling his plate, lips practically touching the rim, and walked back along the river. He kept telling himself: it hasn't all gone wrong yet; there's a long way to go before there'll be dead bodies lying in the grass. That wasn't good enough, of course. He realised he still had the sock: stupid, limp bit of cloth with some dust lodged in the toe. He threw it in the river, and watched it float away downstream, towards the sea.

Aidi and Alces had a lesson the next day. They came back bright with enthusiasm. It was easy, they said, a child of six could do it. Even the servants could do it (Aidi's contribution to the narrative). Six months and they'd have a fortune, and then—

"Excuse me," Kunessin said. "I've got to go and feed the stock."

Not that that took very long; not many animals left, just the draught horses, very little food left to give them. The indentured man, Cerauno, was more or less feeding them all with the venison he brought home; him and Menin, with her daily baskets of forage. They were getting stranger; wild garlic had been bad enough, even when boiled into a sort of green glue so you couldn't immediately figure out what you were eating. The last couple of days, she'd come back with a load of strange, thin brown roots, which strained the jaw and tasted like earth, and a supply of dense, bendy fungus she'd chipped off the trunks of rotten trees. It'll be worms next, Alces had said, meaning it as a joke. "Actually—" Menin started to reply, but luckily Dorun interrupted her, asking her to pass the salt.

All the indentured men who hadn't gone in the sloop, apart from Cerauno the hunter, spent all day in the river. Aidi and Alces joined them, but later; they tended to wait for daylight, by which time the indentured men had already been panning for an hour by lanternlight. It was, of course, time to sow the spring wheat and barley, except that they'd eaten the seedcorn some time ago. So Kunessin started building a fence. The idea was to split the flat meadow directly behind the settlement into two pastures, one to graze and one to rest. He paced out the distance: six hundred yards. One post every five yards; a hundred and twenty six-foot three-inch posts, with straining spurs every twenty-one yards;

two hundred and forty nine-foot half-round three-inch rails. Just cutting and trimming the timber would take two months, and then there'd be carting it down off the hill, before he could even start ramming in posts and nailing on rails. On the other hand, he had nothing better to do.

"I can't see the point," Dorun said to him, as he staggered home one evening and collapsed into a chair in front of the damp, smouldering fire. "By the time the ship gets here, we'll be able to afford to send back to Faralia for all the lumber you could possibly want, all sawn and planed ready."

"I don't like sitting around idle."

She frowned at him. "Fine," she said. "But at the rate you're going, you won't have the timber cut, let alone hauled, by the time the ship could be back here with sawn wood. You'll do yourself an injury, charging away at it like that, and it's just a waste of effort."

Chaere had found a bit of roof slate and a nail, and she was crossing off the days till the sloop got back. All she could think about, she told anybody who'd listen, was food; proper food, from a shop, or a chandler at the very least, and tea (she had dreams about tea, she said) instead of dreary, horrible water that always tasted of mud these days. She was right about that, at least. The river ran dirty all day (the indentured men had wanted to drain all their drinking water through a muslin sheet, just in case a few flecks of gold showed up).

Clea and Enyo fell out about something. Nobody knew what it was, and nobody dared ask; but Chaere and Dorun were on Enyo's side, so Clea refused to do any work if it meant being in the same building as any of them. Menin tended to leave for the woods at daybreak and not come back till dusk. One evening she returned with a basket full of snails, and got very upset when nobody was prepared to eat them. Cerauno the hunter said that all the deer had left the lower woods (that, Aidi commented, or he'd killed them all), which meant he had to go right up the mountain, and then half a mile east, because Kunessin was making so much noise cutting wood that all the mountain deer had shifted to the south side. The sloop was a day late, then two days; then it was a whole week late, and people stopped talking about it.

Each evening, they put that day's gold into a jar, which stood in the corner of the one long room of the main house. It had originally been a storage jar, made to hold flour; it was long and thin, designed to be half buried in the ground. To keep up morale while they were waiting for the sloop, and because he enjoyed being watched, Aidi Proiapsen came up with a little ritual, which quickly caught on and proved extremely popular with the indentured men. First came the ceremony of the weighing, which Aidi performed using a set of home-made scales. The day's weight was chalked on the side of the jar, read out and contrasted (usually favourably) with the previous day's take; then Kunessin would do the arithmetic and announce the grand total, followed by the value of one ordinary share, which allowed everybody to work out how much richer he'd become since the previous day. Finally, Aidi would stand on tiptoe, lift off the stopper, pour in the dust, take a candle and a stick of wax from whoever was acolyte of the day, and seal the stopper in place, using the tails side of his lucky six-thaler piece as a seal matrix. Since his was the only six-thaler in the settlement, it was recognised as a guarantee of good faith, and when it wasn't being used for this purpose, it hung round Aidi's neck on a fine steel chain.

(Where the idea came from, nobody knew; but quite soon it was generally accepted by both the women and the indentured men that once the jar was full, they'd wind up the company, pay off the shares and go home. Aidi maintained that it had been Kunessin's idea, part of the original deal with the workforce. Kunessin denied all knowledge of it. Chaere claimed she'd thought of it and suggested it to Aidi, who put it to the other four, who ratified it. Everybody else knew she'd made that up, but nobody could be bothered to contradict her.)

One day—the sloop was two weeks late—Aidi noticed the six-thaler was missing. There was an immediate commotion. Aidi searched his bed space and his dirty laundry; everybody joined in, turning the main house upside down. A search party retraced his movements for the whole of the previous day, spending the entire morning and losing, at a conservative estimate, seventy-five thalers' worth of production. Of the coin there was no trace, and the consensus was that the chain must have broken while he was working in the river, and the coin had probably been trodden deep into the silt, where it would never be found.

After the search had been abandoned and work was resumed, the only topic of conversation, in the river and back at the house, was the loss of the company seal. Without it, they couldn't seal the jar, which meant the treasury was unprotected and anybody could just stroll in and rob them all. Aidi, who was feeling guilty about being careless, pointed out that this was garbage; before he'd come up with his stupid end-of-day ceremony, none of them had given a second thought to safeguarding the gold. He'd only included the sealing as a nice, showy end to the proceedings, and now he was starting to wish he hadn't bothered. Furthermore, he pointed out, anyone with a little dexterity and a wooden toothpick could fiddle the impression of a copper ten-turner bit to look just like a six-thaler, so it had been a pretty worthless safeguard in any case.

This was news to the indentured men, some of whom instinctively patted their pockets for loose change, and there was a thoughtful silence before everybody started talking at once. In that case, they said, from now on there'd have to be an armed guard posted next to the jar at all times; they'd have to have a rota. The proposal divided the shareholders into two nearly equal factions: those who held that posting just one guard was like leaving the fox to guard the chicken run, and that there had to be a minimum of two sentries at all times; and those who pointed out that guard duty would mean a reduction in the labour force, and therefore a significant fall in production. At some stage, someone suggested that Kunessin should be the guard. After all, he didn't work the river; in fact it was a mystery what he did all day, so why shouldn't he do something useful; and furthermore, if you couldn't trust the general, who could you trust? For some reason Aidi got quite annoyed at that. He'd be interested, he said, to see which of them had the guts to go and tell the hero of Eleonto, the most devastating fighting man on either side of the war, that he was a good-for-nothing layabout. He also undertook to bury the remains once the interview was concluded, assuming enough could be scraped together to be worth burying. They were, he went on, the saddest collection of idiots he'd ever had the bad luck to associate with, and if he heard one more word about guards or seals, someone was going to get a hard smack. That abruptly ended the debate, and nobody said a word for the rest of the day. There was no ceremony that evening. Aidi took charge of the day's take and slept with it under his pillow. The evening meal—watery venison stew bulked out with Menin's indigestible wood fungus—was a tense, muted affair, and the mood wasn't improved when Clea was suddenly and spectacularly sick all over the leftovers, which were to have been the next morning's breakfast. As soon as she was able to speak, Clea launched into a furious attack on Menin, blaming her for picking poisonous mushrooms, carelessly or on purpose. Menin burst into tears and ran outside, Clea had another bout of vomiting (Alces, who'd gone up to her to calm her down, just managed to get out of the way in time; Aidi reckoned it was the neatest bit of footwork he'd seen since the war). Kunessin jumped to his feet and shouted for quiet; he got it, along with the stares of everybody in the room. He sat down again in dead silence, while Dorun picked up the serving dish and put it outside. Clea went and sat in a corner on her own, clutching her stomach and scowling at the whole room. Menin didn't come back for a long time, but nobody suggested going to look for her.

The next day, Aidi found his six-thaler piece. It was in the left toe of his spare pair of boots. He said several times that he'd looked there twice, but nobody seemed interested. The ceremony went ahead as usual that evening, though nobody cheered when the day's weight was announced, or when Kunessin read out the grand total. Dinner was venison stew without the wood fungus; very little of it and mostly water. All in all, it was probably just as well that nobody seemed to have much of an appetite.

The following day, just before noon, the sloop came back. It crept in slowly, listing heavily to one side, and Kunessin, watching from the jetty, saw that it was riding very low in the water. He ran to the river and called the men back to the settlement. They lined up on the jetty, waiting in silence as the sloop crawled towards them. There was practically no wind, and for a long time they couldn't see how many men were on board, let alone recognise faces. Aidi offered to run across to the house and fetch the women. No, Kunessin answered quietly, not just yet.

Right up to the last minute, when Kudei threw Aidi the rope, there was the chance that one of the indentured men — for the life of him, Kunessin couldn't recall his name — was lying down in the sloop's waist, out of sight. But the first words Kudei said to him were, "We lost Picron Oistun," and Kunessin caught himself thinking: that's right, Oistun, it was on the tip of my tongue.

"Lost?" he said.

Kudei nodded. "We ran into heavy squalls on the way home. Things haven't worked out too well, I'm afraid."

"As bad as that." Kunessin frowned. If Kudei had said it was a nightmare, a total fucking disaster, that would have meant seasickness, some tiresome problem with the rigging, squabbling among the crew. "Things haven't worked out too well" was about as bad as it could get.

"Where's Muri?" he asked.

"He'll be all right," Kudei replied. "Really, we should get him to the house as quickly as possible. Aidi'll know what to do."

Muri was sitting in the waist of the sloop, his back to the mast. "I'm fine, really," he protested, but when he tried to get up, he failed dismally. It took three of the indentured men to carry him to the house.

"My own stupid fault," he explained. "Fell out of the rigging, landed on my back, took a bit of a bump."

Aidi leant over him, his face blank. "Can you move your legs?"

"Of course I can," Muri said.

"Two days ago he couldn't," Kudei said quietly. "Now he's got a bit of feeling back in his toes."

"More than a bit," Muri protested. "Mostly itching; it's driving me crazy."

Kudei sighed. "You know Muri," he said. "Discomfort isn't some-thing you hoard; it's for sharing with your friends."

Kunessin looked round. Menin wasn't there, of course; she was out in the woods with her basket. Muri didn't seem to have noticed her absence. "We'd better get the sloop unloaded," he said.

Kudei smiled. "That won't take very long," he replied.

He wasn't far wrong. Afterwards, Kunessin hustled the inden-tured men out of the house, and A Company held a staff meeting.

"The journey out wasn't so bad," Kudei said, "not till we ran into a bit of a squall, third day out, which shook us up and dumped us way off course, about a day's sail north-west. Which wouldn't have been the end of the world," he added, "except then we got becalmed, not a breath of wind for three days. Food all gone, water looking a bit sad; it was just as well the wind suddenly picked up in the middle of the night, ended up taking us straight there. By then, of course, we weren't exactly at our best; also, we'd had to dump quite a lot of the trade goods over the side during the blow-up. Truth is, we didn't manage to strike a particularly good deal with the chandlers, about a third less than we'd hoped for."

Aidi was scowling. Kunessin said, "Not your fault. If you had to dump the stuff..."

"We should have done better," Kudei said. "But anyway, we loaded what we'd got and patched up the sloop as best we could. The locals said we should be all right coming back, so we decided to take a chance and make a run for it. That was a week ago."

Alces nodded. "What happened?"

"Same again," Kudei replied. "Nasty storm second day out. That was when Oistun..." He frowned. "A big wave came up and sort of hooked him off the deck, all very quick, nothing we could do about it. Anyway, that left us short just when we needed every pair of hands, so Muri went charging up the rigging, slipped—"

"I was careless," Muri said.

"Luckily, the wind died down soon after that," Kudei went on. "Trouble was, it went to the other extreme. Stranded us for four days. We'd had the sense to lay in extra water, but we lost a full cask overboard during the storm. Also, ten barrels of flour smashed open and completely spoiled, some other stuff as well. Fact is...Well, you've seen for yourself. What with two storms and making a pig's ear of the trade, I reckon we've got about half of what we were banking on getting, if that. Oh, and you can forget all about the bacon and the salt beef, we lost all that. Flour, oats, beans, I think we salvaged one barrel of malt. Otherwise..."

Silence for a moment or so; then Kunessin said firmly, "It could have been worse. And anyway, we haven't done so badly while you've been away. In fact, I'd say we've proved we can pretty much fend for ourselves if we have to, so it's not nearly as critical as it might've been."

Aidi, who'd been frowning, said: "Exactly how much—?"

Kunessin cut him off. "We'll worry about that later. Aidi, what's the matter with Muri? You're the doctor."

Aidi shook his head. "If only," he said. "Patching up cuts is one thing. Anything I do'll probably just make it worse. Wait and see's all I can suggest, really."

"I'll be fine," Muri said loudly. "It's not like there's any bones broken."

"Tell him to stop being brave, Teuche, before I break his neck," Alces snapped. "Look, this could be serious. We ought to take him to the mainland, find a doctor."

Kudei snorted with laughter. "For crying out loud, Fly," he said. "We only just survived one trip, and you want us to go back? We'll be lucky if any of us makes it. Besides," he added, talking over Alces' objections and Muri's protestations of rude health, "I've been to that town, and I wouldn't trust one of their doctors to butcher a hog. No kidding, Teuche, that's a rough old place."

Kunessin turned to Aidi. "Well?" he said. "What do you think?"

"No," Aidi said firmly. "Too risky. We'll stay here and see what happens."

"Thank you," Muri said gravely. "If I'd had to go back on that bloody boat, I really would've been ill."

"All right," Kunessin said, shaking his head. "We'll give it three days. If you're no better, we'll take you to the mainland. By the sound of it, we need that long to get the sloop fixed up."

In the event, Muri was back on his feet within forty-eight hours, which was just as well. Nobody was prepared to waste gold-panning time on ship repairs. Even Terpsi Cerauno put away his bow and headed for the river, and Clea made quite a scene when Kunessin forbade her to join in. By the time Muri was up and about again (and the first thing he did was grab a tin plate and hobble off down the river-bank), the only man not working the strike was Kunessin himself. He was still going through the motions of cutting timber for his fence, but it was obvious his heart wasn't in it.

"Come with us," Alces urged him. "An extra pair of hands—"

"I'm not just a pair of hands," Kunessin snapped back angrily. "This is my island, in case you've forgotten. You want to spend all day up to your knees in mud, you carry on. I've got better things to do."

Next morning, though, he waited till everybody was gone, then took a tin plate and crossed the yard to Aidi's forge. It was dark inside, so he opened the shutters. Every surface was thick with dust—the floor, the bench, the face of the anvil—and the hearth was white with ashes, like snow on a meadow. He looked round until he found what he'd been looking for: a small swage block and a round-nosed punch.

An hour later, he closed the forge door carefully behind him and followed the well-worn path to the river.

Aidi was the first to see him; he was standing in mid-stream, brown water just over his knees, holding a pan full of sludge. His face was streaked with wet brown silt, and his clothes were sopping wet.

"Teuche," he said. "What brings you here?"

By way of answer, Kunessin handed him the plate. Aidi saw that five evenly spaced concentric grooves had been hammered into it; a neat job, he had to admit. "What's this in aid of?"

Kunessin grinned. "Progress," he said. "The idea is, when you shake the plate around, the heavy gold gets dislodged and falls into the groove. Then, when you sluice it off in the water, you don't have to worry about losing what you've just got out. Ought to speed things up, don't you think? Also, it should take most of the skill out of it."

Aidi was impressed, he could tell; that rather tight-lipped look. "Good idea," he said. "Smart but simple. Better try it and see if it works."

It worked. At the end of the day, Kunessin had sifted more gold dust than anybody else, and all the indentured men were crowding round him to get a closer look at the wonderful grooved pan, imploring him to tell them how he'd made it. Kunessin referred them all to Aidi, their resident craftsman, who'd be happy to make similar pans for all of them.

"I've missed you," she said.

Cerauno looked away. "I had to take my turn in the river," he said. "Otherwise there'd have been trouble."

She frowned. "You're excused, surely. Somebody's got to get the food."

He shook his head. "Not since the boat came back," he said.

"We still need fresh meat," she said. "That little bit of flour's not going to last long."

"That's not how they see it," he said irritably. "Anyway, I've been hitting the deer pretty hard; it's just common sense to rest it a few days. Otherwise they'll cross the valley and be long gone."

She gave him a mildly contemptuous smile. "We're on an island, remember?" she said. "It's not like they can get away."

He shivered impatiently. "Look, I know what I'm doing, all right?" he said. "I don't tell you how to pick mushrooms."

She was silent, hurt, offended. He took a deep breath and apologised. "It's not like I want to work in the river," he went on. "I'd far rather be out here. But I don't want them picking on me, saying I'm not pulling my weight."

"You don't have to excuse yourself to me," she said, looking away. "Doesn't matter to me what you do."

He winced at that, feeling both annoyed and guilty. "Well, I told them I'll be up the woods for the next three days, and they didn't give me any trouble over it, so . . ."

She smiled at him, which made him feel uncomfortable, so he asked: "How's your husband?"

"Oh, fine," she said quickly. "Comes home in the evenings wet through, happy as anything."

"He's a grafter, I'll give him that," Cerauno said. "None of them can keep up with him, not even the general."

"We don't have to talk about Muri," she said.

He felt threatened, and realised it was because she'd said the name; not Captain Achaiois, but Muri, as though Terpsi Cerauno and the captain knew each other as equals. He wasn't quite sure why this should bother him, but to be on the safe side he apologised again.

"You make it sound like he's something special," she said. "He's not. The rest of them treat him like rubbish. Don't let him finish what he's saying, don't listen to him. He does all the work and lets them push him around. He's a fool."

Cerauno wanted to walk away. It wasn't right, her talking like that. He liked the captain. He wasn't right up himself like the other four, and he listened to what people said. He wanted to tell her not to talk like that, but he didn't think he could.

"I've got to go now," he said, and she froze, the way he did when he'd made a noise and the deer lifted its head. He felt a sudden surge of fear, which he couldn't account for.

"See you tomorrow, then," she said. Her eyes were very wide; she was concentrating on him.

"I expect so," he replied, picking up his bow and quiver.

"Good luck."

He nodded clumsily and walked away, not looking where he was going, straight into a tree root, which tripped him and made him stagger. Feeling ridiculous, he lengthened his stride, not caring about making a noise. At that moment, the very last thing he wanted to do was shoot a deer.

When he'd gone, she stood up and walked slowly down the path, swinging her basket by the handle. Deer had made the path, though there weren't any left in this part of the wood now. She'd lost sight of him among the trees, but it was easy to see where he'd gone, if you knew what to look for. She thought briefly about the boy who'd taught her, back in the beech woods above Faralia. He'd been nice, but one day he'd tried to kiss her, and she'd hit him on the side of the head with a stone. He hadn't made any trouble about it, even though she'd hit him quite hard, and he ended up losing the sight in one eye; he was afraid of her after that, and told everyone he'd fallen and banged his head on a rock. Still, he'd been useful. If it hadn't been for him, she wouldn't know how to follow a trail.

She followed him all morning, staying well back and keeping quiet. She saw him shoot a roebuck as it grazed on the sugary buds of a willow, down by the river. She didn't look away as it kicked and stretched on the ground. She noticed that he held back until it had stopped moving, instead of running in and finishing it off. He broke the shaft of the arrow, trying to pull it out. That made her frown. Clearly he didn't know that you were supposed to push the arrow into the wound and out the other side, to keep the barbs from digging in. Her uncle had taught her that. She wondered if there was some way of telling him without letting him know she'd been following him. His clumsiness offended her; a man should know how to do things properly, and she couldn't help thinking just a little bit less of him for breaking the arrow. But, she persuaded herself, he couldn't be blamed if nobody had taught him the right way (though it was perfectly obvious, really, so he should have been able to figure it out for himself).

She watched him paunch and dress the carcass, then quietly drew away and left him, making her way back to the path. She found a big patch of tree fungus, nearly enough to fill the basket, and a bed of watercress where one of the streams had flooded over the winter, so that was all right. She thought about her husband — how could a grown man fall off a mast and hurt himself like that? — and thinking about him made her feel cross and unhappy. It'd have served him right if he'd fallen on his head and broken his stupid neck. He's a grafter, I'll give him that, he'd said. None of them can keep up with him, not even the general. She scowled at the thought. It was stupid to work so hard, much harder than the others, and not get anything extra for it. They took advantage of him, because he was stupid and anxious to please, and the harder he tried, the more they looked down on him. And they'd have let her work in the river along with the men if only he'd stuck up for her; but he'd said no, the work was too hard for a girl (at least, that was what he'd meant; he'd tried to make it sound nice, but she knew what he was really saying). That made her think about the other girls, which made her even more sad. Chaere was spoilt and stupid, Clea was common, Enyo was moody and stressed all the time, and she couldn't stand Dorun—so calm, so sensible, keeping them all in order like a shepherd's dog. She'd seen Dorun looking at her; too shrewd by half. Not that she was ever nasty, not out loud to her face, but she didn't need to be. She was horrible, the worst of all of them, and if something were to happen to her...

No, she thought, mustn't think like that. If you start hating someone it shows in your face; people can tell, no matter how careful you are. Her uncle had always been able to tell just by looking at her. Maybe Dorun was the same, she thought, in which case things could get very awkward indeed. Suddenly she smiled (she had a nice smile, people said). If something were to happen to Dorun, maybe it'd happen to Muri as well—a plague, maybe (she wasn't quite sure what a plague was; some kind of illness), or a fire, or pirates. It'd be so helpful if people could just die sometimes.

She thought about that for a while, turning it over in her mind as if chewing something delicious; she thought about the fire that had burnt up all the food, and imagined someone, the general presumably, gravely announcing to the company that his wife and his dear friend Muri had been killed in the blaze. Then everybody would've been really nice to her, the tragic young widow, and of course Dorun wouldn't be there to suspect her of not really being sad at all. They'd be so kind—people could be very kind, but usually only when something bad had just happened, which was sort of stupid, because you'd be too upset to enjoy it—and so long as you were careful and didn't overdo it, you could make it last ever such a long time. And Terpsi would be nice to her, he'd have to be. She thought about that. Of course, it was wicked to want something bad to happen to anybody, and she took a moment to feel properly ashamed. That said, it wasn't as though Muri, or Dorun for that matter, had any real claim on her, not like family. She'd seen how family could be: sons waiting for their fathers to die so they'd get the farm, daughters hating their mothers for years and years, cooped up in the same house together; husbands and wives were just as bad, brothers and sisters. Compared to all that sort of thing, wanting the death of a relative stranger wasn't really so bad; and it wasn't like Muri was some young man with all his life in front of him. Quite the opposite: he'd been a soldier, after all, and she didn't like soldiers. They were killers, people who came and burned houses and drove off cattle and spoiled everything, so really, you couldn't feel sorry for them. (She thought of her soldier, in the cave, and for some reason that made her think of Terpsi. She wondered: am I falling in love?) And then her mind turned to the gold, the immense fortune, and she found herself speculating: if one of them were to die, would his share in the gold go to his widow? Common sense said no, it wouldn't, it'd be divided up between the survivors; but hadn't the general said something about that — the company, with each of them having so many shares, which could mean it was like a farm or a business, and wives could inherit.

She scowled. She badly needed to know which it was, but of course she couldn't very well ask, or at least it'd have to be done right, and that would mean being nice to Muri, pretending she was worried in case something were to happen to him and she'd be left. Already, she was phrasing the question in her mind, choosing the right tone of voice, the right expression to wear. It'd be awkward, she decided, but she could probably manage it, and then she'd know.

Now she felt quite cheerful, and she picked a small bunch of pretty blue flowers. If something were to happen to Muri (forget about Dorun for the moment), she'd have people being nice to her and possibly a lot of money as well, all of her own, like the rich women in Faralia who'd inherited money from old, ugly husbands. She liked the thought of that; and she wouldn't be horrible like they were, sad and hungry with their hair dyed and their faces plastered with rouge and white lead; she'd just be herself, but with nobody to bully her or tell her what to do. And Terpsi... She scowled again, all her cheerfulness suddenly frozen. It wouldn't be like having her soldier, a secret in the woods. You couldn't just have a living person and keep them hidden away somewhere. Being in love was one thing, but it didn't stay nice for very long. They wanted to kiss you, and all that other stuff, like Muri wanted. She thought: at least when I said no he didn't get nasty or anything; perhaps I'm better off with him after all, and he's going to have lots of money soon. But being alone would be better. Besides, Terpsi was a bit stupid, he couldn't even pull out an arrow without breaking it, and he was scared of the dying deer, which was ridiculous. She'd have to think very carefully about him and decide what she wanted to do.

She felt calmer after that. The cheerfulness had gone, but she wasn't sad either, because now she had something to think about, something to find out, maybe plans to make. It was all a bit stupid, because it all depended on something happening to Muri, and you couldn't just ask for stuff like that to happen; you could wait fifty years, like the sour old wives at home, and a person would still go on resolutely living.

She paused to pick some mushrooms: ceps, the best wild mushrooms of all, and quite a lot of them. Ceps were a treat, wasted on them, she thought; they never appreciated what she brought home. You had to be quite clever to gather stuff, you had to know which ones were good to eat and which were poisonous. They'd all said it was her mushrooms that had made Clea throw up, which was simply not true, and unfair. Of course they hadn't believed her when she'd told them, and now some of them muttered about her and fished the mushrooms out of their food and left them on the side of the plate. People could be so nasty, and she was only trying to help. But they ate the roots, and the wild garlic, which just showed how stupid they were, because mushrooms weren't the only poisonous things in the forest...

She thought about her soldier, in the wood.

TWELVE

The accounts officer was a short, bald, bull-necked man with a weak chin, which made his head look like a thumb. He lived in a small, cramped office in the back annexe of Headquarters, which before the war had been the best inn in Elio. It didn't take much imagination to guess what purpose his office had served. For one thing, the smell lingered. He didn't strike Kunessin as the sort of man who'd relish jokes about it, however.

"Quite a sum of money," he said, with more than a hint of disapproval. "Quite a tidy sum of money, Colonel." He looked down at the ledger, then back at Kunessin, then down at the ledger again. "You've got the affidavits, presumably."

Kunessin smiled, and handed him the sheaf of papers. He went through them slowly, one by one, a man to whom time was largely irrelevant. "They seem to be all right," he said, as though congratulating Kunessin on the quality of his forgeries. "I'll need to check them against the day books, of course. And the requisitions."

"Of course," Kunessin replied.

"Assuming it's all there," he went on, shifting in his seat, "I'll need to know who to make the warrants out to."

"Warrant," Kunessin corrected him. "Just the one. I've got a form of authority signed by the others."

The head went back, the eyebrows went up. "Just the one warrant," he said. "For the lot of you."

"Saves time," Kunessin said.

It was a pretty weak reason, but the accounts officer didn't seem inclined to take the point. "In that case," he said, "I'll need you to sign a pro forma receipt, for yourself and the rest of the company. And," he added, squinting down at the paper, "the estate of the late Major Nuctos Di'Ambrosies. Actually, that complicates matters, if you're taking it all in one warrant. Properly speaking, the executors—"

"That's me," Kunessin said. "Sole executor. He made a will, so it's all in order."

The accounts officer relaxed slightly. "That's all right, then," he said. "You've got it with you, presumably."

Kunessin laid it on the desk. The accounts officer glanced at it. "Fine," he said. "In that case, just sign here, and here."

Kunessin reached out for the pen, a stub of quill sharpened down to the vanes. His hand was perfectly steady as he signed. "Is that the lot?"

The accounts officer nodded. "Apart from the checks, yes. Shouldn't take more than, oh, a week, ten days at the most. When's your actual date of discharge?"

"Tomorrow."

Frown. "You've cut it a bit fine, haven't you?" he said. "When's your shipping date?"

"Tomorrow."

It was rather pleasant, watching him struggle with that. "Then why the hell didn't you...?"

Shrug. "Not up to me," he said. "We've been stuck here for six weeks with nothing to do, and then they tell us we're being sent home tomorrow. So..."

The accounts officer sighed. "That's a pain in the arse," he said. "I don't suppose you'd agree to having letters of credit sent to you at"—he glanced down—"Faralia? I assume there's a bank of sorts there."

Kunessin shook his head. "Sorry," he said. "No disrespect, but I know about military letters of credit. We would quite like our money while we're still young enough to enjoy it."

A slight nod of the head, conceding the point. "I'll see what I can do," he said. "I mean, normally there'd be no way. But since it's not your foul-up..."

"Thank you," Kunessin said graciously. "I can wait while you do it now, if you like."

That, apparently, wasn't possible. Not only was there the actual drawing-up of the warrant—it had to be written on special paper in special ink, to circumvent forgery—it also had to be countersigned by the brigadier and the civilian commissioner, both of whom were busy men with short tempers. "Best I can do you is first thing in the morning, say just after reveille," he said. "I imagine you can skip morning parade, since it's your last day."

Kunessin thanked him and left by the back door, directly into the courtyard. He made sure he was out in the street before he stopped, and looked down at his hands. They were shaking.

Guilt, he supposed, but he wasn't convinced. If he was honest with himself, it was really just the fear of being found out. Not so much by the military; it didn't do to be complacent, but he'd been fooling them long enough to know he could get away with it, so long as he was careful and very, very particular about details. That wouldn't be enough to make his hands shake, for the first time since he'd joined the service.

He made himself walk, though his knees were weak. Muri wouldn't be a problem. Kudei—Kudei was shrewd, but he'd never shown much interest in the money. Understandably; the first thing he'd do when he got home would be to hand it over to his brothers, who'd waste it all in six months and leave nothing to show for it. Fly was very keen on money, and sharp enough to pick up on anything that wasn't quite right, but it'd never cross his mind that one of the company would do anything to cheat the others. It was Aidi who'd be the danger; precise, meticulous Aidi, the man who always added up bills, checked invoices, read documents before signing them; Aidi, with his inherited skill at maths, and his annoying instinct to question every damn thing.

He went back to the barracks, but not to their quarters. Instead, after checking to see that nobody was watching, he darted up the spiral steps to the deputy paymaster's office, long since vacated after the staff had been relocated to Headquarters. Under the bench, in the dust, among the rat droppings and shredded scraps of paper, was an old wooden trunk. He lifted the lid, took out a handful of papers and a clerk's portable inkwell, and sat down on one of the high stools.

The accounts, when he'd finished them, were a work of art. Mostly, he used false deductions to get rid of Nuctos' share. It was a sensible approach, since nearly all the deductions — for clothing, kit replacements, storage, shipping, agency, expenses of sale — were genuine, or would have been if he hadn't figured out many subtle ways of not paying them, or pretending they'd been paid (forged vouchers, forged letters of credit — God bless the service for being so unreliable in its banking procedures — false requisitions and so forth). It was a relatively straightforward matter to write them in, doubling or trebling the amounts, recalculating the running totals and carrying forward the reduced amounts to the summary. Aidi would be furious, of course; he'd complain bitterly about how much the army had screwed out of them for things they should have provided gratis. But he'd believe; he'd often said that nothing the service did by way of underhanded, ungrateful, mean, spiteful deductions would ever surprise him. No problem there.

Next, he systematically devalued the receipts by twenty per cent. Consistency was the great thing here. So long as the market prices for salvaged goods appeared to stay roughly the same, it was unlikely that any of them would be suspicious. It was extremely unlikely that they'd ever be in a position to check the prices actually raised at auction, since as far as he knew the results weren't published anywhere, and the buyers wouldn't tell anybody what they'd paid.

Next, he allowed himself a little daring, and wrote off one entire consignment as lost at sea. He didn't choose the most valuable one, the aftermath of the battle of Synaxa. Instead, he picked a middle-range consignment, one that had gone through about the time the enemy navy had enjoyed a brief spell of success in commerce raiding. That only disposed of a modest amount, but it'd mean he wouldn't have to be so rapacious elsewhere. Little and often was the way to go.

Once he'd finished, he carefully wrote out the fair copy, checked and double-checked it, folded it and put it away in his pocket. That, he knew, would be the great leap of faith: explaining what had become of the detail accounts, and why he only had the main account to show them. He'd thought through various explanations, but decided in the end to tell them that the accounts office were holding the detail papers for examination — which might well have happened, after all, if there wasn't the sudden desperate rush to get the warrant drawn in one day. He was modestly proud of that, and it hadn't been too hard to arrange.

Last of all, the part he'd been both looking forward to and dreading: comparing the true sum of the warrant with the revised version. He did the simple arithmetic, looked at the result and frowned. It was, as the accounts officer would have said, a tidy sum, but it wasn't enough. It would pay for a comfortable retirement, or a nice little business somewhere; it'd more than pay for a good farm (but the only good farm wasn't for sale). For what he had in mind, however, it was simply inadequate.

For a long time he sat with the papers in front of him, staring at the wall. Blessed with a vivid imagination, he'd thought of all manner of ways in which his plan could go horribly wrong, but this wasn't one of them. Not enough money. He suddenly leaned forward, snatched up the summary sheet and checked the calculations yet again. No mistake. The whole miserable business, in other words, for nothing.

Like a weak chairman trying to bring an unruly meeting to order, he tried to clarify his thoughts. For one thing, if the plan had failed, what was he going to do with all the money? The answer to that was fairly obvious: divide it up properly, honestly, so that each of them got his fair share. Yes, he thought, I could do that; and then Kudei's useless brothers would waste his share, buying cattle that died and seedcorn that wouldn't grow, extra land they couldn't work, which would weed over and revert to scrub. Aidi would take his share and invest it wisely; in a few years he'd be a prosperous man of business, with no time for his old friends from the war. Fly would most likely drink himself to death; Muri would lose it all somehow, to a pretty, smart girl or a flock of long-lost poor relations. It would be the end of A Company, and that meant the end of everything he'd had since his father lost the farm. So: not that, then. He was stuck with his involuntary trusteeship, until he could find some way to make good on his unspoken promise.

He thought long and hard, and the more he thought, the clearer the answer became. There was only one thing he could do.

The colonel was surprised to see him. "You're shipping out tomorrow, aren't you?"

He shook his head. "That's what I wanted to see you about," he said. "I changed my mind. I want to stay on."

The food was running out again. Aidi worked out a rationing system that'd stretch their reserves for another six weeks, by which time the ship should have returned from Faralia. Kunessin proposed it to an extraordinary general meeting of the company. The proposal passed comfortably, but not unanimously.

Two days after the meeting, the workers came home from the river to be met by Dorun and Enyo, both looking grim and worried. Apparently, someone had stolen a half-hundredweight jar of flour from the store.

"Are you sure about that?" Aidi said. "You're sure you've counted right?"

Enyo glared at him. Dorun said, "When you came up with the rationing idea, Enyo and I organised the stores so we'd know what we were doing. We chalked numbers on all the flour jars, and we made a tally, so we'd know exactly how much was left in the open jar each day. So yes, we're sure."

Dead silence. Then Kunessin said: "In that case, we'll have to search for it. Aidi, you're with me; we'll do the main house and the outbuildings. Muri and Fly, scout round the yard, and you might take a look up by the jetty, all round there. Kudei, you take someone with you and search the animal pens, it could be stashed in with the feed. If we don't find it tonight, we'll do the woods in the morning."

It was Kunessin himself who found the jar, in a corner of the burned-out grain store, hidden (rather badly) behind a few old sacks. It was empty.

"Which makes it a damn sight harder," he explained to another general meeting later that evening. "Whoever took it's clearly no fool. I imagine he's parcelled the flour up in small pots and bags and hidden it away all over the place." He paused, then went on, "It's up to you what we do now. We can keep looking, but my guess is, it'll take a long time and we may not find anything; that's at least a day's lost production. On the other hand, this is about as serious a crime as you can get. If we don't catch whoever did it, we're practically inviting a repeat performance."

Awkward silence; then Aechmaloten stood up and said: "I agree it's a serious matter, and if we catch the bastard, I vote we kill him. But it's only fifty pounds of flour. A whole day's work lost is a lot of money."

Nobody said anything, and Aechmaloten sat down again. After a very long pause, Kunessin said, "Well, we've got a proposal: forget about it and cut the ration to compensate. All in favour."

Aidi voted against; so did Muri and three of the indentured men. Kunessin abstained. "Vote carried, then," Kunessin said edgily. "Aidi, you're the mathematician. You'd better work out a new ration."

It was a long, silent evening, and they didn't bother with the gold ceremony. Aidi lifted the previous day's seal, dumped the day's proceeds in the big jar and sealed it up again, and nobody spoke. Next day, though, the indentured men had a long whispered debate before setting off for the river, and it didn't take much imagination to guess what they were talking about, or the conclusions they drew. A Company held more or less the same debate during the noon break.

"It's not exactly difficult," Aidi insisted. "We know where we all were yesterday: we were here, up to our waists in cold water and mud. I'm pretty sure I can vouch for all of us and the servants too."

"Fine," Alces snapped. "Problem solved. Nobody stole it. The jar went for a stroll and got mugged by rats."

"I wasn't at the river," Kunessin pointed out.

"And neither were the girls," Kudei said. "Don't look at me like that; it's what you've all been thinking, and so have they, you can bet your life," he added, nodding towards the indentured men.

"Oh come on," Muri protested. "What you're saying is, one of our wives—"

"Yes, that's exactly what I'm saying," Alces said briskly. "Because it had to be. And just think about it, will you? Say one of us steals a jar of flour. What are we supposed to do with it? All the pots and pans are in the lean-to, right? And there's at least one of the girls in there all the time. We couldn't just sneak in and bake a quick loaf or brew up a crafty bowl of porridge. But one of the girls—"

"Who exactly did you have in mind?" Muri asked icily.

"Fly's not naming any names," Aidi interrupted. "But he's got a point, you must admit. A woman cooking: hardly likely to arouse suspicion."

Muri scowled at him. "Well you can cross Menin off your list, for a start," he said. "She was out in the woods, so it can't have been her."

"Unless she came back without being seen," Aidi replied. "That's entirely possible. She does come back early sometimes."

"I think your Chaere's the lead suspect," Muri replied angrily. "She moans enough about being hungry all the time."

Aidi was about to reply to that, but Kunessin forestalled him. "That's not being helpful, Muri," he said. "You're the only one mentioning names."

"Or Clea," Muri snapped back. "Her family's all a bunch of thieves."

"Shut up, Muri," Kudei said quietly. "Look, it could have been any of them. Maybe all of them together for all we know. The fact is, we aren't going to do anything about it. Well, are we? Are we going to hang one of our wives?"

Nobody answered him, and after a long silence Kunessin said: "We've got to drop this, or risk a civil war. I don't know about you lot, but I'd rather get by on a bit less than have this discussion again. Agreed?"

The others nodded; all except Aidi. "It's all very well saying cut the ration and forget about it. I'm not so sure we can do that. Someone's just stolen food, when we're desperate enough as it is. For one thing, what if the ship doesn't turn up when we said it would? We've got no guarantee whatsoever. I tried to make a bit of an allowance when I figured out the ration, just in case, but now that's all gone to hell. If that ship's a week late, we're screwed."

"You're forgetting something," Muri said, still scowling. "We've got the sloop. All we've got to do is make another run to the mainland. All right," he went on, "last time wasn't a raging success. But this time we've got gold dust to pay with. That's got to be better than starving, and accusing each other of stealing."

"We agreed," Kunessin said firmly. "We don't send gold to the mainland. It'd be inviting an attack, letting them know what we've got here."

"Things were rather different when we decided that," Muri replied. "If it's a choice between risking pirates and starving to death, I know what I'll be voting for. Besides," he added, "since when were we scared of a fight?"

"I agree with Muri," Alces said. "Send the sloop out, and then it doesn't really matter. The last thing we need is a civil war."

Kudei said, "Aidi?"

Aidi screwed up his face; if someone had wanted a portrait of Thought to go on the back of a coin, he'd have been perfect. "I don't know," he said eventually. "We don't want to attract attention, I can see that, and paying for groceries with gold dust would be asking for trouble. But if we've reached the stage where someone's stealing food, something's clearly gone badly wrong. We don't want to have to make a big deal out of this, or we'll be at each other's throats. Make sure there's enough food for everybody and we sidestep the problem."

Silence; then Kunessin said: "That's a neat summary, Aidi. Now tell us what you think."

"I just said," Aidi replied. "I don't know."

"Fine." Kunessin stood up. "Then here's what we're going to do. We aren't going to send the sloop out. We all agreed, and that's all there is to it. Aidi, I want you to recalculate the rations. Muri, get a lock put on the store. Kudei, you're quartermaster. Every morning, you unlock and give Dorun the day's supply of flour, then you lock up again. All clear?"

Kudei nodded. Aidi said: "Is that it? What about the thief?"

"We forget about it," Kunessin said. "My guess is, it must've been one of the girls; in which case, we really don't want to know which one it was. So long as it doesn't happen again."

The others went back to work. Kunessin walked up the hill to his lumber pile, looked round to make sure he wasn't being watched, then took the lower path, dead ground, back to the settlement. The women would all be in the various outbuildings; he crossed the yard quickly and opened the door of the main house. Nobody about. He lit a candle from the embers of the fire and used its flame to loosen the wax on the seal of the gold jar. With the tip of his knife, he carefully prised it off without cracking it and put it in his pocket. He took off his coat, spread it out round the base of the jar, lifted the lid, then reached down into the jar until his fingertips located the neck of the flour-sack. Before he lifted it out (a half-hundredweight at arm's length; the effort made him grunt) he shook it, to get as much of yesterday's gold dust as possible out of the coarse weave of the sacking. Out the sack came, sparkling like a newly hooked fish; he dumped it on his spread-out coat and put the lid back, then gently warmed the back of the seal in the candle flame until the wax started to run. Firm pressure and a little more heat from the candle secured it. He let go and stood back. It got easier, of course, each time he did it.

The spilt gold dust from the sack went in a pottery mug, to be added later to his private store. He hid the mug in the usual place, behind the loose brick in the fireplace. The flour sack was more of a problem. His assumption had been that, once everywhere had been thoroughly searched, he'd have no trouble finding a cache for it; but he had an unpleasant feeling that Aidi meant to keep searching, and he was smart enough to figure that the thief might well move the sack once the official search had been abandoned. The logical course of action, therefore, would be to get rid of it: pour it in the river, tip it out in the boggy patch in the wood and tread it in. Logical, but he really didn't want to do that. Fifty pounds of flour was ten days' supply for the five of them, as and when the food ran out. The other alternative was to put it back in the store, but he couldn't be certain that he'd got all the gold dust out of the sacking; that'd be a nasty clue to give Aidi, who'd be bound to notice. Really, the sack had to be burnt. If he wanted to get rid of the sack but keep the flour, he'd need one of the big jars, and the loss of one of them would be noticed, leading to another grand search and more aggravation and risk. Oh well, he thought. It had seemed like a good idea at the time.

Maybe he was preoccupied, and that made him careless. He opened the door, and found Dorun facing him across the threshold. It was no use trying to hide the sack.

"That's it, isn't it?" she said.

He nodded. "You'll never guess where it was hidden."

"No," she said.

"In the gold jar." As he said it, he could see the mistake he'd just made. "The only place none of us thought to look."

She was frowning at him. "But the seal," she said. "Does that mean Aidi...?"

She was looking over his shoulder. From the doorway, she had a clear view. The seal, intact, in place. "That's a neat trick," she said.

For once in his life, he wasn't quite sure what to say. "I lifted the seal," he said. "I didn't want to let him know I'd found out."

"Can you do that? I thought—"

"A candle and a sharp knife," he said. "But don't tell anybody. The last thing we need is anyone getting ideas."

She stood away from him a step or two. "So it was Aidi," she said.

"Let's not talk about it," he replied. "I should imagine Chaere had something to do with it. Rationing isn't her style."

He could see she was thinking about it. "It doesn't make sense, though," she said. "I mean, we've been talking about it, and it can't have been him. He was away at the river, with everybody else."

Everybody else but you, she didn't add. "When we were in the service," he said, "if there was ever any quiet work to be done — taking care of a sentry, something like that — it was always Aidi's job. Never known anybody who could move so quietly. He must've done it while we were all asleep."

"That's..." She shook her head. "What're you going to do?"

"Nothing," he said. "I'm going to put this back where it came from, Muri's going to put a lock on the store, and Kudei's going to be in charge of the key. I can guarantee there won't be a repeat performance."

She nodded slowly. "What are you going to tell everybody?"

"I'm not," he said. "We'll cut the ration a little. No bad thing, actually; this means there'll be a bit of a reserve. Telling everybody's just going to make matters worse."

"I suppose so." She wasn't looking at him. "Aidi, though, of all people. He's so particular about things."

"Think about it," Kunessin said. "Fifty pounds of flour."

She frowned, then said, "Oh, I see. I suppose that makes sense. But—"

"That's enough." He took hold of her arm. "You can come with me, as a witness, just in case this ever comes out. You can tell them you saw the flour go back."

"What puzzles me," Aidi said, "is the quantity."

Alces straightened his back and loaded a shovelful of silt into Aidi's pan. "What's that mean?" he said.

"The quantity," Aidi repeated. "Fifty pounds. Think about it."

"What's there to think about?" Alces said, as Aidi began to twist the pan around. "Well, I guess a half-hundredweight's about as much as a woman can carry without doing her back in."

Aidi shook his head. "Yes, fine," he said. "But if you steal fifty pounds of flour, what're you going to do with it? Look," he went on, draining away the first rinse of black water, "the food runs out, all right? Everybody's starving; except one person, who stays fat and healthy. That's going to be rather obvious, don't you think?"

Alces sighed. "Maybe," he replied, nudging the toe of the blade into the gravel and shifting his weight behind it. "Assuming whoever it was thought it through that carefully."

"Fifty pounds," Aidi went on, "isn't going to go far if there's a lot of you, so the servants probably wouldn't bother. It'd be a hell of a risk for what, a couple of days' extra rations? And if it was just one man, why steal a whole half-hundredweight and get the whole camp up in arms, when you could just keep stealing an extra cup or two every day, and probably not be noticed at all."

Alces pulled a face, to show he was bored with the conversation. But Aidi wasn't looking at him. "All right," he said, "how about this? Fifty pounds is ten days' rations for five people. There are five women in the camp. The likeliest suspect, I think we've all agreed, is one of the girls; they're the only ones who had the opportunity."

Aidi nodded. "That's the conclusion I jumped to, to begin with," he said. "And it sort of makes sense, though I don't see any of them having the nerve to do it. But in that case, where's the stuff now? If it was one of them, it'd have to be hidden in the settlement somewhere, because the girls don't leave camp."

"There's Menin."

"Could've hidden it in the woods, you mean." Aidi shook his head. "She can't lift fifty pounds, let alone carry it all that way. I watched her with a three-gallon bucket once. That's thirty pounds, and she was really struggling."

Alces lifted the shovel out of the mud and slewed off the surface water. "I think Teuche's right," he said. "Forget about it. There's no way finding out who did it's going to make things better."

Aidi sighed. "He's right, of course. It's just... I don't know." He tipped a slug's trail of dust into the pot and replaced the lid. "It's something that shouldn't have happened. If it was up to me, I'd pack it in here and go home."

"What, because of this? One sack of flour?"

"It was Teuche's idea," Aidi said, "his wonderful ideal community; hence the wives, and the servants. Should've just been the five of us. With outsiders along, something like this was bound to happen. And it's all very well saying forget about it, but it's not that easy. The servants won't, I can guarantee that."

"Soon as the ship gets here, they won't give a damn," Alces said. "Besides, soon enough they'll have their money and they'll be gone."

"I'd like to think that," Aidi said.

The reduced rations weren't popular. It was the women who complained most (Dorun excepted); the indentured men didn't say much, but they didn't need to. Some of them started asking why the sloop hadn't been sent out. Kunessin reminded them about the agreement, with the result that they stopped talking about the sloop whenever they saw him coming.

That wasn't the end of it, however. Anculo Metis, a carpenter, and Pollas D'Iphthimous, one of the stockmen, hatched up a plan to steal the sloop and a day's worth of gold, sail to the mainland, stock up with food and use the bargaining power it'd give them to renegotiate the agreement and, with any luck, get rid of the five proprietors. They recruited four rather half-hearted conspirators, one of whom (a tinsmith by the name of Dactylo) lost his nerve and told the whole story to Aechmaloten, who lost no time in passing it on to Kunessin.

The theft of the ship was scheduled for daybreak the next morning. Metis, D'Iphthimous and two of their four recruits crept out of the main house and walked quickly to the jetty, taking with them a sock half filled with gold dust (they'd switched it for another sock containing sand, which had been put in the gold pot the previous evening). Waiting for them at the jetty they found General Kunessin and Captain Gaeon. Neither of them was armed.

"You're up early," Kunessin said. "Going fishing?"

D'Iphthimous had stolen a Type Fifteen sword from the shed where the weapons were kept, and Metis had brought his carpenter's side-axe under his coat. D'Iphthimous took a step forward, said, "Get out of the way, General," and drew his sword, which he then promptly dropped. As he stooped to pick it up, Kunessin kicked him on the chin. He toppled over the side of the jetty, landed in the water, and sank. When Metis went to jump in after him, Kudei stopped him, twisting his arm behind his back and lifting the axe out of his belt. He didn't say anything, just shook his head.

D'Iphthimous' body was washed ashore two days later. It was fished out of the sea and hung up next to those of his fellow conspirators, on the big, splay-branched ash tree on the western edge of the compound. The whole community had been there to see them hanged, in spite of a quick, fierce shower of rain that soaked everybody to the skin. The only man to speak throughout the whole performance was Dactylo the tinsmith, reprieved for informing on the others; he yelled abuse at the condemned men as they were led out, blaming them for putting him in an impossible position and turning everybody against him. Alces eventually shut him up with a kidney punch. Three days later, Dactylo's body was found head down in the latrine, and no action was taken over his death.

"We're going to have to do something," Aidi insisted, at the staff meeting that evening. He'd just finished helping Kudei to dispose of Dactylo's body, in a bog pool out on the edge of the marshes, where Kunessin had hoped to find natural outcrops of iron ore. "Otherwise things are going to get very bad."

Kunessin shook his head. "They've accepted it," he said. "Mostly, I think, because of Aechmaloten. Because he turned the traitors over to us, rather than us going and taking them, the general view is that it was an internal matter which they sorted out themselves."

Alces frowned. "They sure as hell sorted out the tinsmith," he said.

Kunessin shrugged. "Can't blame them for that," he said. "It's like they taught us at college: love treachery, hate traitors. I don't plan on doing anything about it. Believe it or not, I didn't come here to start a career as a policeman."

"Teuche's right," Muri said. "This and the business with the flour; obviously we had to make a show of strength. But with any luck we've nipped it in the bud."

Aidi rolled his eyes: at the sentiments, or the clichés, or both. Kudei got up and threw a log on the fire. "It's going to be awkward making conversation with them for the next day or so," he said. "You can't lynch four men and expect to carry on the same as usual."

"It's the food crisis that's doing it," Aidi said. "Maybe we should send the sloop out, after all."

Kunessin looked at him. "That'd be the worst possible thing," he said.

"Beg to differ," Aidi replied. "Starving to death when we've got a perfectly good boat's the worst possible thing, closely followed by having our throats cut in our sleep over a few mouldy sacks of flour. Sending out the sloop comes a poor third."

"We should hold on till the ship gets here from Faralia," Muri said. "It can't be much longer, for crying out loud. And once it gets here—"

"If it gets here," Aidi snapped. "If it gets here, it's bloody obvious what we do. We unload the supplies, then we march the servants on board and send it straight back home. Then we take the gold and the sloop and clear out ourselves."

There was a long silence. Then Kunessin said: "Why would we want to do that, Aidi?"

"Use your head, Teuche," Aidi replied briskly. "Those four are bound to have family and friends back home. I don't imagine they're going to let the matter drop, especially once they find out there's a large sum of money involved. They'll lodge a complaint with the government, and you can bet the farm they'll take a very close interest in this place, when they learn about the gold strike. Bearing in mind the fact that your title to this chunk of rock isn't exactly watertight—"

Kunessin lifted a finger, and Aidi stopped talking. "You agreed to the hanging," he said.

Aidi shrugged. "Didn't see how we had much choice," he replied. "If we'd let it go, they'd have taken the sloop, news would've got out anyway and we'd have no way off the island. As it is, provided we can hang on here till the ship comes, we're in with a chance." He sighed, and made a sad gesture that ran from his shoulders to his fingertips. "It's a fucking mess whichever way you look at it. Damage control's the best we can hope for now."

"I have no great desire to get into a fight with the government,"

Alces said. "By some miracle we kept out of the stockade while we were in the service. Pushing our luck at this point would be a mistake."

"Agreed," Aidi said. "Where it all started to go wrong was when whoever it was stole that bloody flour."

Kunessin shook his head. "You're all in a tearing hurry to give in and run," he said. "I can't see any call for that. Listen," he went on, softening his voice, "we were entirely within our rights dealing with D'Iphthimous and his lads the way we did. D'Iphthimous tried to draw on me, so that was simple self-defence. Stealing the sloop would've put all our lives at risk, and as the proprietor named in the transfer deed, I've got personal jurisdiction. Suppose the government does want to take over the gold working. So what? Let the fuckers have it. We came here to farm. Let them have the gold; we keep the rest of the island, plus what we've already dug out of the river. If I can't negotiate that, I'll jump off the jetty with a rock tied round my neck."

Silence again. Then Kudei said: "You reckon you could swing that?"

"If it comes to it, yes," Kunessin replied. "For one thing, I know the general staff. They don't just tear up legal documents, they're far too legalistically minded. They may well want the gold works, but they don't give a stuff about the land. And if the worst comes to the worst, I know where the bodies are buried at central command. Nobody's going to want to pick a fight to the death with me; they know me too well. Which is more than you clowns do, if you think I came here without proper insurance."

Muri was nodding. Alces rubbed his chin with his thumb and forefinger, an affectation he'd developed over many years. Kudei sat down and stared hard at his fingernails.

"Aidi?" he said.

Aidi didn't reply for a while, until Kunessin gently said, "Well?"

"I don't know," Aidi said. "I'd have thought the hangings'd be just the pretext they'd need to clear us out of the picture completely, and then there'd be no question of disputed property rights. It's what I'd do, in their shoes."

"Just as well you didn't try staying on in the service, then," Kunessin replied. "Central command doesn't do things like that. Too scared of whose fault it'd turn out to be if something went wrong. Play it by the book's their style; that way nobody gets in trouble."

"Maybe," Aidi said. "But the bastards running the service when I was in wouldn't have passed up an opportunity like a river full of gold, and I don't suppose very much of that gold would've found its way through to the Treasury. You talk about them going by the book and respecting legal documents, Teuche. Maybe so. Maybe they've read through their copy of the transfer deed and seen where there's no reservation of mineral rights. Which makes us a loose end."

Kunessin smiled. "So we do a legal assignment," he said. "Give them the rights, of our own free will; our duty as loyal citizens. Can't say fairer than that."

Kudei frowned. "I'm not so sure about that," he said. "Giving up all that money without a fight. Isn't that a sure way to make them suspect something?"

"You haven't been listening," Kunessin replied irritably. "They couldn't care less about this island. They don't want it. All it meant to them was the trivial cost of keeping a guard here, which they didn't want to pay. If they find out about the gold strike, all right, they'll want the gold." He raised both hands in the air: mock surrender. "We give it to them, and keep the land. Situation back to normal. One thing they won't want to do is make any more work for themselves than absolutely necessary." He paused to draw breath, then looked straight at Aidi. "What do you think?" he said.

Aidi let out a long, sad sigh. "Fine," he said. "Why not? Just promise me we'll send the servants away as soon as the ship gets here. Provided you do that, I'll go along with anything you want."

The next day was the most productive so far. Quite early, an indentured man by the name of Calceo dug into a deep pocket of silt trapped between a tree root and a large stone. The silt was so rich, the gold could be seen sparkling in it as he shovelled it into the pan. He started yelling, as if something was attacking him; Kudei dashed over and saw the gleam.

"Over here," he called out. "All of you."

The pocket proved to be deeper than they'd first imagined. It was soon clear what had happened: a flood current had shifted the stone, and the cavity it left behind had trapped silt as it washed down and got caught in the eddy caused by the root. Further floods, common enough in winter, had lifted away the sand and sludge, but the gold's weight had made it sink, so that in effect the river had already done most of the work of panning for them. As pan after pan came up gold-plated, the pace of work quickened; it was as if everybody expected someone to come along and stop them, and they wanted to get as much out as they could before that happened. As they dug deeper, they started finding nuggets, ranging in size from grape pips to acorns. The sock was full well before noon; Aidi pulled off his left boot, and they filled that by mid-afternoon. The pocket gave out just as it was starting to get dark; white clay from the river bed was coming up on the cutting edges of the shovels, but no colour. They gave it up by unspoken unanimous consent, but instead of washing off their tools and heading home, the entire party stood or sat round on the bank, staring into the water. They were worn out, of course; they'd been working all day at a frantic rate, without noticing the fatigue slowly building. Partly, though, there was an uneasy feeling of a ceasefire about to run out, one that couldn't be renewed because of some technicality of the rules of war, although none of them wanted it to end.

"A couple more like that and we can all go home," someone said; one of the indentured men, but impossible to say who in the tightening darkness. Nobody replied. Hardly a word had been spoken all day.

Eventually Aidi made a move. He walked awkwardly, with only one boot, cradling the other against his chest, like a proud father carrying a baby. Aechmaloten carried the sock, and if anybody noticed that this was the first time an indentured man had brought gold back from the river, nobody commented on it.

"You know," Alces said quietly to Aidi as they headed the procession back along the bank, "it seems a bit feeble. Teuche's approach, I mean."

Aidi took a long time to reply. "Picking a fight with the government..." he said.

"Oh, sure," Alces said. "Couldn't agree more. Except it's there in the transfer deed: we've got the mineral rights. If they'd wanted to keep them out, all they had to do was write in an extra clause."

"You're forgetting," Aidi said quietly. "Teuche drafted the bloody thing."

"I thought he used the standard form of words."

"Maybe." Aidi's shrug dismissed the point as unimportant. "Makes no odds. We can fight them in court or on the beach, we'll lose either way. They're bigger than us."

"A lot of people thought that," Alces said quietly. "Come on, Aidi, since when were we scared of a fight?"

"Me personally? I was always scared."

Alces frowned, as though that was the last thing he'd been expecting to hear. "It just seems a bit of a shame," he said, "quitting, if there's more where that lot came from. Just letting them come here and take it..."

"I guess it depends on how much money you actually feel you need," Aidi said, in a neutral voice. "Got to draw the line somewhere, unless you want to spend the rest of your life here."

"Fine," Alces snapped. "Easy for you, your family always had money. Some of us—"

"That's not the point," Aidi said, and his voice was a door slamming. "For crying out loud, Fly," he went on, his voice soft and worried. "We both of us left home when we were kids, and since then—" He broke off, then started again. "Money's the least of our worries," he said. "If it goes that way, by the time we have to give this lot away, there'll be plenty for everyone. We'll be gentlemen of leisure, sipping wine in a walled garden."

Alces stared at him, then burst out laughing. "I bloody well hope not," he said. "We'd all be dead from boredom inside of a week."

"You know what I mean," Aidi replied, good-humoured-offended. "Besides, when has Teuche ever steered us wrong?"

They saw the lights as they rounded the river bend, where the current had carved an oxbow out of the soft soil. Yellow light streamed out of both doors of the main house; but the doors were always kept shut.

"Wait here," Aidi called out to the indentured men. "Muri, Fly, Kudei."

As the four of them approached the back door, they could hear Kunessin's voice; he was talking much louder than usual, not shouting, projecting his voice so he'd be heard from outside. That and the open doors meant trouble. Aidi crept forward until he could hear.

"It says it here, in clause seven," Kunessin was saying, "and again in clause ten, look. No mention of any rights of redemption."

Another voice, a man's, unfamiliar, much softer. Aidi couldn't catch the words.

"If that's what it's supposed to mean, there'd need to be explicit wording," Kunessin thundered. "You can't just imply a pre-emption clause. I know, you're not a lawyer, and why should you take my word for it? Fine. Go back, get your lawyers to take a look at it, and then we can have a sensible discussion. At the moment, by your own admission . . ."

Aidi had had enough. He waved the other three to join him, then sent Muri and Kudei round the front, while he and Alces came in through the back.

Two men in junior officers' uniform were standing with their backs to the fire; they looked like they'd stopped there because they couldn't retreat any further without getting burnt. Kunessin was confronting them, looking very much like a schoolmaster telling off a pair of troublemakers. The women were all down the far end of the house, watching the show with undisguised fascination. Fair enough; they'd probably never seen Kunessin in full flight before.

"Teuche," Aidi said.

"There you are," Kunessin replied without looking round. "I was wondering where the hell you'd got to. Allow me to introduce some guests. Didn't catch their names," he went on, overriding one of the officers, who'd tried to speak. "Apparently they're from the government. They seem to think we've got no right to this island."

Aidi heard a soft intake of breath at his side. He said, "You've shown them the transfer deed."

Kunessin held up the familiar sheet of paper. "They admit it's a perfectly valid document," he said. "They maintain there's no record of it back in the archive, which I know for a fact isn't the case."

"We're not disputing that," one of the officers said; he sounded very unhappy. "It's just that we've got our orders, and—"

"They insist on taking possession of the island," Kunessin went on. "They've given us notice to quit."

Muri made a sort of soft growling noise (a bit melodramatic, Kunessin thought, but it made the two officers shuffle back a further inch or so). "Is that right?" Kudei said.

"There's no specific time frame," one of them mumbled. "We just..."

They know who we are, Aidi thought; or, more to the point, who we were. He felt sorry for them. "The hell with that," he said briskly. "We've put our life savings into this. We're not just going to walk away."

"I'm sure compensation..." The elder of the two—they both looked like children—caught Kunessin's eye and subsided at once. Muri and Kudei were advancing up the hall, so Aidi began to move as well. They've been to the College, he thought, same as us; they know about tactics. A classic encircling movement, even in miniature, wasn't hard to recognise. He could almost smell the fear, and it made him want to grin.

"Clause seven of the transfer deed clearly states..." Kunessin launched into a massive, lumbering legal exposition, the sort of thing you really needed to concentrate on, or you'd lose the plot straight away. Not something you could easily grasp while watching four feral humans advancing on you from all cardinal points. The two wretched officers were frozen, leaning slightly back, desperately trying to resist the urge to look round to see what was happening behind them, or simply to run. Abruptly, Kunessin broke off his tirade, and barked, "Well?"

The younger officer tried to pull himself together. It was a splendid effort, in the circumstances. "If I could just talk to my colleague for a moment," he mumbled.

"Of course." Kunessin made an overdone hand gesture: calling off the dogs. "Aidi, can I have a word?"

The other three stayed in position; it was just like old times, no need to give orders.

"This isn't so good," Aidi said quietly, his head turned away so the officers couldn't read his lips.

"It's not so bad," Kunessin replied. "They don't know about the gold, for one thing. Send Kudei up to tell the men to stay put."

Aidi nodded. "What's the plan?"

"For now, get rid of them. While we've got them here, get Muri to take a look at their ship. I haven't seen it. I don't suppose they've got back-up, but let's be sure."

Aidi said: "About that. There'll be food on the ship."

He could see Kunessin hadn't thought of that. "What do you reckon?"

"Remember the trouble our sloop had," he said softly. "Ships sink. Maybe they never got here."

Kunessin thought for a moment. "They'll send another," he said. "We'd have to tidy up."

"Load it with rocks and scuttle it in the bay," Aidi said.

"And those two, and the crew." Kunessin frowned. "No, we'd better not."

"All right. What about their stores, though? We need them."

Again Kunessin paused for thought. "Let's not make trouble for ourselves. The men'd better camp out tonight; tell Kudei to keep them out of the way till these two've gone. They'll understand why. I'll write a letter for them to take back to Command. I should be able to buy us some time." He paused, drew breath. "Really, it's not so bad. We knew there'd be something like this to deal with at some point. Sooner's better than later, if you ask me."

Aidi nodded, then added, "We found a big nest of colour today; nuggets, too. Best day so far, ironically."

Kunessin looked bothered by that. "Tell Kudei and Muri what to do," he said. Then he advanced on the two officers, who looked up sharply as he approached. "Well?" he demanded.

"We think it'd be best if we went back to the mainland for further orders," the elder man said in a high voice.

"Just what I was about to suggest," Kunessin replied. "You can take a letter for me." His frown tightened. "Do you want to sleep here, or on your ship?"

"We don't want to put you out," the younger man squeaked. "We'll go back to the ship."

"As you like. Just hold on here while I write the letter."

He took his time over it, to give Muri a chance to carry out his orders, though that wasn't quite so important now. These two weren't going to try and take the settlement by force, even if they had the numbers. He'd never seen two men more scared, not even in a battle. On balance, he took that as a compliment.

THIRTEEN

When Clea Andron was fifteen years old, she'd fallen in love. Typically, both of herself and her family, she hit upon the worst possible man to fall in love with. He was ten years older than her, a soldier, a deserter, on the run, primarily interested in food and somewhere to hide, with sex a very poor second and romance nowhere. As a result he was a half-hearted, rushed, preoccupied lover (not that she knew any better), but she still managed to get pregnant, a condition which started to make itself noticeable at almost exactly the time as the military proctors caught up with him. Just in case the situation wasn't miserable enough, he chose to make things worse. When the proctors' men arrived at the derelict lime kiln where he'd been hiding, there was a brief, messy fight, in the course of which he somehow contrived to smash in a soldier's skull with the poll of the axe Clea had brought him for splitting up kindling. The proctors' men took the axe to the blacksmith, who by sheer fluke recognised it, because of a flaw in the weld between the two halves of the head. He'd made it for a customer who'd rejected it because of the flaw, and Clea's father had taken it off his hands at half-price. When the soldiers asked him about it, Stethessi Andron told them the axe had been stolen from the woodshed; anybody could have taken it, of course, but the date was significant. When Clea heard that the soldiers had been round asking questions about an axe, she panicked and tried to poison herself with sycamore pods. She made a mess of that, too, but (as her mother told the neighbours) at least it got rid of the baby.

Everybody knew, of course; and since it was common knowledge, everybody assumed that Kudei Gaeon knew about it when he agreed to marry Clea. They assumed wrong. The other false assumption they made was that Clea tried to kill herself because of the baby, and for fear of being arrested for giving the deserter the murder weapon. In that respect, they underestimated her. It was the news, casually imparted by the soldiers, that the deserter had been hanged the previous week, rather than the conventional shame or fear of the law, that pushed her over the edge.

"You're mad," Clea said. "You must be out of your heads, all of you."

Kudei turned away. When Clea started yelling, he'd learned to ignore her until she stopped and calmed down. It was how you dealt with fractious livestock, and apparently it worked with women, too.

"That's the decision," he said to the wall. "Not up to me."

"What's wrong with you?" Clea persisted. "There's a fortune in that river, you said so yourself. You can't just let the army take it away from you."

"We'll keep what we've already got," Kudei replied. "That'll be plenty. With my share, we can buy more land, really get the farm on its feet again."

Because he wasn't looking at her, he didn't see the expression on her face. "You're going to give it all to your stupid brothers."

"Not give," Kudei replied.

Clea made a sort of half-swallowed shrieking noise. "For God's sake!" she yelled at him. "Even you couldn't be that stupid. Look what they did with your money you brought home from the war."

"We were unlucky," Kudei said. "Just bad luck. It could have happened to anybody."

"In six months it'll all be gone," Clea said. "All gone and fuck all to show for it, just like the last time. And I'll be stuck there on that pathetic little farm for the rest of my life, with you."

He waited to make sure she'd finished for the time being, then said, "We can't stay here. When the soldiers come back, we'll have to go. There's no two ways about it."

Her brief silence he attributed to speechless rage. "But General Kunessin's got a legal paper," she said. "It means the island belongs to him. Doesn't that mean anything?"

"No," Kudei said.

"He doesn't think so."

Kudei sighed. "His idea is, let them have the gold workings and we keep the rest of the island. Basically, the original plan but with a permanent military garrison on our doorstep. Not what I signed up for. I'd rather go home. The others will just have to get along without me. Don't suppose it'll be the end of the world."

She laughed at him. It was the first time she'd done that. "Don't be bloody stupid," she said. "If they stay, they won't let you go."

"Surely that's what you want," Kudei said mildly. "To stay here."

He yawned, stretched, and rubbed his eyes, and as he moved, she saw, peeping out from under the collar of his shirt, the upper end of the terrible scar that ran from his collar-bone to his navel: broad, shiny, soft, purple against his unusually pale skin, like a river crossing a plain. On their first night together she'd asked him about it; got it in the war, he'd replied, as though she'd asked him about a hat or a pair of shoes. She felt the anger drain away, soaked up by the disgust, and the fear.

"No I don't," she said, almost meekly. "I want to go somewhere—somewhere nice." She winced at her choice of word, but he nodded, and the movement tugged on the end of the scar, stretching the purple skin. "A nice house somewhere, I don't care if it's a farm or in a town. Somewhere quiet. Away from them."

He frowned, as though thinking over a complex proposition. "You said you didn't want to go back to the farm," he said.

"Not with your brothers," she said. "That'd be as bad as being here, with your friends. For crying out loud, Kudei, don't you want to get away? You do really, I know you do."

His face didn't move for a long time; then he grinned. "Not as simple as that, though, is it? Teuche and Aidi and Muri and Fly..." He pulled a face, comic and sad, then shook his head, like a cow shaking off flies. "It's difficult," he said. "I have obligations. Running away's just something I daydream about, so I won't actually have to do it."

He stood up. She turned her back, not watching as he left her and walked away. There was something he did, a tiny mannerism, a slight tilt of the head as he stooped under the lintel, that reminded her of the soldiers who came to ask her father about the axe. It had puzzled her ever since she first noticed him doing it, until eventually she'd overheard Muri and Alces talking about something or other while they sat under a tree, sheltering from a sudden squall of rain. Muri had a heavy cloth bag slung over his shoulder—his carpentry tools, something like that—and as he eased the strap away from the base of his throat, he'd made some remark about old times, and suddenly she knew: the tilt of the head, just the way someone who carried a heavy bag on a strap every day instinctively stretches his neck to shift the strap into a comfortable position. Something a soldier would do, something all soldiers did, such a stupid thing to hate someone for, but she couldn't put it out of her mind; and every time he did it, it pulled up the purple tip of the scar. She'd asked Menin, who'd asked Muri, and he'd said Kudei had got it cutting into a hedge of pikes (the place-name meant nothing to her); the gash went so deep you could see the bone, but it was only after the battle, when the enemy had been routed, herded into a steep-sided combe and slaughtered to the last man, that he'd even noticed it, and condescended to allow the surgeon to pack it with moss and spider's web and stitch it up. Muri seemed to think that was rather fine and splendid, but to her the scar was a line on a map of the place where Kudei and A Company still lived, the place they'd never leave. She thought about that and shivered, and a shadow fell across her face. She looked up, and saw one of the indentured men, Xipho Sideroi.

"You made me jump," she said.

He grinned. "You looked like you were miles away. Didn't mean to startle you."

"That's all right. I didn't expect to see anybody round the house, this time of day."

Sideroi pulled a sad face. "Had to come back for my other boots," he said. "The pair I was wearing split—there, look, right up the seam." He held a muddy, stinking boot under her nose, and the burst seam, with its ripped stitches and frayed holes, looked like an open wound. "Past mending, I reckon. What do you think?"

She shrugged. "Chuck it out, then," she said. "I expect there's some that'll fit you in the general's stores."

He laughed. "Don't think so," he said. "I don't know who he bought them off, but they saw him coming. Sixty pairs he bought for the stores, and they're all the same bloody size."

It took a moment for her to understand; then she snorted with laughter. "You're kidding," she said.

"Perfectly true. All the same, and too small to fit any of us." Sideroi grinned. "You know what I reckon? He bought them off one of the military contractors, cheap; and I think they're from the war, when we were fighting those foreigners from down south, the little chaps. Small feet, see?"

Four days of deep, rich silt, and the lid of the gold jar no longer sat quite straight, even when Aidi pressed it down hard. On the fifth day, around mid-morning, Dorun came running up the river to the workings, to say that there was a ship in the bay. Not a sloop or a cutter; a big ship, as big as the one they came in.

For a long time, roughly as long as it takes to bridle a horse, nobody moved or spoke. Then Aidi dropped his shovel, straightened up with an effort (he'd been digging for four hours) and started giving orders to the indentured men. Muri and Kudei sprinted off towards the settlement. Alces went in a different direction.

Back at the main house, Kunessin put the wooden box he kept his papers in down on the long table, though he didn't unlock it. Then he went to the shed where the weapons and armour were kept. Behind him in the main house, the women were putting up the shutters and filling buckets from the stream.

Kunessin waited for as long as he could bear, then walked out to the jetty. He was unarmed, but under his coat he wore his brigandine: twelve hundred and fifty small plates of proof steel, riveted into buckskin and faced with green velvet, so perfectly articulated that after a while he'd forget it was there. He'd got it from an enemy whom he'd stabbed seven times without any effect before guessing the truth and cutting his throat.

He stood at the end of the jetty and watched the ship grow and take shape. The dot stretched sideways, sprouted tiny points that resolved into masts, which flowered into sails. He stared at it, frowned, then suddenly grinned, clapped his hands together so fiercely that they stung, executed a jumping turn and ran very fast back to the house, just in time to meet Muri and Kudei. He flung one arm around Kudei's neck and the other across Muri's shoulders.

"It's not the government," he roared in Kudei's face. "It's our ship."

It took Kudei a surprisingly long time, maybe as much as two seconds. Then he broke free and jumped in the air, while Muri let out a shrill whoop. "Look for yourself if you don't believe me," Kunessin was saying. "Food and clothes and fuck knows what else."

Kudei feinted a sparring punch at his chin; he parried it open-handed with his left and prodded Kudei's solar plexus with his right forefinger. "You'd better run over and tell Aidi," he said. "Muri, go and get Fly, he's up at the boathouse. We'll meet back here and start unloading."

As luck would have it, a stiff breeze got up and bustled the ship into the harbour. The entire company was there to meet it, wives and indentured men as well as the five proprietors. As the plank came down and the captain stepped on to the jetty, Kunessin's ferocious "Where the hell have you been?" was drowned out by a raucous cheer. He gave up, grabbed the captain, lifted him off his feet and hugged him, nearly crushing him to death against the plates of the brigandine.

It took a whole day to unload the ship. Three quarters of the hold was taken up by barrels of flour; in the remaining quarter, bacon, dried fruit, beer, crates of live chickens, store apples, carrots and turnips packed in sand, salt fish, onions, boots (all different sizes), shirts, coats, tools, nails, roofing slates, sheet iron, billets of hardening steel, wire, staples, hinges, latches, mirrors, crockery and tinware. The company (joint owners of a four-foot-high jar of gold dust whose lid would no longer shut properly) were stunned into silence by the sight of six gallon jars of pickled walnuts and nine gross of five-eighth-inch tallow candles.

The ship brought other things. For Kunessin, two letters. One was from his agent in Faralia, informing him that his account at the bank was now exhausted. The other had been handed to the ship's captain by a wild-eyed second lieutenant, whose sloop had intercepted the ship the previous day; if the captain could possibly deliver this letter, the lieutenant had said, it would save him two days' sailing. The way he'd fought so hard not to grin when the captain agreed to take the letter...

Kunessin took a walk up the hill, and read the letter sitting on the top rail of the two-thirds-unfinished stock pen. It was a notice to quit, referring him to the emergency provisions in the third schedule to clause fourteen of the transfer deed. The emergency wasn't specified; but, fair enough, there was no explicit requirement in clause fourteen that they should do so. All the government had to do was certify that a genuine state of emergency existed, and they had the right to revoke the grant and take back the island.

He frowned. Everybody knew that clause fourteen was only invoked if there was a war, and the land in question was needed for strategic purposes: a base of operations, a shipyard, a garrison. So maybe there was a war; he wouldn't have heard about it, isolated on his little rock. He was, however, inclined to doubt it. His own letter couldn't have reached Central Command yet; neither, by the same token, could the two young officers' report. This notice, therefore, had nothing to do with the recent visit.

Properly speaking, it was the end of the world. A clause fourteen requisition couldn't be opposed or appealed against, there was no defence whatsoever. It was like trying to fight the gods, or an earthquake. It was also incredibly rare. It had to be; if the government made a habit of using clause fourteen in anything but the direst emergencies, no rational man would ever buy land from them. It was a mandatory clause. Every government transfer had to include it, and if some fool of a clerk accidentally left it out, it would automatically be read into the deal by any court. Misuse of it was unthinkable, it simply didn't happen...

Which was why, although the wording of the letter was unambiguously clear and the seal at the foot of the page was unimpeachably genuine, he couldn't make himself believe that it really was the end of the world, the loss of everything. After all, he knew exactly what that felt like (a field full of dead bodies; losing the farm), and this wasn't it. Therefore, it had to be a mistake, a clerical error, a misunderstanding. Like a government refusing to recognise a new regime in a foreign country, he resolved to ignore it, for the time being at least. He folded the letter carefully, and put it in his pocket.

Other letters, too. For Aidi, the death of an uncle he hadn't seen for twenty years, bringing with it a legacy, fifteen thousand thalers, a house and six hundred acres with vacant possession. He grinned as he read it, then screwed it up into a ball and threw it at the fire. He assumed he'd hit the back of the grate, but for once his superb natural aim failed him, and Chaere picked it up after he'd left the house. For Alces, a final demand for the rent on the fencing school, payable within six days (the letter was three weeks old), failing which the house would be repossessed and its contents sold. For Kudei, a letter from his sister-in-law, to tell him that his brother Lusei had had a stroke, and was paralysed from the neck down. For Dorun, a long, chatty letter from her mother. For Chaere, a shorter letter from her father, inquiring after her health and asking, very delicately, for money.

While the last barrel was being rolled across the yard into the stores, Kunessin led the ship's captain out of the compound, up the hill as far as the stock pen. There he told him about the gold strike; about how the settlement was now a merchant company rather than an agricultural estate, and how it would therefore be needing regular supplies of food and essential material.

"It goes without saying," he said, in a bland, everyday sort of voice, "that if word of what we're doing here gets out, it'll ruin everything.

We'll have the government down on us like flies in summer, not to mention pirates and God knows what else. All it'd take would be one conversation in a bar and we'll be screwed. Do you see that?"

The captain nodded warily.

"Excellent. Now," Kunessin went on, "so far, nobody knows about this except us here, and you. We won't be telling anybody, because we're stuck here on an island, with nobody to tell."

The captain was a big man, more than a head taller than Kunessin and broader across the shoulders. But he'd been born and brought up in Faralia; he knew who General Kunessin was. "I swear," he said quickly. "On my life."

"Yes," Kunessin replied. "Fine, I'm glad you see it that way. Now, you'd better keep your men on the ship. Tell them we've got mountain fever or something."

"Leave it to me."

"Of course." Kunessin smiled, then frowned. "Oh, one other thing. I've run out of money, so you'll need to raise a mortgage on the ship to pay for the next consignment. I'll give you a letter of authorisation."

The captain wasn't sure about that. "Is that necessary?" he said. "Surely, if you're digging gold out of this river..."

Kunessin shook his head, like a teacher correcting a simple but fundamental error. "We can't pay for anything with gold. We can't sell any of it. As soon as we do anything like that, the whole world's going to guess what we've got here. It's sort of ironic, really. We're quite possibly the richest men alive, and we're broke. Doesn't matter," he went on. "When we're through here, we can pay off the mortgage out of the stuff that gets trapped in the weave of our sacks. And then you can have the ship for your very own, for all I care."

The captain looked at him and said nothing (like the girl in the fairy tale who marries the prince of the elves, on condition that she never tries to talk to him). Kunessin sighed. He was gazing out over the coastal plain, at the water-meadows on either side of the river. "I hate it here," he said. "When I was in the war, this was my dream; this or something like it. Now I wish I'd never set eyes on the place."

*   *   *

The ship sailed early the next morning; empty, apart from its crew. Aidi tried to get Kunessin on his own, so he could shout at him, but Kunessin was keeping out of his way. So he trudged back to the main house, where his wife was waiting for him.

"I need four hundred thalers," she said.

Aidi sighed. "For crying out loud, let me get my boots off first."

She clicked her tongue, a mannerism which she knew irritated him. "Don't you want to know what it's for?"

He shrugged. "Does it matter?"

"Well, of course it matters."

"Fine," he said, kicking off his left boot. "If it matters to you, then of course you can have the money." Then the right boot. "I take it you need it in Faralia rather than here."

"Well, of course."

"Just asking. In that case, it'll have to be a letter of credit on the bank. Pity you didn't mention it before the ship sailed. It'll be two months before it comes back."

She glowered at him. "I was picking my moment."

"When I'm in a good mood?" He grinned. "Like now, for instance?"

"If I had to wait till you're in a good mood, I'd most likely die of old age first." She scowled horribly at him. "You're not going to ask, are you?"

"Why should I? It's your business, not mine."

"It's for my father," she snarled at him. "He needs to cover a bad debt from a customer, and—"

"Fine." Aidi stood up. "How many times do I have to say it? You can have the money." He opened the door, then turned his head and looked at her. "It's one of your more annoying traits, Chaere. You won't take yes for an answer."

He left her in the porch and went inside, but Kunessin wasn't there. That made him angry. He crossed the room, waddling gingerly in his bare feet, and sat in a chair in front of the cold fireplace. He closed his eyes; then he heard footsteps behind him and sat up.

"Now what?" he asked.

"I want to know why you're in such a foul mood," Chaere said.

"You should be happy. You've been worrying yourself sick about when the ship was going to get here."

"True," he said, closing his eyes again. "And now everything's a whole lot worse. Can't win, can you?"

She hesitated, then knelt down beside him. "What's the matter?" she said.

"Teuche's the matter," he replied, eyes shut, head turned away. "He'd agreed to send the servants back with the ship. And now the ship's gone, and they're still here."

Chaere frowned. "Is that so bad? We need them to get the gold."

He didn't appear to have heard her. "We're only here because of him," he said. "He's only here because he wants a country estate—no, scrub that, he wants a farm, like the one his father lost. Well, fine. Big bloody deal. He can have mine." He paused, then said, "I just learned, from a letter I got—"

"I was wondering when you'd mention it."

"Oh." He pulled a face. "Anyhow, it seems I now own a farm, which I really have no possible use for. Teuche wants one. Splendid. Why don't I just give it to him, and everybody's happy?"

Even with his eyes shut, he could feel Chaere's horrified shock at that suggestion. He savoured it for a moment, then answered his own question. "Because," he said, "stupid bloody Teuche wouldn't take it. Missing the point, he'd say. Probably get offended with me for offering and not talk to me for a week."

"Quite right too," Chaere said quickly. "Aidi, have you any idea what that land'd be worth? You can't just go giving—"

"So instead," Aidi went on, "we stay here. Which should be all right, because we've found the richest gold strike in history. Lucky us. We've dug enough of the stuff out of there in a few months to make us all comfortable for life, even if we share it with the bloody servants. So, we go home, sell it, live happily ever after. Do we hell."

"You should talk to him," Chaere said. "Insist. Get the others on your side, then he'll have to listen."

Aidi turned on her, so fast she didn't have time to flinch. "You don't know anything about us," he said, quiet and savagely intense.

"You don't think we came here because we wanted to, do you? Of course we didn't. But Teuche..." He sighed, and leaned back in the chair. "Teuche gave us a direct order. And if he wants to stay here, we stay." He shifted, as though the chair had suddenly become uncomfortable. "I just wish he'd make up his mind what he really wants," he said. "Then we could see to it that he gets it. That's all we want out of life."

Nothing she could have said could possibly have been more informative than the silence that followed, but he really wasn't interested. He closed his eyes again. He'd just paid four hundred thalers for that darkness. He waited until he'd heard her heels pecking furiously at the floorboards, from the fireplace right across to the door, before opening them again.

Money, he thought; one way or another, it was all about money with Teuche. Losing the farm for want of a few dozen thalers had screwed him up so tight he'd never recovered. In the army, he'd built up an immense fortune — understandable; so much money, security, he could never possibly want for anything ever again — but as soon as he leaves the service, what does he do but spend it all, wildly, recklessly, stupidly (and Teuche Kunessin had never been stupid), almost as though he was desperate to get rid of it, like a thief with his loot hearing the voices of the watch at the door. Well, he'd done that, for reasons best known to himself, and then saw what happened: more money, an even more immense fortune, and he'd never seen Teuche look so lost — so scared — in all the years he'd known him. It reminded him (he had to think to capture the memory) of a dog they'd had once, that would insist on finding dead, decaying birds and rats and bringing them into the house, sitting at your feet during dinner and offering them to you, a worshipper sacrificing to its god. So: Teuche tries to get rid of the money, throws it away, but the dog keeps bringing it back. There was something in that, but just now he couldn't quite see what it was.

He closed his eyes, to help himself concentrate. Teuche got a huge amount of money while he was in the army. Well, that wasn't anything unusual. There were opportunities everywhere: misappropriation of stores, corruption in the allotment of supply contracts, drawing the pay of dead men—there were whole regiments on the paymasters' books that didn't actually exist. A man could make a fortune in the army if he set his mind to it. The thing was, though, that Teuche hadn't ever wanted to be rich—as in luxury, excess, ostentation, conspicuous consumption. Teuche wore his coats till they frayed apart, ate bread and cheese for preference, whined if the bed was too soft, because it hurt his back. Some people wanted money because of the power it gave them, but Teuche had been a general. If he desperately wanted money, it was because there was something he wanted to buy; which, apparently, was exactly what he'd done.

Aidi frowned. He didn't approve of dishonesty. Shrewdness, yes, but cheating, lying for money, made him feel slightly sick. And now they had so much money it really didn't matter, and Teuche was thoroughly miserable, and scared.

Scared; what of? Aidi twisted in his chair. It was like when he'd lost something, and he knew exactly where it should be, but when he went to look for it, it wasn't there. Scared of losing the gold. Rule that out straight away. If that was the case, he'd evacuate immediately, sell what they'd already dug out of the river, be done with it. Scared of losing the land. So what? With the money, he could buy all the land he could possibly want. Scared of losing his four best friends. Aidi slowed his thoughts down so he could keep pace with them. Closer to the mark; something that money couldn't buy. But the simple fact remained that when the war ended, they'd split up and deliberately stayed out of each other's way; Teuche still in the service, the rest of them back in Faralia but scarcely ever meeting, as though by common unspoken agreement. True, all of them (except Teuche) had pretty much wasted their time since they got home; Fly and Muri barely getting by, Kudei stuck on the farm, himself playing at being a shopkeeper when by rights he should've founded a mercantile empire, if that had really been what he wanted to do. That could be explained by a glib generalisation: A Company, the biggest bunch of underachievers the world had ever seen. Then go on to argue that men who'd seen and done what they had simply couldn't be bothered with the trivial business of peace and order, and as for money...

Money, again. He tried to clear it out of his mind, but instead, a fragment of a pattern snagged his attention. Money; they'd had money in their pockets when they came home from the war. Kudei had given his share to his brothers, who'd contrived to evaporate it on money-spinning schemes that fell through, improvements that went bad, land that turned out to be worthless. Alces had wasted his by sheer fecklessness; Aidi wasn't entirely sure what Muri had done with his, but it hadn't taken him long to get rid of it all. For his own part, he'd set up his shop, gone through the motions of running his business, not really bothered, but when the time had come to sell up, he'd still doubled his original stake, making him a wealthy man.

That brick wall again. Missing the point. Money in their pockets when they came back from the war; in his case, enough to buy the shop. His share; his equal share. Something to do with that, but he still couldn't quite see what it was.

Two days after the ship left, Kunessin called a general meeting. The government, he told them, had served notice to quit. He did not intend to comply. He had lodged a formal appeal, and was confident that the notice would be withdrawn. For the time being, however, the threat had to be taken seriously. Given the possibility, however unlikely, that they could be evicted, it was essential that they increase production, to get out as much gold as possible before the government took action to enforce the notice. Since gold could only be extracted in daylight, everybody — himself and the women included — would work in the river from dawn to dusk; other tasks such as cooking, washing clothes and so forth would have to be done after nightfall, by lamp- or firelight. He was working with the other proprietors to plan an emergency evacuation, should one be necessary. That was all.

"Emergency evacuation," Alces murmured, as they walked up the river to the workings. "Sounds very efficient and reassuring. What did you have in mind? Swimming?"

"There's the sloop," Kunessin replied.

"We can't all get in the sloop," Kudei said. "Eight of us, maximum."

"Ten," Kunessin said. "Us five, and the girls, and the jar."

Kudei rolled his eyes. "It'll sink like a stone."

"No it won't. It'll be low in the water, but it can do it."

"I don't suppose you've discussed this with the servants," Aidi said. "Let me know when you do, I'll be interested to see how you go about it."

"I wasn't planning on doing that," Kunessin said, looking straight ahead.

"All right," Alces said. "So what are you going—?"

"I'll tell them the ship's coming back early," Kunessin said. "And then we'll have it stand by on the other side of the island, just in case we need it."

"Where?" Muri objected. "There's nowhere on the far side a ship could—"

"They don't know that, and they'll be too busy working to go and look for themselves. It'll be all right," he went on. "If the government sends troops, they'll just round them up and ship them to the mainland. No earthly reason why they shouldn't be perfectly civilised about it."

Aidi nodded. "Fine," he said. "Then what? Do we all meet up in a bar somewhere and have a grand sharing-out ceremony?"

Kunessin frowned. "Not in a bar," he said. "That'd be rather public for my liking."

"You're going to share it with them, though. That's the plan, is it?"

Kunessin looked straight at him, like an archer at a target. "Of course," he said. "The net proceeds, less our original investment. That's what we agreed."

Chaere didn't like panning for gold. She didn't like standing in water, she refused to handle a shovel and she complained bitterly about the ache in her elbows and wrists from turning the pan.

"Are you listening?" she said, as Aidi stabbed the shovel into the silt. "I'm in pain, damn you, I can't do this any more."

"No such word as can't," Aidi replied absently. "Stop whining and get on with it."

She threw the pan down, splashing water all over Aidi's knees. "No," she snapped. "That's it, I'm going home."

She didn't move. Aidi yawned and retrieved the pan before it could float away. "For one thing," he said, "you're doing it wrong. You're turning the pan like you're trying to wring its neck. Also, if you just let it rest on the surface, the water takes the weight out of it. I did show you, but you always have to know best."

He shoved the pan at her; she grabbed it in self-defence. "I shouldn't have to be doing this," she hissed. "It's man's work. I'm not a man."

"Ah," Aidi said mildly. "That'd explain a lot." Before she could get out of the way, he scooped up a shovelful of silt and deposited it in the pan. She scowled at him, then started twisting it viciously. "Try it like I told you," Aidi said. "Just once, for fun."

She carried on twisting, harder than before. Aidi watched her for a few seconds, then said: "They can do it. The rest of the girls, and the servants. If they can manage it, you can."

She gave him a scowl that would've stripped bark off a log. "I don't want to do it," she said.

With a flick of the shovel blade, Aidi tipped the pan neatly out of her hands. "Fine," he said. "Go and sit on the bank, where they can all see you. I'll explain you're too feeble to work."

Very slowly, she stooped down and picked the pan out of the water. "Tell me again," she said. "This time clearly, so I can understand."

Half an hour later, she'd got it down to a fine art, as he knew she would. "It's like peeling apples," she said. "You've just got to keep turning it and turning it. Nothing to it, really."

Aidi levered out another spit of silt and stood up, letting the water drain off the blade. "Told you," he said.

"Once I'd figured it out for myself," she went on. "The way you tried to show me was hopeless. That's the trouble with you: you make everything much harder than it needs to be."

Aidi grinned at her. "Is that right?" he said.

"Yes. Come on, the pan's empty; don't just stand there."

"Sorry," Aidi said humbly. "Oops," he added, as he spilt muddy water off the edge of the blade down the front of her dress. "Not looking what I was doing."

An hour later she said, "I'm going to stop now, I need a rest."

"Fair enough," Aidi conceded. "We haven't done too badly. You can sit on that rock there."

She sat and watched him as he picked up the pan and tipped the silt into it one-handed from the shovel. He was quicker and more productive on his own, of course, but that wasn't the point.

"So," she said, "what's Kunessin going to do? Really?"

Aidi shrugged. "Ask him yourself," he said.

"I'm asking you. You're his best friend."

He didn't bother to correct her. "You heard what he said. He's appealed against the notice to quit, and he's confident—"

"I can remember what he said without you reciting it for me. What are these evacuation plans you're supposed to be making?"

Aidi paused, looking down into the pan. "We make a run for it in the sloop," he said.

"The five of you?"

"The ten of us."

"And the gold?"

"No, we leave that behind for the government, with a bloody great big ribbon tied round it. Yes, and the gold."

She scowled at him. "That stupid little boat..."

"It'll be fine."

She shrugged. "What about the servants?"

"The government'll give them a ride back to the mainland. Saves us making arrangements."

"Do they know—?"

"They'll be told the ship's come back early," he interrupted her irritably, "and it's anchored off the other side of the island, out of sight."

"Will they believe that?"

"Teuche reckons they will." He started to work the pan, but his usual dexterity seemed to have eluded him; he slopped silt over the rim, and swore. "Anyway, once they're ashore, we all meet up somewhere and share out the takings, and that's that. We all go home."

"Really." A flat tone of voice; he wasn't quite sure what to make of it. "This appeal."

"Waste of time."

"So we're definitely going home? As soon as the government—"

"Yes."

She stood up. "Here," she said, "give me that, you're making a complete mess of it."

Dorun and Enyo had tossed a coin, and Dorun had lost. That meant she got the shovel.

"You're good at this," Dorun said, after they'd been working for a while.

Enyo nodded. "If they can do it," she said, "so can I." She grinned. "I grew up with three elder brothers," she said. "Being too feeble to join in wasn't an option."

"I might have guessed," Dorun said. Then, after a while, "They're back home, then. Your brothers."

She shook her head. "They were killed in the war," she said.

Dorun mumbled something appropriate.

"It's all right," Enyo replied. "They were too young to join up, so they lied about their ages. Gamous and Pinein were twins, they were seventeen, and Bia was very tall for sixteen. Besides, by that stage they weren't fussy. Their ship sank, taking them over there. Stupid, really."

"I lost my cousin Zeuge in the war," Dorun said. "He was a sergeant in the Sixteenth."

Enyo frowned. "Weren't they...?"

Dorun smiled. "That's right," she said. "The big battle right at the end of the war. Teuche and our lot were there, of course. He told me about it, or at least he started to, and then I made him stop. Not that Zeuge and I were close or anything. Anyway, that was the battle where Zeuge was killed. Him and a lot of other men, of course." She furrowed her brow, as though a loose end had just dropped into place. "They never did figure out how it happened," she said. "They think somebody must've told the enemy where they were headed; someone on our side, I mean. But I talked to some of the men who'd been in Zeuge's unit, and they told me it had all been a deadly secret; they didn't know where they were being sent, not even the junior officers. So if there was a traitor, it had to be someone pretty high up." She shook her head. "I asked Teuche what he thought, but he didn't want to talk about it. You can understand that, I suppose."

Enyo shrugged. "You'd have thought," she said. "Thouridos isn't quite like that. Sometimes he's all uptight about it, gets blazing mad if I ask him anything about the war. Other times the problem's getting him to shut up. I know he thinks about it all the time. More since your Teuche came back, I reckon. There's something about it that really bothers him, and that's what makes him clam up. Mind you, I think he's like that anyway: up one moment and down the next. He'd have been like it even if he hadn't been to the war. Oh damn," she added, as she slopped mud over her sleeve. "And I was just thinking how easy it is."

"We're not doing too badly, for beginners," Dorun replied. "I'd like to've seen how they got on, the first time they tried it."

"Mud everywhere, probably," Enyo replied. "Only they'd rather die than admit it. It's no good, I've got to stop for a bit. My wrists are killing me."

Dorun clicked her tongue sympathetically. "Would you like me to take over for a bit?"

"Not likely." Enyo nodded at the shovel. "You were brought up on a farm, I suppose."

"Is it that obvious?"

Enyo sighed. "When I was seventeen they wanted me to marry a farmer. Good bit older than me, but perfectly nice, I wouldn't have minded at all. But then I thought about mucking out cow stalls and killing chickens and shearing sheep and all that constant, never-ending handling food, and that was that. My parents got really upset with me."

"It's not so bad," Dorun said with a smile. "It's like everything, you get used to it."

"Not me," Enyo said firmly. "Cleaning and washing and mending and three meals a day is one thing, but I draw the line at field work, or anything that involves pulling the guts out of something dead. I know about farmers' wives. Their hair always stinks of blood."

Dorun laid the shovel down on the bank. "We haven't done too badly so far," she said, lifting up the pottery cup they were using to hold the gold dust. It sparkled as she moved it. "How much do you reckon we've got in there? Five thalers?"

"Easily," Enyo replied, peering. "Closer to ten." She lifted her head and grinned. "That's not bad," she said. "I never earned five thalers before."

They sat on the bank and watched for a while. The frantic pace had slowed down, and was holding steady, brisker than usual but realistic. Dorun looked around until she found Kunessin. He was shovelling for Muri, further upstream than anybody else. He looked slow compared with the others, but she soon realised that wasn't the case. He looked slow because his movements were short, efficient, unhurried, the minimum effort and the maximum effect. There was something faintly disturbing, frightening even, about it. He reminded her of a predator, a lynx or a hawk: economy of effort, concentration of force. So different, she thought; quite unlike a human being. Certainly not a farmer. Maybe he'd been one once, but he could no more go back to it than he could be twelve years old again.

"I hope we do go home soon," she said, her voice a little shaky. "After all, we've got everything we could possibly want. There's no earthly reason to stay here."

A week later, and they'd been forced to start another jar. It was already nearly a quarter full. The indentured men had asked four times for a slower pace, and Kunessin had got angry with them. Now they hardly spoke, not even to each other. Muri and Kudei had taken to sleeping on board the sloop, just in case anybody took it into their heads to use it for an early private evacuation. There was plenty of food now, but nobody was particularly hungry: too tired to eat, or simply not bothered. Menin hadn't said a word to Muri for a week; she worked with Terpsi Cerauno—she was a first-rate panner—did her share of cooking and cleaning but barely spoke to the other girls, and slept in the corner of the main house furthest from the fire, wrapped up in six blankets and a discarded greatcoat of Kudei's. Chaere, by contrast, had suddenly turned cheerful. She'd taken to panning in a big way, easily keeping pace with the men in both technique and stamina; ever so much better than weaving or embroidery, she told anybody who'd listen, and not all that much harder physically. True, she complained about how being soaked in water all day was playing havoc with her hands; she spent most of the evening massaging sheep's-wool grease into them, from a pot of the stuff that had been intended for waterproofing boots. She got up early to wash her hair every morning, and spent half an hour every evening combing it. Clea argued with Kudei all the time, though nobody was quite sure what about, even though they couldn't help hearing every word. Aidi and Kunessin had taken to wearing swords, catsplitters, on their belts under their coats. They took them off when they were in the river, but put them on again as soon as they stopped work. Aechmaloten went down with a fever, but nobody seemed interested in looking after him. A stomach bug did the rounds for a day and a half. A Company were disdainfully immune, but the women and the indentured men most decidedly weren't. Kunessin refused to suspend work; and, as Alces pointed out, since they were working in a river, a perfect combination of latrine and bath, there really wasn't anything to complain about, except possibly for those working downstream. Production wasn't greatly affected, so that was all right.

"Maybe," Menin said to Cerauno, as she tipped dust into the cloth bag he was holding for her, "they aren't coming after all."

Cerauno shook his head. "It hasn't been that long," he said. "Since the general got the letter, I mean. And he's appealed, hasn't he? I expect all that takes time."

"I suppose," Menin said. "Really, I wish it was all over and done with. Either we go or we stay, I mean. Hanging around like this . . ." She angled the pan to shift the last few speckles. "I'm worn out," she said sadly. "This is hard work."

Cerauno grinned. "You can see the general's point, though," he said. "Might as well make the most of it while we can. Every day extra we're here means hundreds of thalers."

"I guess." Menin stepped back, and Cerauno nudged the blade of his shovel into the silt. "How are you feeling now? Any better?"

"Oh, I'm fine," Cerauno said. "It must just've been one of those things that goes round. Surprised we haven't had more like it, actually; this many of us, cooped up in one place."

"There was that thing a while back," Menin said vaguely. "You remember. And everyone said it was the wild mushrooms."

He looked at her; something in her voice. "Oh, I don't think anybody blamed you."

"Yes they did." She shot the words straight back at him, like a swordsman countering a failed lunge. "They all thought it was me."

Cerauno didn't reply, and neither of them spoke again until Menin needed the cloth bag once more. "Have you thought what you're going to do," she asked. "With your share?"

He shook his head. "Go home," he replied. "Buy a place of my own. Maybe I'll start a lumber mill. There isn't one for miles where we live; people have to go right up the valley to Sharf and it's a long way with wagons. Plenty of good timber up the top; old beech and holm oak mostly, and some birch on the south side. I don't think I'm cut out for farming," he added. "Too much work."

She nodded. "A sawmill's a good idea," she said. "Is there a fast river where you are?"

"Oh yes." He was smiling. "The Redwater. Comes down off the moor at a hell of a lick, specially in the spring. But if you dug leats and put in gates, you'd have good pressure all year round."

"Sounds like you've figured it all out already," she said gravely. "I thought you said you hadn't thought about it."

"I haven't. Well, not really. It's an idea I've had for years, actually, but I never thought I'd be able to do anything about it: too much money. Now, though...Well," he went on, heaving the shovel out of the water, "we'll wait and see what happens. No point getting all excited about it yet."

Menin slopped off the excess water and began to twist. "I think a mill's a really good idea," she said. "People always want lumber, and it's a real business if you've got to plank it up yourself by hand. I watched some men sawing out planks in a sawpit once; it took hours."

"It's bloody hard work," Cerauno agreed. "Specially if you're the one down in the pit. Working above your head, see. After a bit, you get this horrible cramp in your shoulders."

She was looking into the pan, as if it was a mirror. "And once you've got the mill," she said, "there's all sorts of other things you can do as well. In the summer and autumn, I mean, when people aren't building and don't want timber. There's a mill just outside town where I used to live. Winter and spring they sawed lumber, and in the autumn they put up a couple of big stones and ground everybody's corn for them, so there was always something to do. I'm sure we could do that. I wish I could remember how the stones were rigged up. It wasn't a big job to change them round, I know that."

He'd heard the word, one little word. At first he'd assumed it was a mistake. Then he realised it wasn't. We, she'd said. We could do that.

"Terpsi? I need the bag. Come on."

He came to with a shudder, leaned the shovel against the bank, let it slip so it fell in the water; fished it out, stood it upright, fumbled for the bag and dropped it. Gold dust flopped out and heaped up round the roots of the grass, like snow.

"Terpsi..."

He stood quite still, suddenly unable to think what to do. She pushed past him and started scooping up dust with her fingers. "Sorry," he said.

"It's all right," she said; patient, forgiving voice. "Hold the bag for me." She was scrabbling in the soil with her fingernails, like a dog digging. "That's most of it," she said. "If you dig up that chunk of turf, we can put it in the pan and wash the dust out."

He made his mind up. His instinct had been to pretend it hadn't happened, but he knew that would only make things worse. He had no idea what he was going to say.

"Menin."

She was busy with the pan, and didn't look up. "Yes?"

"A moment ago." He hesitated. Things were going to be bad whatever he did or said. "I think you said, when you were talking about grinding corn..." He couldn't think how to put it, but he couldn't leave it now. "You made it sound like, well, we'd be running the mill together."

Her head was bent over the pan. She was twisting it; strong wrists and forearms. The last stage of the movement made the muscles stand out.

"I'm sorry," he said. "That was what you said, wasn't it?"

"Well?"

As if he was making a fuss about something that didn't really matter. "Menin," he said, and he could feel the fear in his voice. "Your husband..."

"Don't worry about him," she said.

"Menin..."

She stood up straight, turned and looked at him. "What about it?" she said.

"Menin, I can't..."

An impatient look. No such word as can't. "You know why he married me. Because they were all going to be farmers, and farmers need wives. But we're all going home now, so they won't need wives any more. I'll just tell him, and that'll be that." She studied him for a moment, as if deciding whether to pick him or tread on him. "You're not scared of him, are you?"

"That's not the point," he said awkwardly; he wasn't a good liar. "It's not right, Menin; you're his wife."

A hard look, scornful, disappointed. "You should've thought about that before, shouldn't you?"

He felt as if he'd just put his foot through a rotten floorboard. He wanted to say: but nothing's happened, I never...but he knew it'd just make things worse. In her mind, things were different, things had happened differently. Then she said, "Leave it all to me, I'll deal with Muri," and he knew that something was badly wrong. They all thought it was me, she'd said; he could hear her voice in his head, aggrieved, because it wasn't fair. Because...(she was waiting for the next shovelful of silt, impatient; quickly he stabbed the bright edge of the shovel into the red water)...because she'd thought about it, and decided not to, and still they'd blamed her, which really wasn't fair at all, no way to reward her for being good and doing the right thing. So, if they were going to blame her anyway, why not do it?

For a moment, it crossed his mind that he could swing the shovel, while she was looking down at the pan; she wouldn't see it coming. One swing; the thin edge would split her skull and she'd be dead, nipped in the bud, stop it before it gets out of control. And he'd explain, tell them all the truth; and of course, nobody would believe a word of it, and they'd hang him. So, that was no good; and the moment passed, and from then on he knew he wouldn't be able to find that quick spurt of courage again. She's going to murder her husband, he thought, and I can't stop it, there's nothing I can do about it. The only thing that might possibly keep it from happening would be if the soldiers came, right now, and pushed us all on to a ship.

He waited, as if he actually expected soldiers to jump up out of the clumps of briars. They didn't. It was settled, then.

His fault.

They couldn't actually be certain until they got back to the settlement and weighed up, but they were pretty sure it had been the best day yet. A fat bar in midstream, which Alces and Kudei had spent all day on; a deep pocket where a boulder had been washed away; nuggets the size of hazelnuts in an undercut hollow of the bank. They crowded round to empty their cups and bags and socks into Aidi's sack; he made a show of buckling at the knees as he took the weight, and they laughed. The best day yet, almost certainly.

They didn't talk much on the way back down the river, but it was an easy silence rather than a strained one. Someone started to whistle a tune. Aidi and Chaere were holding hands, which made Kudei smile; he nudged Alces and nodded at them, and Alces rolled his eyes.

It was dark by the time they reached the yard, which explained why they didn't see the soldiers.

FOURTEEN

There were twenty-three of them: two platoons comprising twenty men-at-arms, each with a sergeant, making up a full-strength company and led by a second lieutenant. As politely as was possible in the circumstances, they herded the settlers into the main house. Five men and a sergeant took position in front of the door, while the rest fanned out round the walls. They wore half-armours of munition plate, with cabasset helmets, steel bucklers and Type Nineteen swords. They were quite obviously terrified.

("Stands to reason," Alces muttered to Aidi. "After all, we outnumber them by nearly minus five to one.")

There was also a civilian; a short, stocky man with curly grey hair and cheeks like a pig, who didn't look the least bit scared. He cleared his throat and asked for their attention.

"My name," he said, slowly and clearly, as though dictating notes to students, "is Garana Straton. I'm an assistant commissioner in the enforcement directorate of the department of public lands and property. Could I speak to General Teuche Kunessin?"

Dead silence, and Aidi could have sworn Kunessin hesitated before walking through the scrum towards him. He stopped seven feet away, and said, "I'm Kunessin."

Straton looked at him, then down at a piece of paper in his hand; a description of Kunessin, Aidi guessed, to make sure the man in front of him wasn't an impostor. Pause while he glanced through the paper, then he lifted his head and took another long look. "General Kunessin," he said, "I have here a warrant for your arrest and immediate removal to the mainland. You have the right to remain silent and to be represented by counsel."

"No thank you," Kunessin said quietly. "What's the charge?"

Straton shuffled the papers in his hand until he found the one he wanted. "Unlawful occupation of government land," he said. "Unlawful damage to public property. Unauthorised use of military stores, equipment and facilities. Making unauthorised landfall at a restricted naval installation. Failure to secure appropriate permits before crossing a restricted maritime area. You are not obliged to enter a plea at this time; however, a guilty plea and early co-operation with the authorities may be taken into account in sentencing."

Kunessin looked at him, as though trying to decide if he was real. "This is all nonsense," he said. "I've lodged an appeal."

Straton nodded. "Your appeal in the eviction proceedings has been noted. Those proceedings are, however, in the civil jurisdiction and have no direct bearing on the criminal charges you now face." He cleared his throat, looked quickly round the room, then went on: "You and your associates will be shipped to the mainland first thing in the morning. Until then, nobody is to leave this building without my express permission. Anybody granted such permission will be closely attended by two guards." He paused for a moment, then raised his voice a little and continued: "I must ask all of you to keep away from the door and walls. Any attempt to leave and any disturbance will be met with appropriate force." He paused again, said, "Thank you for your attention," and took a step backwards; two soldiers immediately stood in front of him, covering his retreat to the far corner. Apart from Straton, everybody in the room was perfectly still and quiet, watching Kunessin; and Aidi thought: they don't know about the gold. This is all about something else, and they've got no idea what's in the two big jars.

Kunessin was moving again, and Aidi felt his muscles tense (not at his command; it was as though the brain controlling his movements was Kunessin's, not his own. Ah, he thought. Back in the army again). The soldiers reacted too; they seemed to shrink away without actually moving, a sort of speeded-up desiccation. "Commissioner," Kunessin said; his parade-ground voice. "Can we discuss this in private?"

Straton slowly turned round. He was frowning slightly. "I don't see that there's anything to discuss."

And then Kunessin seemed to grow, just as the soldiers had shrunk. "I'm sure we can think of something," he said. He wasn't smiling.

Straton was thinking. He reached a decision. "If you like," he said, and raised his left hand, with the thumb folded inwards. Four soldiers stepped away from the wall and closed in round him, like a glove round a hand. "Outside?"

Kunessin nodded, and Straton and his guards advanced through the room towards him. Two guards took position behind him (Aidi saw him not-move, a deliberate act in response to the tactical disadvantage), and then Straton led the way.

It was cold outside, and Straton had taken off his coat. Kunessin saw him tense up against the chill. "Well?"

"Commissioner," Kunessin said. "What the hell's going on?"

Straton took a moment to reply; choosing his persona like someone deciding which shoes to wear. When he spoke, he sounded almost human. "The government needs this facility, I'm afraid. You've got to go."

"What for?"

Not quite so human: "I can't tell you that."

"Yes you can. I'm a general."

"Retired."

"But still on the active list."

Clearly Straton hadn't been told that. He frowned.

"Which means," Kunessin went on, "I'm not subject to civilian criminal jurisdiction. If you want to bring charges against me, they'd have to come through the provost marshal's office, and I'd need to see a proper warrant. Without which," he added smoothly, "I'd be within my rights to resist arrest, as a matter of prerogative. Well?" he snapped. "Is that right?"

Straton thought about it, then nodded.

"Good," Kunessin said. "Glad we've got that straight. Now," he went on, and his voice was softer and richer. "What's all this really about?"

Straton changed; a complete metamorphosis, from head to foot. Now he was one important, put-upon man talking to another. "They want Sphoe for a dockyard," he said. "At least, the navy does, but the joint chiefs don't; they want to expand the base at Krinoisin, which means it'd come under the army, and the army could control the budget."

Kunessin nodded briefly; a tiny movement, like a close-in stab.

"To cut a long story short," Straton went on, "Central Command refused to authorise repossession, so the only way the navy can get Sphoe is if it's forfeited land following a criminal conviction. Then it'll pass to the Treasury—"

"And the Treasury can give it to the navy as ordinary requisitions without going through the joint chiefs," Kunessin said quickly. "Understood." He smiled. "That's rather clever. Your idea?"

Straton pulled a face. "Nothing personal."

"Of course not." Kunessin sighed. "It's a shame you didn't check the active lists. Spoilt the whole thing."

Straton breathed out, like a diver surfacing. "Attention to detail," he said. "Of course, we could have your name removed."

Kunessin gave him a nice-try smile. "Not without leave from the army," he said.

A dip of the head, by way of acknowledgement. "We're stuck, in other words," Straton said. "So, what are we going to do?"

Kunessin smiled at him. "Go home," he said.

"Can't," Straton replied. "Come on, General Kunessin, let's be realistic. I have a flawed case but actual possession. You've got a forged transfer deed. Let's help each other out of this."

Kunessin's face didn't change. "It's not forged," he said.

"No, strictly speaking it isn't. Improperly obtained; better?"

Kunessin nodded. "But still valid until revoked by Central Command," he said. "Which isn't going to happen, with all this politicking going on." He smiled. "It's nice to know I'm helping the army."

"Fortuitous," Straton said drily. "But that's beside the point. As I see it, your transfer deed and my procedural lapses cancel each other out. What's left is the fact that I've got twenty armed men, which gives me actual possession."

Kunessin beamed at him. "Fine," he said. "If you want a bloodbath, I'll be delighted; it's years since I slaughtered a whole platoon before breakfast. Then all we have to do is fill your ship with rocks and scuttle it in the bay, and there'll be nothing to show you ever reached here. Lost at sea with all hands, a maritime tragedy. Please, remember who you're talking to. Now, shall we be sensible and start again?"

Straton thought about that. "Make me an offer," he said.

Kunessin nodded. "There's something quite important you don't know about yet," he said. "Take a look at this."

From his inside pocket he took...

"A sock," Straton said.

"Yes." Kunessin untied the knot and spread the sock open on the palm of his hand. A faint yellow sparkle gleamed in the moonlight.

"What am I supposed to be looking at?" Straton asked.

Kunessin grunted. "Get one of your men to open the door just a bit."

Enough to let a beam of firelight out; and Straton's eyes opened very wide. "Is that...?"

"Yes."

"Here? On Sphoe?"

"Yes. The river—have you seen a map? Half a mile upstream from here. We think it could well be a substantial strike."

For a long time, Straton seemed to freeze, like an animal hibernating. "You'll excuse me for saying so," he said, his voice low and soft, "but surely that makes things worse for you, not better. There's no way they'll let you—"

"Quite," Kunessin said. "And I don't want it. You can have it, and welcome." He moved away a little. "Even though the transfer deed quite explicitly includes the mineral rights."

"The forged transfer deed."

"We've been into that," Kunessin said. "Don't say you're one of those tiresome people who won't take yes for an answer. Listen to me. I could make it very awkward for you to get vacant possession. It could easily take a year, and by then, who knows? We're hard grafters, Commissioner, we could clean the river out in a year. But that wouldn't be right. Like I said, you can have it. Free, gratis, absolute in possession."

Straton looked at him. "Go on," he said.

Kunessin turned his head aside, looking over his shoulder. "It stands to reason," he went on, "that if the government's going to work this strike, it won't want a dockyard on Sphoe. Too much risk, temptation; too easy for dockyard workers to nip out after dark and help themselves. Ships coming and going all the time. A security nightmare, in fact."

"Quite."

Smile. "So that puts paid to the navy's plans, then. I'm sorry for all your hard work and ingenuity, but as an army man, naturally I'm biased. Of course, you won't come out of it too badly, if you can give them a gold mine."

Straton frowned. "Make your point."

"Simply this." Kunessin's turn to pause. "Two documents," he said, "two pieces of paper, and everything's dealt with. I execute a transfer of mineral rights to the government, in return for a new transfer deed—a genuine transfer deed, as you would say—confirming my ownership of the freehold land. Which is all I want," he added. "The land, to build a farm on, for my friends and me. That's all I ever wanted."

Dead silence; Kunessin could hear the guards breathing. Straton didn't need air, apparently. Then he said, "I think we can come to an agreement along those lines. Just to recap: we get the gold strike, you keep the farmland." He frowned. "Is that really what you want?"

"Yes," Kunessin said firmly.

"You're an interesting man, General," Straton said. "That's all—"

Kunessin laughed. "All right, then, I'll add something else. Just as well you reminded me. I'd like a general pardon for any and all criminal acts and infringements of regulations, just in case it occurs to you to try the trumped-up-charges idea again at some point. I like things straightforward, you see. The less fuss, the better."

For the first time, Straton smiled. It was a poor effort and didn't mean the same as most men's smiles. "I think I can do that for you," he said. "I do have a certain amount of leeway. The documents..."

"You can draft them if you like. Or my colleague, Aidi Proiapsen; he took law at the Military College."

"I'll do it," Straton said firmly.

"Tonight?"

"Why not?" A small shrug. "They're both relatively simple. I used to do that sort of thing all the time when I was a young clerk."

Kunessin yawned. "That's settled, then," he said. "Once the paperwork's out of the way, we'll all know where we stand. I'm glad we were able to sort it out."

Straton pushed open the door, then turned back. "Your friends," he said. "They'll..."

"That's fine," Kunessin said. "Don't let me hold you up."

Straton went back into the house, closing the door behind him. Kunessin stayed where he was for the best part of a minute, then walked very quickly round the side of the house, to the lean-to where some of the tools were kept. He found what he was looking for, even though it was too dark to see properly: a long wooden box with rope handles and a plank lid. He opened it and knelt beside it, searching by feel, until his fingertips made out the shapes he'd had in mind. He took out five hand-axes—long, narrow heads on eighteen-inch handles, the special pattern made for splitting willow branches into withies for making hurdles and baskets. Very carefully he tucked them into his belt, the heads overlapping, with folds of his shirt wedged between the heads to stop them clinking as he walked. Then he replaced the lid and buttoned his coat up to the neck.

The second lieutenant was waiting by the door as he came back in. He still looked very scared, but he spoke loudly, as if he wanted everybody in the house to hear him. "You were a long time," he said.

Kunessin smiled at him. "I went for a shit," he said. "That's all right, isn't it?"

Somebody laughed. The lieutenant stood aside and let him pass.

"Well?" Aidi said, as soon as he'd joined them.

"Stand up, all of you," Kunessin replied, his voice calm and quiet. "Follow me."

He led them towards the corner nearest the door, where the women were sitting on the floor. "I can't sit down," he told Aidi. "Knock a table over, or something."

Aidi thought for a moment, then nodded. Chaere was sitting next to Dorun, though they weren't talking; behind her was a stool with a big pitcher of water resting on it. Aidi nudged the stool with his hip, spilling the jug into Chaere's lap. She yelped and jumped up, then started yelling at him.

"Sorry," he said. "Get a cloth, someone. I'm terribly sorry, wasn't looking where I was going."

Chaere told him various things about himself, some of which were true, while he tried to look suitably ashamed, and Clea got a dish-cloth from somewhere. "This is stupid," Chaere was saying, "I can't sit here in these wet things all night; I need dry clothes or I'll catch my death. Make those soldiers go away while I get changed."

Still with the sheepish look clamped on his face, Aidi backed away and joined the others, sitting in a knot near the middle of the room. Kunessin's coat was lying on the floor next to him.

"Sit down," Kunessin said. "Nicely done."

Aidi acknowledged the tribute with a tiny nod. "What's up?" he said.

Looking straight at him, Kunessin lifted a coat sleeve one inch; just enough to let him see a tiny sliver of steel underneath. "Just to make us all feel better," he said.

"Nice to know it's there, you mean," Aidi replied. "Got you. Now, what did you and the civil servant find to talk about?"

Kunessin smiled at Aidi's choice of words. "We're staying," he said.
"You're kidding me," Alces said. "How did you—?"
Aidi held up his hand. "Go on," he said.
Kunessin explained briefly about the procedural flaw in Straton's warrant. Muri laughed. Aidi nodded slowly. "That's a good point," he said. "So what do you want us to do?" he went on, glancing down quickly at the coat, then back up again.
"Not that," Kunessin said pleasantly. "Not yet, anyhow. I did a deal with our man there. He nearly fell over when I suggested it."
Kudei leaned in a bit closer. "I smell nettle soup," he said. "What've you done, Teuche?"
Kunessin concentrated on a crack between two floorboards. "Traded," he said. "They get the mineral rights, we keep the island."
Muri started to say something, but broke off without actually framing a word. The others looked at him.
"You told him about the strike," Aidi said.
"Showed him a sample," Kunessin replied. "He's over there drawing up the paperwork right now."
"Teuche..." Alces paused, then shook his head. Muri was frowning. Kudei's face was completely blank.
"What about the jars?" Aidi said.
Kunessin shook his head. "He didn't seem to have taken that point," he said. "Or maybe he didn't want to upset the deal; I don't know."
For a full minute, nobody spoke. Then Aidi said, "You really shouldn't have, Teuche."
Kunessin was still gazing at the floor. "It's what we came for," he said. "And now we'll have a cast-iron title, everything fair and square. It's a good deal, in the circumstances."
"Teuche's right," Muri said. "The gold was just... And we've still got the jars."
"For now," Aidi muttered. "That man's not thick. He'll want to know what we've been doing."
Alces shifted a little, so he could look at the two jars out of the corner of his eye. "How much do you reckon those things weigh?" he said. "Aidi?"

"Enough," Aidi said. "Really, Teuche, you should at least have told us first. That's—"

"Wasn't time," Kunessin interrupted. "In case you hadn't noticed, Aidi, they're holding the high ground, I had to do something quick. It's a good deal," he repeated. "It solves a lot of problems."

Aidi frowned. "That's true," he said, glancing sideways at the end of the room where the indentured men were gathered. "We should never have brought them in the first place."

"Oh, sure." Alces grinned. "And then we'd never have found the gold, let alone—" He broke off. "They've been useful," he said. "But I'll give you that, Teuche. It's a neat way of getting rid of them."

A pause; waiting for Aidi to speak. Then, when he didn't, Kunessin said, "That's settled, then. Which just leaves us with a transport problem." He lifted his head. Nobody who didn't know him well could have told he was looking round. "There's no reason to suppose they know about the sloop," he said.

Alces nodded. "Nice," he said. "Well, at least we've whittled it down a bit. Now it's just an engineering problem. Aidi, you didn't answer my question. How much do you think those jars weigh?"

Aidi closed his eyes: mental arithmetic. "The full one's got to be a ton," he said. "Quarter-ton for the other one. Tucking them under our coats as we go past isn't really an option."

"Agreed," Kunessin said. "Aidi, you're the metalworker. Those jars are pretty solid. Do you think they could act as crucibles?"

Aidi blinked; then, almost immediately, smiled beautifully. "That's not a bad idea," he said. "There's still the business of moving so much weight, with those buggers watching."

"Easier, though," Kunessin said.

"They'll have other things on their minds, I grant you," Aidi replied. "All right, why not? And if it screws up, we'll kill them and sink them in their ship. Agreed?"

Kunessin hesitated, then shrugged. "It won't screw up," he said. "Right, we'll need some straw."

Commissioner Straton woke up with a mouth full of smoke. Instinctively he tried to get to his feet, but a body lurched into him and shoved him back down again. As he opened his eyes, he heard a woman screaming. He could barely see across the room.

He scrambled to his knees, then stopped, pinned down by a violent burst of coughing. He was looking at a red glow, soft and hazy through the grey smoke. He could feel the heat. I'm not going to get out of this, he thought, and the certainty both shocked and calmed him. He tried to breathe in, but it was as though someone heavy was sitting on his chest. His head began to swim, like being drunk, and the fact he couldn't breathe didn't seem to matter so very much. This is where I get off, he thought, and his eyes closed.

Someone, some oaf, some idiot was manhandling him, hauling him about; he wouldn't have minded, except the sudden movement made him swallow a big mouthful of smoke, which set off the coughing again. He could taste the raw lining of his own throat, and his whole chest burned, like indigestion only much worse. His weight was on his feet; he felt his knees buckle, and then the interfering fool lifted him before he could fall over, hit the floor, get some desperately needed peace and quiet. At least he was suffering too, the busybody; he was coughing horribly. You'd have thought someone in so much distress would have better things to do than molest a dying man. Stupid, he thought, and if he had the strength he'd have given whoever it was a fat lip. Ridiculous and uncalled for. If such things could happen in the world, he was glad to be leaving it.

Then a tearing sensation, as though his lungs had burst and split into shreds, as though he was sucking in iron and ice, and the pain in his throat blotted out everything else, so that he'd cycled two lungfuls of clean air before he realised it. And wet: some bloody fool had splashed water over him, he was drenched, soaked to the skin...

He landed on his back and opened his eyes, to see a pair of legs stepping over him, a boot narrowly missing his head. His eyes were cruelly painful, and he closed them again. The last time he'd felt anything like this was thirty years ago, when he'd run long-distance races. Like he'd been kicked in the chest by a very big horse.

He lay back. It made him sickeningly dizzy, but he no longer had the strength to move at all. To take his mind off the pain, he tried to listen to the noises all around him—shouting, mostly, with some unexplained thuds and crashes, cracking noises that could be timbers breaking under enormous strain, a noise that could have been axes. His head was splitting.

The house was on fire. It dawned on him like the solution to some abstruse, long-considered problem. The house he'd been in, the house on Sphoe, where he'd come to handle a nasty mess about a land transfer. He'd done a deal with General Kunessin, and then it was time to sleep: no bed, just a space on a hard plank floor and a few inadequate blankets. While he'd been sleeping, the house had caught fire. He'd nearly died in the smoke. Someone must've pulled him out.

Quite extraordinary, he thought; I nearly died. Would quite definitely be dead right now, if someone hadn't... He was choking again; so stunned by what had just happened, forgotten how to breathe. Choking hurt like hell. He made an effort to stop.

But someone had got him out of there; someone who must also have been breathing in smoke, tearing his lungs to bits on the hard grey obstruction, but who nevertheless took the time and trouble to drag a living dead weight from the far end of the room to the doorway and out into the clean, sweet air. What a remarkable thing to have done. And if he hadn't...

More coughing, driving out everything while it lasted, which was much too long. When the coughing stopped, he felt shattered, as though he'd just been in a fight. A fire, he thought; well, just the sort of thing that happens, though usually to other people. I nearly died, he thought, and shuddered.

Must have fallen asleep; woke up with bright light burning his scratchy, raw eyes. Tried to breathe in, hurt, coughing. Remembered.

"He's awake," someone yelled (loud enough to take the top of his head off. Headache, very bad, like a hangover). He could smell wood ash, and the metallic taste of water, and the revolting stink of burnt flesh. "Get the general."

Curious, he thought. The general would have to be General

Kunessin, but the voice sounded very much like one of the sergeants of his own detachment—who didn't, it went without saying, answer to Kunessin. Or did he? He tried to think, but it was like trying to lift an anvil one-handed.

"Commissioner." Kunessin's voice, and here was Kunessin himself, his face, abnormally large, hovering over him. "How are you feeling?"

Outside, he realised; I'm lying outside in the yard, on my back in the dust. "What happened?" He knew the answer, of course, but the question sort of asked itself.

"There was a fire," Kunessin said. "We lost the main house and a couple of outbuildings."

"Anybody...?"

"Yes." Kunessin frowned. "Two of your men, I'm sorry to say." Then his face changed; it set, the way concrete goes off, but instantaneous. "And my wife."

"I'm sorry."

"You should be," Kunessin said. "It was your fault. At least," he added, "she'd still be alive if it wasn't for you." He looked away, his face thoughtful, intense. "While I was pulling you out of there, a rafter came down on her, pinned her down, and then the smoke got her. By the time I'd dragged you out and realised she was still in there, it was all over."

Straton wasn't quite sure he'd understood. "You...?"

"That's right," Kunessin said irritably. "I woke up, figured out what was going on; the first thing I thought of was: is Commissioner Straton all right? So I looked round and there you were, choking to death, and none of your precious marines the slightest bit interested. So..." He shrugged. "They say it's the ultimate test of your true priorities," he said, his voice light and brittle. "If the house catches fire, you instinctively save the one you value most. If you'd died, the deal would've gone up in smoke with you." He was looking down at his hands, as if he blamed them for something. "It's funny," he said. "If you'd asked me: what's the most important thing to you, I wouldn't have said it was the deal, keeping this island. Probably I'd have said it was the others, my friends, and Dorun after that. But apparently not. Where's Commissioner Straton? Just that one thought in my mind. Well."

Straton was trying not to stare at the raw red weals on Kunessin's hands; he'd been looking straight at them while he'd been talking, but Straton would have been prepared to bet he didn't even know they were there. "Thank you," he said stiffly. "You saved—"

"Yes, fine," Kunessin snapped. "A shame I just spoiled it by telling you it was a mistake. But there it is. You'll excuse me, I've got every bloody thing to see to."

Kunessin left Straton and crossed the yard, pausing every few paces to give an order or direct an operation. Back in the army again, he thought. He quickened his step to get him past the log shed, where the bodies were laid out under sheets. Two of the women, Enyo and he couldn't quite make out who the other one was, were in there with them, but he couldn't see what they were doing. He didn't want to know.

The others were waiting for him by the gate of the stock pen. Kudei looked up as he approached and muttered something. They all turned round to look at him.

"Well?" he asked.

"Teuche—" Muri started to say, but Kunessin cut him off.

"Well?" he repeated.

Aidi was studying him; there was a long pause before he spoke. "It's all right," he said. "Nearly wasn't, the heat cracked the big jar two thirds through, but somehow it stayed in one piece."

Kunessin pushed past him and leaned heavily on the rail. "Has it cooled down yet?"

"God, no. I mean, it's solid on the outside but the middle's almost certainly still molten."

"Can we move it?"

Aidi thought for a moment. "Not till tonight," he replied. "But that was the plan anyhow, so..."

"That's fine," Kunessin said. "That's what we'll do, then. Kudei, you get the levers."

"Teuche." This time it was Kudei, and Kunessin stopped and listened. "I'm...we're sorry."

He shrugged. "Couldn't be helped," he said. "People die in war. She should've cleared out straight away."

"She hung on to make sure the other girls were all out safe," Alces said quietly. "Enyo told me. She was just about to leave when that rafter—"

"Like I said." Kunessin rode over him. "Should've got out, instead of being all noble and brave."

Aidi took a deep breath. "We should have told them," he said.

Kunessin turned on him like a dog fighting. "That would've been a mistake," he said, soft and fierce. "They'd have done something stupid if they'd known, like all leaving the house just before we set the fire. It'd only have taken one thing like that, and Straton would've figured it out, and we'd be screwed. No, we couldn't have told them, and even if we had, who's to say it'd have turned out different? End of subject," he said firmly. "We did what we set out to do; now let's give our minds to the next stage. Agreed?"

Uncomfortable pause, then Alces said: "It's not going to be easy. Getting the jars up on the cart's going to be the biggest headache, followed by unloading them at the other end and getting them on the sloop."

"I've been thinking about that," Aidi said quickly, like someone making conversation to cover someone else's unfortunate gaffe. "If we get four of those long posts you cut for fence rails, Teuche, with a bit of rope, we could rig up a crane; I'm not saying we'll be able to lift them off the ground, but we can take a lot of the weight, make them much easier to manhandle."

He was about to expand on that, but Kunessin shut him up with a brisk nod. "Fine," he said. "You're on to it, Aidi, so I'll leave it to you. We'll meet up here as soon as it's properly dark, all right?"

He left them without looking back, and crossed the yard to organise the covering-over of the grain sacks. As he worked, he allowed his mind to probe the operation so far; delicately, like the tongue testing a painful tooth.

Objective achieved, he thought; both objectives. By burning down the house, they'd broken up Straton's tactical stranglehold without needing to use obvious force, and they'd solved the tricky problem of getting the gold-jars out without Straton realising what they really were. He was quite proud of that. Problem, to remove the jars from the house. Solution: get rid of the house. Sub-problem: to get the jars out without spilling half the dust. Solution: melt the dust into a solid lump inside the jars. Further problem arising: to get the jars on to the sloop. Solution delegated.

And the other business? Well, he said to himself, people die in war, and at least the five of them were all right, which was all he'd ever considered important. Put it in those terms and he could cope with it. Otherwise—he didn't want to think about that. Not now, at any rate, when he had so much to do.

People die in war. Define war. It could be argued, he had to concede, that the war was over; that it had been over for many years, and therefore Dorun's death wasn't war, it was a horrible, stupid, wretched, meaningless, pointless mess, his fault, his stupidity, his weakness. But that objection wouldn't lie—he knew he was right about this—because as long as A Company was still alive and together, as long as the five of them were together, the war could never end. It was part of them, their core, their reason, what they were for; they kept it alive and it kept them alive, which was why it, they had lasted so long, against all the odds. A Company could no more die in war than a fish could drown in the sea. Dorun—well, that was the deal, it always had been. Other people die, the good, the innocent, the inoffensive. The war goes on. We survive. That was the deal. That was why he'd made the choice, Straton or Dorun, the woman who was so much more than he deserved, or the good of the company. Actually, you couldn't call it a choice. No choice, no need to stop and think. The good of the company, and don't whine about the price.

He washed out his mind with activity. There was plenty to do.

When he'd formed the idea of setting the fire, his main concern was that it wouldn't work: that the fire wouldn't take hold quickly enough, and Straton's soldiers would put it out before it had a chance to pass the critical point; or that it wouldn't cook up hot enough to melt the gold in the jars. Needn't have worried there. A stiff breeze had come up off the sea at just the right time, blowing in just the right direction; the fire had gone straight up into the thatch, then come down through the smoke-hole in the roof, burnt its way through the floorboards and travelled under them, fanned by the marvellously convenient through-draught, so that the house had burnt from on top and underneath simultaneously. The smoke (smoke was the essential ingredient, to drive Straton's men out before they could do any useful fire-fighting) had blown in right from the start. If he'd been an engineer designing a fire-trap, with enormous industrial bellows instead of the wind, he couldn't have done a better job.

A bit too successful, of course. Apart from the deaths, there were other complications. The flames had spread to several of the outbuildings. Loss of stores burnt or spoiled by smoke was trivial, but those stores were now uncovered and vulnerable to wind and rain. He got them moved and protected. Next was the awkward question of where they were going to sleep, now that the main house was gone; also such issues as clothing, since all their personal effects had gone up in the fire. The second problem was no big deal: there were barrels and crates full of coats, shirts, trousers, boots stacked up in one of the lean-tos. Unfortunately, there hadn't been enough covered space for everything. The damp had got into the crates, and everything came out mildewed and stinking, which didn't improve morale. As for somewhere to live, he decided on the long building on the edge of the compound that was to have been the hay barn. It hadn't had a roof for quite some time, and inside it was wet and overgrown with thick tangles of briars, but it was the only structure still standing that was anything like big enough to house them all. He set Straton's soldiers to clearing out the briars, and sent the indentured men to cart sand and gravel from the river to stamp down into a floor. A Company was given the rather more skilled job of cutting, shaping and fitting rafters and thatching them over. Useful: it meant that carts and long poles would be on hand for the night's work, and that (with any luck) the soldiers and the indentured men would be so exhausted by nightfall that they'd sleep like dead men.

As usual, Muri was the master carpenter. Aidi, chief engineer, rigged up an extremely ingenious and efficient crane out of poles, cart chains and rope. For thatch, they used bracken and briar vines stuffed into the branches of birch loppings and brash from Kunessin's abortive lumber yard up on the hill, where he'd cut the poles they used for rafters. Amazingly, they had the job done by nightfall, and were able to help finish off the stamping-down of the floor, using some of the big flour jars as rollers. The result was no palace, but it was habitable; and, as anticipated, everyone was too worn out by the time they'd finished to care too much about the accommodations.

Everyone, of course, except A Company. It wasn't long before everyone else was asleep. They got up quietly, slipped out of the barn and set to work. Aidi had dismantled the crane when the roof was put on, so all they had to do was carry the timbers across the yard to the burnt-out house and reassemble it. Kudei had left a cart handy; he and Alces fetched in the horses. The cart groaned ominously as they lowered the ton-weight jar on to it, and they decided not to risk loading the quarter-ton jar as well. They hadn't bargained on making two trips, but there should be enough time in hand. Aidi quickly unstepped the crane and loaded it on to the cart. Twenty minutes after creeping out of the barn, they were ready to leave for the inlet on the other side of the island where the sloop was moored.

Things didn't go quite as smoothly at the other end. As Aidi pointed out, they hadn't thought that stage through properly. They couldn't get the sloop in tight enough to use the crane, so they had to use the crane beams to form a ramp. With desperate expenditure of effort they managed to roll the quarter-ton jar up the ramp by brute force, but they knew better than to try that with the big jar; if it slipped and rolled back, the least they could expect was crushed legs. For once, Aidi had nothing to suggest; it was Muri who pointed out that there was a perfectly good winch in a crate in the large pigsty, unused, still packed up and in its grease. Kudei and Alces went back a third time and fetched it. As Kunessin had feared, the wet had got into it and seized the ratchet; they built a fire and heated it up to dull red, then quenched it in the sea; that and some straining eventually broke the rust, and thereafter things went reasonably well. Even so, they were cutting it fine for time. It was Alces' suggestion to fill the cart with cobbles from the beach before turning back. Inspired: when they reached the yard, just as the sun was rising, it was accepted without question that they'd got up early and gone to fetch the makings of a proper floor. Luckily, nobody seemed to have noticed that the crane had disappeared.

"It's not the crane I'm concerned about," Kudei muttered, as they watched the cobbles being hauled into the barn in wheelbarrows. "Can't be long before someone starts wondering what's become of the jars."

Kunessin didn't turn his head as he replied. "No one's going to say anything," he said. "Not in front of the soldiers."

Aidi said: "How long will they be here?"

Kunessin didn't smile, but he allowed himself a little relish in his reply. "Long enough."

Aechmaloten had been lucky to survive the fire. The mystery fever that had kept him in his bed left him too weak to move. One of Straton's men had pulled him out.

Kunessin saw to it that he was installed, as comfortably as possible in the circumstances, in the barn, close to the fireplace, under a heap of foul-smelling blankets. "Doesn't look like they've been taking proper care of you," he said, and handed him a cup of water.

"Too busy," Aechmaloten said, with just a hint of resentment. "Getting the—"

Kunessin frowned, and Aechmaloten took the hint. "Not so good, then," Kunessin said. "How are you feeling now, anyway?"

"About the same," Aechmaloten said.

"I'll get Aidi to take a look at you," Kunessin said. "He was always the closest thing we had to a medic. Got me through a nasty dose of fever once." He pulled up an empty box and sat down. "We need you on your feet again," he said, lowering his voice a little.

Aechmaloten shook his head. "Don't reckon I'll be up to much digging for a while yet."

"I wasn't meaning that," Kunessin said, quieter still. "I need you to get your people ready for something." He was looking at one of Straton's sergeants, standing by the door, taking a rest from hammering cobbles into the barn floor with the poll of a splitting-axe.

Aechmaloten frowned; then his face went blank. "Oh," he said.

"You know they've served us notice to quit," Kunessin went on. "You do realise that's not just us, it's your people as well."

Aechmaloten had to gather his strength to answer. "Yes, but that doesn't matter. We've got—"

Kunessin said: "We saw something interesting while we were loading up those cobbles this morning. Ten of the soldiers, down at the jetty, and they'd got Aidi's crane with them. And another thing." He stopped, made a show of looking round. "There's some things missing, from the main house. Two jars."

Aechmaloten's face stayed frozen. "They took them, you reckon. Put them on the ship."

"Well," Kunessin said, "that'd explain why they wanted the crane."

Aechmaloten closed his eyes for a moment. "Those bastards," he said.

"Well." Kunessin took another look round. "I can't see there's much that can be done about it. Straton's keeping me and my men pretty closely marked, and there's only the five of us, when all's said and done. As far as we're concerned, they've won that round."

No reply. Kunessin poured more water into the cup.

"You're just going to let them—"

"What choice have we got?" Kunessin said bitterly. "They're armed, we're not. We can't fight without weapons. Looks like our best shot is to take them to law for our out-of-pocket expenses, once we get home."

Aechmaloten was thinking. Eventually he said: "The soldiers aren't watching *us*."

Kunessin turned his head sharply. "Don't even think about it," he said. "They're regular soldiers, and what have you got? Picks and shovels. You wouldn't have a hope in hell."

Aechmaloten smiled. "There's all that gear you got stashed in the sheds," he said.

"You know about that, then." Kunessin frowned.

"They wouldn't be expecting any trouble," Aechmaloten went on. "My lads aren't regular army, but five of us were in the war. What do you call it, element of surprise?"

"I wouldn't if I were you."

"What, so we just let them steal it off us? I don't think so." Aechmaloten tried to move, gave up. "After all the work we put in. No, I don't think so."

Kunessin sighed. "You're on your own, then. I'm not getting my men involved."

"Then don't expect us to share," Aechmaloten said angrily. "Thought you boys were the hero type."

But Kunessin smiled at him. "We don't do that any more," he said. "Got some sense as we got older. You'd do well to follow our lead."

"All right for you," Aechmaloten said. "You've all got money of your own. No, fuck that. We worked hard for our chance."

Kunessin stood up. "Good luck, then," he said. "I'd rather you had it than the government, at any rate."

That'll keep Aidi quiet, he thought, as he walked back across the room.

Aechmaloten talked to his people. During the meal that evening, three of the indentured men slipped out without the soldiers seeing them and broke into the barrels and packing cases in the shed next to Aidi's workshop. They found helmets, enough for everybody, but the chainmail shirts had taken the damp badly and were rusted solid. They cracked open a case of Type Fifteen swords and another of steel thirty-inch bucklers. They filled three wheelbarrows and took them round the back of the barn; at which point, they were arrested by half a dozen of Straton's men and dragged back inside. There they found the rest of the indentured men herded together in the far corner, surrounded by soldiers with drawn swords.

At Kunessin's insistence, Straton held a formal trial, or the closest approximation possible in the circumstances. Kunessin was the chief prosecution witness. He gave evidence that the ringleaders of the conspiracy to steal Straton's ship had approached him for support, which he'd naturally refused; then, at the earliest opportunity, he'd told Straton all about it. He also accused Aechmaloten and his men of stealing all the gold that had so far been dug out of the river; a considerable sum, he pointed out, which properly speaking belonged to himself and the other four proprietors, though he was realistic enough to realise that it would inevitably be claimed by the government, a claim which he did not intend to contest. The gold, he went on, had been kept in a large clay storage jar — maybe the commissioner recalled seeing it in the main house, before the fire. It had since disappeared, along with the crane built by Major Proiapsen to lift the rafters for the barn roof. Presumably the plan had been to load it on board the ship, once Aechmaloten and his gang had murdered the soldiers, himself and his fellow proprietors with the weapons stolen from the stores by the three men captured by the guards. Compared with the murder plot, Kunessin said, the theft of the gold was relatively unimportant, though if it was now government property, it was clearly Straton's duty to take all possible steps to find where the conspirators had hidden it — he asked, no, he insisted that the island be thoroughly searched until the hiding place was found, and of course the proprietors would help with the investigation in any way they could.

There was one last thing, Kunessin said. Ever since the fire, he'd been asking himself how it could have started. There had been a disastrous fire a few months earlier; it had nearly led to all of them dying of starvation, and after that they'd taken great pains to make sure nothing of the sort ever happened again. He briefly listed the fire precautions they'd been taking, and concluded that it was highly unlikely that a fire could have started accidentally. Of course, he had no proof to back up such a serious charge; but he felt it was his duty to ask the commissioner to consider whether the conspirators might have set the fire deliberately, intending either to kill the commissioner, his soldiers and the proprietors, or as a way of getting the gold away from the house, or both. Kunessin repeated that he had no direct proof to offer; but since two soldiers and his own dear wife had died in the blaze...

At this point, he broke down and was unable to testify further. Commissioner Straton excused the witness, asking that the record should show that General Kunessin had personally rescued him from the said fire. He then called on Aechmaloten to testify on behalf of the accused. Aechmaloten's evidence, which was barely coherent, consisted mostly of wild accusations against General Kunessin and his men; he didn't deny the conspiracy, but claimed that it had been Kunessin's idea, and that if the gold had been stolen, Kunessin and his men must have stolen it.

Commissioner Straton was clearly unimpressed. In his summing-up, he pointed out the glaring inconsistencies and downright impossibilities in Aechmaloten's claims; in particular, he poured scorn on the notion that five men could have spirited away a ton and a quarter of gold, unassisted and unnoticed, in the course of a single night, after an exhausting day's work roofing and thatching the barn. It simply wasn't possible, he said; and if that was the best the prisoners could do, he had no hesitation in finding them guilty as charged. He also believed that they were guilty of arson and the murder of two soldiers and Kunessin's wife, but was forced to rule that there was insufficient evidence to support a conviction. His inclination, he went on, had been to order their summary execution; however, General Kunessin had most generously and eloquently interceded on their behalf, and therefore (against his better judgement) he was prepared to commute their sentence to life imprisonment in a penal colony. Given the difficulty of holding the prisoners on Sphoe, he and his men would evacuate them to the mainland at once, where they would be handed over to the garrison commander at Haema-toenta; given the urgency of the situation, he proposed sailing first thing in the morning. As for the search for the stolen gold, that could wait until his return. By revealing the existence of the gold, which he needn't have done, General Kunessin had displayed great integrity, and could therefore be trusted. Furthermore, Straton pointed out with a smile, there was no way the gold could be taken off Sphoe in his absence, since Kunessin had no ship.

Kunessin watched the ship fade into the horizon, then turned to the others. Muri and Alces were grinning; Aidi looked thoughtful. Kudei had one of his unreadable faces.

"Well," Kunessin said, "that's that. It's just us now."

FIFTEEN

Out loud they said they weren't expecting a hero's welcome, and didn't want one. Faralia's not like that, they said: either nobody would have noticed that they'd been gone, or else they'd be shunned for swanning off to foreign parts and leaving honest men to do their work at home. If anybody was pleased to see them, it'd only be because they had money to spend. Not that they gave a damn, they said, one way or the other.

It was raining hard when the ship docked. The quay was deserted apart from two very sad customs men, strangers, who tried to charge them duty on various small, valuable items tucked away at the bottom of their kitbags. Kudei treated it as a joke, but Aidi couldn't see the funny side.

"Do you know who we are?" he said.

One of the customs men looked up at him from under the curtain of water dripping from his hood. "Should we?"

"Yes."

Shrug. "Well, we don't."

"Leave it, Aidi," said Fly. "Give them their money, and let's get out of this bloody rain."

Wasting his time; he recognised Aidi's matter-of-principle look.

Never a good sign. "I'm not paying excise on legitimate spoils of war. They're specifically exempt, under article sixteen of the revenue charter, paragraph eight, subsection—"

"Army boys, are you?" one of the customs men said.

"That's right," Fly said politely. "Just got our demob, and we're anxious to get home. You know how it is."

Apparently, the customs man didn't. He was already soaked to the skin, for which he blamed them, and it was fairly obvious he didn't like soldiers. "In that case," he said, "I'm going to have to do a full body search. If you'd care to follow me to the customs house."

"Hold on," Aidi said, and the low rumble in his voice made Kudei stop grinning. "What's all that about?"

"Got to search all returning service personnel for weapons," the customs man said. "Things have changed since you've been away. Civilians aren't allowed to carry weapons any more." He grinned. "You boys haven't got anything like that on you, I don't suppose."

Before Aidi could say anything, Fly stepped in front of him. "As a matter of fact," he said, and with a flick of his wrist he shook off the length of old blanket wrapped round the bundle he'd been carrying and, in a continuation of the same movement, gently rested the flat of the blade on the customs officer's shoulder. "You said civilians," he went on pleasantly. "Right?"

The customs man had gone completely rigid, like a corpse. His colleague nodded quickly.

"That's all right, then," Kudei said, stretching past Aidi to lift the blade off the man's shoulder. "Doesn't apply to us. Reservists," he explained. "Still on the active list for the next twelve months. Which, I fancy, exempts us from excise duty as well," he added. "Is that right?"

The customs man knew perfectly well that it wasn't. "That's right," he said. "You boys get along now. Sorry you were bothered."

They'd walked halfway into town by the time Kudei spoke. "They hadn't got a clue who we are," he said.

"What did you expect," Fly grunted back, "a brass band?"

"They're new in town," Muri said doubtfully. "Drafted in from somewhere, I guess. Can't be expected to know us from a hole in the ground."

"Let's go to my place," Aidi said angrily. "It's nearest."

They went to the Proiapsen house by way of the bank, where they presented their cash warrants to the boy clerk sitting in the front óffice. He took one look at them, slid awkwardly off his stool, mumbled something about getting somebody, and fled up the stairs, stumbling twice and nearly doing himself an injury.

"Hero's welcome," Fly muttered.

They could hear doors banging, and heavy footsteps in a hurry; then a short, fat man came bounding down the stairs, barefoot, with a napkin round his neck and soap covering one cheek. There was a slight cut on the other.

The fat man introduced himself as Acherunte Brotoenta, the branch's partner in residence. He was so very sorry to have kept them waiting, and would they please take a seat, and would they care for some mulled wine and biscuits?

Aidi scowled at him. "Is there a problem?" he said.

Brotoenta caught sight of the warrants, lying on the desk where the boy had left them. "May I?"

"Sure," Aidi said. "But look sharp about it, could you? We're in a hurry."

Brotoenta glanced at the warrants and his face went wooden. "I'm terribly sorry," he said. "I can't cash these."

"Now just a moment—" Aidi started to say, but Brotoenta spoke quietly over him. "I do apologise," he said, "but we simply don't hold this much cash on the premises. Now, I can open accounts for you and credit these to them, or I can write you letters of credit, which you can present at one of our larger branches, Boirea, say, or Csiphon City. They'd probably be able to raise the money if you let them have a week or so. Otherwise..." He lifted his shoulders in a heartbreaking shrug. "I really do apologise most sincerely."

Aidi looked at him. "I don't know you," he said. "What happened to Diosuios Hemin? He used to be the resident here."

Brotoenta looked mildly startled. "He died," he replied. "Six years ago. You're from around here, then?"

In the end, they opened accounts. Brotoenta liked them a whole lot better after that. They had, he explained happily, doubled the funds controlled by his branch, which meant he now had the liquidity to lend to the many exciting new enterprises starting up in Faralia now that the war was over. It would be, he said, the dawn of a glorious new day for Faralia, and they could quite justifiably consider themselves public benefactors. They had every right to feel very proud.

"Which means," Fly said, as they splashed through the puddles in Broad Street, "we can't have our money, but every halfwit who wants some can come along with a wheelbarrow and help himself. Not quite sure I follow that."

"Nice to know we've done something right," Aidi replied grimly. "Apparently killing the enemy gets you arrested at the dockside, but thieving from the dead makes you a public benefactor. I think it's called peace."

Muri grinned. "Hero's welcome," he said.

No building looks at its best in the rain, but the Proiapsen house looked different, somehow. The shutters were up, their paint cracked and peeling; the gilding had worn off the raised points of the carved frieze over the lintel, and the brasswork on the door was plum brown. "Odd," Aidi said, as they waited for someone to answer the bell. "Dad's always so fussy about things being neat and shiny. Used to drive me mad when I was a kid. Of course, it was always my job to—"

He broke off. He'd noticed a discoloured patch on the door frame, where the brass plate proudly announcing that this was the Proiapsen house had been removed. It occurred to him that it had been a long time since he'd had news from home; reasonably enough, since they hadn't been in the sort of places where letters could easily reach. Also, none of his family had ever liked him very much.

"Doesn't seem like there's anyone home," Muri said.

"The hell with this," Aidi said. "Let's go round the back."

To do so, they had to thread their way through a complex system of alleys, entries and snickets, which eventually ended, to Aidi's complete surprise, in a brick wall.

"This shouldn't be here," he said.

Fly looked at him. "Looks like they've been redecorating while you've been away," he said. "Muri, give me a leg up."

He cleared the wall easily and perched on the top. "Aidi," he said, "this is somebody's garden."

"It can't be," Aidi replied. "There's our store on the corner, and a passage that leads into our yard."

Fly looked down at him. "See for yourself," he said.

So Aidi scrambled up and sat straddling the wall, like a boy about to steal apples. He saw a pleasant formal garden, with a raised lawn edged with lavender and box, framed by herb and flower beds, with ornamental fountains at each corner. A row of cherry trees screened the side where the back of the Proiapsen house should have been. Aidi didn't know much about gardening, but he guessed the trees were about six years old.

"You sure it's the right house?"

"Piss off, Muri," Aidi snapped, and dropped down off the wall. "Come on," he said, and marched across the flower bed. The others followed at a slight distance.

Behind the cherry trees was a trellised fence. No gate, but Aidi solved that problem by kicking a hole in the fence and ducking through. He found himself opposite the familiar back door. No porch, and the door was boarded shut.

"Let's go to my place," Muri said awkwardly. "Assuming it's still there, of course. I mean, it's not much, but at least it's in the dry."

Aidi launched a ferocious kick at the door, but it was rather more solid than the fence, and he hurt his foot. "Fine," he snapped. "Let's all go round to Muri's."

The forge was at the bottom of Well Street: a heavy gate opening on to the street, wedged between two long, blank walls. The stink of coal smoke reassured them that someone was at home, at any rate.

"Morning, gentlemen," someone called out to them as they entered the yard. "What can I do for you?"

A short, solid, bald man in a leather apron was standing in the doorway of one of the many sheds. Muri pushed past the others. "Who the hell are you?" he said.

The smith raised his eyebrows but didn't move. "I'm Ouden Menei," he said. "This is my place."

Muri opened his mouth, but nothing came out. Fly edged in front of him and said, "We're looking for the Achaiois family," he said. "I take it—"

"Ah." The smith nodded. "Got you." He turned to Muri and said, "You'll be Muri Achaiois, then. Just back from the war, are you?"

Muri nodded. "I'm sorry," he said. "It was a surprise, that's all."

"Of course." The smith's voice was dense with sympathy. "I get the impression you haven't heard." He hesitated, then added, "You'd better come inside. No point standing round getting drenched."

The forge had changed. It was tidy. There were racks for all the tools on the walls, with outlines drawn in charcoal to show where everything should go. The iron and steel billets were piled up neatly against the far wall, sorted by width and profile. Within living memory, someone had swept the floor. Aidi and Muri sat on the workbench, while Fly perched on the edge of the anvil. Muri stayed stranded in the middle of the floor, as though unable to move; as though constrained by the memory of his father's clutter, which would have prevented him going further.

"I'm sorry to have to tell you," the smith said, "your parents are both dead."

Muri frowned. "Oh," he said.

The smith looked away. "Your father died about five years ago," he said. "Your mother sold me the business, but she died about six months later. I don't know where your brother is now. Last I heard, he'd gone to Csiphon, but that was some time ago. I'm sorry," he added. "This must come as a nasty shock to you. I assumed..."

"It's all right," Muri said quietly. "Thank you," he added. "Sorry we burst in on you like that. Come on, Aidi, we'd better be going."

The smith looked as though he was about to say something, but changed his mind. Muri started towards the door, but Aidi cleared his throat and asked, "You wouldn't happen to know what's become of the Proiapsens?"

The smith turned his head and looked at him. "Are you Aidi Proiapsen?"

344   K. J. Parker

"Friend of his," Aidi said. "I've got a letter from him to deliver, but the house is all closed up."

"That's right," the smith said. "They moved out, couple of years ago. Old man Proiapsen made a heap of money in war salvage."

Aidi frowned. "War salvage?"

"Loot." The smith grinned. "He bought cheap from the military—boots, shirts, socks, belts, armour, you name it; all the stuff they take off the dead bodies after a battle—then he sold it back to them at five hundred per cent mark-up. Shortages, see. Don't ask me how it works, but Proiapsen had it all figured out, did very nicely, thank you very much. Bought a fine estate a way down the coast—the Di'Ambrosies place, don't know if you've heard of them. They sold up when their son got killed in the war. Last I heard, old Proiapsen's retired, having a high old time playing the fine gentleman. Presumably his son's coming home soon. Well, you'd know all about that."

Aidi shook his head. "He won't be back for a while," he said. "What about the town house? Any idea what they figure on doing with it?"

The smith shrugged. "For sale, I guess," he said. "Trouble is, what with the war and everything, there's not many in Faralia as can afford a big old place like that, even with prices as low as they are. I seem to remember hearing they sold off some of the land—the yard, some of the buildings. If you ask around, I expect there's someone who knows the details."

"Thanks," Aidi said. "I might just put in an offer myself. I always fancied living there."

Once they were back out in the street, Fly said, "Don't look at me. My dad threw me out when I was fifteen, never darkened my door again, so we can't go there."

"We'll go to the farm," Kudei said. "You never know, maybe they've all pissed off too. Fingers crossed, right?"

No such luck. The Gaeon boys were still there, still more or less the same, except that three of them were now married; tidy, sullen women, rarely seen and never heard, who made up three beds in the barn for Kudei's army friends and gave them their dinner in the kitchen. The next morning, they appeared to have forgotten that Kudei had ever been away. It was, as Fly pointed out, scarcely a hero's welcome, but it was better than sleeping in a ditch. The day after that, the remainder of A Company split up, for the time being. Fly went into town for a drink and didn't surface again for two years. Muri was unlucky in his investments. Aidi bought the old Proiapsen house under a false name, started a business from scratch and prospered hugely, somehow never finding the time to write to his father and let him know he was back. Kudei worked on the farm and quickly became invisible.

The next time A Company met was at Fly's wedding, three years after their return. The first thing they asked each other was: heard from Teuche lately? In each case, the answer was the same.

Eventually, Aidi Proiapsen wrote to his father; or at least, to his father's agent. He wanted detailed figures for the family's speculations in war salvage.

First things first. Aidi and Muri buried Dorun's body in a small hollow near the stock pen, out of sight of the house. The women hung round while they filled in the grave. Nobody said anything.

Kunessin, Kudei and Alces, meanwhile, hurried across the island to the inlet where the sloop was moored. Getting the jars off the ship was much easier, a simple matter of rolling them across the deck and down the beams-tied-together plank.

"Now what?" Kudei asked.

Kunessin frowned. "I'm not sure," he said. "Best thing would be to break it up into small chunks. Easier to handle."

Alces shook his head. "Gold's soft, not brittle," he said. "What we need is a saw."

"What we need," Kunessin corrected him, "is Aidi. He knows about this stuff."

Aidi, when consulted, gave it a few minutes' thought and decided the best thing would be to melt the gold down again and draw it off into ingots. He made it sound easy.

"Not here," he said, looking down the beach. "Over there."

Over there was a stretch of white sand, a bald patch in the shingle.

They knew better than to ask questions, so they helped him roll the jars the hundred yards or so up the beach, a long, hard job that took all their strength, even when Muri joined them later. Then Muri was sent back to the settlement for the bellows from the forge, the carpenter's augur, axes and a cartload of charcoal ("We haven't got nearly that much," Muri protested. Aidi looked grim. "Yes we have. Rafters and floorboards from the burnt house. Charcoal."), while the others built an improvised hearth out of middling-sized stones, and Aidi scratched about in the sand with a stick.

"The idea is," Aidi explained, once Muri had come back, "we've got our fire here" — he pointed to the charcoal heaped up between two flat rocks — "blown by the bellows here — Muri, your job — and we put the jar on top, just resting in its own weight. The jar is the crucible. First, though, we bore a hole in the bottom of the jar and block it up with a stone bung. When the gold's melted, we knock out the bung, and the melt pours out of the jar and runs along this channel in the sand, and into these here." He indicated the brick-sized trenches that branched off the main channel. "Technical term is pigs," he said, "because to an active imagination they look like piglets suckling a sow. Once it's all cooled down, all you do is break the pigs off the sprue, and you've got your ingots, then chop up the sprue and that's the job done. And that's all there is to it."

Aidi's productions were always spectacular. There was the breathy roar of the fire, the deep, pale glow of the molten gold, the cloud of steam as the hot melt running down the channels evaporated the residual damp in the sand, the occasional crackle and lethal spit as a droplet of condensation landed on the surface of the molten metal; a feast of sensations, sound, colour and movement, like a masque or a pageant. Everything went according to plan and Aidi was in complete control, anticipating each development in good time, giving his orders calmly and clearly, warning of the dangers, conducting the whole affair like an orchestra. When at last the great golden frame had cooled to solid, they set about butchering it with axes, hacking the ingots off the sprue, like soldiers dispatching the enemy wounded on a battlefield. The result was a shining stack of bars with gashed ends, a fortune, a king's ransom.

"Now what?" Alces said.

"Good question," Kunessin replied. "Not sure, to be honest with you."

Muri looked at him. "We've got to get it back on the sloop," he said. "In case those buggers come back early and start searching for it."

Aidi pulled a face. "And then the sloop slips its anchor or sinks, and that's two hundred and fifty thousand thalers lost and gone for ever. No, I don't think so."

"It's obvious, surely," Kudei said. "Get it across to the mainland, quick."

"And run into Commissioner Straton on the way to the assay office." Alces shook his head. "I'm not too keen on that idea. We want to get this lot back to Faralia, where it'll be safe. Then we can get rid of it discreetly, without starting an almighty fuss."

"There's nothing discreet about a quarter of a million thalers," Kunessin said. "Even in Csiphon City you'd have a job disposing of that much all at once without making yourself a bit conspicuous. No, we need to stash it somewhere safe and get rid of it nice and gradually. Otherwise, we're going to attract a lot of attention."

"Not here on the island," Aidi said.

"Agreed." Kunessin closed his eyes; the utmost concentration. "The logical place would be Kudei's farm; bury it up in the small copse, say, somewhere nobody goes. But we'd never get that far in the sloop, so that'd mean waiting for the ship to get back, and we haven't got that long. And we can't leave it here, as Aidi says, because of Straton, so it's got to be on the mainland, as close as possible, really: somewhere we can get to in the sloop and be back in time for when the government people show up." He shrugged. "It's a tricky one, and I don't know the coast opposite here nearly as well as I'd like. All in all," he said, turning and scowling at the stack of bricks, "this stuff is turning out to be a bloody nuisance."

"We've still got the quarter-jar to deal with, don't forget," Aidi said.

Kunessin shook his head. "Don't worry about that for the moment," he said. "I've got an idea about that. Let's concentrate on the matter in hand."

Suddenly, Aidi smiled. "What we need," he said, "is a house."

Pause. Then Alces said, "Say that again."

"We need to buy a house," Aidi said, "on the mainland. Small cottage would do. Look, the main problem with just burying it somewhere is if some bastard comes along and digs it up. So, we buy a house, dig down deep under the floor, bury it there; then we board the place up and walk away. Nobody's interested in an old cottage gradually going to rack and ruin; there's any number of them everywhere you look since the war ended."

Kudei nodded. "Safe as houses, you might say. It's not a bad idea. Teuche?"

"Money," Kunessin replied, after a pause. "Even an old ruin's going to cost at least a hundred thalers."

"I've got that," Muri said.

"It's not a problem," Aidi said. "I can cover a couple of hundred. What do you reckon?"

"It's better than just dumping it in the corner of a field somewhere," Kunessin said. "Yes, why not? We'll need to get a move on, though. Talking of which: Kudei, what's the supply position like?"

Kudei shrugged. "Fine," he said. "We just got rid of a lot of hungry mouths. So we won't need to go shopping while we're over there."

"Good. In that case, you and Muri get provisions for two weeks loaded on the sloop. Aidi, we'll need your wife. Fly, if you wouldn't mind clearing up here, just in case Straton knows a foundry site when he sees one." He hesitated; frowned as though considering some loose end he couldn't quite call to mind. "Right," he said. "Let's get on with it."

The stranger and his wife were clearly nice people, well-spoken, good manners, though obviously fallen on hard times, which they couldn't be induced to talk about, no matter how hard the farmer's wife tried to put them at their ease. Understandable, she felt. Probably something to do with the war: he was of an age to have been in it, and so many dreadful things had happened. She was confident they'd make good neighbours; not that her husband really cared too much about that. He was too excited at the prospect of getting good money for the fallen-down old stockman's cottage. Just as well, he told her, that he'd never got around to knocking it down and using the stones to patch up the Long Reach barns. Ninety-five thalers, and the man had hardly haggled at all. Of course, he and his wife were both townies, you could tell soon as look at them.

"I've got some friends coming in to help make the place habitable," the stranger said apologetically. "That'll be all right, won't it?"

Of course it would, the farmer assured him, and mentally absolved himself of his resolution to offer the services of a couple of his men. No trouble at all. And help yourself to any sand or lumber; there's a nice stand of ash just on the corner there you could use, but not the beech. The stranger thanked him politely, and would it be all right if they got started straight away? His friends were in a hurry to get finished and go on to the city. That'd be fine, the farmer said; and yes, the hire of a cart and a team wouldn't be a problem either. Say, five quarters a day?

When they'd packed up and gone, the farmer and his wife took a stroll up that way and peeked in through a crack in the shutters. They'd made a fine job of putting in a new floor, and so quickly, too. Shame they hadn't had time to do the thatch, or the door frames, or that crack in the east wall where the water came through.

Thoroughly nice people, they agreed, and forgot all about them.

Just the three of them, on Sphoe.

It'll be all right, Kudei had told Clea; we'll only be gone a few days, and nothing's going to happen while we're away. There's plenty of food and logs. Just take it easy till we get back.

But Clea had an imagination, and she didn't mind sharing it with the other two. What if the soldiers returned? What if the sloop sank? They'd be stranded, and nobody would know they were there; the food would run out, and — Enyo reminded her about the ship, from Faralia. Yes, but what if the ship sank too? Well, it could. It happened. Ships sank all the time. Her grandad's brother had drowned at sea, and nobody ever found out what had happened. A sudden storm, pirates...

The ship won't sink, Enyo told her. And even if it does, we're not going to be stranded here to starve to death. The government men will be here soon enough. Yes, Clea replied, and that's another thing. Government men and soldiers, and everybody knows about soldiers.

"Well, yes," Enyo said. "I married one. So did you."

That, Clea pointed out, wasn't what she meant. Enyo knew what she meant. And what if pirates showed up, before the men got back or the soldiers arrived? What the hell could they have been thinking of, swanning off like that and leaving them? What if something happened? What if there was another fire?

"There won't be," Enyo said firmly. "I promise, there won't be another fire."

Clea scowled at her warily. "That's easy said," she replied. "There's been two already, so why shouldn't there be another one? What if the sheds catch fire and all the food gets burnt up?"

"There won't be another fire," Enyo said. "Now, why don't you stop trying to scare yourself to death and make a start on the cornmeal."

"Do it yourself," Clea snapped. "You're not in charge round here."

"Fine." Enyo got up and walked away, out of the barn and into the sunshine. As soon as the daylight warmed her skin, she felt herself relax, and not a moment too soon. Clea, she told herself, had been right about one thing. She was indeed in grave danger, and more likely than not to die a violent death, though not at the hands of pirates. The man must be a saint, she thought, or stone deaf.

Something to do. Well, there was always something to do. She looked round, and saw the patch of turned-over earth, fifteen yards by ten, next to the pigsties. Muri and Kunessin had dug it, not long before the gold strike, with the intention of sowing vegetables. Nobody had so much as looked at it since the gold rush started, and there was a soft, lush cover of weeds; also, it was a bit late to start sowing now. Even so, a few rows of peas, turnips, cabbages might just come to something, and she had a feeling the season started a bit later here than it did at home. She'd missed the garden when she'd lived in town. It'd be something to do.

She scrabbled about in the sheds until she found the tools: a rake, a long-handled shovel for scraping off the weeds. Never been used and rusty already; the sea air, of course, and a not particularly marvellous roof. A ball of twine. It occurred to her to wonder, not for the first time, where Menin had got to. Off in the woods again, presumably. There was something wrong with that girl.

The fire, she thought. Her hair stank of the smoke, even though she'd washed it four times, and her clothes, her one dress (because she'd rather wear rags than the horrible mildewed things Kunessin had issued her with, creased and damp and greasy to the touch, hauled out of a crate and flung at her; what had she done to deserve that? she wondered). Poor Dorun. Clea was shocked because Kunessin had acted as though nothing had happened; she was wrong about that: he was acting as though Dorun had never existed, which was entirely different. Of course, you couldn't imagine a man like the general being in love, the same way you couldn't picture a bull making an omelette. Even so, Clea was quite wrong if she thought he didn't care. There'd be trouble there somewhere along the line.

What Enyo couldn't quite figure out (she'd done her best, but it wouldn't unravel, like badly tangled wool) was whether they were going home or not. The government men had come to throw them out. Kunessin had outsmarted them, she was pretty sure of that, but surely they'd been planning to leave anyway; the decision had been taken before the soldiers turned up. Which reminded her. What on earth had become of the big pot of gold? It had been there the night of the fire, but in all the panic and fuss it seemed to have disappeared, until the general made his accusation against the indentured men; which the soldiers had taken at face value, but she wasn't so sure. At any rate, the gold had gone, and the government had taken the mining rights; so did that mean they were staying now, and if so, why?

I'll ask, she thought; then laughed at herself. Asking would be a waste of time. Thouri—how she hated the name Fly; she couldn't help thinking of flies and maggots and rotting food, but he evidently preferred it, thought of himself as Fly; sometimes she said his name and there was a brief pause before he realised she was talking to him—Thouri had never been the sort of man who answered questions. A hangover from the war, she'd always assumed; so many things that weren't to be talked about there, and after a while he'd got into the habit of dodging any sort of question. Also, she considered, there was the real possibility that he didn't know—that Kunessin either hadn't made his own mind up, or held that the others didn't need to know what he'd decided. It'd be so easy for her to start hating the general, holding him responsible for everything that'd gone wrong. Clea obviously did. She hadn't got the faintest idea what Menin thought, about Kunessin or anything else.

On balance (not, of course, that she'd have any say in the matter), she'd rather they gave up now and went home, even though they'd have lost all their money and had nothing to show for it. Not as though they'd had anything worth losing to begin with. Staying here—well, the idea had always been to have a farm: hard work but a good life; she'd always believed deep down that that was how people were meant to live, not piled in on top of each other in towns. Different here, though. A farm—she frowned, refining the thought out of vague feelings—a farm isn't something you can just call into being, by marking out fields and buying tools and livestock. In order to be a real farm, a proper farm, it needs to have been there for at least two hundred years. You need old buildings, old ways of doing things, tried and tested, everything done the way your grandad used to do it. That was the only way a farm could work. Everything new, everything being done for the first time. That's not what the general wants.

She frowned. The truth is, she realised, he doesn't actually know what he wants. Fine; his problem, except they all get dragged in too. Wouldn't have mattered so much if Dorun hadn't died; she was the only one outside of their little closed gang who could say anything he'd actually hear. She was the sort of person who tried hard to make things work. Now he's on his own again, and it's not like it was when they were in the army.

She thought about that: why isn't it the same? Answer, because there's no enemy. The gang, A Company, needs an enemy; but the general's too smart to try fighting the government, and the indentured men are gone, so he can't fight them. The thought disturbed her; for A Company, everything would always be sharply divided: them, and everybody else the enemy. Does that, she asked herself, include us?

You can't be a soldier without an enemy. Kunessin's gang can only be soldiers; they can't cope with being anything else. But we're on an island; so if they won't fight the government, who does that leave?

(She thought about the stories: shipwrecked sailors drifting in an open boat, no food. Starving. Unless they get food, they'll all die. So they draw lots, and so on until there's just one left . . .)

The end of a row. She marked it with a piece of stick, and paced out the next line. If they were going, of course, she was wasting her time. For now, though, she was happy to go though the motions, pretend that what she was doing had some value. An hour's work now would mean food in a few months' time. It wasn't up to her whether or not there'd be anybody here to eat it.

"What are you doing?" She winced. Clea.

"Gardening," she replied, not looking up. "Are you going to help me?"

"Waste of time," Clea said, as though it was self-evident. "You don't want to bother with all that."

"It relaxes me," Enyo said mildly. "You should try it."

"Not likely."

"Suit yourself," Enyo said.

"Thought you were going to do the cornmeal."

"Later."

Clea came across and stood over her, watching. "What's that you're planting?"

"Beans."

"Hate beans. Give you wind."

"Don't eat them, then."

"Nobody's going to eat your stupid beans," Clea said. "We'll all be gone by the time they're ready."

"You think so?"

"What the hell would we want to stay here for? It's just a stupid rock in the middle of the sea."

Enyo stood up, took the hoe and started to mark out a drill. "We came here to farm," she said.

"Not to do the work ourselves," Clea replied. "That's what the servants were for, and now they've gone. Who's going to do all the work? Not them."

"You think he means to leave, then."

"He must do. Nobody in his right mind'd want to stay here."

Enyo finished the drill. "Seen Menin today?"

Clea shook her head. "Off again," she replied. "Up in the woods, I suppose."

She carried on standing there, like an inconvenient tree. "What happened to the gold?" she asked.

Enyo kept her eyes on what she was doing. "I was asking myself that," she said.

"I think they took it," Clea said. "I think that's what they went to the mainland for, with Chaere. I never trusted her," she added viciously. "I think they've gone off with the gold and dumped us here, like so much rubbish."

Enyo paused, her knees ground down into the soft dirt, a small heap of bean seeds in her cupped hand. "I don't think so," she said.

"I do."

"Yes, thank you, I'd gathered that. But I don't believe it. Why would they?"

Clea made a soft, angry noise. "Don't want us any more, do they? When they were going to be farmers, they wanted farmers' wives, so they got a job lot, like weaners at market. Now they've got the gold and they're off and away. Think about it."

That was the last thing Enyo wanted to do. "That doesn't make sense," she said calmly. "The general went to a lot of trouble to do a deal with the government man, so he'd keep the land, and the government—"

"That was just to fool them," Clea said scornfully, as though pointing out the painfully obvious. "It was the gold he was after all along. And look what happened. Everybody goes away—the soldiers, the servants—and suddenly the gold's disappeared. Use your head."

Cautiously, as though probing a painful tooth, Enyo thought

about it. If I was Kudei Gaeon, she thought, would I sneak off and abandon this shrill, stupid, suspicious woman, with whom I couldn't possibly have anything in common? Or Muri Achaiois, whose wife was almost certainly strange in the head. Or Thouri...

"I don't think so," she said.

"And there's another thing." Clea looked round for something to sit on, but there wasn't anything. "What do you think happened with the servants? I don't think they stole the gold. When could they have done it? Load of nonsense."

"I've got my doubts about that," Enyo confessed. "But you made the point yourself. Without them, who's going to do all the heavy work? Surely the general would want them here, if he means to stay."

(But that didn't figure, she knew. If the soldiers hadn't turned up, the indentured men would have taken their share of the gold and gone. If the soldiers had taken the gold, would they have stayed, just gone meekly back to the original deal? She doubted it. No, as things had turned out they'd been a hindrance, and now they were gone. Fortuitous.)

"Enyo."

"Hm?"

"I'm scared." Her voice had changed. "Really, do you think they'd go off and leave us?"

Enyo paused. "No," she said. "Thouri wouldn't leave me." She let that sink in. "Now, Aidi took Chaere on this trip to the mainland. If they weren't planning to come back, Thouri would've taken me. Therefore," she went on, speeding up a little, "they do plan to come back, which means they do plan to stay, which means they need us as, well, as breeding stock, for when they're too old to work. That's what we were for to start with." That's what *you* were for, she didn't say. "I don't know what's going on with the gold or the indentured men, but I'm quite certain they're coming back and they plan on staying here." She took a deep breath, then added, "So if I were you, I'd start thinking up some way you can smuggle yourself on board the supply ship from Faralia when it gets here without them noticing you're missing, at least till the ship's sailed with you on it. And I'd say the same to Menin, if I knew where the hell she was."

She could feel Clea looking at her. "Run away?"

"If I were you." Carefully, she began placing the beans in the drill. "I think you're right about one thing," she said. "I think that if they had to, Muri Achaiois and your husband would dump you and Menin, without a second thought, if the general told them to. You'd be better off back in Faralia."

"Oh, right." Clea sounded furious. "But not you."

"No."

"Fine."

Just to be on the safe side, Enyo counted to ten before she looked round, and satisfied herself that Clea really had gone. She sighed, then carried on planting beans.

The fire, she thought. No doubt about it, the general was a shrewd negotiator and a cunning man generally, but if Clea was right about the gold, the fire had been a real stroke of luck. No, of course it hadn't. Dorun had been killed; General Kunessin wouldn't have killed his own wife.

Accidents happen.

She decided not to think about it any more.

Menin came back from the woods. She was in a dreadful state, though she didn't seem aware of it herself: muddy, green with lichen-stains, bits of stick and twig in her hair, her face and hands dirty. She had her basket, the one she always carried. It was full.

Enyo met her at the barn door. Before she could say anything, Menin asked her: "Where are they?"

"What, you mean . . . ?"

"My husband, and the others."

Handle with care, Enyo thought. "They went to the mainland," she said. "In the sloop. They've been gone for ten days."

"Oh." Menin frowned. "When will they be back?"

"I'm not sure. Quite soon."

Menin looked at her basket. "That's a nuisance," she said. "They won't keep more than a day or so, unless I dry them, and that's not the same as having them fresh."

Enyo smiled, a little bit too much. "That's all right," she said. "We'll have them tonight, for supper, with the cornbread."

"No." Harsh voice. "It doesn't matter. I can find more, I guess. Only it's late in the season."

"That's right," Enyo said helplessly. "Now, why don't you go inside and...?"

Wasting her breath. Menin walked away, back the way she'd just come. Marvellous, Enyo thought, exactly what we need, on top of everything else. "Menin," she called after her, but she carried on walking, a slow, functional trudge, taking the basket with her.

Three days later, the sloop came back to Sphoe.

They'd had a miserable crossing from the mainland: becalmed for two days, then caught in a series of violent squalls, then becalmed again.

"Actually," Alces told his wife, "the getting blown about wasn't so bad. It drowned out the noise of Aidi and Chaere yelling at each other. Three days of sitting dead still on a perfectly flat sea with those two..." He shrugged. "Thank God the war was never as bad as that. Don't think I could've handled it."

She smiled at him. "What were they...?"

"The stupidest bloody thing," Alces replied, peeling off his sodden, salt-caked clothes. "She says, maybe if we jettison the cargo, the ship'll go faster. Aidi says, perfectly reasonably, if there's no wind it won't make a blind bit of difference. She says—"

"What cargo?"

Alces grinned. "Artichokes."

"Arti—"

"Artichokes," he repeated; then he frowned, and added, "You know: not the round spiky things like a giant thistle. The lumpy white roots. Stuff you feed to pigs."

She paused before asking, "Why?"

"That's what Chaere wanted to know," Alces said, trying to ease the boots off his feet. "Which means Teuche has to butt in and say, we'll be planting them for winter fodder for the stock; and she stares at him like he's mad, and starts nagging at Aidi again. Teuche doesn't like that, as you can imagine—doesn't take kindly to being ignored—which makes Aidi get all pompous and up himself, and he says, I think you ought to apologise to Teuche, and then she really gets wound up. And so on, for days on end."

She hesitated, as though she wasn't quite sure she understood. "About artichokes."

"Among other things," Alces said, dragging off his left boot. "But all directed at Aidi, mind you, as though the rest of us weren't actually there. Lots and lots of stuff about his personal shortcomings." He sighed. "I'll say this for him," he said, "he's a patient man. If it'd been me, I'd have pushed her off the ship."

She turned her head away from him a little. "I guess," she said in a neutral voice, "if he's planning for spring fodder, that means we're staying here."

He looked at her. "Well of course we're staying here. I mean, it's what we came for, isn't it?"

She nodded slowly. "And that's what you went to the mainland to buy, was it? Artichokes?"

It gave her more pleasure than she'd expected to see him twitch slightly, caught out by one little slip. "And other stuff too."

"Can't have been much other stuff, if the boat was stuffed full of artichokes."

He grinned. "Quite right," he said.

She waited for him to go on, but he didn't; so she said: "Did you sell it?"

"No, of course not." He shook his head vigorously. "We've got it stashed away, in a safe place. Our rainy-day fund, I guess you could call it."

She handed him a shirt. She'd washed and pressed it while he was away, carefully worked out the marks of mildew and rainwater with soaked wood ash and two round stones. He didn't look at it, just hauled it on, like a tarpaulin. "And we're definitely staying," she said.

He nodded. "Confirmed," he said. "We're now officially farmers,

Teuche says so. Tomorrow, first thing, we celebrate by planting the artichokes. Won't that be something to look forward to."

She thought about her twelve rows of beans. "Yes," she said.

"It gets better." He stood up, fetched his other pair of boots, knelt to lace them. "After that, we get to mend the stock pen rails and dig a root cellar. You know," he added, standing up again, "practically like real life."

Enyo looked at him cautiously. For once, she wasn't quite sure what he wanted to hear her say. "The gold," she said. "He's glad to be rid of it, isn't he?"

"Of course," Alces replied, as if it was self-evident. "Just so long as nobody else gets it, which would constitute a defeat. As far as he's concerned, it was never anything but a bloody nuisance." Suddenly he grinned. "He's been smart, you know," he said. "Things haven't gone the way he expected, but he's dealt with it well. Got rid of the gold, and the indentured men, once he'd realised he couldn't handle them any more, and he's squared things up with the government. As far as he's concerned, it couldn't have turned out much better."

Apart from Dorun, she didn't say. Instead: "All that money, though."

"Oh, that." Alces grinned broadly. "You don't know him like we do. Teuche's not like that; not like Aidi, or me, for that matter. He never could give a toss about money."

SIXTEEN

From now on, Kunessin let it be known, we do everything for keeps.

They planted the artichokes—three days' hard labour with mattocks and rakes; they had six fine undercut ploughs packed in unopened crates, but no oxen to pull them with. They mended the fences, which weren't in such a bad state anyway. They dug the root cellar, a long, miserable job that involved tearing up half the cobble, gravel and sand floor they'd been to such pains to lay in the barn, digging down six feet into the clay, shoring up with lumber and puddling the floor and the walls till they were hard as stone to keep the damp out. "I'd forgotten," Kunessin said, when the job was almost done, and they were so tired they could barely stand, "how easy ordinary work is, compared to all the other shit we've been doing lately." They found other chores to occupy themselves with, all labour-intensive, all of them needing five men working together as a team, all of them necessary, more or less; and as each task ended and turned into something accomplished, they seemed to pause, as if waiting for the other party to recognise their cue. But the soldiers hadn't come back yet; and so Kunessin found them something else to do.

*   *   *

Menin hadn't said a word to any of them since they got back, so it came as something of a surprise when she announced that she was going to cook them a special dinner, to celebrate both their safe return and the decision to settle permanently on Sphoe. She had, she told them, been planning it for some time. Nearly all the ingredients would be things she'd gathered herself: doves' eggs pickled in rosemary vinegar, honey-glazed upland hare stuffed with minced nuts and early berries, served with wild onions, sweet roots and forest dumplings...

A kind of puffball, she explained, that grows on fallen trees; but don't be put off by that. Think of a cross between the best white flour dumplings and smoked beancurd. Back in Faralia, rich buyers from the mainland paid a thaler a pound for it, which was presumably why they hadn't come across it before; it was quite rare back home, and far too valuable for country people to eat themselves. Here, though, you'd be hard put to it to walk ten yards through the woods at this time of year without treading on at least half a dozen good-sized heads. Which only went to show, she added, what a really special place Sphoe was; and this dinner would be (she blushed as she said it) sort of like the island's way of welcoming its new owners.

"I can't believe he's letting her do it," Chaere repeated. "He must be mad."

Aidi gave up pretending he couldn't hear her over the chink of his mattock blade on the stones. "What was he supposed to do?" he said wearily. "Say 'No thanks, we think you've gone crazy and you'll try and poison us all'? I don't think so."

Chaere sighed at him. "You heard what Enyo said. She's been acting really strange while we were away. And let's face it, she wasn't exactly normal before that. Do you honestly want to sit down to a meal of God only knows what, concocted by a woman who spends her entire time roaming about in the woods like a tinker?"

"I don't know," Aidi said. "Depends on whether she's a good cook, I suppose." He straightened up, arched his back, then stooped again. "Hasn't it occurred to you that it may just be a rather nice gesture on her part?"

"No." Chaere scowled at him. "I think she's strange."

"Shy," Aidi amended.

"And why now?" Chaere went on. "It's not like we've just arrived, or it's the first anniversary, or anything like that. No, she suddenly announces—"

"Like she said," Aidi said patiently, "it's because we've decided we're staying. Nice thought on her part, I approve. Oh come on," he added wearily. "We've been eating her toadstools and dandelion roots and stuff practically since we got here, and nobody's died yet. In fact, after the stores got burnt, it was her and that servant who kept us going. You didn't make a fuss then," he added, "or at least you did, but only because of how it tasted. Why should she take it into her head to murder us all now, when she could've done it any time in the last—?"

"She's changed," Chaere hissed back. "Since we went to the mainland. Got worse. Clea thinks she had some sort of a thing going with one of the servants, the deer-hunter person. Don't you see? This is to get back at us for sending him away."

Aidi frowned. "Please don't go saying things like that where Muri might hear you," he said. "He's a bit of an innocent in some ways; I don't think he really understands about female gossip. He might be inclined to believe there could just possibly be a grain of truth to it. All right? Promise me."

It took Aidi rather longer than usual to get Chaere to lose patience with him and go off in a huff. Once she'd gone, he turned over what she'd said slowly in his mind and decided that, on balance, she'd put up a case that needed to be referred upwards. So, when they stopped at midday, he talked to Kunessin about it.

"Well, we've agreed now," Kunessin said. "We can't very well say no. Muri'd wonder what we're playing at."

"Fine," Aidi said. "I'd rather offend Muri than die in agony, thanks all the same. You've got to admit, it's a bit odd, suddenly deciding she wants to treat us all to a grand banquet."

Kunessin took his time before answering. "I'm not saying she's the most rational woman in the world," he said. "That doesn't make her a mass poisoner. Anyhow, if she wanted to kill us, she could have done it any time. Could do it today, or tomorrow, come to that; slip something nasty into the cornmeal and then not turn up for dinner. We'd none of us know till it was too late. Why make a big song and dance about it, and risk putting us on our guard?"

"I don't know, do I?" Aidi said impatiently. "I don't know how mad women think. Sane ones are hard enough going, God knows."

"And," Kunessin went on, "if she's doing us this big spread, she'll have to eat with us, which means if it's poisoned . . . "

Aidi nodded. "Maybe she doesn't care. In fact, that's more likely, if you ask me. Look, I'm not saying she's definitely planning on doing the lot of us in; it's not a court of law or anything. I'm just saying there's a danger, even if it's just a slight one, so surely it'd be a good idea not to take the risk, just in case. Well?"

Kunessin sighed. "So what's the logical inference?" he said. "We decide we don't trust her. Well, we can't very well leave it at that. It'd mean we'd have to stop her going foraging, we'd have to get the other three to keep her away from all the cooking and food handling, we'd have to put locks on all the stores; and even then, if she's set her heart on it, she'd find a way. And she's Muri's wife, don't forget. What's he supposed to think while all this is going on? He's got quite attached to her."

Aidi couldn't help but grin at the choice of words. "So basically you'd rather die than make a fuss, is that it?"

Pause; then Kunessin nodded. "I guess so," he said. "I'd rather run what I reckon is a smallish risk than tell one of us that I don't trust his wife not to kill us all." He lifted his head and grinned suddenly. "Of course it's a risk," he said. "Everything's a risk. If we'd let risks put us off doing dangerous things and trusting each other, we'd none of us have survived the war. Funny," he added, "I'd almost forgotten. You know, what it was like when a one-in-four chance we'd make it was good odds. We weren't the least bit worried then. We just knew."

He shook his head. Aidi frowned, then said, "That was different. That was in a war. It's like swimming. If you're in water, you swim, you've got to, or you drown. On dry land, though, swimming's completely out of place, it'll get you nowhere and you'd be stupid to try.

The war's over, Teuche. We don't have to do that sort of thing any more."

Kunessin looked at him; almost a pitying look, as from a wise teacher to a promising but occasionally misguided student. "That isn't how I remember it," he said. "But then," he went on abruptly, and the smile on his face wasn't entirely friendly; it was an expression they all knew well, "the day you and I actually agree on something, I'll be sure to wear a very big, wide hat, in case the flying pigs shit on my head."

Aidi shrugged and walked away, and there the matter rested. That evening, however, Kunessin caught up with Enyo as she went to fill the log basket.

"This banquet idea," he said.

Enyo nodded. "Chaere, I take it."

"Correct," Kunessin said. "But I suppose she's got a point. Look, could you do me a favour? Could you find a way of watching her like a hawk while she's cooking up this wonderful feast of hers, just in case there's something not quite right about it?"

Enyo pulled a face. "Trouble is," she said, "I wouldn't know what I'd be looking for. That's the problem. She's the only one who knows about that stuff."

Kunessin nodded. "Quite right," he said. "But I remember when my mother used to cook for us, and when it was something fancy she was going to a lot of trouble over, she'd be forever sticking her finger in and licking it, or slurping a bit off the ladle, to make sure it tasted right. That's what you do when you're cooking, isn't it?"

Enyo laughed, then nodded. "But it's just a taste..."

"Sure," Kunessin agreed. "But somehow I don't think you'd do that if you knew for certain it was poisoned. It'd be instinct. You just wouldn't want that stuff in your mouth. Well, would you?"

Enyo frowned; then she shrugged. "I can watch her, if you want me to," she said.

"Thanks, I'd be obliged. Here," he added, picking up the log basket. "Let me take that for you." And he carried it back to the house like a trophy.

*   *   *

Enyo watched while Menin cooked the dinner (Kunessin grabbed her arm as she brought in the dish of doves' eggs. "Well?" Enyo smiled at him. "I've learned how to make short-base pastry," she said), and very good it was, too. Menin and Enyo served up, while Clea sulked and Chaere made faces. Kunessin made sure Menin got plenty to eat. They washed it down with a jar of red wine the farmer had given them to seal the house purchase—Alces and Muri had water—and after a few drinks Menin loosened up considerably and started prattling: about the recipes, what all the ingredients were and where you found them and what the seasons were and what her grandmother had told her about a wide range of related topics, and in the end it was all they could do to persuade her to shut up.

"That's the end of the mushrooms," she said sadly. "There won't be anything fit to eat now till early autumn."

"Is that right?" Kunessin said politely.

"Oh yes. Nothing now till the early ceps. Now they're really nice, really, really nice, in a sauce, though you can just fry them in a little green oil, but I think that spoils the flavour. There's really nice ceps here, they're quite scarce back home but not here, there's plenty." She paused to drink another half-cup of wine. "No, you don't want to go eating any mushrooms between now and the start of harvest."

Aidi looked up. "Really?"

She nodded gravely. "Oh no," she said. "They could make you really ill. Really ill. I knew someone once who died from eating poisonous mushrooms."

Kunessin looked in her direction; not at her, just past her. "As bad as that, then."

"Really bad," Menin said. "Of course, there's some mushrooms that're bad for you even in the mushroom season, but it's all right so long as you know what you're looking for. I mean, you have to know, but once you do, it's perfectly all right."

"You'll have to teach us," Kunessin said with his mouth full.

"Sure," Menin chirped, and her hand located the wine cup and lifted it to her mouth. "I can do that. My gran taught me, when I was a little girl. We used to go out to the woods together, and she showed me which ones you could eat and which ones are bad for you. It's quite easy to tell, once someone's shown you."

"Pity we'll have to wait till autumn," Muri said.

"Well, I can tell you," Menin replied, "but that's not the same as showing you, because it can be hard to say the difference in words, but when you see for yourself it's quite easy, really. But in the autumn I'll show you, sure, and then you'll know too."

After the meal, Aidi muttered to Kunessin, "I liked her so much better when she was sinister and didn't talk," and moved away to sort out Chaere, who was defiantly trying to feel ill in a corner, though without success. Menin, meanwhile, slipped out into the yard and crossed to the burnt-out house. Quickly looking behind her to make sure she was alone, she knelt down beside the ruins of the fireplace, pulled back her sleeve and searched by feel up the chimney until she'd found what she was looking for. She could only touch it with her fingertips, but that was enough to make her smile. Then she went to the woodshed, gathered an armful of logs and went back to the barn.

A ship came in. No soldiers; it was a sloop, slim, fast and expensive, a government courier, and it had come all that way just to deliver a letter. Kunessin opened it, read it, quickly glanced through the enclosures to make sure they were all there.

"Thanks," he said. "No reply."

The ship sailed away the same day, having taken on a little drinking water and the quarter-jar of fire-melted gold. The covering letter explained that this was the sum total of the proceeds of the mine prior to the agreement with Commissioner Straton; it had been stolen and hidden away by the mutineers, but had since come to light. Properly speaking, it belonged to the proprietors, since its extraction pre-dated the assignment of mining rights; as a gesture of goodwill, however...

"Teuche." Aidi, stunned and bewildered. "That was sixty thousand thalers."

"About that, yes." Kunessin was sitting at the only remaining good table with three of the six remaining oil lamps lit beside him, and the wad of legal papers that had been in with the letter spread out side by side in front of him. "The question being, was that enough? And yes, I'm inclined to think it was. The important thing to remember is, they've got no way of knowing for sure when we first made the strike. I told them we'd only been going a few weeks, which made sixty thousand a good return. I'm not sure they believed me, but my guess is they won't want to rock the boat over a few unprovable suspicions."

"Teuche..."

"Meanwhile," Kunessin went on, without raising his voice, "here we've got the counterpart land transfer deeds, properly sealed by the registrar, a deed of rectification and indemnity—strictly speaking it's not necessary, since all that's superseded by the new transfer, but it can't do any harm—and a nice long letter of comfort setting out the ancillary terms I agreed with Straton. You're the lawyer, Aidi. That pretty well covers everything, doesn't it?"

He slid the documents across the table in Aidi's direction, but Aidi ignored them. "You should have asked us first," he said. "It's a lot of money."

Kudei, who'd been cleaning his boots a few yards away, stopped and turned his head a little. Alces saw him, and came over to stand beside him.

"Agreed," Kunessin said. "So what?"

"So we should've talked about it first, before you gave it away like that."

Just the slightest shift on Kunessin's face, a flaw or crevice between the eyebrows. "I just explained about that," he said. "Weren't you listening?"

Aidi took a deep breath. "That's not the point."

The crease became a definite frown. "Of course it's the point," Kunessin said. "Sorry, don't you agree with my approach? You think we should've done something else."

Aidi shifted nervously, like a horse at the start of a thunderstorm. "I'm not saying that."

"So if we had discussed it, you'd have supported my decision? Or did you have a plan of your own you'd have liked us to consider?"

Behind them somewhere, Clea knocked over a jug. It hit the floor with a bump, didn't break, rolled away under a bench. Clea swore at it and asked Menin to fetch her a mop. All that happened, and still Aidi hadn't answered Kunessin's question. Neither had he moved; and Alces, watching him carefully, thought about an arrow hanging in the air at the end of its ascent. Then someone did speak, but it was Kudei.

"Sixty thousand's a lot of money, Teuche," he said.

Slowly, Kunessin stood up and carefully moved his chair; like an artilleryman shifting the lie of his piece so that his arc of fire covers two targets. "Maybe I'm the one who's missing the point," he said mildly. "Perhaps you'd care to tell me what the big deal is, Kudei."

Kudei was sitting very still, his eyes wide open, his hands at his sides, perfectly relaxed. "Maybe it would've been a good idea if we'd talked about it," he said. "After all, we've had plenty of time. It's not like you had to make a snap decision in a hurry."

Kunessin nodded slowly, like a judge. "Fine," he said. "If this is going to be a formal staff meeting, someone had better fetch Muri. Anyone know where he is?"

"Hold on, both of you." Alces had shifted his position just a little; not obstructing Kunessin's view of Kudei, but impinging on it. "We don't want to get all uptight about it, and besides, it's done now, no use crying over spilt milk."

Kunessin said: "Do you know where Muri is, Fly? If we're going to talk about this—"

"Muri always takes your side," Aidi snapped. "We don't need him here to know what he'd think."

Kudei frowned, as though taking a point away from Aidi for a misjudged move. Alces said, "I don't think this is about sides, Aidi. And yes, I think it'd have been nice if you'd told us first, Teuche. It came as a bit of a shock."

Kunessin smiled. "Just to clarify," he said. "You'd have liked to have been told, or you'd have liked to have been asked? You'll agree there's a difference."

"Can we stop this?" Kudei said. "Like Fly said, what's done is done. No point starting a civil war over it."

"I think we should have discussed it first," Aidi said. "That's not unreasonable, is it?"

Kunessin moved round to face him. "It's funny," he said. "I remember a time when I made decisions for all of us, and it wasn't about money, it was our lives, whether we'd get killed or not. And I don't seem to remember having to refer every single fucking order to committee before people did as they were told."

Kudei tried to speak, but Aidi was quicker. "That was in the war," he said.

Kunessin paused, as if waiting for the rest of the argument. "That's right," he said. "I'm not quite sure I see what you're getting at."

Alces was looking down at the floor. Kudei noticed that, at some point, the women had left the barn. "Don't you?" Aidi said. "Sorry, I thought you knew: the war's over. I assumed they'd have told you, you being a general."

Kunessin smiled; dry, angry. "All right," he said. "Granted, the soldiers who want to throw us off our land and take it away from us are from our own government, not some enemy overseas we've never heard of before. If you think that really makes a difference, maybe I can begin to understand why you're turning on me like this. Personally, I don't see there's a whole lot in it." Aidi started to reply, but Kunessin cut him off. "When Nuctos died, I seem to remember you wanted me to take over, make the decisions, be the officer commanding. Isn't that right, Fly? Kudei?"

"I'm not disputing that, for crying out loud," Aidi said, and he knew his anger was making him sound weak. "This isn't—"

"Aidi?" Kunessin said. "You wanted me to take over, didn't you? When Nuctos died."

If Aidi hesitated just for a moment, maybe Kunessin didn't notice. "Of course I did," Aidi said. "And yes, I entirely agree: in the war you gave the orders and we didn't discuss everything, and yes, it's quite true that we were in a sticky situation when Straton was here, and you handled it and got us out of it, and I agree with every decision you made. I agree that giving the government that stupid jar of gold will most likely keep them off our backs and head off any trouble we might've had on account of it." He paused, drew breath.

"I still think you should've told us first. After all, you had plenty of time. It wasn't a spur-of-the-moment decision."

Kunessin looked at him, face blank, for three seconds. "Apology accepted," he said.

Muri Achaiois came back from the sawmill drunk. His hair and beard were floured with the same pale yellow dust that clogged his nose and made his eyes watery and red. He'd cut himself on the fore-arm, hadn't noticed doing it, but there was caked blood and a big black scab. He tripped over the door frame and fell into the house, instinct guiding his fall so that he landed on his shoulder, rolled and regained his feet as nimbly as a front-rank fighter; then he staggered again, slammed the table with his knee and roared, not so much because of the pain but because he was so angry with himself for being idiot-clumsy and waking his wife, and most likely the neigh-bours as well.

"Muri?" Her voice, muffled and snarly with spoiled sleep.

"It's all right," he growled back, furious at her for having been woken up by a pathetic drunk who couldn't even open a door any more. A couple of houses down, a dog started barking. Wonderful.

He knew what she'd do next: pretend to go back to sleep, to spare him further dishonour, but her back would be tense like a bow at full draw, and her breathing would be all wrong. So he said, "Go to sleep" at her, then sat down on her feet and tried to get his boots off.

Once upon a time he'd vaulted the pike hedges and tightrope-walked the depth of a battalion on the shoulders of the enemy, smash-ing heads and lopping arms at will as he went. Now, he was being wrestled to submission by a bootlace. That was too great an insult to be endured, so he stuck his finger under the lace and yanked at it with all his legendary strength; but the lace held and sawed into his finger like a stonemason's rope, and he yowled. Once upon a time, at the Military College, he'd solved all six of Holoenta's Paradoxes, when all the rest of his year were still struggling to understand simul-taneous equations. Now all he could do was suck his finger where a bit of string had drawn his blood and tasted his flesh.

"Iero," he whined, "I can't get my boots off."

"All right." A sad, patient voice, one that expected nothing more from him. "Light the lamp." Then, very quickly, "No, it's all right, I'll do it."

Not the right thing to say. Muri Achaiois had been a mathematician and a scientist before this woman was born. "I'll light the lamp," he said, and caught her soft hand like a wasp on its way to the bedside table, and held it under arrest while his other hand fumbled for the lamp and the tinderbox. He knew he was gripping on it a little bit too tight, but he took his time letting go. She didn't say anything.

He found the lamp; found the tinderbox but knocked it off the table on to the floor, heard it bump and skitter. "Now look what I've fucking done," he roared (Muri Achaiois, trained as a blacksmith and cabinet-maker, who could file a perfect circle by eye and plane two complex curves so they'd glue together flush). "Stay there," he moaned, in a crude imitation of her patient voice. "I'll find it."

Down on his hands and knees, his stomach raging like the sea, his brain sliding about in his head like the bubble in a spirit level, scrabbling for the stupid tinderbox; banged the bridge of his nose into the side of the bed, swore, found the damn box, stood up, barged into the table, just managed to grab the lamp, by perfect instinct, before it rocked over and smashed; with infinite care stood it upright again, fumbled off the glass mantle and set it down, knocked it over with his sleeve as he reached for the tinderbox and heard it tinkle-smash, a sniggering sort of noise, on the floor. Broken glass crunched under him as he moved. Just as well he still had his boots on.

He heard her say nothing, louder than shouting. Well, he thought, glad I managed to live down to your expectations. He wanted to hit her for putting up with him, but instead he thumbed open the tinderbox lid, prodded down the crunchy dry moss, let the lid flop shut and turned the handle. Turned and turned and turned, but couldn't hear the tiny crackle and fizz of the tinder catching. Turned harder.

"Shit," he said. "I broke the handle."

"Let me—"

"No." Once upon a time, he'd believed that she loved him; but she must've been lying, because who could possibly love a clown like Muri Achaiois? "It's all right, I'm perfectly capable..." He felt his arm swat against the lamp-oil jug, felt it topple, tried to grab it, missed, heard it smash, splat; and, in that small, frozen second of sober perception, realised he'd dropped the tinderbox, and that he had managed to get it going, after all.

A white spear of flame shot up from between his feet, sprawled up his legs and licked at his face like a bad dog; he jumped backwards before it could ignite him, landed badly, lost his feet and fell backwards on to his bum, jarring his spine and rattling his teeth.

"It's all right," he shouted, as the flame swelled and blossomed, hiding her from him, and she screamed. It was all right, because he knew what to do, in this as in all genuine emergencies. He scrambled to his feet—the flame was impossibly tall, licking its sharp yellow tongue against the bare thatch—and lunged at the fire, eager to club it to death and stamp on it and defeat it, and stood on his trailing untied bootlace and came down on his nose like a hammer on the head of a nail, and the darkness came and took him away for a while.

Then he was awake, sitting in a chair, with a pounding headache and a horrible stinging pain where the air was eating into his raw cheek, and he could smell the foul stink of burned hair, and for some reason Aidi Proiapsen was there, standing over him, looking down at him as though he was all the leading problems and issues of the day. So he assumed he must be dreaming, until Aidi leant in closer and said, "Muri?"

(Which was the first thing Aidi, or anyone from the old days, had said to him for three years. He blinked. He had an idea he was missing the point.)

"It's all right," Aidi said. "You're all right. You've had a bang on the head and your face is a bit burned, but nothing much at all. Other than that, you're fine."

Aidi, you're such a piss-poor liar. "What happened?" he asked.

Aidi looked blank for a moment. "There was a fire," he said. "At your place. Don't you remember?"

Then, suddenly, he remembered. He felt his stomach lurch at the shame, the total humiliation: Muri Achaiois, who once sacked the citadels of the enemy, burns down his own stupid little house. Of course, Iero would leave him now, and she'd tell everybody why—

"Where's Iero?" he asked, and there was a split second before Aidi answered, and by the time he spoke there was no need.

Utterly ridiculous, of course; because he was the one who'd fallen on his face and knocked himself out cold, been lying there a great inert lump on the floor of the burning house, inches from the heart of the fire, and he'd made it out alive (death doesn't apply to A Company), and his hangover hurt worse than his burns; and she'd been the one who died. That wasn't just ridiculous, it was deliberately, gratuitously insulting.

The smoke killed her, Aidi was saying; you were right down on the ground, and that's where the air is, in a fire. Standing up, you're in the smoke. But of course, she hadn't known that, so by the time the neighbours...

He wasn't interested, but it was all he could think to ask: "How did I get here?"

Aidi paused again. "One of your neighbours remembered that I know you," he said; a curious choice of words. "So they sent for me, and I had you fetched back here."

And here he was; but Aidi's lying, he thought. I always know when Aidi's lying. It unsettled him, enough to cut through all the mess and junk lying on his mind and reach down to the basic soldier instincts, danger and fight and escape. He noticed in passing that Aidi was directly between him and the door, which was shut and bolted.

"I want to go home," he said.

"I'm afraid there's not much left," Aidi said. "They did what they could, but once it'd got into the thatch..."

"I want to go home," he repeated, and tried to stand up, and just about managed it. He noticed that both his feet were bare.

"I'm afraid that's not possible." Aidi's face was completely frozen. "Please, Muri, just stay put for now. You need to rest. That bang on the head you took..."

Bad lie; poor quality throughout. He knew all about bangs on the head, the sort that could kill you and the sort that just gave you a headache. "Aidi," he said.

"I'm afraid you'll have to stay here for now," Aidi said, and his voice was cold and filled with self-hate, and Muri remembered that Aidi was, among other things, a magistrate.

"Oh," he said.

Aidi closed his eyes, then opened them again. "It's her family," he said. "They've filed a complaint. Apparently the neighbours heard some things..."

(Drunken Muri Achaiois crashing about; glass breaking...)

"Oh," he repeated.

By now Aidi was looking desperate, as though he was the wanted man frantic to escape. "You really do want to stay here," he was saying. "Come on, Muri, you know what they're like, better than I do. If I let you leave this house, they'll be after you with a rope. If you stay here, they won't dare try anything. It's just till everybody cools down." Please, Muri, he didn't add. Aidi Proiapsen didn't plead, not out loud, and to anybody who knew him well, he couldn't lie worth spit.

Later there was an inquest, Coroner Proiapsen presiding. Allegations of culpable negligence amounting to manslaughter were raised by the deceased's relatives, but dismissed as not proven. An open verdict was returned.

Thouridos Alces was at the inquest. Kudei Gaeon didn't attend; it was a busy time on the farm, and he couldn't get away. Muri lost his job at the sawmill, and spent the next few months sleeping in fallen-down barns and sheds. Aidi told Alces he'd offered him money, a job or both, but Muri hadn't been interested.

It was while Muri was sleeping rough and begging or stealing his living that his wife's family made their move. They'd hired six men, ex-soldiers, nominally for the apple-picking; there were also her three brothers, her father, two uncles and two cousins. They armed themselves with hand-axes, knives, billhooks and a scythe blade, and tracked him to a charcoal-burner's camp where one of the uncles knew the gang master, who arranged for the rest of the burners to be somewhere else, and for a gallon of strong cider to be left lying about where it could easily be found. He also gathered up all the axes, saws, hooks, mauls, froes, hammers and other edged and striking tools and hid them in the bed of a wagon, so that when the search party found Muri asleep under a tree, there were no convenient weapons of necessity available to him, and he had to make do with a stick. He did just fine.

Two of the hired men, one brother and both uncles got away, all of them in more or less of a mess. Muri threw the others on the fire when he'd finished with them, and some of the charcoal-burners later claimed that they could smell the bodies burning half a mile away. Then he sat down under his tree and went back to sleep.

Aidi woke him up some time later. He opened his eyes and yawned. "Hello," he said. "Come to arrest me?"

"Don't be bloody stupid, Muri." Aidi was scowling at him, at his gashed face and bloodstained fingers. "Obviously it was self-defence. Even you wouldn't pick a fight with thirteen men."

He smiled. Aidi had always had that knack, of getting it right and then spoiling it, and not realising. "You know all about it, then."

Aidi nodded. "I heard about what they were planning to do. I came as soon—"

"Thank you, Aidi," Muri said.

"I was going to try and stop it," Aidi said, his school-prefect voice.

"Oh well. It's the thought that counts."

Aidi was rubbing his knuckles with his thumb, a danger signal from way back. "Well?"

"Well what?"

"So what were you planning on doing?"

"Not sure." The big, slow shrug. "Haven't decided. I could read for the bar, I suppose, or try the diplomatic corps, or there's always architecture, or the priesthood. Or I could run away and join a circus. What do you think, Aidi?"

Aidi looked at him, then turned and started to walk away. "Goodbye, Muri," he said, over his shoulder.

He walked five yards, but nothing. He kept walking, slowing his pace just a little. Ten yards, fifteen. He wondered how far Muri would let him go before calling him back. Twenty. He nearly stopped. Of course Muri would call him back. Muri was weak; in the final analysis he was one of life's followers, a great man to have at your side or watching your back, but a born sidekick. He'd worshipped Nuctos, then Teuche, and now he'd be drawn, like filings to a magnet, and Aidi Proiapsen would take him on and look after him, and that was how it should be. One word would do it, and now he'd gone thirty yards. Once again he very nearly stopped, but he couldn't do that.

Fine, he thought, as he walked back to town. He'll come, tomorrow or the next day, once he's pulled himself together. And (ten yards further on) if he doesn't, if he's determined to be difficult, I'll just have to go and fetch him, won't I? It's not like Muri Achaiois will ever be hard to find.

Five days later, he was in his office checking bills of lading when the boy told him Thouridos Alces was outside waiting to see him.

"What the hell did you do to Muri?" Fly snapped at him before he could open his mouth.

"Me? I didn't do anything. What are you...?"

(Fly had changed the most of all of them, he thought: thinner, slower, edgier. He could imagine walking into a room full of people and not immediately noticing Fly was there.)

"He's gone," Fly said angrily. "Gone off somewhere."

Aidi frowned. "Big deal. Off somewhere's been his official address for years."

"On a ship," Fly said, and Aidi felt like he'd been slapped. "Someone I know saw him get on a ship, day before yesterday."

"Going where?"

Fly shrugged. "No idea. He wasn't paying attention, he said, just happened to recognise him, and then mentioned it to me in passing when I ran into him just now."

Aidi scowled, as if tightening the focus of his mind with his eyebrows. "All right," he said. "I can find out which ships were in that day and where they were going."

"Shut up, Aidi," Fly said.

He hadn't been expecting that.

"I thought you wanted me to—"

Fly turned his head away, a typical Alces give-me-strength gesture. "It's a bit late for taking charge now, Aidi," he said.

"What's that supposed to mean?"

Suddenly Fly seemed to have lost interest. "I heard about what he did to the lynch mob," he said. "He's not in trouble over that, is he?"

"Self-defence," Aidi replied. "I told him that."

"So that's not the reason, then." Fly pulled over a stool and perched on it, precisely, like an angel on the head of a pin. "What did you say to him?"

"Nothing. I asked him what he was going to do."

"And?"

Aidi shook his head. "I was going to...well, I don't know. I'd have put him back on his feet, if only he'd asked. I didn't think he'd just go."

Fly sighed, a long, weary getting rid of breath. "See what you can find out," he said. "If you can trace him, I'll write to him. Don't suppose it'd do any good, but you never know." He stood up: a short, thin, worried man who looked older than he was. "Well," he said, "I won't hold you up any longer. You know where I'm living now."

Aidi realised he didn't. That made Fly smile.

"The old Kouroi house on the Ropewalk," he said. "I took the lease. Going to start up a fencing school."

Aidi frowned. "Are you sure that's a—?"

"No, not really." Fly grinned at him. "But the money's run out and I need to earn a living, and I have absolutely no useful skills whatsoever. Enyo's right behind me, of course. Enyo," he repeated. "My wife."

"Yes, I know," before he realised Fly was teasing him. "How is she, by the way?"

"Depressed," Fly replied. "Worried about money. Thought she was marrying a rich man. Well, she did. But I spent it all." He grinned again. "She thinks I did it just to spite her. I think she may be right. Thanks for your time, Aidi. Let me know if you find out anything."

When he'd gone, Aidi went upstairs, lay down on the bed and closed his eyes. Command, he thought; being in charge, being responsible. He mused for a while on the nature of command, and how it was transmitted, outside of a formal structure. In the beginning (once the officer had been killed; and he'd never been in charge anyway, not of them) it had been Nuctos, by light of nature. There had been no need to choose him, in the same way that nobody chooses the sun as their principal source of light. Then Nuctos had died (he thought about that; moved on) and immediately Teuche had taken charge; like water flowing into the gap when you pull a rock out of a river bed. They hadn't discussed it or voted on it; there had been no interregnum. Then Teuche stayed on when they came home, and... He sat up and rubbed his eyelids. A Company couldn't exist without a leader, just as you couldn't have shadows without light. He'd assumed that he was the leader, had been since they got back, because he'd settled down and got on with things and made money and succeeded, while the other two (Kudei didn't count) had gone on a sort of extended R&R, time off for bad behaviour. But that hadn't, shouldn't have altered the fact that he, Aidi Proiapsen, was in charge; and once they'd finished messing around and got it out of their systems, he'd have fallen them in, taken charge, led them...

Apparently not. He could see it now, looking back after the event. Muri Achaiois had got himself in trouble while on leave, and instead of standing in front of him while he was down, ready to demolish any-body who so much as scowled at his fallen comrade, Aidi Proiapsen had arrested him. Not, he decided, what Nuctos or Teuche would have done. No; his first thought, when they'd brought Muri to his house on the night of the fire, was I'm a magistrate, I can't just...

Now look what you've done, he said bitterly to himself. The end of A Company; in other words, the end of the world. Suppose Muri were to die abroad; the thought made him shudder. Or not even that; suppose he just stayed away, untraceable. He composed his report. Command passed to Major Aidi Proiapsen, who failed in his duty, whereupon the company disbanded. It is the finding of this commit-tee that Major Proiapsen is entirely deficient in leadership and unfit-ted to hold a commission in this service...

A month later, he got some news. Muri Achaiois had taken a ship to the mainland, where he'd tried, unsuccessfully, to re-enlist. Since then, he'd dropped out of sight and nobody knew where he was. So Aidi wrote to Fly (the old Kouroi house was just down the road; he could see it from his bedroom window) and got no answer; and six months later, someone happened to mention that Muri Achaiois was back in Faralia, working at the tannery, of all places. He made a mental note to go and see him sometime, but never actually got round to it.

"Apology accepted," Kunessin said.

There was a moment (brief as the interval between pulling a rock out of a river bed and the water rushing in to fill the hole) when Aidi was so angry he could have killed Teuche, or at least tried to. Instead, he breathed out long and slow, like a man laying down his weapons...

Laying down his weapons, all but one. That one was still there, concealed, ready for immediate use, but only if the situation escalated to the point where it was worth destroying the whole world just in order to have won. It had crossed his mind when Teuche said what he'd just said that the point had finally come; he'd considered it seriously, gone so far as to apply the relevant criteria, found that they didn't in fact apply in this instance, although there had indeed been a case to answer.

He knew they were all looking at him. He chose to ignore it; a bit like ignoring the sea when you're drowning.

"Right," Kunessin was saying, "I think that's everything. Let's have some dinner." He was controlling the space, the way he always did, the way the moon draws the tides. By my sufferance, Aidi thought; by my indulgence, my permission. I could smash him with a few words. But he knew perfectly well that he wasn't going to, not today, not until and unless the moment came when he had no choice; no, belay that, don't lie to yourself. Until and unless the moment comes when I want to.

Old story, halfway house between history and myth, about a prince who hated his elder brother so much, he betrayed the kingdom to the enemy rather than let his brother take the throne. To get to that point, Aidi had always thought, must've taken a massive dose of motivation. Himself, he couldn't see it; because what would be the point?

The night after Teuche came home, he'd actually cried, great big wet girlie tears, because Teuche was back and A Company would be saved and restored, and his dereliction of duty hadn't been fatal after all. Actually cried, which was pathetic, but he hadn't been able to help it. But even then, while the hot tears were rolling down his cheeks (shameful as pissing himself), he'd instinctively checked to see that the weapon was still there, still handy, ready for use at a moment's notice. Of course he'd never use it, never want to use it. But it was nice to know it was there.

SEVENTEEN

Menin Aeide was gathering flowers. She'd found a dense thicket of rhododendrons, half a mile inside the woods and over on the west side, and today her basket was full of the fat red blooms, which grew so well here (not like at home); particular favourites of hers, for a reason she hugged close to herself, and which made her smile every time she thought of it. The air was still and cool this far into the wood, and all she could hear was the dull, soothing hum of bees, busy robbing the flowers, like miners working a claim.

They liked it when she brought flowers home. Even General Kunessin made a point of thanking her, saying how nice they looked, how they brightened up the barn. She knew for a fact that none of them gave a damn about flowers (men didn't), but she realised that what gave them pleasure was Menin Aeide acting normally, doing an accepted female thing—not acting crazy, in other words. Fine: she could do that, if that was what it took. Cooking nice meals, picking flowers, chattering, dusting. Any fool could do that.

She'd found the hive the day before she gave her dinner party. It was an ugly growth on the trunk of a dead tree, hollowed out by damp and rot, now teeming with construction and industry. The busy bee: epitome of all the female virtues. She grinned like anything when she thought of that; almost wished there was someone she could share the joke with.

Since she was both cautious and patient by nature, she hadn't stripped the combs of every last drop. Instead, she'd taken a little honey each day, just enough to fill her little horn cup, and each evening she'd added that day's achievement to the store, which she kept in a jar hidden in the chimney of the burnt-out house. She didn't bother with a ceremony, the way Aidi Proiapsen did, and there was no need to seal the jar, because nobody else knew about it. It was her secret, the second beautiful secret thing in her life, and today, if she'd judged it right, the jar would be full.

Danger was, of course, that the bees would swarm and move away. You couldn't tell with bees, sometimes they just upped and went, abandoning their settlements and their workings and their store of hard-won gold. It all depended on the whim of the leader, so she'd heard, because bees were violently loyal; they lived for the queen, unquestioning, devoted. She'd always wondered about that, but she understood it perfectly now.

The bees were still there. As she approached the dead tree she could hear them. She walked right up close, knowing they wouldn't sting her, even though they must suspect she had designs on their treasury. She laughed; maybe she could do a deal with them. They could keep the wood if they gave her the honey.

She stood and listened to them for half an hour, until she fancied she was beginning to understand their language — not worth the effort, she had to admit; all bees have to talk about is work, where the flowers are, how much pollen we got today, weigh it and store it in the comb, how rich we're getting, how rich we'd be if we all flew away tomorrow with our individual shares smeared on our legs. She realised that there was a great big happy grin all over her face, but it didn't bother her. She'd learned that the bees weren't planning on going anywhere; their queen had brought them here from far away, right the other side of the wood, to this corner where the rhododendrons bloomed, and here she intended to stay. So that was all right.

Instead of going home the direct way, she followed the edge of the wood on the seaward side, so she could look out from the top of the round, pudding-shaped hill; a pudding with a slice out of it, where the wind and tides had undermined its base, and all the crumbs had fallen into the sea. It was the best lookout on the island—Kunessin and the men hadn't found it yet; they used the watchtower or the tall rocky spike down on the coast by the bay when they wanted to watch for ships, but Pudding Hill gave a clear view right out to sea. If a ship came, she'd see it from here a full two hours before they could. She'd proved that, the day the courier sloop came.

On the edge of Pudding Slice, the cliff that had fallen down, there was a little platform of rabbit-cropped short grass, practically a lawn, and she liked to sit there when she came here to watch. Later, there would be flowers in the grass, buttercups and angel's eyes and small, shrewd white daisies, but of course she wouldn't be there to see them.

As usual, she occupied her mind as she stared at the wide blue sea by making the list. It varied from day to day, according to her moods. Some days there were two: Enyo and either Chaere or Clea, if she was feeling particularly charitable. Some days, nobody at all, if something had happened to upset or annoy her. On the days when there was just one, it'd be either Enyo or Chaere. It was never just Clea, though. She hated Clea.

She yawned. Peaceful. In summer, it'd be quite delightful here. As usual, having done the list for the day (Enyo and Chaere; she was particularly good-natured today), she ran once through the sequence of events and schedule of Things to Do, and then fell to musing about recipes; though, if she was honest with herself, that was overambitious and unnecessary. When all was said and done, you couldn't beat just plain fresh cornbread, smeared with lashings of rich golden honey.

And (secret smile) the barn decorated with great big bunches of rhododendron flowers, purely for her sake. Private joke.

She must have dozed off. She opened her eyes, and there it was: a white speck on the blue sea, like spit. She looked again. Two specks. Her eyes opened wide, and she laughed out loud. Two ships! Two ships, and how many soldiers would there be on each? Obviously the government wasn't taking any chances. Or—mild disappointment, as she rationalised—one ship full of troops, the other one carrying the miners for the gold works. Even so and never mind. She jumped up, did a little twirl for sheer joy of living, and skipped down off the Pudding back into the woods.

The bees didn't sting her when she robbed them. It was as though they understood.

It was pure chance that she found them all together in one place. Aidi had convened the meeting. The issue being debated was his latest pet project, the scud mill. The idea was to build a simple waterwheel on the river, where a fast-running branch stream forked off and ran down to the beach about two hundred yards from the settlement perimeter. The wheel, Aidi said, would power all sorts of things: grindstones to grind corn, a take-off to run a circular saw for planking and slabbing lumber, a triphammer for ironworking. How they'd planned to survive on Sphoe without it, he simply couldn't understand. All that remained was the simple, straightforward business of building it, and there'd never be a better time, when they had nothing to do except wait for the artichokes to grow.

Aidi Proiapsen, Nuctos had once remarked, was the sort of man who wouldn't take yes for an answer. Kunessin had approved the project in outline, leaving Aidi to get on with it. Aidi had drawn up plans, using the coarse brown paper used to line the seedcorn chests and a stick of alder charcoal. He'd insisted on showing and explaining the plans in detail to the assembled company, and they'd been approved. Now he'd been at the mill site, marking out the footprint with wooden pegs and twine, and he'd marched them all down there—the women too—to give their blessing to his proposals. Kunessin, who'd said, "Yes, that's fine" at least a dozen times without seeming to make any impression at all, was standing with his weight on one foot, gazing back at the settlement. Kudei was yawning, fidgeting; he'd never managed to find a way to cope with being bored. Muri was following it all very carefully, squinting along the lines of twine. Alces was trying to think up objections to raise and problems to point out, just for the hell of it. The women just looked cold.

"There you all are." She smiled indiscriminately at them, and held up the broad wooden trencher. "Oh, sorry, am I interrupting?"

Aidi would've said yes if he'd had the chance, but Kunessin was too quick for him. "Hello," he said, moving abruptly in her direction. "What've you got there?"

"Cornbread and honey," she replied cheerfully. "I'll put it down here and you can help yourselves."

"Honey," Kunessin echoed. "Where'd you find that?"

Just a fraction of a second before she answered. "There's a wild hive up in the woods. First of the season," she added seductively. "I managed to fill four pint jars, so we'll be all right for a while."

Kunessin was already chewing; she knew how much he liked honey, and sweet things generally. Kudei had scooped up a slice. He held it at nose height and turned his head so the drips off the side of the bread would drop into his mouth. Clea and Enyo were scoffing; no other word for it. Alces bit his slice of bread in half, then used the severed edge to wipe up pooled honey off the trencher. "Go on, Muri," she said. "There's plenty to go round."

He was still fussing round Aidi's bits of string and stick. "I'm not all that hungry, thanks."

"Don't be silly," she said, then grabbed a slice and shoved it in his mouth. Golden globs dripped down his beard on either side of his chin.

"Aren't you having any?" Chaere asked with her mouth full. But she'd already thought of an answer to that.

"Already had three slices," she replied. "One slice left. Now, who wants it?"

Aidi had already had a slice and a half, but he shot out a thumb and forefinger and snatched the last slice off the plate. "This is good honey," he pronounced. "Particularly delicate flavour."

"It should be," she said, taking a long step back, away from them all. The last corner of Aidi's last slice was vanishing into his mouth. "It's always better when the bees've been feeding on just one type of pollen. You get a purer taste, my aunt used to say."

"I'm glad there's more of this," Kunessin said. "So, what's the secret ingredient?"

And she smiled; she produced the smile like a weapon and covered them all with it. "It's rhododendron honey," she said.

Kunessin was still smiling. Aidi and Muri were chewing. Chaere was trying to get stickiness off her hands with the edge of her shawl. It was Kudei who looked up—he was smiling too—and said, "Oh. But isn't rhododendron honey supposed to be poisonous?"

"Yes," Menin said.

Kunessin's face was good-natured, interested. "So what've you done to it to make it edible?"

"Nothing."

Silence. Their faces didn't change. Don't pull faces, or the wind'll shift and you'll be stuck like it. Dear God, she thought, have I got to spell it out for them?

"You've all been poisoned," she said. "Quite soon, you'll all be dead. Oh, and there's two ships in the bay. I had to wait for the ships, to take me home."

Kunessin was about to say something along the lines of a joke being a joke; then it was as though someone had stabbed him, just above the navel. He knew about being stabbed: the sudden weakness, the mind coming apart. He tried to breathe, but it was like drinking mud. He saw Aidi take a huge stride in Menin's direction, then stop dead, as though he'd hit an invisible wall, and slowly double up, the exaggerated slow movement of a falling tree. Enyo was standing staring. Clea had her fingers down her throat—far too late for that. Chaere was clutching her stomach, rocking backwards and forwards. Another stab—he felt that one—and he had no strength left at all.

She'd thought of all sorts of things to say at this point: bitter speeches, gloating speeches, explanations, accusations. She'd thought how proper it would be for them to die with her savage, justified complaints in their ears, so that the last thing that crossed their minds was that she'd been right to kill them; it was only fair, what they deserved. But that was based on the assumption that she'd be the centre of attention, that they'd actually be listening, and she didn't think they were. Oh well, she thought, not that it matters. She took a few more steps back, though none of them showed any further signs of coming after her, and composed herself to watch.

Aidi kept his feet the longest. She'd thought it would be Kunessin, but he went down before Kudei. It was the knees that went first, she noticed, in every case. She sat down on the grass beside the stream, and settled herself comfortably. She'd brought a chunk of bread — no honey, ha, ha — and a fistful of stale cake, for herself.

She watched as Enyo, then Chaere, then finally Clea drained to clay white and stopped twitching. It would have been nice to leave at least one of them alive — she'd given so much thought to the list — but in the event it simply wasn't practical. Muri had rolled over on to his side and she could only see the back of his head. Kudei was rolled up in a ball, still moving. Alces had tried to crawl over to his wife (sweet) but hadn't got far. He was lying on his chest, his elbows drawn up under him, which reminded her of a dead spider, and each breath he drew was like a saw in green wood. Kunessin looked like he was asleep on his back, breathing very shallow, just sips of air every now and again. Aidi was still trying to get up.

She frowned. Of all the things she'd expected it to be, she hadn't counted on dull.

Time passed. She thought: they're fighting. Everything's got to be a battle where they're concerned, even something so everyday as death. It was almost admirable in a way, but time was getting on; the ships would be at the quay before too much longer and she still had things she had to do. She got up, brushed crumbs off her front, and walked delicately between them, looking down, feeling more than a little impatient. She'd wanted so much to see them actually die, but now it looked like she'd have to leave before the end. Of course, she reflected, some people are like that. Some people just go out like snuffed candles; others drag on and make a meal of it. She bent down to look at Alces, almost sure he'd gone, and saw him blink. Damn the man. Stubborn.

She walked away, feeling cheated, like a child who's been promised cake.

*   *   *

Major Thumos Anogei had fought in the war. He'd been in the Pharous campaign, where he saw action in all the major battles, and he'd been assigned to General Euteuchida's expeditionary force, although he hadn't joined it in time and was therefore not among the thousands who died in the ambush. That, among other reasons, was why he'd been given this job. He knew all about A Company, of course. He fancied he'd seen them once, at some transfer depot in some place whose name he couldn't remember, one early evening in the rain, and someone had pointed at a clump of weary-looking men sitting on boxes. The incredibly famous A Company, he'd been told, Di'Ambrosies' men. He'd glanced, seen a clump of men sitting on boxes, slumped forward, too far off to make out details of faces, and he'd had other things on his mind. Since then, since the end of the war, he'd improved on that. Many times, when the conversation in the mess or with civilians had thrown up the exciting name, A Company, he'd looked very modest and said, I knew them, actually, when I was out east; and eyes had widened, and men had bought him drinks.

About Sphoe he knew nothing at all. It was an island, it had been one of those nothing-doing postings during the war, the sort of place you secretly longed to be sent to, but you were ever so scornful about men who'd spent their war there. Now, apparently, they'd found gold here, which of course changed everything. That, fortunately, wasn't his concern.

His feet itched in his boots, and he went and found the captain.

"How much longer?" he asked.

The captain gave him a patient look. "You tell me," he said. "Can't do anything without the wind. Soon as it picks up, we'll put in. Till then," and he shrugged, a tradesman's shrug, a waiting-for-the-parts shrug. "Just got to be patient."

Major Anogei tried to think like a soldier. "How about launching a boat?" he said. "Could we do that?"

The captain thought about it. "Could do," he said. "Take, what, four hours to row in from here. Wind should've got up by then, I'd have thought, and we'd get there before the boat. But it might not, you don't know."

Major Anogei looked away, at the thin string of smoke rising from the blur that presumably marked the settlement. No hurry, of course. It was an island, and the targets didn't have a ship, so they weren't going anywhere. "We'll launch a boat," he said.

He went below and announced the change of plan: he wanted a dozen volunteers who could row. Nobody moved. It was, of course, a nuisance that word had got out about why they'd come here. He couldn't blame the men.

"All right," he said, and reeled off a dozen names. He had no idea whether any of them could row; they were names he happened to be able to remember. Then he stumped back on deck, unrolled his map of the island, and tried to think.

The Military College; amphibious landings. Opposed or unopposed? Well. He had no reason to believe that A Company suspected anything. They knew soldiers were on their way; they'd done their deal with the civilian commissioner, Straton. That said, if things got nasty, as he was fairly certain they would, it'd be plain common sense to take a few basic precautions, such as drop off half a dozen men on the way in, to act as a reserve in waiting. On the other hand, he ought to work on the assumption that A Company were watching, and if they saw him doing that, they'd immediately know he was up to something.

In the boat, cramped up in the stern with the rudderman's elbow in his ribs, he did the arithmetic yet again. He had twenty men, and there were five of them. He didn't like that at all. Bloody fool, he thought; should've waited for the wind, landed both ships together at the quay, made his deployments with the advantage of overwhelming force. Instead, here he was bobbing about on a stupid little boat with twenty men, on his way to pick a fight with A Company. At least the sea was calm. He'd suffered on the way out—not conducive to proper military spirit, watching your commanding officer barfing his guts out over the rail—and he was glad that he wouldn't have to land and develop precise tactical solutions with his mouth full of refluxed acid. Both his feet had gone to sleep. He felt totally unprepared and generally unfit for duty. It reminded him of the old days.

The captain's estimate of four hours proved to have been optimistic; the sea was flat, but there were currents coming out of the bay, which kept trying to nudge them sideways, as if some kindly god was trying to tell him he really didn't want to do this profoundly stupid thing. No sign of anybody on the beach, at any rate. Maybe they weren't at home—out working in the fields (Major Anogei had been brought up in a town; he wasn't entirely sure what people did on farms, but he knew they did most of it out in fields) or having a last binge in the gold-beds before the government came to take possession. He fervently hoped so. Secure the settlement, hide men in advantageous positions, a smooth, clean trap. He ran it through in his mind and it still ended in a ghastly bloody mess, like bringing a wild boar into the living-room.

He made himself remember why he'd volunteered for this job. It was harder, in a boat, sailing down the throat of death, but the reason was still valid; and as for the mess and the fear and the sharp edges, it wasn't as though he was fresh out of the College. Context was everything. This was a job worth doing (he told himself; and, to his great surprise, he still believed it).

She watched the boat grow, from speck to shape, from shape to recognisable miniature. She checked to see if she was feeling nervous. Just a little bit. She wondered if they were dead yet. Must be, by now. She wondered why the soldiers had come in a little boat, but there was bound to be a good reason, too technical for her. She cramped and flexed her hands, like a little girl about to recite.

Not to the quay after all; the steersman had done his best, but the sea insisted they should land on the beach. Major Anogei stood up, his legs wobbly, feet shot through with pins and needles. "This as close as you can get?" he asked. No answer; it was clearly a stupid question. Oh well, he thought. He climbed up on the bulwark and hopped off into the water.

Splash. A man always feels a clown, jumping into water with his clothes on, instantly reduced to a small boy who's going to get a telling-off from his mother. He felt his boots fill up, and knew with a sinking heart that he was going to be squelching rather than striding up the beach to meet his destiny. He died with his boots on, they'd say of him, but his boots were full of water.

Someone stood up, fifty yards or so away, among the rocks. He hadn't seen whoever it was; bad start. But it was just a woman.

He stopped for a moment, then advanced. A woman; odd. She was waving. Was there an indigenous population? Not according to the briefing, which meant precisely nothing. She looked cheerful; cheerful and plain and half-witted and cunning, as though she was going to try and sell him local craftware.

"Hello there," he called out. Of course, he had no idea what language she might speak, since she wasn't even supposed to be there.

"Hello," she called back.

He closed the distance. She was quite young, shabby clothes but clean hair, slab-fronted peasant face. "Could you tell me where I might find General Kunessin?"

For a moment he thought she hadn't understood; then she made herself look very sad. "He's dead," she said.

No, surely not. Like arriving at the battlefield and being told the battle had been cancelled, on account of the weather. "Excuse me?"

"They're all dead," the girl said mournfully. "My husband and all the others. Thank goodness you've come," she added, remembering her line a fraction of a second too late.

"Dead?" Does that word mean what I think it does? "What happened?"

"I don't know," she wailed (and in her eyes there still lurked the little gleam that had made Anogei think he was about to be offered a very nice basket, very cheap). "I think it must've been something they ate. They just suddenly—" And then she broke off, covered her face with her hands, made some very dry tearing noises.

Anogei hadn't the faintest idea what to say. The whole thing was absurd. "Are you sure?" he heard himself ask.

"Of course I'm sure," the strange girl snapped back at him, fast as a cat. "I came out of the house and there they all were, lying on the ground." Her eyes narrowed. "You can come and see for yourself if you don't believe me."

He remembered that he was a leader of men, and that his men should by now be right behind him. "I'm sorry," he said. "Who are you?"

"I'm—" She stopped short. "I'm Chaere," she said. "Chaere Proiapsen."

Kunessin opened his eyes.

The knife, or spear or arrow or whatever it was, was still there. He could feel it very distinctly, cutting into him, doing damage; but it wasn't quite as bad as it had been, and if he was going to die, he doubted whether it'd be slackening off. In which case, he was probably going to live. He could feel the sweat; soaking, as if he'd been out in the rain. His throat felt as though he'd swallowed a rasp. Oh, and there's two ships in the bay. Two ships. He groaned quietly. For one ship, he wouldn't make the effort. Two ships.

He jerked his knees and pushed with his arms, bouncing himself off the ground. That made the pain worse, and he pulled a sad face. It was hot, like the desert. He was in terrible pain. He'd been poisoned. He was excused duty. No, he wasn't. He crouched, huddled, and stabbed at the ground with his feet. The leverage got him upright, and he caught his balance just in time. The next stab was so violent that he staggered, as though absorbing the impact of a real blow. Now then, he thought.

"Aidi." He couldn't hear himself. He was sure he'd just spoken, but he hadn't heard it. So this time he shouted, and this time he heard a little tiny voice, a very long way away, whispering. A child's voice, a little lost child who's wandered off at the fair. He was exhausted.

He could see Aidi, or a dead body; no idea which, but he supposed he'd better find out. Trouble was, the body was three yards away. Two ships. It's all right, he told himself, I can walk from here.

Three enormous yards. Imagine picking up something really big and heavy and awkward, an anvil, say, or a big block of masonry. Just holding it's bad enough, but you try actually walking with it. All that pressure, crushing down on one flimsy, wobbly knee joint. It'd never cope with the shearing force. One step. His head swam, his eyes lost focus, it was like trying to stand up in a howling wind. He kept his balance. Next step.

"Aidi?"

No good. Aidi could just be ordinary asleep; he wouldn't hear a pathetic little whimper like that. He took the third step (stabbing so sharp he was sure the point must've come out through his back). Can I stop now, please? He stretched out his toe and prodded the side of Aidi's neck.

"Aidi? Are you alive?"

He waited. He'd give it till the count of twenty, and then pronounce Aidi officially dead. On seventeen, Aidi's neck twitched. A nod.

"Then fucking well get up." He felt his stomach lurch. Any minute now...

"Any minute now," he said, "I'm going to throw up right where you're lying. I suggest you move."

The warning proved timely. Aidi rolled over on to his side just as the contents of Kunessin's stomach reached the ground.

"Aidi. How are you feeling?"

Stupid question; he issued a mental apology. "You've got to get up," he said. "Didn't you hear what she said? Two ships."

Sick as he was, he couldn't help but be impressed by the way Aidi stood up. It was a bit like watching someone draw water out of a well without a bucket. He'd overdone it, of course, and as soon as he was on his feet, he fell forward, and Kunessin had to catch him.

"Come on," Kunessin said. "You've got to help me with the others."

Aidi shook his head, like a drunk. "They're dead."

"I don't think so."

"That mad bloody woman," Aidi croaked—his face was the colour of flour. "She poisoned us."

"Two ships," Kunessin reminded him. "Come on."

"What's so special about two ships?"

Alces was already stirring when they reached him. "Teuche, that bloody woman..."

"We know," Aidi said, reaching out a hand. Alces nearly pulled him over, and Kunessin had to rescue both of them. Kudei got up slowly but steadily, groaning and asking over and over again what had happened, without seeming to hear their replies. Muri was breathing—light, short sniffs—but they couldn't bring him round, not even when Aidi kicked him in the ribs.

"Fine," Kunessin grunted. "We'll have to carry him."

They tried, but they didn't have the strength. "We can't just leave him here," Aidi said. So they dragged him, head and shoulders off the ground, the rest trailing. They had to stop every five yards; but by the time they reached the settlement, all of them felt a little stronger (though Kudei was having trouble staying upright, and Alces threw up over his boots). They reached the barn, shouldered open the door, and collapsed in a heap, like tired dogs after a long day. At some point, Kunessin dragged himself up again, filled a jug with water and handed it round.

"How's Muri doing?" he asked.

"I'm not happy about the way he's breathing," Aidi replied. "That's not just asleep. I think he's pretty bad."

"He'll be all right." Peremptory, as though he was issuing an order. "If we've pulled through, he'll be all right too."

"Why did she do it?" Aidi demanded. "It seems such a strange thing to do, pointless."

Alces laughed. "Far as I can tell, a better question would be: why did she wait so long? She was always going to be trouble."

Kunessin sighed. "If she was telling the truth about having seen ships in the bay, I guess that's the answer to your question. She wanted to be sure of her ride home."

"You think that's why?" Kudei put in.

Kunessin shrugged. "Just a theory."

"A bit—well, rational," Alces objected. "Either she's crazy and that's why she tried to kill us, or she's cunning and practical, in which case why'd she do it?"

"Money?" Kudei suggested.

Kunessin shook his head. "If she'd done it earlier, then quite possibly," he said. "But now we're broke."

"There's the gold..."

"Which is buried on the mainland, and only we know where it is. If we'd died, that'd have been that."

Alces sighed. "Crazy, then. Well, I'm not entirely surprised."

The water jug went round again; then Kunessin put on his best serious face. "Aidi," he said, "I take it you saw. Chaere..."

Aidi nodded, a small, economical movement.

"Fly..."

Alces nodded too, and Kudei grunted, "Thanks, I saw. They weren't so lucky."

It was a phrase they used in the army, a kind of incantation to mark the passing of the fallen. None of them had used it when Nuctos died; they'd never been comfortable with it, and the acceptance it implied. Other than when Nuctos died, of course, they'd never had occasion to use it. Dismissive; a charm to cut someone out of your mind. Unimportant; because in spite of everything, once again A Company had survived.

"Two ships, Teuche," Aidi said.

Kunessin closed his eyes for a moment, then opened them again. "At the very least, the second ship's to carry the miners, which would mean there's enough soldiers to fill one ship. Or it could be they're both carrying soldiers. At any rate, it's not a good sign. You can bet they haven't fetched along at least five companies just to guard the works. That's a full-strength garrison. Or an assault force."

"Can't just be for us, either," Kudei said. "Come on, Teuche, you're the officer. What are they up to?"

Kunessin frowned. "I wish I knew," he said.

"Arrest her," Anogei said.

Immediately two men appeared behind her and caught hold of her elbows. At first she was too shocked to resist.

"What's going on?" she demanded. "I haven't done anything."

"On the boat," Anogei said. "Set a man to guard her. No, better make that two."

The pressure on her elbows increased, gentle but very strong. She tried to pull away, but it was like pushing a wall, so she stamped down with her heels, trying to crush the tops of their feet. Apparently they'd been expecting that. They sidestepped her, and she squealed angrily, and they marched her away.

Now that, Anogei thought, was a stroke of luck; assuming, of course, that Proiapsen loved his wife. Rather a substantial assumption, of course. Still, it gave him another line of approach beside straightforward frontal assault. He turned his head and looked back at the ships, which hardly seemed to have moved. Back-up, he decided, wasn't arriving any time soon. Not that he needed it: he outnumbered them five to one. He pulled a face, and wondered what on earth had possessed him to come ashore in a boat, rather than wait for the wind.

Well, he thought. Might as well get on with it.

The settlement, as he approached it, looked to be in a bad way. Signs of considerable damage by fire; he knew about the blaze in the main house from Straton's report, but the other burnt-out shells were too far away, in his view, to have been part of the same incident. Signs of activity, too: a freshly dug patch of earth, with bits of stick marking out rows, so somebody had been planting vegetables. A stack of rails, recently cut out of green timber, leaning up against a wall to season. No livestock that he could see, other than a pair of carthorses in an overgrazed paddock; overbred, too big and too unsteady to pull a plough. A thin line of smoke drifting up from one of the barns, which looked as though it had been thatched recently, in a hurry, using improvised materials, by ingenious but unskilled men. The smoke suggested an untended fire rapidly burning itself out, implying that nobody was inside the building. No other signs of life. He thought carefully for a minute or so, then gave the order to fan out and secure the perimeter.

(The sergeant's face said: secure it against what? Well, fine. Better overcautious than the other way about.)

The operation didn't take long; and when he saw it was complete, he asked himself: what's all that in aid of? He'd secured the perimeter because in a police action that's what you do. You seal off the edges so fugitives can't slip away. The idea that twenty men could seal in the legendary A Company was so ludicrous it made him smile. Truth was, he admitted to himself, he hadn't the faintest idea how he was supposed to do this. In which case...

He gave the signal to move in. Under standard procedures, this meant searching the buildings, moving from the outside towards the centre. The barn, which was the only building that showed any signs of recent occupation, wasn't in the centre. Going about it all wrong. He gave the signal for hold it, stay where you are, and tried to think logically.

The logical thing to do was wait till the ships got in, then use all the men at his disposal to seal the perimeter properly; then, backed up by at least twenty men in plain view, advance on the barn and knock on the door. Unfortunately, it was a bit late for that now. If A Company weren't at home, if they were off in the woods or the hills somewhere, they'd be sure to have seen his men moving about inside the compound. If they were in the barn, everything he'd done so far had actively weakened his position. The only advantage he still retained was that A Company most likely neither knew nor suspected the purpose of his mission; and he'd significantly weakened that advantage by deploying his men in a manner calculated to arouse the deepest suspicion. If he'd marched up to the barn and knocked on the door, he might have been in with a chance. What he'd done instead was scatter his forces and show his hand. All in all, he was hard put to it to think of a mistake he hadn't made.

Assuming, of course, that A Company was still alive. The woman, Proiapsen's wife, had said they were all dead: food poisoning, or something of the sort. He hadn't believed her at the time, because he'd been looking at the smoke from the barn, which he'd taken as an indication that someone inside the compound was very much alive. In other words, he'd jumped to the conclusion that the woman's statement was some sort of cunning ruse designed to put him off his guard, so he'd go blundering into the yard and get caught in an ambush. But that, he realised, was a bloody stupid thing to assume, since A Company had no reason to suspect that he was anything more sinister than Straton's representative, and that he'd come to take over the gold mine. Stupid, he thought. Another stupid mistake.

But if he'd assumed wrong, and the woman was telling the truth...

A gleam of light glowed warm and beautiful inside his head. Maybe the woman had been telling the truth. Maybe they really were all dead, and all he'd have to do was find Proiapsen's body, pack it in salt and load it on the ship. Wonderful thought, and, therefore, presumably too good to be true.

The hell with it, he thought, and called over one of the two sergeants.

"Take three men," he said, "and get up as close as you can to that barn, see if there's anybody alive in there. Don't be too obvious about it. If there's anybody home, I'd rather they didn't know we're here."

The sergeant gave him a pained, is-that-all look, for which he couldn't help feeling a certain degree of sympathy. Go over there, just the three of you, and see if the enemy's home. No, he wouldn't care to do it himself. Tough.

He watched them from the cover of a doorway. They did the job well, the right balance of caution and expedition. He watched the sergeant arrive at the barn door, which was shut, and lean in close to it, listening for voices; then a brisk nod of the head and the signal to withdraw.

"Definitely somebody in there, sir," the sergeant reported. "At least three of them."

Not dead, then. Anogei scowled, trying to make his mind work. At least three of them; in which case the woman had been lying, and it was such a peculiar lie to tell: they're all dead. He tried to account for it, but all he could come up with was a rather basic, rather crude ruse to get him to march blithely into a trap (so crude it had to be a double bluff, which made it ingenious and clever). Only, he'd done that, and there wasn't one. Instead, at least three of them were inside the barn. Funny sort of a trap. He had an idea that he was missing the point somewhere along the line.

Never mind. At least he knew now what he had to do. Wait for the ships to come in, wait for his overwhelming superiority in numbers, and in the meanwhile keep out of sight and hope A Company didn't know he was here (but if they'd sent out the woman and she hadn't come back, they must suspect something by now. Oh God, he thought, what a complete mess).

Muri came round, eventually, and was immediately, expressively sick.

"What happened?" he asked.

"Your wife," Aidi replied.

"It looks rather as though she tried to kill us," Kunessin said. "Poison. Poisoned honey, of all things."

Muri opened his mouth, then shut it again.

"Enyo's dead," Alces said. "And Clea and Chaere. We're just very ill. We thought you'd had it, but apparently not. How are you feeling?"

"Not so bad," Muri croaked. "Is that really...? I mean, she tried to kill us?"

Kunessin nodded. "Apparently," he said. "That's what she told us, in so many words."

Muri stared at him, then looked away. "I had no idea," he said.

"Well of course you didn't," Aidi snapped." Anyway, that's what seems to have happened. She's made herself scarce, needless to say; she must've figured out by now that we're not dead after all. If she's got any sense, she'll be up in her beloved woods."

"What are we going to do? About her, I mean."

"Guess," Aidi said.

"But not now," Kunessin interrupted. "We're in no fit state to go crashing about in the woods. After all, she's not going anywhere. Not unless she can teach herself to sail the sloop single-handed. She'll keep."

Muri looked as though he wanted to say something, but didn't. Instead, he nodded, a fine, economical, military expression of understanding and agreement. Kunessin yawned, then winced. Aidi said, "In the meantime..."

"The best thing we can do is stay put here and get some rest," Kunessin said. "The main thing is, we seem to have got away with it. I'm assuming so, anyway, I've never been poisoned before. When we've got our strength back, we can figure out what we're going to do."

"Has it occurred to you she might try something else?" Aidi said.

Kunessin nodded. "She could try and set fire to this building," he said. "But on balance I'm inclined to think not. It'd be a hell of a risk, and she's got no way of securing the door from the outside, to keep us in here. My guess is, she's scared stiff and hiding, so for now at least we can forget about her." He frowned. "I'm more worried about what she said about two ships."

"She was lying," Aidi said firmly. "If they existed, they'd be here by now, and we'd be up to our necks in soldiers."

"What's wrong with that?" Kudei asked. "They'd be the government men, presumably. We don't mind them, do we?"

"Teuche's got some bee in his bonnet about there being two of them," Aidi replied. "Apparently, two is sinister."

Kunessin raised his hand, the quelling gesture. "Odd, rather than sinister," he said. "I'm just inclined to be careful, that's all. I wouldn't trust them as far as I could spit."

"Fair enough," Alces said. "Not a great deal we can do about it, though, is there?"

"We can stay here still and quiet and conserve our strength," Kunessin said. "That's about it." He paused, then added, "If there is something going on, we're more or less limited to making a dash for the sloop and getting off the island. Right now, speaking purely for myself, I don't feel in absolutely peak condition for anything strenuous like that." He sighed. "Quite likely there's no ships," he said, "or we'd have had company by now, like Aidi says. And if there are ships, I'm sure there's absolutely nothing to worry about, and they might even have a doctor, which'd be nice. But, just in case, there's no harm in being paranoid, specially when you're playing hardball with the government." He pulled a face, as a surge of pain swept through him. "Talking of which," he said, "I don't suppose we've got any weapons in here."

Aidi frowned, then shook his head. "All that stuff's in the sheds," he said.

"I've got mine," Alces said.

"You would. Doesn't help the rest of us much."

"No matter," Kunessin said. "But when we're feeling a bit stronger, it might be an idea to nip out and get a few things."

"There's a bow," Kudei said, "and a few arrows."

"Fine." Kunessin had his eyes shut, and a pained expression on his face. "More to the point, is there anything resembling a bucket?"

The ships, at last. Anogei sent a man down to the quay to tell them what to do.

First things first. Twenty men to reinforce the perimeter, making forty in all. The remaining thirty to make up the assault party. He played the worst possible outcome through in his mind.

If everything goes wrong, he told himself, A Company will break through the thirty men at the barn door, killing maybe five or six. Then they're most likely to head for the quay, with a view to seizing a ship, and terrifying the crew into sailing it for them (or would they be able to handle a ship themselves?). They have to get off the island. If I anchor the ships out in the bay, will that help? No, they'll take the boat, or swim. Assume another two or three dead when they break through the perimeter; say ten, all told.

Or, assume they break out but we head them off from the ships. So they go inland, up into those woods. Assume they've got stores of food up there, so it's not as simple as just starving them out. Hunting down A Company in dense woodland, which they presumably know like the backs of their hands; he revised his assessment. In Kunessin's place, he'd head straight for the woods, not the quay. If they got to the woods, a numerical advantage of seven to one (six to one by that point, of course) would be no advantage at all. Quite the reverse. The more targets offered, the easier it'd be to hit something.

Fine. Kunessin gets to the woods, but we don't go after him. We stay here, in the settlement, sixty men besieged by a superior force of five. Kunessin would like that. A series of night raids; hit and run, between five and ten men killed, the pressure mounting on him to strike back as morale plummets; he'd end up having to go into the woods after all, but by now he'd be down to fifty men, or forty…

All right, Anogei thought, look at it another way. If he was in my shoes, what would Kunessin do?

Simple.

They took her to the quay, where two ships were tied up. "I don't understand," she protested. "I haven't done anything wrong. What's the matter with you?"

"Don't ask us," the soldiers told her. "Nobody tells us anything."

They escorted her, respectfully but firmly, up the gangplank and on to the deck, where a tall, dark young man in civilian clothes—rather dashing civilian clothes—met her and dismissed her guards. He smiled as he asked who she was.

"I'm Chaere Proiapsen," she said.

"Ah." The young man raised both eyebrows. "In that case, I'd be obliged if you'd follow me. This way."

He walked quickly, so she had to skip to keep up with him. He had nice eyes, but a rather offputting mouth: clever, sarcastic. He led her down a flight of stairs in the deck into a narrow hold stacked with barrels. "Please, do sit down," he said, quite charmingly, as though he was talking to a lady. "So you're Major Proiapsen's wife," he said.

"That's right."

He nodded slowly. "In that case," he said, "I'm afraid I've got some rather bad news for you. My name's Scapho, by the way, I'm with the adjutant general's department. That's the army's lawyers."

She waited for a moment, then said, "What's the bad news?"

He studied her for three seconds. "I'm here with a warrant for your husband's arrest," he said.

"Oh." Then: "Are you sure you don't mean General Kunessin?"

He shook his head slowly, like a pendulum. "I'm afraid the charges are very serious," he went on. "In fact, they're about as serious as it's possible to get. We have good evidence that your husband's guilty of treason."

He saw her face lock up, as though a catch had been pressed. Not such a simple little thing after all, he thought.

"What's he done?"

Scapho took a deep breath. "At the end of the war," he said, "our forces landed in what was thought to be neutral territory with the aim of striking at one of the enemy's most strategically important cities. It should have won us the war, and we weren't expecting any trouble. We were sure the locals would let us pass through their country without bothering us. Do you remember?"

"Vaguely," she said. "I was only a child."

"Of course." Scapho smiled, bleakly gallant. "Anyway, it all went disastrously wrong. We were ambushed by local militia, far stronger, better armed and better trained than we'd imagined possible. What really did for us, though, was the exact knowledge they had of where we were going, the route we were taking. Thousands of our men were killed; only a handful got away. Your husband was one of that handful." He paused, looked at her sideways, and said, "He's told you about this, perhaps?"

"He never talks about the war."

Scapho nodded. "At the time, we were pretty sure that the enemy had got hold of one of our people and extracted the information from him somehow." His face darkened, and his eyes weren't nice any more. "We recently found out who the traitor was. Your husband."

If she reacted at all, it was a very slight widening of the eyes, which hadn't blinked, he realised, for a long time. He could almost hear her mind working behind those closed shutters: a busy mind, not brilliant but able to concentrate very intensely. "How do you know it was him?"

"Ah." Scapho broke eye contact—a bit like looking straight into the sun, but more like staring down a deep well shaft; wearing, in any event. "We've never stopped investigating, of course; something like that can't just be let drop and forgotten about. Six weeks ago, one of our agents managed to get close to the top men in the enemy militia, and he found out who'd carried out the interrogation of the traitor. We managed to capture the interrogator and get him back our side of the border. Then, not to put too fine a point on it, we beat it out of him. It took a long time—he was determined to be difficult, from sheer bloody-mindedness mostly—but we got there in the end. He told us the man he questioned was a linebreaker: 'one of the famous

404   K. J. Parker

ones,' he said, which could only mean your husband's old unit, A Company. We pressed him a little harder, and he said it was a tall man, well over six foot, with broad shoulders and fair curly hair." He shrugged. "He's still alive, so he can identify your husband at the court-martial. I'm sorry," he said, "but it's as clear-cut a piece of evidence as anyone could wish for."

She hadn't blinked yet. "That's very bad, isn't it?"

Scapho nodded. "I'm afraid so, yes. Also," he went on, "from the description of the interrogation that this man gave us, we have a pretty good idea of where to look for some rather distinctive scarring on your husband's arms and back." He pursed his lips. "Maybe you could tell us about that."

She was looking at him as though he was a window. "Am I going to be in trouble?" she said. "Because he's my husband."

"You needn't concern yourself about that," Scapho said. "All this happened long before you married him, so obviously you've done nothing wrong."

She nodded sharply. "What's going to happen to him?"

The right question, but not the emphasis he'd have expected. "There's only one penalty for a crime like that."

"Afterwards." She paused. "It won't affect me, will it? I mean, I'll still inherit his property and everything."

He wanted to laugh, but that wouldn't have done at all. "I'm afraid not," he said. "The estate of a convicted traitor forfeits to the state. The government takes it," he translated. "I'm very sorry, but that's the law."

"Yes, but what if he doesn't..." She stopped, and when she spoke again, it was a much smaller voice. "If he's never actually convicted, I mean. If he died first."

Scapho frowned. "If he dies resisting arrest, you mean?"

"He's already dead," she said quickly. "All of them, they died not long before you got here. It must've been something they ate."

"They're dead?" He felt as though he'd just been punched in the mouth. "That's..."

She was nodding eagerly. "And if he's dead," she went on, "then he can't stand trial, and your witness can't identify him, so it wouldn't be fair at all, would it? I mean, it's so important, isn't it, a fair trial. Aidi always used to say, that's the sort of thing we fought the war for. I mean," she went on, talking quickly, "he might not have been guilty after all; you can't really prove it if he's not there. And if he's dead..." She let the words hang in the air, like a fat ripe plum from a tree.

Scapho stood up. Suddenly he was very anxious indeed to leave the cargo hold and get away from this extraordinary creature, small and bright-eyed and intense and vicious as a rat in a live trap. "It's not up to me, I'm afraid," he said. "I'm not the prosecutor. It'd be his decision. I'm sorry."

"But you could talk to him," she persisted. "I mean, it can't really be important, can it? Not compared with all that stuff you were talking about."

All that stuff. "I'll see what I can do," Scapho said, and that, apparently, was enough to get him away from her and back into the fresh, clean air.

"Guard that hold," he said to the first man who passed him. "Make absolutely sure she stays in there, and don't let her talk to anyone."

He went back to his cabin, a small, curved-sided box wedged in behind a bulkhead at the stern of the ship. He opened his trunk, scrabbled about under various shirts, found a bottle, uncorked it and glugged four big mouthfuls. Then he sat down to write a letter to his superiors, recommending that forfeiture of property be waived in the Proiapsen case. It wasn't, he couldn't help feeling, as if he had any choice in the matter.

Major Anogei also wrote a letter. He had to send back to the ship for paper and ink and a pen.

He wrote:

Major Aidi Proiapsen is under arrest on charges of treason, in that [he wasn't sure if that was the right turn of phrase, but he hoped it would do] *he betrayed troop movements to the Stethessi militia, thereby enabling them to ambush and wipe out our forces. We have identification*

evidence and an eyewitness, namely the militia officer who conducted the
interrogation. Surrender Major Proiapsen and you will not be harmed.
You have one hour. Signed, Thumos Anogei, major, 6th Marines.

He dusted it with fine sand to blot it, then folded it lengthways, crept up to the barn, slid it under the door and ran away.

EIGHTEEN

"What's that?" Aidi asked.

Teuche frowned. "It looks like a sheet of paper," he said. "Fly, you're nearest."

Alces groaned, rolled off the pile of sacks and blankets that served as his bed, levered himself on to his feet and staggered to the door. "It's a letter, I think," he said.

"Well, don't just stand there, give it here."

As Kunessin opened it, Muri said, "Who the hell can it be from? We're on an island..."

"Teuche?" Kudei said.

Kunessin was reading. Alces said, "If it's from your fucking wife, Muri, apologising..."

"It's not from her." Kunessin was staring at the paper, as though it was too bright to look at.

"Come on, then," Aidi said irritably. "Who's it from?"

"The government, presumably," Kudei said. "But why a letter, of all things? Why don't they just knock on the door and talk to us, if—?"

"See for yourself," Kunessin said, and handed him the letter.

"Teuche," Aidi protested, lifting himself on one elbow, "stop mucking about and tell us what's going on. Have they gone back on the deal or something? Talk to me, for crying out loud."

No reply; dead silence. Kudei, Aidi noticed, had actually stopped breathing. "Kudei," he said. "Teuche won't talk to me for some reason; you'd better tell me. What is all this? Kudei?"

But Kudei had passed the letter to Alces. He was grinning when he took it, and the grin didn't really fade; it stuck (the wind'll change and you'll stick like it), so that he looked rather like a fox pelt nailed up on a door to dry and cure, with the head left on, and the drying-out shrivels the flesh of the jaw, drawing it open in a grin...

"Someone talk to me," Aidi said angrily. "Fly, for crying out loud."

Alces lifted his face away from the letter, and it was whitish-grey, like low-grade pipe clay, and his eyes were very wide. Without looking away, he shoved the letter towards Muri, who was just out of arm's reach. "Screw you, then," Aidi snapped, and he lunged at the paper in Alces' hand; it was whisked away before his fingers could close on it, and he felt Kunessin's hand on his shoulder. He stopped where he was.

"Leave it," Kunessin said. "Let Muri read it."

Muri read it; and then his hands dropped to his knees, and he said, "It's not true. It can't be. Teuche?"

Kunessin was looking at Aidi, thinking, doing some sort of complex mental calculation. "Let him see it," he said.

Muri shook his head, like a horse shying. "It's just the government playing games," he said. "It's not possible."

With a sound somewhere between a grunt and a roar, Aidi sprang forward and snatched the letter from Muri's hand, darted back to where he'd been and glanced at it. Then there was a moment when his eyes seemed to slip off it, like a rasp off hardened steel. His lips parted, but he made no sound.

"It's not true, is it?" Muri said. "It's just a stupid lie."

Nobody moved, apart from Aidi, who swallowed, the way you do when you wake up after sleeping with your mouth open.

"Is it true?" Kunessin said.

The hand holding the page slowly drooped; it hung at Aidi's side as though it was broken. "No," he said, "of course not."

"Are you sure about that, Aidi?" Kunessin said.

Silence. Perhaps it was as quiet as that at the beginning of the world. Then Alces said: "Odd that they chose to pick on you, though. You don't own the island, Teuche does."

"It's not true," Aidi repeated; and the others, who knew him so well, knew that he was lying. Always was a piss-poor liar. He saw it in their faces. They were watching him...

Years ago, when he was a boy, he'd heard his uncle's story about the time he'd gone to Allogloss, the land of scrub and burning skies, where there are still lions; how his uncle, stupid drunk after a session round the campfire, had stumbled off into the bush to piss; how he'd crossed the rim of a small dip in the ground and suddenly realised he was five yards away from six fully grown lions, which stood absolutely still and watched him, with the most perfect concentration imaginable; how he'd frozen, knowing that the slightest movement would mean his death, a clown caught balancing on one foot, suddenly cold deadly sober, looking back at the lions, a mirror to their intensity; how he'd hung there, impossibly, for a lifetime of ten seconds before slowly putting his left foot on the ground, slowly taking a step back with his right foot, slowly taking a step back with his left foot, keeping his head perfectly, perfectly still, until his heel told him he'd made it to the top of the rise; how he'd slid down the back face of the escarpment on his nose and belly, scrambled, run so fast he was practically flying, back to the campfire where the other drunks were singing...As a boy, Aidi had had nightmares about the cold, quick, keen eyes of the lions, so that he imagined they were watching him all the time, waiting for the slightest movement, which would entitle them to spring...

"Aidi," Muri said.

"It's not true." (And he felt cold, in his elbows and knees and knuckles, and his stomach clenched tight and stabbed him, like the spasms from the poison.) "You believe me, don't you?"

And nobody answered, which was like the absolute stillness of the lions before they sprang, and Aidi knew that everything had suddenly gone wrong.

"So that's where you got to," Teuche said, his voice flat. "When we all got split up."

Aidi nodded. "I wound up at a farmhouse," he said. "They asked me in, made a fuss of me; what nice people, I thought. And I went to sleep, and when I woke up—"

Kunessin held up his hand. "I don't want to know," he said.

"Teuche..."

"I said, be quiet." The last word flicked out at him, like a slap, like a punch, so fast it couldn't be warded against or ducked or side-stepped; like a lion, so much faster than any human. He actually tried to dodge the word, shifting his head to one side, as if it was an arrow or a javelin. It was one of those words, he knew, that changes everything; like, no, I don't love you any more, or yes, it's terminal, one of those words that mark the end of the world. So he tried to avoid it, the way A Company had always managed to avoid that sort of thing. A Company had the knack of skiving off death, sneaking past defeat, worming their way into salvation without paying for a ticket; they had reactions faster than any arrow, footwork and moves that could beat any man living; fire couldn't burn them, even poison didn't seem to work on them, as though they had a note, a safe conduct, diplomatic immunity or some other loophole or technicality. But not, apparently, when the word was launched by one of them at another of them, as though the lions had turned on each other.

But Aidi Proiapsen, outnumbered four to one, had a concealed weapon, and in that cold moment, suddenly cold deadly sober, he chose to draw it, knowing it couldn't be sheathed again without drawing blood. It was the hardest decision he ever took. He didn't hesitate for even a split second.

"All right," he said. "I admit it. What are you planning to do about it?"

Kunessin was nobody's fool, and he knew Aidi Proiapsen very well. So he hesitated, trying to understand the stab of intuition, the prick of a knife at his throat, the sudden all-destroying awareness that in the moment of committing his forces to all-out attack, he'd been out-thought and outflanked and was running into ambushes and pitfalls and caltrops and checkmate; that he'd lost, without yet knowing how.

"Well?" Aidi said.

"If it's true..." Kudei said slowly.

"It's true," Aidi said.

"But that's not..." Muri was drowning, sinking into quicksand. "Nuctos died," he wailed. "Aidi, how could you do that?"

"You weren't there," Aidi replied. "You don't know anything about it."

"You betrayed us," Alces said, the faintest growl from the lions.

Well, Aidi thought, this is it. "I wasn't the only one," he said.

Major Anogei gave his orders. Over there, by that lean-to, a big stack of cordwood. Of course, he knew better than to ask for volunteers.

"Get a couple of long poles," he said, "and brace the door. Actually, make it half a dozen. Get 'em jammed in really good and firm. Then I want you to pile that cordwood tight up against the door. Think you can do that?"

There was also sacking, and packing straw from the barrels and crates, a nice store of small, dry kindling. He took a long, hard look at the thatch, which wasn't thatch at all; it was compressed bundles of dead bracken and briar. A quick burn, very hot, but would it burn itself out too quickly, and would it burn too clean, without smoke?

At which point, one of the junior lieutenants reported that they'd found another large logpile on the far side of the compound: five cords, still green, but all ash, and ash will burn unseasoned. Anogei closed his eyes for a moment. "Fetch it," he said. "I want it piled up against the walls on the two long sides."

He glanced up at the sun. One hour he'd given them. Of course, he doubted very much whether they had anything to measure a precise hour by; and suppose he cheated and only gave them fifty-five minutes, what exactly were they going to do about it?

"Make up a dozen torches," he ordered.

Kunessin said nothing.

It was as though a spring had broken, and the mechanism had

stopped. Aidi waited for his cue, which was a long time coming. Eventually Kudei said, "What's that supposed to mean, exactly?"

He felt better now, much calmer. He'd been afraid his voice would crack, or come out squeaky, or he'd stammer and trip over the words. "Teuche?" he said.

Kunessin lifted his head. There was no need for words; he was saying: Don't do it, Aidi. Between us we can sort this out. We can handle them. Don't.

But it was too late for that, Aidi decided; it was a choice, rather than a conclusion drawn from an assessment of the evidence. Actually, he believed Teuche might be able to handle it, if he asserted his full authority, gave them a direct order. But—now here was a surprise, which only went to show; he hadn't realised it, right up to this moment. He'd found the weapon; of course, Teuche hadn't been there, he'd still been in the army, miles away, no reason to assume he'd ever come back, so what earthly good would it do, to destroy him with it and bring them all down? So he'd put it away, carefully, wrapped it in oilcloth in his mind, not realising when he did so that Teuche's crime was something he could never, ever forgive, even if it meant the end of the world. His own guilt, oddly enough, had nothing to do with it. He didn't feel bad about it. If he hadn't given in, they'd have put his eyes out, and his life would have been unbearable. Besides, he hadn't killed Nuctos; it was some enemy archer who'd done that. But Teuche (Teuche who was guilty, rotten to the core, unforgivable) wouldn't let him explain, had never let him win an argument, had listened to him all these years and over-ridden him every single time. So it was the end of the world. So what?

"Teuche stole from us," he said, and such a blessed relief to get the words out. "All through the war. He stole our money, embezzled. He took Nuctos' share. He cheated us. He shaved the prize money. He sold cheap to his agent back home, and then the agent sold on at full price, and he kept the difference. All the time we were fighting for our lives, when we were thinking it was just us, the six of us against the whole world, he was screwing us for pennies on the thaler, just like he was screwing the government." He ran out of words. He felt empty, as though he'd just sicked up his soul. So he waited. The next words Teuche would say would be the end of it, the unforgivable statement, the foot in the snare, the trap sprung. He knew him so well.

"It wasn't for me," Kunessin said, and Aidi barked like a dog for pure joy. "It was for all of us. It's what paid for us to come here. Every penny..."

"Light the torches," Anogei said, "and set fire to the cordwood."

"Yes, sir," replied the lieutenant; then he checked himself, hesitated, and asked, "Aren't you going to give them a chance to surrender?"

"No," Anogei said.

"Teuche," Kudei said.

Kunessin swung round and hit him. His fist caught the side of his head, just above the ear. Kudei went down with a crash, knocking over a chair. Alces jumped up, took a step back, but he was up against the wall.

"It's true, isn't it?" Alces said. "It's true, what he just said."

"He betrayed us to the enemy," Kunessin shouted. "He killed Nuctos."

"You stole Nuctos' share," Aidi said, delighted, enjoying himself so much. "Do you remember, Fly? He was so coy about it: oh dear, someone's got to do this boring job of sorting out the money, I really don't want to, but if you insist..." He took a pace forward, inviting attack. "Nobody made you do it, Teuche; nobody was torturing you, forcing you into it. No, you thought: here's all this money, and they'll never know. You might as well have pulled the boots off his feet."

"Oh, it was torture, was it?" Kunessin grinned scornfully, all his teeth. "What did they do, Aidi? Break your arms and legs, pull your teeth out, smash your ribs in with a pick handle? I don't think so. I think we'd have noticed if they had. I seem to remember you came back and there wasn't a mark on you."

Alces was about to lunge forward, but Muri stopped him, a massive hand on his shoulder, pushing him down until his knees folded. Alces wriggled free, flipped sideways, caught Muri's wrist and tried to wrench it into a lock; failed and let go. He expected Muri to do something, but realised Muri's attention was elsewhere. He was frowning.

"They said they'd put my eyes out," Aidi replied; unwillingly, because it sounded so weak. "It's the one thing I've always been scared of. I just couldn't bear the thought of it. Being dead, fine, so what, comes to us all. But that..."

"You killed Nuctos," Muri said slowly.

"Nuctos died in the war," Aidi snapped. "Some bastard on a horse shot him and he died. It could've been any time, in any of the battles. It just so happened—"

"I think you'll have your work cut out getting us to believe it was an accident," Alces said quietly. "I wouldn't bother trying, if I were you."

"Fine," Aidi spat. "I was a coward. I was chicken. I sold out my friends to save my own skin because I was shit scared, because I was so fucking terrified I couldn't control myself. At least I've got that excuse. What he did—"

Kunessin swung round to face Aidi. "For crying out loud, I just told you, it wasn't for me. Every last quarter, I put into this place—"

"He's lying," Aidi said, smug, happy. "He wanted the money to buy Kudei's farm. That was nice, wasn't it? He was going to buy Kudei's farm with Kudei's own money. Of course, he could never forgive the Gaeons for buying it, when his dad lost the place because he was such a useless farmer he couldn't make a living."

"It was the war," Kunessin screamed at him. "It was the bloody war."

"So was what I did," Aidi said. "You can't have it both ways, Teuche."

"Just a minute," Muri said. "Can you smell burning?"

"We didn't choose to have a fucking battle on our doorstep," Kunessin roared back. "It was all right for you, safe in the town, sat on your arse counting your money."

"I'd keep off the subject of money if I were you."

Kunessin went for him. Like a lion, Aidi thought, as he moved to dodge the punch. He fully expected to get out of the way in time, but he didn't. His eyes blurred, and he was falling, and Teuche was standing over him, kicking him in the ribs, killing him. Too quick, like the lions.

But Alces was quick too; he jumped on Kunessin's back, linked his hands under his chin and pressed back as hard as he could, to crush the windpipe. Kunessin slammed backwards over his shoulder with the palm of his right hand, estimating to perfection where Alces' jaw was likely to be; he felt the bone crack, and the pressure on his throat slacken. He kicked Aidi's ribcage, as hard as he could. It was like breaking up sticks for kindling. Then he felt a finger in his left eye, which was more than he could afford. He twisted away, stumbled back until his heel hit the wall, and slammed himself backwards against it to crush the enemy.

Aidi was on his feet. He'd got hold of a length of wood, a stave from the barrel he'd been sitting on. But Muri was suddenly there, and he kicked it out of his hand, and Aidi punched him in the chest. Muri staggered back, took three steps to get his balance, then charged, head down, crude, stupid move but Muri was very big and very quick; Aidi was expecting something clever. He screamed as Muri's head thudded into his cracked rib, tripped over his own feet and went down, catching his head a horrible crack against the leg of the table. Then Muri was on top of him, hammering his fists into Aidi's face, just as Alces relaxed his hands and fell off Kunessin's back.

Muri stopped hitting, leant back and stared up at the roof. Aidi's eyes were full of blood, but he took the opportunity; he twisted sideways, throwing Muri off him, rolled clear, and used the momentum to bounce himself on to his feet. For a moment he couldn't get his balance; he could hardly breathe and his vision was wretchedly blurred, as if the room was full of smoke. But then Kunessin came hurtling at him; he turned his shoulder and charged. They collided, crashing into each other so hard that they both staggered, clutched at each other for support, found it and shifted their grips, each scrabbling for the other's throat.

"The house is on fire," Muri shouted.

Then Kudei was sitting up, blood trickling from his nose, eyes squinting in the bitter smoke. Through his blurred vision he saw

416   K. J. Parker

Kunessin; he skipped and hopped through the fallen and smashed furniture and slammed his fist into the small of Kunessin's back; lost his footing, clutched, both arms round Kunessin's throat, hanging on to him like a toddler and strangling him at the same time.

Above the crackle of the bone-dry briars and the hiss of damp steaming out of the walls, Anogei could hear thumps and crashes, like fractious steers being herded into stalls at the market. His heart fluttered, and he yelled for all his men to come up and form a ring round the barn. "Sounds like they're busting through the wall," he told his senior lieutenant. "If they get out, they'll be through us like a needle."

The lieutenant turned his face away; it was stinging and raw from the heat.

Trying to shout a warning, Muri sucked in a mouthful of smoke. Coughing it back up again was like vomiting gravel. It felt like it had taken half his throat with it.

They'd done this at the Military College, of course. When you're trapped in a smoke-filled room, remember there's always one lungful of clean air inside your shirt. He sucked it in, savoured it, and used it to yell, "Come on, for God's sake, we've got to get out."

His last shout of air, and he'd wasted it. They hung together, like the four legs of a table, supporting each other and the thing itself; even as they fought, every second inflicting some further real and permanent damage (they'd gone through the war pretty much unscathed), they made up one mutually supporting structure, twined round each other, a fabulous creature with four bodies, eight arms, eight legs, four heads. Like a statuary fountain, or the pedestal for some great overblown bronze monument; all four applying the maximum force at his disposal, four perfectly balanced forces cancelling each other exactly out.

Muri Achaiois, who'd never fitted in quite as well, who was never listened to, hurled himself at the group, trying to break in, to force them apart, to make them stop fighting and understand that the barn was on fire. It was an accident that he got the heel of

Aidi's hand in his face, Kudei's knee in his crotch, Teuche's elbow
in his solar plexus. He grabbed for support and hung from Aidi's
and Teuche's shoulders, while they hammered him with their fists,
believing (because they could no longer see) that they were hitting
each other. He felt a rib splinter, an overpowering sharp spike as the
jagged blade of the bone pricked his lung. He was yelling, the barn is
on fire, but he couldn't even hear it himself.

A section of rafter, burned through at both ends, fell across his
shoulders, hit the side of Alces' head, rested its red-hot, bellows-
blown embers on Aidi's outstretched, braced arms as he gripped
Muri's throat. Kudei got his hands under the other end and heaved it
out of the way. Before he could get back to the job in hand, however,
a pitch of blazing thatch landed on top of his head, lighting his hair,
and Aidi's, and Muri's.

Anogei was surprised at how well the barn went up. In his report,
he gave the credit to a sudden stiff breeze off the sea, which was
drawn in under the eaves by the short, intense blaze in the thatch.
His explanation was that the fire on the roof, fanned by said breeze,
cooked up hot enough to ignite the two-inch-thick side planking,
which then burnt freely from the top down. Unsupported, the rafters then fell in, flushing a dense, thrilling covey of orange sparks. Of
course, nothing could have survived that.

Even so, he kept his men back for as long as the flames continued to dart and lick; for fear that they'd get burnt, sure enough,
but mostly just in case A Company came bursting out of the fire
and pulped them, like apples under the millstone. After all, he said
nervously to himself as the sparks flew upwards, there's no hurry. If
they're dead now, they'll still be dead in ten minutes' time, maybe
even twenty.

It came on to rain while the flames were still as tall as a man,
and the smoke blended with steam, and the white and grey ash
dissolved into filthy black mud, and there was no sign of anything
living, or anything that had ever been alive, under the splayed ribcage of fallen rafters. Even so, Anogei held his men back a little
while longer, during which time a soldier reported having found the

bodies of three dead women, a little to the west and just up from the beach.

But when the last glowing coals had died out, and the light was beginning to fade, Anogei sent his men in to search the charred beams and the black sludge, just in case. He himself held well back and out of the way, a fact that didn't go unnoticed. In particular, he said, he wanted bones; failing which, rings, buttons, belt and shoe buckles, any solid item that could give a positive identification; weapons, he added, something distinctive, like a catsplitter, or Thouridos Alces' famous zweyhander sword, from which it was well known that he was extremely reluctant to be parted.

In his report, he rationalised the absence of solid evidence by pointing out that the fire, fanned by the freak wind referred to above, became extremely hot. The bones must have been consumed, the metal artefacts melted and drained away into the ground. He could assure Central Command quite categorically that nobody and nothing had passed through the cordon of armed men he'd placed round the burning barn. It was equally certain that nobody had left the building before the fire took hold. It was even possible, if the statement of the widow Proiapsen was to be believed, that all five were dead already (and the discovery of three dead women, all apparently poisoned, corroborated her story to some extent). As to the woman Chaere Proiapsen, he'd delivered her into the custody of the civil authorities, in case they wished to question her further about the women's deaths. Personally, he could see no point in such enquiries, since nothing could be proved. Further to a promise made by his civilian revenue officer, he was enclosing on the widow Proiapsen's behalf a formal notice of appeal against the confiscation of her late husband's assets, for what it was worth.

On a more positive note, he was pleased to be able to report that the gold workings were now ready to be reopened, and he trusted that the revenue derived therefrom would be reserved exclusively for funding the expeditionary force against the old enemy, which he understood was to be launched in the near future. If such an expression were not out of place in a formal report, he would be most grateful to be considered for any command in said force that might become available, so that he might have further opportunities of serving his government and his country.

There is a legend about A Company, elusive but remarkably persistent: that they survived the fire by hiding in the root cellar, breathing through a channel cut through the clay to the surface by Thouridos Alces, using his long zweyhander sword (which would account for the fact that it was never found); that when the ashes had cooled and the soldiers had gone away, they crept out, hurried across the island to the place where the sloop was moored, set sail for the mainland; ran into one of those sudden, unpredictable squalls and were driven on to the murderous reef that surrounds the volcanic island of Oudenos, making that wretched, treeless scrap of lava and ash inaccessible to the outside world; that there they remain to this day, living on crabs and gulls' eggs and semi-edible roots, the way Menin Aeide taught them to, and fighting each other to a standstill every day from sunrise to sunset, five against five, with no particular alliances and all the anger and hate in the world; that if ever they are found and rescued and brought back to the mainland, the war will come again and sweep through the land and the continent and the entire planet, and it will last for ever and ever, world without end, amen.

ACKNOWLEDGEMENTS

I am most grateful to Jim Gibb, late of Imperial College, London, for the specifications of the gold-jar. If anyone doubts the accuracy of Mr. Gibb's calculations, I'd be happy to test them by practical experiment.